TIAMAT'S WRATH

By James S. A. Corey

THE EXPANSE
Leviathan Wakes
Caliban's War
Abaddon's Gate
Cibola Burn
Nemesis Games
Babylon's Ashes
Persepolis Rising
Tiamat's Wrath

THE EXPANSE SHORT FICTION
The Butcher of Anderson Station
Gods of Risk
The Churn
Drive
The Vital Abyss
Strange Dogs

TIAMAT'S WRATH

BOOK EIGHT OF THE EXPANSE

JAMES S. A. COREY

www.orbitbooks.net

Copyright © 2019 by Daniel Abraham and Ty Franck
Cover design by Lauren Panepinto and Kirk Benshoff
Cover art by Daniel Dociu
Cover copyright © 2019 by Hachette Book Group, Inc.

Orbit
Hachette Book Group
1290 Avenue of the Americas
New York, NY 10104
orbitbooks.net

First Edition: March 2019

Orbit is an imprint of Hachette Book Group.
The Orbit name and logo are trademarks of Little, Brown Book Group Limited.

The publisher is not responsible for websites (or their content) that are not owned by the publisher.

The Hachette Speakers Bureau provides a wide range of authors for speaking events. To find out more, go to www.hachettespeakersbureau.com or call (866) 376-6591.

Library of Congress Cataloging-in-Publication Data
Names: Corey, James S. A., author.
Title: Tiamat's wrath / James S. A. Corey.
Description: First Edition. | New York, NY : Orbit, 2019. | Series: The
    Expanse ; book 8
Identifiers: LCCN 2018054213| ISBN 9780316332873 (hardcover) |
    ISBN 9780316332866 (ebook (open))
Subjects: | GSAFD: Science fiction.
Classification: LCC PS3601.B677 T53 2019 | DDC 813/.6—dc23
LC record available at https://lccn.loc.gov/2018054213

ISBNs: 978-0-316-33287-3 (hardcover), 978-0-316-33286-6 (ebook)

Printed in the United States of America

LSC-C

10 9 8 7 6 5 4 3 2 1

To George R. R. Martin
Good mentor, better friend

Prologue: Holden

Chrisjen Avasarala was dead.

She'd passed in her sleep on Luna four months earlier. A long, healthy life, a brief illness, and she left humanity very different than she'd found it. The newsfeeds all had obituaries and remembrances prerecorded and ready to spin out across the thirteen hundred systems to which humanity was heir. The chyrons and headlines had been hyperbolic: *The Last Queen of Earth* and *Death of a Tyrant* and *Avasarala's Final Farewell*.

No matter what they said, they hit Holden just as hard. It was impossible to imagine a universe that wouldn't bow to the little old woman's will. Even when the confirmation came to Laconia that the reports were true, Holden still believed deep in his bones that she was out there somewhere, irritated and profane and pushing herself past all human limits to bend history just another fraction of a degree away from atrocity. It was almost a month between the moment he heard the news and the first time he let himself accept that it was true. Chrisjen Avasarala was dead.

But that didn't mean she was finished.

A state funeral had been planned on Earth before Duarte intervened. Avasarala's time as secretary-general of the United Nations had been a critical period in history, and her service not only to her world but to the whole human project had earned her a place of honor that could never be forgotten. The high consul of Laconia thought it only right and proper that she find her final resting place at the heart of the new empire. The funeral would be at the State Building. A memorial would be built to her so that she would never be forgotten.

The part where Duarte was complicit in the vast slaughter on Earth that defined Avasarala's career got skipped over. History was in the process of being rewritten by the winners. Holden was pretty sure that even though it didn't make it into the press releases and state newsfeeds, everyone remembered that she and Duarte had been on opposite sides, back in the day. And if they didn't, he certainly did.

The mausoleum—her mausoleum, since there wasn't anyone else of sufficient stature to share it with her yet—was white stone polished micron-smooth. The great doors were closed now, the service concluded. A portrait of Avasarala filled the center panel on the north face of the structure. It was etched into the stone along with the dates of her birth and death and a few lines of poetry he didn't recognize. The hundreds of chairs arrayed around the podium where the priest had spoken were only about half-filled now. People had come from across the empire to be here, and now that they were, they mostly broke into little clumps with whoever they already knew. The grass around the crypt wasn't like the stuff back on Earth, but it filled the same ecological niche and behaved similarly enough that they called it grass. The breeze was warm enough to be comfortable. With the palace behind him, Holden could almost pretend that he might walk out to the wilderness beyond the palace grounds and go wherever he chose.

His clothes were of Laconian military cut, blue with the spread wings that Duarte had picked for his imperial icon. The collar was high and stiff. It scraped the skin along the side of Holden's neck. The place where his insignia of rank would have gone was blank. Empty was apparently the symbol of the honored prisoner.

"Will you be going in to the reception, sir?" a guard asked.

Holden wondered what exactly the escalation tree looked like when he said no. That he was a free man, and rejected the hospitality of the palace. Whatever it was, he was pretty sure it had already been practiced and rehearsed. And he probably wouldn't enjoy it.

"In a minute," Holden said. "I just want to..." He gestured vaguely at the tomb as if the inevitability of death was a kind of universal hall pass. A reminder that all human rules were tentative.

"Of course, sir," the guard said, and faded back into the crowd. Holden didn't have any sense that he was free, though. *Unobtrusively confined* was as much as he could hope for.

One woman stood alone at the base of the mausoleum, looking up at Avasarala's portrait. Her sari was a vibrant blue that was just close enough to the Laconian color scheme to be polite and just far enough from it to make it perfectly clear that the politeness was insincere. Even if she hadn't looked like her grandmother, the subtle-not-subtle *fuck you* would have identified her. Holden ambled over.

Her skin was darker than Avasarala's had been, but the shape of her eyes when she glanced over at him and the thinness of her smile were familiar.

"I'm sorry for your loss," Holden said.

"Thank you."

"We haven't been introduced. I'm—"

"James Holden," the woman said. "I know who you are. Nani talked about you sometimes."

"Ah. Well, that must have been something to hear. She didn't always see things the way I did."

"No, she did not. I'm Kajri. She called me Kiki."

"She was an amazing woman."

They were silent for the space of two long breaths together. The breeze made the fabric of Kajri's sari ripple like a flag. Holden was about to step away when she spoke again.

"She would have hated this," she said. "Hauled into the camp of her enemies to be celebrated now that she can't crack their balls anymore. Co-opted as soon as she couldn't fight back. You could power a planet by hooking a turbine to her right now. That's how much she's spinning in this grave."

Holden made a small sound that could have been agreement.

Kajri shrugged. "Or maybe not. She might have just thought it was funny. I could never be sure with her."

"I owed her a lot," Holden said. "I didn't always realize it at the time, but she did what she could to help me. I never got the chance to thank her. Or...I did, I guess, but I didn't take it. If there's anything I can do for you or your family..."

"You don't seem to be in a position to do people favors, Captain Holden."

Holden looked back at the palace. "Yeah, I'm not really at my best these days. But I wanted to say it all the same."

"I appreciate the sentiment," Kajri said. "And from what I've heard, you've managed to have some influence? The prisoner with the emperor's ear."

"I don't know about that. I talk a lot, but I don't know that anyone listens. Except the security detail. I assume they listen to everything."

She chuckled, and it was a warmer, more sympathetic sound than he'd expected. "It isn't easy, having no part of your life for just yourself. I grew up knowing that everything I said would be monitored, cataloged, filed, and judged for its potential to compromise me or my family. There's a record in the intelligence service archives somewhere of every time I've had my period."

"Because of her?" Holden said, nodding to the tomb.

"Because of her. But she gave me the tools to live through it too. She taught us to use everything shameful in our lives as a weapon to humiliate people who would diminish us. That's the secret, you know."

"What's the secret?"

Kajri smiled. "The people who have power over you are weak too. They shit and bleed and worry that their children don't love them anymore. They're embarrassed by the stupid things they did when they were young that everyone else has forgotten. And so they're vulnerable. We all define ourselves by the people around us, because that's the kind of monkey we are. We can't transcend it. So when they watch you, they hand you the power to change what they are too."

"And she taught you that?"

"She did," Kajri said. "But she didn't know it."

As if to prove the point, a guard moved across the grass toward them, keeping a respectful distance until he was sure they'd seen him and then gave them time to finish what they were saying before coming closer. Kajri turned to him, lifting her eyebrow.

"The reception is going to begin in twenty minutes, ma'am," the guard said. "The high consul specifically hoped to meet you."

"I wouldn't dream of disappointing him," she said with a smile Holden had seen before on other lips. Holden offered his arm, and Kajri took it. As they walked away, he nodded toward the tomb and the words written on it. IF LIFE TRANSCENDS DEATH, THEN I WILL SEEK FOR YOU THERE. IF NOT, THEN THERE TOO.

"It's an interesting quote," he said. "I feel like I should recognize it. Who wrote it?"

"I don't know," she said. "She only told us to put it on her grave. She didn't say where it came from."

Everyone who was anyone had come to Laconia. That was true on several levels. Duarte's plan to shift the center of humanity away from Sol system to the heart of his own empire had found a level of cooperation and consent that shocked Holden at first and then left him with a permanent sense of mild disappointment in humans as a species. The most prestigious scientific research institutes had all moved their headquarters to Laconia. Four different ballet companies threw off centuries of rivalry to share the same Laconian Institute of Art. Celebrities and scholars rushed to new, palatial, state-subsidized estates in the capital city. There were already movies being made there. The soft power of culture set on speed scrub, ready to flood the networks and feeds with the reassuring messages of High Consul Duarte and the permanence of Laconia.

Business came too. Duarte had banks and office campuses prebuilt and ready for tenants. The Association of Worlds wasn't just Carrie Fisk in a shitty office on Medina Station anymore. It was a cathedral in the center of the capital city with a lobby bigger than a hangar bay and stained glass walls that seemed to rise up forever. The Transport Union's central authority was there too, in a lesser building with fewer amenities so that it was clear physically and socially who was in favor and who was on notice. Holden watched it all from the State Building that was his home and his prison, and it left him thinking of living on an island.

Within the boundary of the city, Laconia was cleaner, newer, brighter, and more controlled than most space stations Holden had been on. Just outside it was wilderness like he'd only seen in storybooks. Ancient forests and alien ruins that would take generations to tame and explore. Holden had heard gossip and rumors about the remnant technologies brought to shambling life by the early work with the protomolecule: boring worms the size of spacecraft, doglike repair drones that made no distinction between mechanism and flesh, crystalline caves with piezoelectric effects that induced hallucinations of music and crippling vertigo. Even as the capital city became synonymous with humanity as a whole, the planet around it stayed alien. An island of the profoundly familiar in a sea of we-don't-understand-that-yet. In a way, it was reassuring that Duarte, for all his god-emperor reach, couldn't achieve everything in just a few decades.

In another way, it was terrifying.

The reception hall was grand, but not overblown. If Laconia had been built in Duarte's image, there was a weird thread of personal restraint in the high consul's soul. However grand the city was, however overwhelming his ambitions, Duarte's palatial compound and home wasn't gaudy or even particularly ornate. The ballroom was all clean lines and a neutral palette that reached for elegance without being too concerned with what anyone thought. Couches and chairs were placed here and there where people could rearrange them. Young people in military uniform served glasses of wine and spiced tea. More than power, Duarte made everything that surrounded him seem born of confidence. It was a good trick, because even after Holden saw through it, it still worked.

Holden accepted a glass of wine from a young woman and strolled through the shifting crowd. A few of the people, he recognized instantly. Carrie Fisk of the Association of Worlds, holding court at a long table, with the governors of half a dozen colonies fighting to be the first one laughing at her jokes. Thorne Chao, the face of the most popular newsfeed coming out of Bara Gaon. Emil-Michelle Li in the flowing green dress that was her trademark when she wasn't in a movie. And for every face Holden could put a name to, there were a dozen more who looked vaguely familiar.

He moved though the thin social fog of polite smiles and nods of recognition that fell short of actual engagement. He was here because Duarte wanted him seen here, but the Venn diagram of people eager to curry favor with the high consul but also willing to risk his displeasure by cozying up to the state's highest-profile prisoner didn't have much overlap.

But it did have some.

"I'm not drunk enough for this."

Transport Union President Camina Drummer leaned against a standing table, her hands wrapped around a glass. Her face looked older in person. He could see the lines around her eyes and mouth more clearly when there weren't a camera, a screen, and several billion kilometers between them. She shifted a degree, making room for him at the table, and he accepted the invitation.

"I'm not sure what drunk enough for this looks like," he said. "Blackout drunk? Fighting drunk? Weeping-in-the-corner drunk?"

"You don't seem even tipsy."

"I'm not. I'm mostly off of alcohol these days."

"Keeping your wits about you?"

"And it bothers my stomach."

Drummer smiled and coughed out a laugh. "They've let the honored prisoner out among the people. Makes me think you're not as useful to them anymore. Have they squeezed all the juice out of you?"

The way she said it, it could have been teasing between two old colleagues, fallen from power together and living in the twilight of political acceptability. Or it could have been something more. A way to ask if he'd been forced to betray the underground on Medina yet. If they'd decided to break him. Drummer knew as well as he did who was listening, even here.

"I've been helping as much as I can with the alien threat issue. Anything else he asks me about, all my answers would be yesterday's news anyway. And I assume I'm here now because Duarte thinks I'm useful to him here."

"Just part of the donkey show."

"Dog and pony," Holden said. Then, seeing her reaction. "The phrase is dog and pony show."

"Sure it is," she said.

"What about you? How's the dismantling of the Transport Union going?"

Drummer's eyes brightened and her smile widened. She answered in a perfect newsfeed-ready voice, crisp and warm and false as a carved acorn. "I am very pleased with the smooth transition to fuller oversight by the Laconian authority and the Association of Worlds. Our focus is to keep all of the old practices that were working and streamline and integrate new procedures that will cut away the dead wood. We have been able to maintain and even increase the efficiency of trade without compromising the security that the greater destiny of humanity requires."

"That bad?"

"I shouldn't bitch. It could be worse. As long as I'm a good little soldier and Duarte thinks I'll be useful bringing Saba in from the cold, I won't end up in a pen."

A murmur rose from the main entrance, and a disturbance in the crowd. All through the ballroom, attention shifted like iron filings aligning to a magnet. Holden didn't have to look to know that Winston Duarte had arrived, but he did anyway.

Duarte's uniform was almost the same as Holden's. He had the same affable calm that he seemed to carry everywhere. His security detail was more obvious than whatever surveillance was on Holden, though. Two thick-bodied guards with sidearms and eyes that flickered with implanted tech. Cortázar had arrived with him too, but stood apart with the air of a teenager pulled away from a game for family dinner. The actual teenager—Duarte's daughter, Teresa—walked at her father's side like a shadow.

Carrie Fisk scurried up to Duarte, her coterie of governors abandoned, and shook his hand. They talked for a moment before Fisk turned to Teresa and shook the girl's hand too. A little crowd had started coalescing behind Fisk as people tried to be unobtrusive about jockeying for a position to meet the great man.

"Creepy son of a bitch, isn't he?" Drummer said.

Holden grunted. He didn't know what she was talking about. It might have been just the way everyone around him was so trained to obeisance. That would have been enough. But maybe she saw something of what Holden did: the stuttering of his eyes, the pearlescent shadow under his skin. Holden had seen the proto-molecule in action as much as anyone who wasn't in Cortázar's lab. That was probably why the side effects of Duarte's treatments were more obvious to him.

He realized he was staring. More than that, he realized that everyone was staring, and he was being drawn along by the pressure of their attention. He looked back at Drummer, making the conscious effort to turn away. It was harder than he liked to admit.

He wanted to ask if there was news of the underground, whether Duarte's reign seemed as inevitable out in the wide vacuum between the worlds as it did here in his home.

"Any news of the underground?" he asked.

"There are always going to be some malcontents," she said, walking the line between innocuous and meaningful. "What about you? How is the famed Captain James Holden spending his days? Going to parties? Waving tiny fists in impotent rage?"

"Nope. Just plotting and waiting for my moment to strike," Holden said. They both grinned as if it had been a joke.

Chapter One: Elvi

The universe is always stranger than you think.

That had been the favorite phrase of a professor of Elvi's back in her graduate study days. Professor Ehrlich, a grumpy old German with a long white beard who'd always made Elvi think of garden gnomes, repeated it every time someone was surprised by the results their lab test delivered. At the time, Elvi had found the catchphrase true to the point of triteness. Of course the universe had unexpected surprises.

Professor Ehrlich was almost certainly dead. He'd been at the edge of what anti-aging technology could achieve when Elvi was in her early twenties. She had a daughter older than that now. But if he'd still been alive, Elvi would have sent him a lengthy and heartfelt apology.

The universe wasn't just stranger than you knew, it was stranger than you could know. Every new wonder, no matter how astonishing, just laid the foundation for an even more astounding discovery later. The universe and its constantly shifting definition of what was considered strange. The discovery of what everyone thought was alien life when the protomolecule was found on Phoebe had shaken people to their foundations, and was somehow still less disturbing than the discovery that the protomolecule wasn't an alien so much as it was an alien's tool. Their version of a wrench, only a wrench that converted the entire asteroid station of Eros into a spaceship, hijacked Venus, created the ring gate, and gave sudden access to thirteen hundred worlds beyond.

The universe is always stranger than you think. God damn right, Professor.

"What," her husband Fayez said, "is that?"

They were on the bridge of her ship, the *Falcon*. The ship that the Laconian Empire had given her. On the screen in front of them, a high-resolution image of what everyone was calling *the object* slowly filled in. It was a planetary body a little larger than Jupiter and nearly transparent, like an enormous crystal ball with a faintly greenish hue. The only structure in the Adro system.

"Passive spectrometry says almost entirely carbon," Travon Barrish said, not even looking up from his work screen as the data scrolled by. He was the team's materials scientist, and the most literal person Elvi had ever met. Of course he gave Fayez the factual answer to his question. She knew that wasn't what her husband had been asking. He'd been asking, *Why is that?*

"It's packed into a dense lattice," Jen Lively, the team's physicist, said. "It..."

She trailed off, so Elvi finished for her. "It's a diamond."

When she was seven years old, Elvi Okoye had returned to Nigeria with her mother when her great-aunt, a woman Elvi had never met, died. As her mother worked to take care of funeral arrangements, Elvi wandered through her house. It became a game of sorts, seeing how much of a picture of the dead woman she could create by looking at the objects she'd left behind. On a shelf next to the bed, a picture of a smiling young man with dark skin and pale eyes who could have been a husband, or a brother, or a son. In the tiny bathroom, among the scattered packages of cheap soaps and cleansers, one beautiful crystal bottle filled with mysterious green liquid. Perfume? Poison? Without having known the woman herself, all the objects she'd left behind were fantastic and compelling.

Many years later, while rinsing her mouth, the smell triggered a memory and she realized the green liquid in the bottle had almost certainly been mouthwash. One mystery solved, but new questions arose. Why had she put mouthwash in such a beautiful bottle instead of just leaving it in the recyclable container it came in? Where had the bottle come from originally? Had she used it as mouthwash, or was there some hidden function mouthwash could perform that Elvi had never thought of? Without the dead woman to explain, it would forever remain a mystery. Some things could only ever be understood in context.

On the view screen, a single faintly green diamond with a machine-perfect smooth surface floating in a solar system with no other planets, orbiting one fading white dwarf star. A bottle of mouthwash in cut crystal, surrounded by cheap soap on a dirty bathroom counter. Fayez was right. The only question that mattered was *why*, but everyone who knew was dead. The only answer she had left was Professor Ehrlich's.

The *Falcon* had been specially designed at the request of High Consul Duarte specifically for her, and it had only one mission: to visit the gate network's "dead systems" and see if they held any clues about the nameless enemy that had destroyed the protomolecule builders' civilization or the weird nonphysical bullets that they—or it, or whatever pronoun you used for an extradimensional alocal antecedent—had left behind.

The *Falcon* had visited three of those systems so far. Every time it had been a wonder. Elvi didn't like the phrase *dead system*. People had started calling them that because they contained no planets capable of sustaining life. She found the classification annoying and simplistic. Yes, it wasn't possible for any life they understood to live on a Jupiter-sized diamond floating around a white dwarf. But there was also no conceivable natural process that could account for such an artifact. Someone had made it. Engineering on a scale that was awesome in the classical sense of the word. Inspiring both wonder and dread in equal proportion. To write it off as *dead* because plants didn't grow on it felt like the dread winning out over the wonder.

"They swept up everything," Fayez said. He was flipping through telescope and radar images of the solar system. "There isn't even a cometary belt clear out to a light-year from the star. They grabbed every bit of material in this entire solar system, turned it into carbon, and mashed it into a fucking diamond."

"People used to give diamonds as gifts before proposing marriage," Jen said. "Maybe someone wanted to be sure the answer wasn't no."

Travon's head snapped up from his console, and he blinked at Jen for several seconds. His rigid literalism meant he was also chemically free of anything resembling a sense of humor, and Elvi had watched Jen's flippant irony put him into vapor lock more than once.

"I don't think—" Travon started, but Elvi cut him off.

"Stay focused on the job, people. We need to know everything about this system before we bring the catalyst online and start breaking things."

"Copy that, boss," Fayez said, and gave her a wink no one else could see.

The rest of her team, the very best scientists and technicians from across the empire, handpicked and placed under her command by the high consul himself, turned back to their displays. In scientific matters related to their current mission, her orders had the full force of imperial law. No one on the team ever argued.

The caveat being, of course, that not everyone was on her team, and not everything was considered a scientific matter.

"You want to tell him that we're pushing the rollout," Fayez said, "or should I?"

She looked at the screen again with a kind of longing. There were probably structures in the diamond. Traces like pale ink in a dead script that could point them a little further toward the next mystery, the next revelation, the next unutterable strangeness. She didn't want to tell anyone about anything. She wanted to *look*.

"I'll take care of it," Elvi said, and headed for the lift.

Admiral Mehmet Sagale was a mountain of a man with coal-black eyes in a dinner plate–flat face. As the military commander of their mission, he mostly left the scientists alone. But when something fell into an area where his orders specified he was in charge, he was as implacable and immovable as his size suggested. And something about sitting in his spartan office always felt disciplinary. Like being sent to the headmaster for cheating on a test. Elvi hated playing the role of supplicant to a military figurehead. But in the Laconian Empire, the military always sat at the top of the authority chart.

"Dr. Okoye," Admiral Sagale said. He rubbed the bridge of his nose with the tips of sausage-sized fingers and gazed at her with the same mix of affection and patronizing annoyance she had once given her children when they were doing something stupid. "We are woefully behind schedule, as you know. My orders are to—"

"This system is incredible, Met," she said. Using the nickname was a little aggression, but one he tolerated. "It's too incredible to just throw away out of impatience. We need to spend time really studying this artifact before you trot out the catalyst and wait to see if something blows up!"

"*Major* Okoye," Sagale replied, using her military title to not so subtly remind her of their relative positions in the chain of command. "As soon as your team finishes their preliminary data collection, we will bring out the catalyst and see if this system has any military value, as per our orders."

"Admiral," Elvi said, knowing aggression would fail on him when he was in this mood and trying for a placating respect instead. "I just want a little more time. We can make up the schedule on our trip out. Duarte gave me the fastest science ship in human history so I could spend more time on the science and less on the travel. Exactly like I'm asking you to do now."

Reminding Sagale that she had a direct line to the high consul, and that he valued her work enough to build her a ship for it. How was *that* for not so subtle.

Sagale was unmoved.

"You have twenty hours to finish gathering your data," he said, folding his hands across his wide belly like a Buddha. "And not one minute more. Inform your team."

"This sort of rigid thinking is *precisely* why it's impossible to do good science under Laconian rule," Elvi said. "I should be running a university biology department somewhere. I'm too old to be good at taking orders."

"I agree," Fayez said. "But here we are."

She and Fayez were in her quarters to shower and catch a quick bite of food before Sagale and his storm troopers trotted out their live sample of protomolecule and risked destroying a billions-of-years-old artifact just to see if it went boom in a useful manner. "If it won't build them a better bomb, who cares if they break it!"

She whirled toward Fayez as she said it, and he took a half step away from her. She realized she was still holding her dinner plate in one hand. "I'm not going to throw it," she said. "I don't throw things."

"You have," he replied. He'd gotten older too. His once-black hair was almost totally gray now, and laugh lines spread out from the corners of his eyes. She didn't mind. She liked that he smiled more than he frowned. He was smiling now. "Things have been thrown."

"I never—" she started, wondering if he was actually afraid she'd throw a plate at him out of frustration or just teasing her to lighten the mood. Even after decades together, she sometimes couldn't tell what went on in his head.

"Bermuda, just after Ricki left home for university, we took our first real vacation in years and you—"

"There was a roach. A roach crawled on my plate!"

"It nearly took my head off when you hurled it."

"Well," she said, "I was startled."

She laughed. Fayez was grinning like he'd won a prize. So, of course, making her laugh had been the goal all along. She put the plate down.

"Look, I know saluting and following orders isn't exactly what we had in mind when we got our degrees," Fayez said. "But this is the new reality as long as Laconia's in control. So—"

It was her own fault, really, being swept up into the Science Directorate. Laconia by and large left people alone. Planets elected their own governors and representatives to the Association of Worlds. They could establish their own laws, as long as they didn't directly contravene imperial law. And unlike most dictatorships in history, Laconia seemed uninterested in restricting higher education. The universities of the galaxy functioned pretty much like they had before the takeover. Sometimes even a little better.

But Elvi had made the mistake of becoming humanity's leading expert on the protomolecule, the vanished civilization that had created it, and the doom that had wiped it out. As a much younger woman, she'd been sent to Ilus as part of the first scientific mission to explore the biology of an alien world. Until then, her specialization in exobiology had been theoretical, mostly focusing on bathypelagic and deep-ice life that had seemed like good analogs for bacteria one might find under the surface of Europa.

They'd never found any bacteria on Europa, but the gate network opened, and suddenly exobiology was a real thing with more than thirteen hundred new biomes to explore. She'd gone to Ilus expecting to study lizard analogs, and instead run face-first into the artifacts of a galaxy-wide war older than her species. She'd become obsessed with understanding. Of course she had. A house the size of a galaxy, filled with rooms full of fascinating things, and the owners dead for millennia. She'd devoted the rest of her professional life to figuring them out. So when Winston Duarte invited her to lead a team to explore exactly that mystery, and gave her a bottomless grant to do it, she hadn't been able to say no.

At that point, she'd seen only the Laconia everyone was presented in the newsfeeds. Impossibly powerful, militarily unbeatable, but not interested in ethnic cleansing or genocide. Maybe even with humanity's best interests at heart. Taking their money to do science hadn't given her many qualms. Especially since there also hadn't been many options. When the king says, *Come work for me*, there aren't many paths to *No*.

The qualms came later when she was inducted into their military and learned the source of Laconia's overwhelming technological advantage.

When she met the catalysts.

"We should get back," Fayez said as he finished clearing away the last of their dishes from dinner. "The clock is ticking."

"I will. In a minute," she replied, stepping back into the tiny private bathroom they shared. One of the privileges of her rank. In the mirror over her sink, an old woman stared back at her. The woman's eyes were haunted by what she was about to do.

"You ready in there?" Fayez shouted.

"You go ahead. I'll catch up."

"Jesus, Els, you're not going to go see it again, are you?"

It. The catalyst.

"It isn't your fault," Fayez said. "You didn't design this study."

"I agreed to oversee it."

"Sweetheart. Darling. Light of my life. Whatever we call Laconia in public, when you take its clothes off, it's a dictatorship," Fayez said. "We never had a choice."

"I know."

"So why do you do this to yourself?" Fayez said.

She didn't answer, because she couldn't have explained it even if she wanted to.

"I'll catch up."

The catalyst holding area was in the heart of the *Falcon*, surrounded on all sides by thick layers of depleted uranium shielding and the galaxy's most complicated Faraday cage. It had become clear very quickly that the protomolecule communicated at faster than light speed. Some application of quantum entanglement was the leading theory, but whatever the mechanism, the protomolecule defied locality, much like the ring gate system it had created. It had taken Cortázar and his team years to figure out how to keep a sample of the protomolecule from talking to itself, but they'd had decades and they'd eventually come up with a combination of materials and fields that tricked a node of protomolecule into locking itself off from the rest.

A node. It. The catalyst.

Two of Sagale's Marines guarded the door to its chamber. They wore heavy blue power armor that whined and clicked when they moved. Each was equipped with a flamethrower. Just in case.

"We're going to use the catalyst soon. I want to check on it," Elvi said to the space between the two guards. For all that she had a military title, she still often couldn't figure out who was the ranking officer in any given room. She lacked the indoctrination of boot camp, and the lifetime of practice the Laconians took for granted.

"Of course, Major," the one on the left said. She looked too young to be the senior officer, but that was so often true of the Laconians. Most of them looked too young for their titles. "Will you need an escort?"

"No," Elvi said. *No, I always do this alone.*

The young Marine did something on the wrist of her armor, and the door behind her slid open. "Let us know when you're ready to come out."

The catalyst's room was a cube, four meters on a side. It had no bed, no sink, no toilet. Just hard metal and mesh drains. Once a day, the room was flushed with solvent and the liquid was sucked away to be incinerated. The Laconians were obsessive about contamination protocols where the protomolecule was concerned.

The node, it, the catalyst, had once been a woman in her late fifties. What her name had been and why she'd been selected for protomolecule infection was not in the official record Elvi had access to. But Elvi hadn't been in their military for long before she found out about the Pen. The place where convicted criminals were sent to be deliberately infected, so that the empire would have a limitless supply of protomolecule to work with.

The catalyst was special, though. Through some work of Cortázar's or through some accident of the woman's genetics, she was only a carrier. She showed early signs of infection—changes to her skin and skeletal structure—but in the months since she'd been brought on board the *Falcon*, those changes hadn't progressed at all. And she never entered what everyone called the "vomit zombie" phase, puking up material to try to spread the infection.

Elvi knew that she was perfectly safe in the same room with the catalyst, but she shuddered every time she entered anyway.

The infected woman looked at her with blank eyes and moved her lips in a soundless whisper. She smelled mostly of the solvent bath she received every day, but under it was something else. A morgue stink of decaying flesh.

It was normal to sacrifice animals. Rats, pigeons, pigs. Dogs. Chimpanzees. Biology had always suffered the cognitive push-pull of proving that humans were just another kind of animal while at the same time claiming to be morally different in kind. It was okay to kill a chimp in the name of science. It wasn't okay to kill a person.

Except, apparently, when it was.

Maybe the catalyst had agreed to this. Maybe it was this or some other, more gruesome death. Whatever that would be.

"I'm sorry," Elvi said to her, as she did every time she came into the catalyst chamber. "I'm so sorry, I didn't know that they did this. I would never have agreed to it."

The woman's head lolled on her neck, nodding forward as if in mock agreement.

"I won't forget that they did this to you. If I can ever make this right, I will."

The woman pushed at the floor with her hands as though she wanted to stand up, but her arms lacked the strength, and her hands flopped bonelessly. It was just reflexes. That's what she told herself. Instinct. The woman's brain was gone, or at least changed into something that wasn't by any sane definition a brain. There wasn't anyone really alive in that skin. Not anymore.

But there had been once.

Elvi wiped her eyes. The universe was always stranger than you expected. Sometimes it was full of wonders. Sometimes full of horrors.

"I won't forget."

Chapter Two: Naomi

Naomi missed the *Rocinante*, but then she missed a lot of things these days.

Her old ship and home was still parked on Freehold. Before they'd left, she and Alex had found a cavern system on the edge of Freehold's southernmost continent with a mouth big enough to edge the ship into. They'd put it down in a dry tunnel and spent a week running seals and storage tarps that would keep the local flora and fauna out. Whenever they got back to the *Roci*, it would be there, ready and waiting. If they never did, it would be there for centuries. Still waiting.

Sometimes, on the edge of sleep, she'd take herself through it. She still knew every centimeter from the top of the cockpit to the curve of the drive cone. She could think her way through it on the float or under thrust. She'd heard about ancient scholars back on Earth making palaces of memory that way. Imagine Alex in the cockpit, holding an hourglass for time. Then down to the flight deck, where Amos and Clarissa were tossing a golgo ball with the numeral 2 painted on it back and forth for initial and final velocities divided by two. Then down to her cabin, and Jim. Jim by himself. Jim who meant displacement. A simple kinematic equation, three things that were all the same, easy to remember because they all stung her heart.

That was one reason she'd agreed to the shell-game plan when Saba and the underground had reached out to her. Memories were like ghosts, and as long as Jim and Amos were gone, the *Roci* would always be a little bit haunted.

And it wasn't only Jim, though he had been the first. Naomi had also lost Clarissa, who would have died from the slow poisons in her implants if she hadn't chosen to die by violence. Amos had taken a high-risk mission from the underground, deep in enemy territory, and then gone silent, missing pickup window after pickup window until they all stopped expecting to hear from him again. Even Bobbie, healthy and well, but in the captain's seat of her own ship now. They were all lost to her, but Jim was the worst.

Freehold, on the other hand, she didn't miss at all. The experience of being under a vast and empty sky had its charm for a while, but the unease lasted longer than the novelty. If she was going to live as a fugitive and outlaw, she could at least do it in something where the air was held in by something visible. Her new quarters—spare and terrible as they were—at least had that going for them.

From the outside, her bunk looked like a standard cargo container made to transport a low-yield planetary fusion reactor. It was the kind colonists in the thirteen hundred new systems would use to power a small city or a medium-sized mining station. With its actual cargo gone, there was enough room for a gimbaled crash couch, an emergency support recycler, a water supply, and half a dozen modified short-burn torpedoes. The crash couch was her bed and her workbench. The support recycler was her power and food and her waste disposal. The kind of thing that would keep the crew of a stranded ship alive for weeks, but not in anything like comfort. The water supply was for drinking, but also part of the stealth, connected to small evaporation panels on the exterior of the container to bleed off her waste heat.

And the torpedoes were how she spoke to the larger world.

Except not today. Today she was going to see actual people. Breathe their air, touch their skin. Hear their living voices. She wasn't sure if she was excited about that, or if the energy stirring in her belly was foreboding. The one could seem so much like the other.

"Permission to open?" she said, and the crash couch's monitor hesitated, sent the message, and then a few breaths later came back with CONFIRMED. DEPARTURE AT 18:45 STANDARD. DON'T BE LATE.

Naomi unstrapped herself from the couch and pushed to the inner door of the container, securing the helmet on her suit as she went. When the suit showed solid seals, she double-checked them anyway, then cycled the air in the container into her emergency recycler, bringing the interior down to near vacuum. When the pressure reached the efficiency limit of the unit and stopped dropping, she popped the container doors and pulled herself out into the vastness of the cargo hold.

The *Verity Close* was a converted ice hauler acting as a long-haul shipping vessel for the colonies. The hold around her was as wide as the Freehold sky, or it felt that way. The *Rocinante* and eleven more like her could have fit in it and not touched the sides. Instead, thousands of containers like Naomi's were locked into place and ready to be hauled out from Sol to any of the new cities and stations that humanity was building. Taming the new wilderness of planets that didn't know humanity's genetic codes or tree of life. And most of the containers were what they claimed—soil, industrial yeast incubators, bacterial libraries.

And then, like hers, a few were something else.

This was the shell game.

She didn't know if Saba had come up with the idea, or if his wife, the figurehead president of the Transport Union, had found some covert way to tell him. With Medina Station and the slow zone firmly under Laconian control, the greatest obstacle the underground faced was moving ships and personnel from one system to another. Even something as small as the *Roci* couldn't hope to pass by Medina's sensor arrays unnoticed. Traffic control through the gate network was too important to ever let that happen.

But as long as the Transport Union was still in charge of its own ships, the records could be forged. Cargo containers like hers could be moved from ship to ship, making it difficult if not impossible to track her communications—or Saba's or Wilhelm Walker's or any of the other organizing heads of the underground—to any one vessel.

Or, if the reward seemed to justify the terrible risk, something larger could be smuggled. Something dangerous. Something like the captured warship *Gathering Storm* could be snuck into Sol system. And with it, Bobbie Draper and Alex Kamal, who she hadn't seen in over a year. And who, right now, were waiting for her at a private rendezvous.

She launched herself along the row of containers, skimming past them with accuracy born of a lifetime's practice. The guide lights blinked at the containers' edges, marking the ever-changing maze of access and control and leading her toward the crew hatch. The actual crew space was probably smaller than the *Rocinante*'s. Her secret cargo container, as spacious as the crew cabins.

She didn't know the crew of the ship that had carried her for the last months. Most of them weren't aware she was there. Saba arranged things that way. The fewer people knew, the less they could say. The old Belter term for it was *guerraregle*. War rules. It was how she'd lived as a girl, back in the bad old days. It was how she lived now.

She found the airlock into the ship and cycled through. Her contact was waiting for her. She was a young woman, not more than twenty years old, with pale skin and wide-set dark eyes. Her shaved head was probably meant to make her look tough, but it just reminded Naomi of baby fuzz. Her name might not have been Blanca, but that was how Naomi knew her.

"You're clear for twenty minutes, ma'am," Blanca said. She had a good voice. Musical and clean. A Martian accent that reminded Naomi of Alex. "After that, I'm off shift. I can stay around, but I can't keep the next guy from coming on."

"More than enough," Naomi said. "I just need to get to the habitation ring."

"Not a problem. We're going to be transferring your container to the *Mosley* in berth sixteen-ten. It's going to take a few hours, but the work order's already been approved."

The pea slipping into a different shell. By the time Naomi was ready to send out her next set of orders and analysis, the *Verity Close* would be past the Sol gate and off toward some other system. And Naomi would be in her same little hole, sleeping on her same little couch, but traveling with a different ship. Blanca would be replaced by her new contact waiting for her at the docks. Naomi had lost track of how many times she'd done this. It was almost routine.

"Thank you," she said, and started to pull herself through toward the dockside airlock.

"It's been an honor, ma'am," Blanca said, spitting the words out quickly. "Meeting you, I mean. Meeting Naomi Nagata."

"Thank you for everything you've done for me. I appreciate it more than I can say."

Blanca braced. It felt like theater, but Naomi saluted the girl all the same. It meant something to the girl, and for Naomi to treat it with anything less than equal seriousness would have been rude. Worse, it would have been cruel.

Then she pulled herself into the cramped green corridor of the *Verity Close* and left Blanca behind. She didn't expect ever to see her again.

Deep Transfer Station Three lived between the orbit of Saturn and Uranus, locked in position with the Sol gate. Its architecture was familiar: a large spherical dock capable of accepting several dozen ships at maximum capacity and a habitation ring spinning at one-third g. It was both a critical central hub for traffic in and out of Sol system and a glorified warehouse complex. Ships from across the system brought cargo here ready to send out to the colony worlds or came to pick up incoming packages. At any given time, there were probably more alien artifacts on the transfer station than anyplace else in the system.

All told, the station could hold twenty thousand people, though the traffic rarely if ever demanded full capacity. A permanent staff and the crews of whatever ships came and went, along with contractors to run the hospitals, bars, brothels, churches, stores, and restaurants that seemed to follow humanity everywhere it went. It was a base where crews from across the system and from the other systems on the far sides of the rings could get away from each other for a few days, see unfamiliar faces, hear voices they hadn't lived with for months, climb into bed with someone who didn't feel like family. It created a constant fraternization that had led to the station's ring getting the unofficial name "Paternity Row."

Naomi liked the place. There was something reassuring in the stability of human behavior. Alien civilizations and galactic empire, war and resistance: They were there. But also drinking and karaoke. Sex and babies.

She walked through the public corridor of the habitation ring with her head bowed. The underground had a false identification for her in the station system so that her biometrics wouldn't raise an alarm, but she kept from making herself too obvious all the same in case a human might recognize her.

The rendezvous was a restaurant in the lowest and outermost level of the ring. She'd expected to be ushered into a storeroom or freezer, but the man at the door led her back to a private dining room. Even before she stepped though the doorway, she knew they were there.

Bobbie saw her first and stood up, grinning. She wore a nonde-script flight suit without identifying tags or patches, but she wore it like a uniform. Alex, rising with her, had an older cut. He'd lost weight, and his remaining hair was trimmed close. He could have been an accountant or a general. Without words, they stepped into each other, arms raised. A three-way embrace with Naomi's head on Alex's shoulder, Bobbie's cheek against hers. The warmth of their bodies was more comforting than she wanted it to be.

"Oh, God dammit," Bobbie said, "but it is good to see you again."

The embrace broke, and they moved to the table. A bottle of whiskey and three glasses waited, a clear and unmistakable sign of bad news to come. A toast to be made, a memory to be honored, another loss to carry. Naomi asked her question with a glance.

"You heard about Avasarala," Alex said.

The relief came in a little rush followed by chagrin at feeling relief. It was only that Avasarala had died. "I did."

Bobbie poured out shots for each of them, then raised one. "She was a hell of woman. We won't see her like again."

They touched glasses, and Naomi drank. Losing the old woman was hard—harder for Bobbie, probably, than any of the rest of them. But they weren't mourning Amos yet. Or Jim.

"So," Bobbie said, putting down her glass, "how's life as the secret general of the resistance?"

"I prefer 'secret diplomat,'" Naomi said. "And it's underwhelming."

"Wait, wait, wait," Alex said. "Can't talk without food. It's not family unless there's a meal."

The restaurant did a good Belt/Mars fusion menu. Something called white kibble that was related to the real thing, but with fresh vegetables and bean sprouts. Rounds of vat-grown beef-pork hybrid cooked in the shape of a Petri dish and touched with a sweet hot sauce. They leaned on the table here the way they had on the *Rocinante* in their previous incarnations.

Naomi hadn't realized how much she missed Bobbie's laugh or Alex's way of sneaking another small helping onto her plate when she was almost finished eating. The little intimacies of living in close quarters with someone for decades. And then not living there anymore. It might have made her sad if it weren't for the pleasure of being there in the moment with the two of them.

"The *Storm*'s crewed up pretty well," Bobbie was saying. "I was worried for a while that it would be straight Belters. I mean, that's where Saba's bench is the deepest. Two Martian vets running a crew full of folks who still call us inners?"

"Could have been a problem," Naomi agreed.

"Saba pulled a whole sheet of UNN and MCRN vets," Alex said. "Young ones too. Weird being around people who were the age I was when I mustered out. They look like babies, you know? All fresh-faced and serious."

Naomi laughed. "I know. Anyone under forty looks like a child to me now."

"They're good," Bobbie said. "I've been running drills and simulations the whole time we've been parked."

"There've been a couple fights," Alex said.

"It's just nerves," Bobbie said. "When this mission's done, that shit will evaporate."

Naomi took another bite of white kibble so that she wouldn't frown. It didn't work, though. Alex cleared his throat and spoke in his changing-the-subject voice. "I'm guessing there's still no word from the big guy?"

Two years before, Saba had found a chance to slip an operative onto Laconia itself with a pocket nuke and an encrypted recall-and-retrieve transmitter. A long-odds mission to get Jim back, or destroy Laconia's rule by cutting off its head. Saba had asked Naomi who she would trust with something that important. That dangerous. When Amos heard about it, he'd packed his bags in the same hour. Since then, Laconia had built new defenses. The underground had lost most of its presence in Laconia system, and Amos had gone silent.

Naomi shook her head. "Not yet."

"Yeah, well," Alex said. "Soon, probably."

"Probably," Naomi agreed, the same way she did every time they had this conversation.

"You two want any coffee?" Alex asked. Bobbie shook her head at the same time Naomi said *Not for me*, and Alex popped up. "I'll go settle up, then."

When the door closed behind him, Naomi leaned forward. She wanted to leave the moment where it was—a reunion with family. A bright spot in the darkness. She wanted to, and she couldn't.

"A mission with the *Storm* in Sol system is a hell of a risk," she said.

"It stands a real chance of getting some attention," Bobbie agreed, not making eye contact. Her tone was light, but there was a warning in it. "It's not just me, you know."

"Saba."

"And others."

"I keep thinking about Avasarala," Naomi said. There was still some whiskey in the bottle, and she poured herself a finger. "She was a hell of a fighter. Never backed down from anything, even when she lost."

"She was one of a kind," Bobbie agreed.

"She was a fighter, but she wasn't a warrior. She was always leading the struggle, but she did it by finding other ways to get the work done. Alliances, political pressure, trade, logistics. Her strategy was always that violence came last."

"She had leverage," Bobbie said. "She ran a planet. We're a bunch of rats looking for cracks in the concrete. We're going to do things differently."

"We have leverage," Naomi said. "And more than that, we can cultivate leverage."

Bobbie put down her fork very carefully. The darkness in her eyes wasn't anger. Or it wasn't just anger, anyway. "Laconia is a military dictatorship. If you want anyone to stand against Duarte, we have to show people that he can be stood against. Military action is what shows people that there's hope. You're a Belter, Naomi. You know this."

"I know that it doesn't work," Naomi said. "The Belt fought for generations against the inner planets—"

"And won," Bobbie said.

"We didn't, though. We didn't win. We held on until something came in and knocked over the playing board. Do you really think we'd have gotten something like the Transport Union if the gates hadn't appeared? The only way we succeeded was by something totally unexpected changing the rules. Only now we're acting like it'll work twice."

"*We're* acting?"

"Saba's acting," Naomi said. "And you're backing him."

Bobbie leaned back, stretching the way she did when she was annoyed. It made her seem even bigger than she was, but Naomi was a hard woman to intimidate. "I know you disagree with the approach, and I know you're not happy that Saba didn't put you in on the details, but—"

"That's not the issue," Naomi said.

"No one's arguing against leverage. No one's saying that we shouldn't be looking for political angles too. But pacifism only works when your enemy has a conscience. Laconia has a deep tradition of discipline through punishment and I know—No, hear me out. I know that because it's a Martian tradition too. You grew up with the Belt, but I grew up with Mars. You tell me that my way doesn't lead to victory? Okay. I believe you. But I'm telling you that your soft approach doesn't work on these people."

"So where does that leave us?"

"Same place as always," Bobbie said. "Doing the best we can for as long as we can and hoping something unexpected happens. On the upside, something unexpected almost always does."

"That's not as comforting as you think," Naomi said with a chuckle, trying to lighten the mood.

Bobbie wasn't having it. "Because sometimes the thing we don't expect is that we lost Clarissa and Holden. Or that we lost Amos. Or that we lose me. Or Alex. Or you. But that's going to happen. We're all going to lose each other eventually, and that's been true since before we were a crew. That's what being born means. Everything else is just specifics. And my specifics are that I'm leading a top-secret military mission in Sol system using the enemy's captured ship against them, because even if it's a bad plan, it's the only plan I have. And maybe my risk will get you your leverage."

But I don't want you to risk anything, Naomi thought. *I've lost too much. I can't stand to lose anything more.* Bobbie's features softened, just a little. So maybe she understood.

The familiar tap of a footstep outside the door was Alex as clearly as if he'd said his name. Naomi took a deep breath and forced herself to relax.

She didn't want to spoil the reunion for him too.

Chapter Three: Alex

Bobbie and Naomi were at it again.

They played it cool when Alex came back into the room, but he could tell a heated conversation had been going on while he was away. Naomi was dipping her head, letting her hair fall in front of her eyes the way she did when she was upset. Bobbie's face was a shade darker than usual, flushed with excitement or anger. Alex had lived on the same small ship with Naomi for decades, and Bobbie only a little less. There was almost nothing they could conceal from each other.

It hurt his feelings a little that they were even trying to hide it because that meant he had to hide it too.

"All settled up," Alex said.

Bobbie nodded and drummed her fingers on the table. Naomi gave him a small smile through her hair.

Alex would have put money that their argument was the same

one they'd been rehashing since they'd left Freehold. Pretending like nothing was wrong was the only safe choice. A wise man doesn't get between two fighting animals, but even a dim bulb didn't step into an argument between Naomi Nagata and Bobbie Draper. Not if he wanted to keep all his fingers. Metaphorically speaking, of course.

"So...," Alex started, letting the word draw out until it became awkward.

"Yeah," Naomi answered. "I've got a lot to do before I climb back into my storage crate."

Bobbie nodded, started to speak, and then stopped. In the blink of an eye she'd crossed the distance to Naomi and swept her up in her massive arms. While the two women were close to the same height, Bobbie outweighed Naomi by at least forty kilos. It was like watching a polar bear grapple a coatrack. But it wasn't the beginning of a fight, because both women were crying and patting each other on the back.

"It was good to see you," Bobbie said, hugging Naomi a little tighter and lifting her off the deck.

"I miss you," Naomi answered. "Both of you. More than I can say."

The *both of you* felt like an invitation, so Alex moved in and threw his arms around the two of them. A moment later, he was weeping too. After a while, when it felt right, they separated. Bobbie wiped her eyes with a napkin, but Naomi ignored the streaks down her face. She was smiling. Alex realized it was maybe the first real smile he'd seen from her since Holden had been taken to Laconia. It made him wonder how lonely her life was now, hidden away in her cargo container, moving from ship to ship and station to station. Even though it was the choice they'd all made together, he felt a pang of guilt for leaving her alone like that. But Bobbie had needed a pilot, and Naomi, in her wandering-statesman role, didn't. And didn't want one.

"When will we see you again?" Bobbie asked.

"I wish I knew," Naomi replied. "You guys going to be in Sol long?"

"Not up to me," Bobbie said with a shrug. In this case it was true, but even if it hadn't been, the answer would have been the same. You never knew who was listening, and even here on a Transport Union station in the back room of an OPA sympathizer bar, the habits of secrecy died hard.

As if on cue, Alex's hand terminal buzzed an alert at him. They were getting ready to transfer the *Storm* from its current ship to the new one. Naomi wasn't the only one living inside a high-stakes shell game.

"Boss, gonna go oversee the transfer," he said to Bobbie.

"I'll come with," she replied, then grabbed Naomi for one last fierce hug. "You stay safe, XO."

"That's all I do nowadays," Naomi said with a sad grin.

Leaving her behind felt wrong. The way it always did.

Alex would never admit it out loud, but the *Gathering Storm* scared the shit out of him. The *Rocinante* was still his first love. Like a hand tool that grew to fit the shape of the hand that held it, the *Roci* was comfortable, familiar, safe. For all that it was a dangerous warship, it still felt like home. It felt *right*. He missed it terribly.

The *Storm* was like living inside an alien creature that was pretending to be an overpowered racing ship and then someone had strapped a shit-ton of firepower onto it. Where flying the *Roci* felt like a collaboration, the ship an extension of his will, flying the *Storm* felt like a negotiation with a dangerous animal. Every time he sat in the pilot's chair he worried about getting bitten.

Bobbie had gone over the ship with her techs from stem to stern and reassured him that there was nothing in the specs that made the *Storm* dangerous to her crew, or at least not more than *all* spaceships were dangerous to their crews. Alex remained unconvinced. There was something about using the controls that felt like the ship wasn't reacting to his inputs; it felt like the ship was interpreting them and agreeing with them, but also making its own damn decisions. The only person he'd ever confided this to was his copilot, Caspar Asoau.

"I mean, yeah, the controls feel a little loose I guess, but not sure that means the ship is fighting back," Caspar had said, giving Alex a suspicious side-eyed glance. Alex hadn't brought it up again. But Alex had been flying spaceships for a lot of years now, and he knew what he knew. There was more to the *Storm* than just metal and carbon and whatever that crystal-looking shit was. Even if no one else could see it.

Still, it was a damn beautiful ship.

Alex stood at a small observation window and watched as it was carefully moved from the open hangar bay of their old transport ship to the new one. The two massive transports flanked the *Storm* as it moved, and the enormous bulk of the transfer station's central hub overshadowed them both. It was all very deliberately done to block line of sight to all the known government telescope and radar stations. For all the Laconian Empire would ever know, two heavy freighters had briefly docked at the same transfer point, dropped off or picked up some cargo, and then gone their separate ways. That a stolen Laconian warship had been moved from one to the other wouldn't appear on any official records or in any video feeds. And the *Storm* and her crew would be free to live and fight another day. Assuming they hadn't overlooked anything.

The gleaming crystal-and-metal flanks of the ship seemed to glow with their own inner light even in the box canyon shadow that two freighters and the transfer station created. Bright white puffs of superheated gas flashed and disappeared as the maneuvering thrusters fired. Caspar would be at the controls, gently nudging the Laconian destroyer out of the open cargo bay of their old ship and into the new with practiced ease. They'd played this game a lot, and both pilots had become expert at moving the ship in very confined spaces.

As a former military man, Alex was always surprised that they could actually manage to keep the conspiracy a secret. They were sneaking a stolen imperial warship through the gate network hidden in the bowels of Transport Union ships. At least dozens and maybe hundreds of people were directly involved. Somehow, they kept getting away with it.

The Occam's razor argument to nearly all conspiracy theories was that people were really shitty at keeping secrets, and large groups of people were exponentially worse. But with the help of their former OPA friends in the Transport Union, they'd been sneaking and peeking for months without getting caught. It was a testament to how bred to insurgency the Belters had become over the last century or two. Hiding a rebellion from vastly superior military forces was in their DNA. During his twenty years as a member of the Martian Navy and then later fighting the Free Navy, he'd had a part in hunting their more radical factions. Alex had often found the Belter capacity for subterfuge and guerrilla fighting infuriating. Now it was literally keeping him alive.

Alex wasn't sure if that was ironic or not. Funny, maybe.

The *Storm* finished buttoning down in their new freighter. It was a cow of a cargo hauler shaped like a fat bullet and named the *Pendulum's Arc*. Its doors slid shut and locked, and Alex felt a tiny tremor in the deck as they did. A pair of doors bigger than a destroyer had some mass to them.

Alex pulled out his terminal and opened a channel to Bobbie. "The baby's tucked in. We can be oscar mike on your word."

"Copy that," Bobbie said, and killed the channel.

She was off doing final prep with her team. Saba's chain of whisperers hadn't told them what their mission in Sol was, but Bobbie kept her troops so drilled on the fundamentals that the specific mission just became a checklist of shit to get done. Alex had been skeptical when Bobbie took a mixed bag of old-guard OPA, stuffed them into Laconian Marine power armor, and said she was going to turn them into a legit covert ops strike team. But damned if she hadn't done exactly that. They'd run three different operations with a hundred percent success rate and a zero percent casualty rate. It turned out that as formidable as Gunny Draper was, she was even scarier when you let her train her own backup.

There had to have been a moment when this had become the new normal. Playing their cargo ship version of three-card monte with the *Storm* while Saba and Naomi and the rest of the underground picked mission targets for them. He couldn't say when it had passed. Only now he was back to being the bus driver he'd been in the MCRN a few lifetimes ago. Every day carried the risk of discovery and capture or death. Every operation sent Bobbie and her team into the meat grinder of the Laconian dominion. For all their successes, they were walking on the edge of a razor blade. If he'd been twenty and unaware of his own mortality, he'd probably have loved it.

He turned away from the observation window and picked up his gear bag. As he walked, his terminal squawked at him. "Locked and powered down," Caspar said.

"I was watching. Elegantly done. The gunny will be drilling the troops, and I'm headed that way. Ship's yours for the duration."

"Copy that."

The corridors of the transfer station were spare and functional. Smooth taupe ceramic walls and a floor just padded enough to keep the occupants from getting shin splints in the habitat ring's one-third g rotation. Alex trudged along one for half a kilometer, then rapped at a door marked STORAGE 348-001.

A grizzled Belter opened it a crack and looked up and down the hallway around Alex. He had gray hair in a military-style buzz cut and flat gray eyes of almost exactly the same color. Alex could see the heavy black pistol he held behind his thigh as he checked to see if the corridor was clear. His name was Takeshi Oba, and he was one of Bobbie's killers.

"All clear," Alex said with a smile, and Oba let him in with a grunt.

It was an empty room of about five by ten meters with the same plain ceramic walls as the corridor outside. Bobbie's team was standing in loose ranks facing her as she addressed them. She gave Alex a tiny nod as he entered, but didn't stop her speech.

"Make no mistake," she was saying, "the Sol system is the most dangerous theater we've operated in. Its threat level is second only to Laconia for our style of covert op. Nearly every rock or chunk of ice bigger than a troop transport has a station, telescope, or radar emplacement on it. There are eyes everywhere."

A mutter passed through the group, but Alex couldn't tell if it was grumbling or agreement.

"And," Bobbie continued, "the Earth-Mars Coalition fleet is entirely under Laconian control. Which means the Laconians' relatively small number of ships—the one fact that has allowed us to operate up to this point—is *not* going to help us here. To make matters worse, the Laconians have left the dreadnought *Heart of the Tempest* in orbit around Earth. It's there primarily as a threat to keep the inner planets in line, but if it detects us, we are in a world of hurt. The *Storm* cannot survive an engagement with a *Magnetar*-class battleship. End of story."

"Any word yet on the target?" Jillian Houston asked. She was the daughter of Freehold's governor, Payne Houston, and had been one of the first volunteers for Bobbie's team. She was tall and rangy, with white-blond hair, the muscles and bone structure of a born Earther, and a perpetual scowl line between her eyes. She'd become Bobbie's unofficial second in the time they'd worked together. Alex worried about that. Jillian was mean as a snake. When he'd told Bobbie that, she'd responded, *I just make sure she never runs out of mice.* He still didn't know quite what that meant.

"No. The kids upstairs are playing this one close to the vest," Bobbie said. "It's starting to feel like we'll know when we're already doing it."

"Outstanding," Jillian said.

"The *Storm* is buttoned up, and we'll be heading Solward on the *Pendulum* in thirty hours," Bobbie said. "Enjoy your time on Paternity Row, but make sure you're on the ship and squared away twenty-four hours from now or find my foot uncomfortably up your ass."

That drew a good-natured chuckle from the crowd.

"Dismissed."

A few chaotic moments later, Bobbie, Jillian, and Alex were the only three left in the room. Bobbie still wore the nondescript flight suit she'd had on when they met with Naomi, but Jillian wore the black jumpsuit adopted by Bobbie's strike team as its unofficial uniform. She also had a large pistol in a holster. Alex had never seen her without it. For Freeholders, wearing a gun was like wearing pants.

"I don't like Saba giving us the runaround on this," Jillian said. "It feels like he's fucking improvising."

"There could be a lot of legitimate reasons why the mission details are still being formulated," Bobbie replied. Her voice was gentle, but firm. *I understand your concern, but do it anyway* was implicit in it.

"It has to be Callisto," Jillian continued as if she hadn't heard the quiet warning in Bobbie's tone. "Only thing worth a damn that's far enough away from that battleship to be a realistic target."

Bobbie took a half step toward her and straightened up, magnifying the size difference between the two women. Jillian stopped talking, but didn't back down at all. *Mean as a snake, and with giant brass balls*, Alex thought.

"That sort of speculation is unproductive. And, frankly, dangerous," Bobbie said. "Keep it to yourself. Go get a drink or five. Get in a bar fight if you have to. But get it out of your system and be back at the *Storm* tomorrow. We'll know more then.

"Dismissed."

Jillian finally seemed to get the message. She threw Bobbie a half-mocking salute and sauntered out of the room.

Alex opened his mouth, and Bobbie pointed her finger at him. "Don't fucking say it."

"Copy that," he said instead. "A day on station with nothing to do. Wish Naomi was hangin' around. Could've done more than eat shitty kibble with her."

"She's got her mission too," Bobbie said. Her lips pressed thin and pale.

"So," Alex said, "you gonna tell me what went on between you, or am I gonna have to beat it out of you?"

Caught off guard, Bobbie let out a bark of laughter just the way he'd hoped she would. It was like a Chihuahua threatening an office building, and Alex grinned to show he was in on the joke.

Bobbie sighed. "She still thinks we should negotiate our way out of this. We disagree on that point. Same shit, different year."

"She's lost a lot," Alex said. "She's afraid of losing it all."

Bobbie grabbed Alex's upper arm and gave it an affectionate squeeze.

"And that's the point I keep trying to make with her, my friend. In a fight like this, unless you're willing to lose everything to win, you lose it all by losing."

Chapter Four: Teresa

We don't know what they called themselves," Colonel Ilich said, lying back on the grass, his hands pillowing his bald head. "We don't know that they called themselves anything, really. They may have done without language at all."

Teresa had known Colonel Ilich her whole life. He was a fact of the universe, like stars or water. He was a calm, thoughtful presence in a life full to spilling with calm, thoughtful people. What made him different was that he was entirely focused on her. That, and that he wasn't afraid of her.

He shifted, stretched. "Some people call them 'the protomolecule,' even though that was really just a tool they made. It'd be like calling humans 'wrenches.' 'Protomolecule engineers' is closer, but it's kind of a mouthful. 'Initial organism' or 'the alien society' or 'the architects.' They all get used to mean more or less the same thing."

"What do you call them?" Teresa asked.

He chuckled. "I call them 'the Romans.' The great empire that rose and fell in antiquity, and left their roads behind."

It was an interesting thought. Teresa turned it over in her mind for a few seconds like she was getting the taste of it. She liked the analogy not because it was accurate, but because it was evocative. That was what made analogies useful. Her mind wandered down that rabbit hole for a few breaths, seeing what was there, what was interesting in it, and decided to ask Timothy what he thought. He always had views that surprised her. It was why she liked him. He wasn't afraid of her any more than Colonel Ilich was, but Ilich's respect tasted like respect for her father, and that made it...not *lesser* exactly. Just different. Timothy was hers.

She felt the quiet stretching on too long. Ilich would be expecting her to say something, and Timothy wasn't something she talked about. She found something else.

"So they built all of this?"

"Not all of it, no. The gates, the construction platforms, the repair drones. The *artifacts*, yes. But the living systems existed on the other worlds first. Stable replicators aren't as rare as we used to imagine. A little water, a little carbon, a consistent stream of energy from sunlight or a thermal vent? Add a few million years, and more often than not something will happen."

"Or if it doesn't, then the Romans don't have anything to work from."

"One thousand three hundred and seventy three times that we know of," Ilich said. "That's a lot." The colony worlds—Sol system included—were only on the gate network because there had been life for the Romans to hijack. A few hundred systems in a galaxy of billions. Ilich was old enough that anything more than one was miraculous to him. Teresa hadn't grown up in a lonely universe the way the colonel had. She'd grown up in a lonely universe the way *she* had, and the two didn't compare.

She closed her eyes and turned her face toward the sun. The light and heat felt good on her skin. The brightness pressed through her eyelids, turning everything red. Nuclear fusion filtered through blood.

She smiled.

Teresa Angelica Maria Blanquita Li y Duarte knew that she wasn't a normal child the way she knew that light reflected off a level surface became polarized. A not-particularly-useful academic fact. She was the only daughter of High Consul Winston Duarte, which all by itself meant her childhood had been strange.

She'd lived her whole life in—or occasionally and clandestinely just outside—the State Building on Laconia. Since she'd been a toddler, other children had been brought in to be her friends and classmates. Usually from the most favored families of the empire, but sometimes because her father wanted her to know a variety of kinds of people. He wanted her to have as close as she could get to a normal life. To be as close as she could be to a normal fourteen-year-old. And it worked as well as it worked, but since she only had her own life to judge from, she couldn't really say how successful it had been.

She felt more like she had friendly acquaintances than actual friends. Muriel Cowper and Shan Ellison particularly treated her best, or at least most like they treated other students in her peer group.

And then there was Connor Weigel, who had been in her classes almost as long as she'd had them. He had a special place in her heart that she found herself curiously unwilling to examine.

If she was lonely—and she assumed she was—she didn't have anything to compare it against. If everything in the world was red, no one would know it. Being everywhere was just as good a way to be invisible as not being anywhere. It was contrast that gave things shape. Brightness made darkness. Fullness made emptiness. Loneliness defined the borders of whatever not-loneliness was called. They were comparative.

She wondered if life and death were like that too. Or life and not-life, anyway.

"What killed them?" she asked, opening her eyes. Everything looked blue. "Your Romans, I mean."

"Well, that's the next step, isn't it?" Colonel Ilich said. "Figuring that out and then building a strategy around what to do about it. We know, whatever it is, it's still out there. We've seen it react to things that we do."

"The thing on the *Tempest*," Teresa said. She'd seen the briefing on it. The first time Admiral Trejo used the *Magnetar*-class ship's main weapon in normal space, something had happened that knocked out people's consciousness all through Sol system for a few minutes and left a visual distortion on the ship itself, locked to its frame of reference. It was why James Holden had come to the palace, which was really the aspect of it that had the biggest impact on her.

"Exactly," Ilich said. He rolled onto his belly and propped himself up on his elbows to look at her. Eye contact was how he signaled that something he said was important. "It's the most serious threat to our security. Either the Romans died because they ran up against some natural force that they weren't prepared for, or because an enemy killed them. That's what we're finding out first."

"How?" she asked.

"We don't know how they killed the Romans. We're still just at the edge of understanding what they were compared to us."

"No. I mean how are we finding out if it was an enemy or a natural force?"

Colonel Ilich nodded to say it was a good question. He pulled out his handheld, tapped on it a few times, and brought up a grid.

	TERESA COOPERATES	TERESA DEFECTS
JASON COOPERATES	T3, J3	T4, J0
JASON DEFECTS	T0, J4	T2, J2

"Prisoner's dilemma," Teresa said.

"You remember how it works?"

"We both decide without talking whether to cooperate or defect. If we both cooperate, we both get three points. If only one of us cooperates, they don't get any points and the defector gets four. If we both defect, we both get two. The problem is that no matter what you choose to do, I'm better off defecting. I get four instead of three if you cooperate or else two instead of nothing if you defect. So I should always defect. But since the same logic applies to you, you should always defect too. And then we wind up both making fewer points than if we'd cooperated."

"So how do you fix that?"

"You don't. It's like saying 'This statement is false.' It's just a hole in logic," Teresa said. "I mean...isn't it?"

"Not if you play it more than once," Colonel Ilich said. "You play it over and over and over for a really long time. Every time the other player defects, you defect the next time. And then you go back to cooperating. It's called tit for tat. There's a pure game theory analysis of it I can give you if you want, but you don't need it for this."

Teresa nodded, but slowly. Her head was thick, the way it got when she was thinking about something without quite being conscious of what it was. Usually something interesting came up shortly afterward. She liked the feeling.

"Think of it like you were training Muskrat back when she was a puppy," Ilich said. "The puppy wets the rug, and you scold it. You don't go on scolding it forever. Just once, when it happens, and then you go back to playing with it and petting it and treating it like a puppy. It defects, then you defect, then you go back to cooperating."

"Until it figures out that there's a better strategy," Teresa said.

"And it changes its behavior. It's the most basic, simplest way we can negotiate with something we can't talk to. But what if you do the same thing with the tide? Punish the waves for getting the rug wet?"

Teresa scowled.

"Exactly," Colonel Ilich said as if she'd spoken aloud. "If you scold the tide, it doesn't matter. It doesn't care. It doesn't learn. And most of all, it doesn't change. Your father is going to play tit for tat with the force that killed the Romans. And we're going to see if it changes its behavior. If it doesn't, we'll take the hypothesis that they ran up against a law of nature like gravity making tides or the speed of light. Then we can study it, and find ways around it. But if it *changes*..."

"Then we'll know it's alive."

"That's the difference between exploration and negotiating," Colonel Ilich said, pointing at her. She felt the bloom of pleasure that she always got when she'd answered a knotty problem well, but something nagged at her.

"But it *killed* the Romans."

"War's a kind of negotiation too," he said.

Teresa's rooms were in the north wing of the State Building, as were her father's. It was the only home she'd ever had. A bedroom built to military specifications, a private bathroom, and the room that had been her playroom and was now her office, the difference being mostly cosmetic. When she'd been ready to strip away the decorations of cartoon dinosaurs and puppies, she'd said so, and the next day a designer had come to help her choose a new color scheme and layout. Her corner of the State Building wasn't large or ostentatious, but it was hers to customize and re-create. Her little bubble of autonomy.

She'd chosen to make the office look like a science station. Her desk was tall enough to stand at, but also had long-legged stools along the side if she chose to sit. The east wall was a single screen set to run animations of simple mathematical and geometrical proofs when she wasn't watching a news or entertainment feed. It wasn't that she understood all the math, but she thought it was pretty. There was an elegance to the proofs, and having them there made her more aware of her intelligence. She liked being aware of her intelligence.

But she also had a couch long enough that she could lie down on it and still have room for Muskrat, her Labrador, to curl up at her feet. And a real glass window that looked out over a ceremonial garden. There were whole days when, if she wasn't with Colonel Ilich or in class, she'd curl up on the couch with Muskrat and read books or watch films for hours at a time. She had access to everything the censors approved—her father was very liberal about giving her access to literature and film—and she gravitated to stories about girls who lived alone in castles or palaces or temples. For such a specific genre, it turned out there were quite a few.

Her present favorite was a ten-hour feed made on Mars back before the gates opened called *The Fifth Tunnel*. In it, the hero—who, at twelve, was now younger than Teresa, but had been older when she first watched it—discovered a secret tunnel under a city called Innis Deep and followed it to a whole buried community with elves and fairies who needed help getting back to their dimension.

It all seemed wildly exotic, and the idea of a girl who lived her whole life underground captured her imagination so much that she'd put a blanket over her windows and pretended that the darkness was made of Martian dirt. When her father told her that part was true—that there was an Innis Deep and that Martian children did live in tunnels and buried cities—and that only the elves and fairies were inventions, it had astounded her.

She was watching it again when her father came by. She'd just gotten to the part where the girl—whose name was never mentioned—was running through a dark hallway with the evil fairy called Pinsleep chasing her, when the knock came. She was just getting up to answer it when the door opened. Only her father opened the door. Everyone else made her get it.

The treatments had changed him over the last few years, but just growing up had changed her. It didn't seem weird. His eyes had developed more of their oil-on-water shimmer in the whites and his fingernails had gone darker at the cuticles, but that was all just looks. In every way that mattered, he was the same.

"Am I interrupting?" he asked, the way he always did. It was half a joke, because she didn't have anything to interrupt, but only half. If she'd ever said yes, he would have let her be.

The nameless girl shrieked as Pinsleep lunged for her. Teresa paused the feed, and prey and predator both froze. Muskrat huffed, tail thumping against the couch as her father scratched the dog's wide ears.

"I have a briefing in two hours," he said. "I'd like you to attend."

Teresa felt a little prick of annoyance. She'd meant to go out and visit Timothy as soon as the feed was done. If they'd found out she was leaving the grounds without permission...

"Did I do something wrong?"

Her father blinked, then laughed. Muskrat pushed her head up into his hand, demanding more attention. He went back to rubbing her ears. "No, not at all. It's Admiral Waithe's report on the expansion plan for Bara Gaon Complex. You aren't expected to contribute, but I'd like you to listen. Then afterward, we can talk about it."

Teresa nodded. If it was what he wanted, of course she could, but it sounded dull. And strange. Her father's eyes went unfocused for a moment, the way they did sometimes, and then he shook his head like he was trying to clear it. He leaned against the arm of the couch, not quite sitting but not standing either. He tapped Muskrat's side firmly twice in a way that meant petting time was over. The dog sighed and flopped her head down on the cushion.

"Something's bothering you," he said.

"You've been asking me to do this more often," she said. "Am I doing it wrong?"

His laughter was warm, and it made her relax a little.

"When I was your age, I was pushing for early entrance to upper university. You're like me. You learn fast, and I want to keep up with you. I'm bringing you in more because you're old enough to understand things now that you weren't able to when you were a child. And Colonel Ilich says that your studies are on track. Even advanced."

She felt a little glimmer of pride in that, but also confusion. Her father sighed.

"It's hard work, keeping people safe," he said. "Part of that is that we've come up against very dangerous, unknown things. I can wish that weren't the case, but I can't take it back. And the other part is that we're working with people."

"And people are terrible, terrible monkeys," Teresa said.

"Yes, we are," her father said. "We have a very close horizon almost all the time. Including me. But I'm trying to get better."

The way he said it, he sounded tired. She leaned forward, and Muskrat took it as a sign that she was looking for someone to pet. She shifted, breathing hot on Teresa's face until she gently pushed the dog back.

"Is the Bara Gaon Complex expansion really important, then?" Teresa asked.

"Everything's important. All of it," her father said. "And so every part of it needs to be able to fail without destroying the whole project. Including me. Which is why I've been asking you to come to the briefings more often."

"What do you mean?" she said.

"I'm fine," her father said. "Everything's fine. There isn't a problem. It's only that…if there were to be, sometime later. Decades from now. Someone would need to understand the shape of the whole plan, and be able to step in. And people trust what they already know. Having a new high consul would be difficult under any circumstances, but it would be less difficult if there were a story with it. A succession. I want to train you to be that, if—God forbid—something happened to me."

"But why should I be good at it just because you were?" Teresa said. "There's no reason to think that. That's dumb."

"It is," her father said. "But it's a mistake people have made all through history. And since we know that, the two of us can use the tool we've been given. Come sit in the briefings and the meetings. Listen. Watch. Talk to me afterward. This is the next phase of your education. So that if you need to step in, you'll actually be the leader they need you to be." It took a few seconds to really understand what he was saying. The huge moments in life seemed like they should have more ceremony and effects. The important words—the life-changing ones—should echo a little. But they didn't. They sounded just like everything else.

"You want to train me up to be the next high consul?"

"In case something happens to me," Duarte said.

"But just in case," she said. "Only just in case."

"Just in case, princess," he said.

Chapter Five: Elvi

A few decades earlier and about two hundred thousand trillion kilometers from where she currently sat, a tiny node of active protomolecule in a biological matrix had entered the orbit of a planet called Ilus, hitchhiking on the gunship *Rocinante*.

As the uncanny semisentient intelligence of the protomolecule tried to make contact with other nodes in the gate builders' long-dead empire, it woke up mechanisms that had been dormant for millions—or even billions—of years. The end result had been an ancient factory returning to life, a massive robot attack, the melting of one artificial moon, and the detonation of a power plant that nearly cracked the planet in two.

All in all, a really shitty experience.

So when Elvi's team took the catalyst out of isolation in unexplored systems to do a similar if slightly better-controlled reaching out to the artifacts and remains, she made sure they were careful. They watched what happened, they were ready to put the catalyst back in its box, and they didn't get too close to anything.

"*Falcon* in position," the pilot said.

If anything went terribly wrong, the pilot or Sagale or Elvi could give a single spoken order—*Emergency evacuation*, their name, and the delta-eight authorization code—and the ship would take it from there. Given the *Falcon's* oversized engine and massive acceleration, anyone not in one of the ship's specially designed high-g couches would be injured or killed, but the data they'd already collected would be preserved. Laconia had a lot of fail-safe logic like that. It wasn't her favorite part of the job.

"Thank you, Lieutenant," Admiral Sagale replied. He was strapped into a crash couch on the bridge too. Another sign of how seriously everyone took this part of the mission. "Major Okoye, you may proceed."

"Take her out," Elvi said into the comm. In this situation, there was only one *her*.

Elvi sat in her custom Laconian crash couch, surrounded by screens. The instruments could be yanked away in under a second, and the couch chamber filled with a breathable fluid for high-g burn shortly after. She was one of the few people important enough that efforts would be made to keep her alive. It felt like working inside a torpedo. She kind of hated it.

On one of her screens, a camera tracked the movement of the catalyst as she was wheeled out of her storage room on a high-tech gurney covered in sensors. Protomolecule communication went both ways. What happened to their sample was just as important to their study as what happened to the dead system that they might be about to activate.

The catalyst's gurney moved on magnetic wheels down the corridor to a compartment in the skin of the ship, away from all the radiation shielding and whatever high-tech wizardry Cortázar's team had come up with to lock their sample away from the rest back beyond the gate.

Nothing happened.

"No response yet," Travon said.

"Gee, really?" Fayez replied, the sarcasm in his tone meant for everyone else. Travon wouldn't hear it.

While the protomolecule might communicate in ways that looked like they were faster than light once it got going, it didn't start it right away. Since locality wasn't a big deal for the protomolecule, but the speed of light was, Elvi suspected it was some slower-than-light handshake as the two network nodes agreed on the protocol to be used. That was somewhere between a guess and a metaphor, but it helped her to think about it.

Her sample came out of Cortázar's laboratory pens. It hadn't existed until the recent past. Everything they were trying to interact with here had been waiting since humanity had been a kinky idea that two amoebas came up with. So somehow, when her node came into physical proximity—meaning somewhere in the same solar system—for the first time, they were creating some kind of relationship to each other on the fly. Which was awesome, but also weird. And not how quantum entanglement worked, unless somehow it was.

In her study of the protomolecule and the civilization that had created it, Elvi often found herself glad she wasn't a physicist. What the protomolecule did biologically, while not entirely explicable yet, at least seemed like it might be fully understood some day. The mechanisms by which it hijacked life and repurposed it were incredibly advanced, but not totally dissimilar to things like viruses and parasitic fungi. She didn't understand all the rules yet, but she felt like she could, given enough time and research.

What the protomolecule did to physics looked less like a variation and refinement of the standard models and more like kicking the game table over and scattering the pieces across the floor. Elvi wondered if Jen Lively's constant lighthearted joking was so she didn't go insane as her understanding of reality was ripped to shreds in front of her on a daily basis.

"Getting a reaction," Travon said.

"Yeah," Jen agreed. "Something's happening in the object."

"What was the delay on that?" Elvi asked.

"Eighteen minutes."

They were nine light-minutes from the structure, so that made a handshake propagating at or near *c* plausible. She really needed to write that hypothesis up and run it past the nanoinformatics staff.

Elvi's screens went wild with readings from the catalyst's sensor package. It was too much data to be analyzed in real time, so Elvi let it wash over her like a wave of numbers and graphs. There would be plenty of opportunity later to figure out what it all meant.

"Looking stable so far," Travon said.

"Always glad when things don't immediately blow up," Elvi said, but no one laughed.

"You know what makes a diamond green?" Jen asked everyone and no one. "I looked it up."

"Radiation," Fayez said. Of course he knew. He'd been on the Ilus team too, as its geologist. While the opening of the proto-molecule gate network had given Elvi more than thirteen hundred new biospheres to study, it had given Fayez ten times that many new geologies to explore. Some of them as exotic as a great huge lump of carbon crystal that was a really pretty color. "Diamonds that form in the presence of radiation can get that green color. Some people mistake them for emeralds. But totally different mineral. Emeralds are beryl, not carbon."

"Stealing my thunder there, sport," Jen said. "But I'm betting it means that this star was a lot more active when the object was formed. My best guess, based on stellar decay, is that the object is almost five billion years old. That's been hanging out for about a third of the time the universe has, you know, *existed*."

"That would make it one of the oldest artifacts we've found," Travon said, suddenly interested. "Maybe something from the very beginning of their civilization."

"Fascinating," Sagale said, his clipped tones the only sign of his impatience. "What's it doing?"

What's it doing that helps us fight ghoulies from beyond time and space? was the implied question. For all her bottomless budget, for all the cream-of-the-crop science teams she'd been given and her custom-built state-of-the-art ship, there was only one result the high consul and his Science Directorate cared about. *How do we stop the things that eat ships passing through the gates?*

"I don't know," she said. "Let me take a look."

Eighteen hours into their data collection, Elvi retired to her cabin. She'd learned early on that the military discipline of the Laconians didn't extend to forcing people to work on no rest. Duarte wanted everyone at peak efficiency. Baked into that was the idea that most people would spend a third of their day sleeping. When Elvi climbed out of her couch and said she needed to rest before she began her analysis, Sagale didn't bat an eye.

It was a trick she'd started using to buy uninterrupted work time. She'd been able to go twenty-four hours straight since grad school. Some caffeine tablets and hot tea, and she could go forty-eight if she needed to. Not sleeping bought her eight or nine hours without Sagale's questions about results and timetables.

But the gag only worked if everyone pretended that she actually was sleeping, so for Fayez to burst in meant he had something big.

"It made a copy."

Before Elvi could ask what had made a copy and what it had made a copy of, he'd floated over to the dining table in the middle of her cabin and slapped his terminal down on it. The electromagnetics in the table kept the terminal from floating away, but the impact sent Fayez tumbling gently toward the wall. He was an Earther, born and raised, and no matter how much time he spent in space, he never seemed to lose that instinctive expectation of gravity. As he drifted away, he yelled at the table, "Show her! Show her...the thing! Display last file, volumetric display."

A holographic map of what looked like a human brain appeared, floating above the table. The brain sparked with flashing synaptic

paths, probably an fMRI or fNIRS scan. Elvi had seen this particular brain often enough to know it belonged to the catalyst. That
it had been a woman, once upon a time. Fayez hit the bulkhead
and pushed off with one foot, rejoining her at the table.

"A lot of activity," Elvi said. "But taking her out of her pen
might be causing her stress, or physical discomfort. Nothing here
is all that unusual."

"That's just her being her," Fayez said, shaking his head and
tapping away at his terminal. "Look at this."

A second image appeared. It took Elvi a moment to recognize
that it was a copy of the catalyst's brain activity, but without the
physical structure of the brain.

"I don't understand. What's that second image from?"

"That," Fayez said with a grin, "is coming from the object."

"What, the whole thing is mirroring her brain activity?"

"No, it's very localized," Fayez said, and tinkered with the
controls. The second image zoomed out for a long time until the
entire object was in view. A tiny white dot appeared. "That dot
is not to scale, of course. It'd be the size of Greenland at this distance. But that's the approximate location of the image."

He tapped some more, and the image was replaced with long
strings of sensor data. "Jen started picking up some EM fluctua-
tion in the surface of the object. I mean, in context it's tiny, but the
object is totally inert, and the sensors on this boat are as sensitive
as a galactic tyrant's money can buy."

"Okay," Elvi said. "What does she think we're looking at?"

"At first it just looked like some photons bouncing around,
until Jen put together this map. No one knew what we were looking at until Travon said, 'Hey, that looks like an fMRI.' I pulled
up the catalyst's monitor, and boom, there we were."

Elvi didn't mind space, but the one thing it lacked that she
needed right then was the ability to collapse into a chair. She felt
a rush of adrenaline that made her hands tingle and her legs go
numb.

"So they're echoing each other?"

"Like looking in a mirror."

"Oh," she said. Then, "Okay. That's huge."

"Oh, it gets huger," Fayez said. "All across the object we're now seeing radiation hotspots"—he zoomed in on one, and a new rush of numerical data splashed across the image—"like this."

He was looking at her expectantly. Waiting for her to make the connection. She didn't think she was all that tired, but whatever flash of insight he was looking for just wasn't there.

"I give up."

"It took us a minute too," Fayez said. He pulled up a third image. Elvi recognized a ring gate. "This is the same kind of radiation that sprays out of the gate during a transit."

Almost before the numbers hit her screen Elvi had it. "That correlated to the catalyst."

"Yes. Catalyst brain, green diamond-thing copy, and weird distributed gate-like radiation. Three things, all with the same pattern," Fayez said.

Elvi pulled the image of the huge green diamond back until she could see the whole thing at once. It seemed to flicker with tiny stars of light appearing and disappearing where the computer marked the radiation spikes for her.

"This thing is filled with...gates? Like, in the physical structure of the object itself?"

"We have a theory," Fayez said. He was grinning like he had the first time she agreed to sleep with him. He was a goofball, but she liked what made him happy: knowing things, and her.

"It's too early for theories," she said.

"I know, but we have one anyway. And by we, I mean Travon first, but we're all on board. This thing comes in contact with a protomolecule-infected mind, it makes a copy of that mind, then these gate signatures start showing up all over the object. Travon starts talking about how secure data storage works. You take the physical imprint that's the encoded data and you scatter it. You put it in a bunch of discrete storage locations with tags and code built in so that if any portion of the storage system is lost, the rest of it knows how to rebuild the lost portion from the scattered fragments."

Elvi, who was a lot more computer literate than Fayez, started, "That's not exactly—"

"So then Jen says, 'A diamond is a super-dense and incredibly regularly structured mass of carbon atoms. If you had a way to shift things around without damaging the overall structure, it'd make a great data storage material.' "

Elvi paused, her mind ticking through the implications.

"A way like tiny, tiny wormholes," Elvi said.

"Right? We know that the protomolecule builders seem to have had a hive mind. Or one brain. However you want to parse that. Instantaneous nonlocalized communication across all the various nodes and entities, all across their corner of galaxy. But shit happens, even to them. Asteroids hit planets or earthquakes or volcanoes or whatever. Anything that's stored in a single node is lost forever when that node is destroyed. So what if what we're looking at is the backup drive for their entire civilization? Everything they ever knew, packed into a carbon lattice the size of Jupiter?"

"That," Elvi said, "is one gigantic fucking logical leap."

"Yeah." He nodded, but his grin remained undiminished. "Totally unfounded. Complete guesswork. We'll need generations of scientific studies to verify what this thing is, and then generations more to crack the code on how to dig out the data, if any such data exists.

"But Els," he said, almost breathless with excitement. "I mean, *what if?*"

Admiral Sagale floated beside his desk, looking over navigational charts on a large wall display. Elvi could see a course plotted from their current position, through the Kalma gate and into the hub, then out again through the Tecoma gate and into the next dead system on their galactic tour.

"Tell me that this system is the most important scientific discovery of all time," Sagale said, not even looking up when she floated into his office.

"It might very well—" Elvi started.

"But the big crystal flower in Naraka system was the most important discovery."

"It was an astonishing artifact," Elvi agreed. "But compared to—"

"Before that, it was the trinary star system in Charon, and the planet where it rained glass shards."

"That was more just really cool. You have to admit, it was pretty spectacular."

He turned to give her his full attention.

"I'm hearing you say—*once again*—that there are artifacts in this system that are critical to future investigation," Sagale said. He seemed weary, and vaguely disappointed. "Just like the big crystal flower."

Elvi went through it for him, and as she said it, Fayez's theory seemed more and more plausible. Sagale stared at her through half-closed eyes as she spoke. When she told him that the diamond outside might actually house every piece of information the gate network builders had ever had, a muscle in his cheek twitched, but that was his only sign of surprise.

"That is interesting. Please write up that theory and include it with the data dump when we send everything back to Laconia during the transit. I apologize for lumping this in with the flowers and glass rain. This actually does seem impressive."

His grudging admission stung a little, but she let it go.

"Sir," Elvi said. "Met, this might be everything the high consul sent us on this mission to find. This might be it."

"It is not," Sagale said, but she pushed on.

"I strongly encourage you to send word back to the admiralty asking for more time. There are a thousand more tests we can be running while we wait for additional personnel and ships to join us. Leaving now gains us nothing."

"And you believe you will be able to access this data if I give you that time?" Sagale said.

Elvi almost lied, hungry for the chance to stay a little while longer and learn a little bit more, but...

"No. I can't say that. In fact, it will almost certainly be the work of decades, maybe centuries, to solve this problem. If it even is solvable. But this is our best shot. Nothing we find in Tecoma will be as important as this. I feel pretty safe guaranteeing that."

"Then we'll keep to our schedule, and see whether you're right," Sagale said, already turning away. "Get secured. We burn for Tecoma in eighty minutes."

Seventy-eight minutes later, Elvi lay in her crash couch, waiting to drown.

The problem with space travel had always—from the very beginning—been the fragility of human bodies. In spite of these limitations, humanity had done itself pretty proud even before Laconia. Now they were improving by leaps and bounds. The *Falcon* could make the travel time from one system to another almost trivial by comparison to the standard science vessels and freighters of the civilian fleet. A journey of weeks could be accomplished in days. The *Falcon* would even give most of Duarte's military ships a run for their money. But the price of all that acceleration was the full-submersion crash couch. A diabolical device that completely surrounded the human body in shock-absorbing gel, and filled the lungs with highly oxygenated fluid to make the chest cavity as incompressible as possible. For days.

"I don't understand what he wants," she said.

"He is a complicated man," Fayez said from the couch next to hers.

"It's like he doesn't want us to find anything interesting. Every time we do, he gets grumpy."

"You took your preflight meds?"

"Yes," she said, even though she wasn't sure she'd actually remembered to. They weren't critical. "I feel like he's got some other agenda he's not telling us."

"Almost certainly because he's got some other agenda he isn't telling us," Fayez said. "That can't be surprising, Els."

"It can't be something more important than this," she said. "What would be more important than this?"

"To him? I don't know. Maybe he just hates learning. Traumatized by a science fair when he was young. Ten seconds. I love you, Els."

"I love you too," she said. "I remember when juice was something they injected you with, not something you breathed. I remember I didn't like it at the time."

"Price of progress."

She was looking for something clever to say back, but then the fluid poured in the way it always did and silenced her.

Chapter Six: Alex

The *Gathering Storm* was the absolute state of the art in Laconian naval technology. The first ship of her class to be fielded, she was intended to be the prototype of an entire fleet of fast attack destroyers that could patrol the many systems of the gate network and project Laconian power to every corner of the empire. She had a keel-mounted rail gun capable of firing a three-and-a-half-kilo slug every five seconds at velocities that would punch a hole through smaller moons. She had two separate batteries of torpedo launchers with four rails on each and a fast reload system that could have another eight fish in the tubes and ready to fire less than seventy seconds after the first barrage was let loose. She was defended on all sides by a network of twelve rapid-fire point-defense cannons, and every angle of approach on the ship was covered by at least four of them. She was, as Alex's copilot Caspar liked to quip, a couple thousand tons of fuck-up-your-day stuffed into a five-kilo sack.

Nestled inside the massive cargo hold of the *Pendulum*, she was also defenseless.

Sitting in the pilot's couch, waiting for the go signal, and knowing that if someone realized they were there and started firing he wouldn't even be able to see it on radar made Alex's scalp itch. The *Pendulum* fed them her scopes, so they weren't completely blind, but she was a lumbering heavy freighter. Her threat detection was mostly so she didn't run into a stray hunk of rock. The low-res radar and grainy telescope shots he had to look at did little to calm his nerves.

"So you and the boss go way back, right?" Caspar said.

He sat second couch on the *Storm*, behind and to the right of Alex's chair. Caspar Asoau was a short, skinny kid with a motion tattoo of a running cheetah on one shoulder and the wispiest hint of a goatee. In spite of looking way too young for the job, he was a hell of a good pilot. Quick to obey an order and perfectly charming company. Alex had rapidly discovered that they had nothing in common outside of a love of flying, so other than a casual greeting, the only time they ever seemed to talk was sitting at the *Storm*'s controls.

Alex didn't hold it against the kid. He remembered being a young pilot and trying his hardest to hide his nervousness by chatting up the older officers.

"Yeah. The gunny and I have known each other for a long damn time."

"See, that's funny. She's the captain of this ship, but you guys all call her Gunny. That was a rank or something, right? Back on Mars?"

"Something like that," Alex replied. "She'll always be Gunny to me."

Caspar was running the preflight as he talked, fingers tapping softly on the screens. On Alex's monitor the checklist rolled past, each system verified and reporting green before Caspar moved on to the next, with Alex giving the final okay to his work. His copilot was thorough and efficient. He took his job seriously. It kind of made Alex wish the kid were thirty years older so they could be friends.

"She give you any hint on what this op is about?" Caspar asked, then threw the weapon stores inventory to Alex's screen for his double check.

"I show two hundred slugs in the rail-gun mag, eighty fish in the pipes, all PDCs show green and full," Alex said, sliding his finger down the inventory list as he went. "And no, she's an old operator. Keepin' your mouth shut gets drilled into those guys pretty hard."

"Copy, two hundred in the rail gun, eighty torpedoes, PDCs full and greens across the board, verified," Caspar said. "Yeah, but I figured since you guys were friends, maybe she gave you some kinda heads-up."

"She did not. And I wouldn't ask. We'll know when we need to know, and that's good enough for me," Alex said, then, with the preflight complete, spun his couch around to face Caspar. "It's okay to be nervous."

Caspar nodded. He didn't look embarrassed at all to be discussing his fear. Alex felt another little rush of affection for him. He was a good kid. Alex hoped he'd make it through to the other side of the Laconia business, but the odds on that were pretty short for all of them.

"I knew a guy on Pallas," Caspar said. "It wasn't like we were tight. We never seriously dated or anything. But when I'd go through the station on cargo runs, we'd hook up. Ben Yi. I liked him." A tear formed at the corner of his eye and then failed to be pulled down his cheek in the gentle quarter-g burn of the *Pendulum*'s drive.

"He didn't make the evacuation?"

"Nope," Caspar said, then wiped his eyes. "They say that the *Tempest* turned the station into rubble so fast no one would even have seen the actual attack coming. I guess, if you have to go, that's not the worst."

"I'm sorry," Alex said. Everyone on the *Storm* had their reason to hate the Laconians. Everyone had a story. The only answer for most of them was *I'm sorry*. It felt pretty limp.

"If this op gets blown up," Caspar said, turning his attention back to his screens and going through his checklists one more time, "I want you to know. You don't have to worry about me. If that big bastard *Tempest* comes after us, the only thing I'll be thinking is how can I make a hole in it."

"I know, man," Alex said, then patted the kid's knee before turning around. "No doubts."

"Kamal?" said Bobbie's voice in his ear, where the comm bud was inserted. Bobbie only called him Kamal when they were on an op and other ears were listening. It meant go time.

"Kamal copies from the flight deck, Cap," he replied, sitting up straight in his couch. From the hiss of the gimbals behind him, he knew Caspar was doing the same. Even the crash couches on the *Storm* sounded slick.

"I need a go, no-go for deployment," Bobbie said. "*Pendulum* cuts us loose on your word."

"We are all greens up here on the flight deck, go on your command."

"Outstanding," Bobbie said. "Okay, kids, word came down, and here's the op. Listen close, because I don't have time to repeat myself."

Alex hated flying ballistic. No drive meant he had maneuvering thrusters at most. No active sensors was like piloting with his eyes half-closed.

The *Storm* had a tiny radar profile for such a large ship. Something about the hull materials just absorbed or bounced off at an angle almost any radar that hit it. She could also dump all her waste heat into internal heat sinks for several hours and run liquid hydrogen through capillaries in her skin, keeping the hull temperature pretty close to zero. Unless someone was really looking for her, she'd just show up as a slightly warmer spot in space with a radar profile not much bigger than a bunk bed. Alex could remember when a destroyer with similar technology had killed his old ship the *Canterbury*. How terrifying it had been when a gunship seemed to materialize out of the dark of space and started firing torpedoes. Apparently that came standard now. Still, he could relate to what their intended targets were about to experience.

"One minute," Caspar said. There was no time for sympathy.

"Copy that, one minute," Alex replied, then switched channels over to Bobbie. "Cap, we're go in sixty seconds. Your team ready?"

"Kids are belted in and ready for a roller-coaster ride," she replied.

"Copy that," Alex said, then watched the countdown timer on his screen drop toward zero. "Three...two...one...mark."

"Mark," Caspar said, and the *Storm* flared to life around them. The screens switched to active sensors and telescope shots of their target: a fat Transport Union freighter, escorted by two Laconian frigates. Behind the freighter lay Jupiter's vast bulk.

And that was, according to Bobbie's pre-mission brief, the reason for all the secrecy beforehand. Whether or not they could make their attack run depended on the resistance partisans on the freighter's crew getting the signal out on the ship's course and date of entry into the Sol system, all while working around a Laconian political officer who had been stashed on board. Because for the attack to work, it had to all happen while Jupiter blocked line of sight to Earth and the *Magnetar*-class battleship parked there.

It was a lot of moving parts, any one of which could have failed out at a moment's notice, and launching the attack meant burning some spies in the union. If things hadn't panned out, the *Storm* would have just climbed back into her berth on the *Pendulum* and flown away, her crew none the wiser and the spies on the freighter undiscovered.

But the prize was worth the risk. A ship directly from Laconia with highly sensitive cargo attached to some secret Laconian project and replacement parts for the *Tempest* itself. Hopefully also some of the weird fuel pellets the Laconian ships used that couldn't be manufactured anywhere else, and which the *Storm* was getting dangerously low on. Ammunition for the *Storm*'s weapons and for the power armor suits Bobbie's team wore. Taking the freighter meant keeping the underground's best weapon armed and operational, possibly for years.

And—best of all—the political officer. Taking them alive would be a huge intelligence win.

If Alex could take care of two escort frigates and deliver Bobbie's dropship to the freighter.

"They've spotted us," Caspar said. No surprise there. With the *Storm* pinging away with active radar, she was lit up like a Christmas tree.

"Jammers on," Alex said, and the *Storm* drowned the little fleet in static, cutting them off from each other and from any outside help. The three ships didn't change course, apparently deciding the smartest move was to try to get around Jupiter. It was their best strategy. Alex would have done the same.

Which was why he'd prepared for it.

"Cap, launching you now. Make sure you come back," Alex said, and hit the button that hurled the strike team's high-speed breaching pod at the freighter. Bobbie and her boarding party throwing themselves at the enemy ship like pirates. While the pod burned hard toward the Transport Union ship, Alex fired two precisely angled shots from the rail gun past it and through the freighter's drive cone. The shots covered the thousands of kilometers separating the ships in a handful of seconds, and the freighter's drive winked out.

"Get ready, they'll be coming for us now," Alex told Caspar, and almost as if on cue the *Storm* buzzed an angry target lock warning at them.

"PDCs hot," Caspar said. Alex was surprised at how calm his tone was. For all the sadness and fear the kid had expressed in the moments before the fight, now that the battle was on, he'd become almost machine-like. "Ready for incoming. Tubes two and four are locked."

"We should close a bit, cut off their options," Alex said. The two frigates were not a trivial threat, but the *Storm* massively outclassed them in tonnage and firepower, and he didn't worry too much about flying straight at them fangs out and trying to end the fight quickly.

"Copy that, one and three loaded and locked if we need them."

Acceleration pressed Alex back into his couch as he closed the gap. In the distance, Bobbie's pod had reached the crippled freighter and was firing grapples to lock the two ships together. The frigates couldn't talk to each other, but their crews had some emergency plans already on the books, because they split up and flew away from the freighter in opposite directions as if they'd coordinated the maneuver.

"They're trying to get on both sides of us," Alex said, but Caspar was already on it. He was tasking half their PDCs with one ship and half with the other. Didn't matter if they came from both directions at once, the *Storm*'s flak screen could handle it.

Down at the freighter, Bobbie's pod suddenly flared to life in a massive deceleration burn. Alex had crippled the freighter's drive, but the ship was still hurtling along with whatever velocity it'd had before the engine went out. Bobbie's pod was programmed to push back against that speed on a vector that would keep the freighter safely hidden behind Jupiter. Part boarding pod, part secondary, aftermarket temporary braking thruster.

"We're on board," Bobbie said, her voice phase shifted into a robotic screech as it cut through the static from their jamming.

"We have fast movers," Caspar said at the same moment the alerts showed up on Alex's threat board. The two frigates unloaded their tubes. Alex ignored them, waiting for the missiles to get into PDC range so the *Storm* could chew them up.

"Let's go ahead and start shooting back," Alex said, and a moment later the *Storm* shuddered as if with pleasure as she fired four torpedoes of her own.

Before the rapidly closing missiles could even pass each other, two of the incoming torpedoes veered off in a wide turn.

"Worry about the two that are still coming at us," Alex said to Caspar, and then stopped thinking about that. The other two Laconian torpedoes were now winging in a wide arc toward the freighter. And the two frigates had also flipped and started a hard burn back toward their former charge.

They hadn't been able to draw the *Storm* away or shoot it down. Their plan B appeared to be scuttling the freighter. Bloodthirsty, but not unexpected. Alex threw the throttle down to catch the swiftly slowing freighter as quickly as possible, shifting from attacking their prey to protecting it. For a moment, everything was falling toward a central point in space defined by the crippled ship. The *Storm*, eight torpedoes on wide looping courses to find their targets, the two frigates burning back. On the threat board, it looked like the freighter had turned into a black hole, and its gravity was sucking everything, large and small, into its event horizon. In its way, it was beautiful.

Then everyone was shooting.

Caspar's PDCs cut down all four of the Laconian torpedoes in an instant, even as two of the *Storm*'s impacted on the nose of one of the frigates and the plasma warheads turned the front half of the ship into glowing slag. The other frigate spun and slewed sideways and shot down the torpedoes chasing it, then continued its rotation and gave the freighter and Bobbie's attached breaching pod a full broadside from its PDC array. The freighter was riddled with holes, and plumes of escaping atmosphere jetted out, looking a bloody pink in the reddish light coming off Jupiter. Or maybe there was some actual blood mixed in there. As many holes as the freighter had taken, it defied belief that no one on board had been hit.

"Splash that one," Alex ordered, but Caspar was already saying, "I got that motherfucker."

The frigate killed its rotation with a massive blast from its maneuvering thrusters, then kicked on its drive. Even though it only slowed down, it seemed to leap straight at the approaching *Storm*. The two ships passed at high speed, every PDC blazing.

The much smaller frigate was hit by half a dozen of the *Storm*'s cannons all at once, and seemed to just come apart into a cloud of chaff as it passed by. But it unleashed a barrage of its own before it died that cut along the *Storm*'s flank.

Suddenly the ship was a cacophony of alarms, sirens, and alerts from the control panel.

"Damage!" Alex yelled over the din. The noise was getting gradually quieter, which meant at least the flight deck was in the process of losing its atmosphere. He grabbed his helmet from under his couch and locked it into place. He could see Caspar doing the same.

"Damage!" he yelled again, but heard only static on his suit's speakers. He banged his fist on the side of the helmet in frustration, then spun around. Caspar was pointing at his mouth and ears, signaling that his suit radio seemed not to be working either.

Alex flipped through the pages of damage reports popping up on his screen and found the culprit. A PDC round had cut through the computer nexus that controlled all intraship and intership communications, and for whatever reason the backup wasn't taking over. Maybe it was fucked too. It looked like there were a lot of flashing red lights on the engineering panel.

But the *Storm* would heal the hull breaches, just like it always did. And damage control teams were already on the move to bring their other systems back online. The *Storm* would survive, Alex had no doubt.

But the freighter with Bobbie and her strike team on it was tumbling through space, out of control and empty of atmosphere, and with the radio down, there was no way for him to know if anyone on it was still alive.

Chapter Seven: Bobbie

"Cap, launching you now. Make sure you come back," Alex said. The breaching pod shook as the *Storm* cut it loose. The drive came on a moment later, slamming Bobbie back into her couch and leaving her with nothing to do while the battle raged around her.

The *Storm*'s breaching pod was a little more high-tech than the Martian version Bobbie had trained on, but there was only so much you could do with something so simple. The basic concept was a small troop carrier with an engine on one end and an airlock that could blow holes into enemy ships on the other. The interior was a close-walled metal box fitted with crash couches. The "flying coffin" joke Marines had been making for centuries would have made perfect sense even to the ancient soldiers who rolled into battle in armored personnel carriers with wheels: If you die before you get to the fight, you're already boxed up for eternal rest.

People always claimed that waiting for the fight was the hardest part of fighting. Bobbie had said it herself, as a younger woman. When the fight is coming, when it's inevitable, let's just fucking get to it. Once the battle starts, things happen too fast to worry about. The fear is all instinctual, not intellectual. Somehow, that used to feel better.

Age had changed that. Bobbie had learned to see the quiet moment before the fight as a blessing. A gift. Very few people who were headed toward death even knew it was happening, much less had time to sit and reflect on their life. What they'd done that mattered. Whether it would be a good death.

Bobbie's father had already been a legendary Marine in the MMC before she was born. When his family started to grow, he left the front lines and became an even more legendary training sergeant. An entire generation had learned what it meant to be a Martian Marine under Sergeant Major Draper at Hecate base. A giant of a man, with a face that looked like it had been cut from flint, he had always seemed invincible. An immutable fact of nature, like the avatar of Olympus Mons, come to life and walking among the mortals.

When he'd died, he'd been a tiny shriveled husk. Lying in his bed, hooked to the tubes and monitors that only prolonged the inevitable, he'd held her hand and said, "I'm ready. I've done this a dozen times before."

She hadn't understood at the time, but now she thought he was talking about sitting right where she was now. In the transport, heading toward battle, examining his life as he rushed toward its possible end. Who am I? Did the things I accomplished matter? Will I leave the universe a better place than I found it? If I don't come back, what are my regrets? What are my victories?

It was a thing maybe only a warrior could understand. Only those who made the choice to run toward the fire, instead of away from it. That made it feel sacred to her. "This far, and no farther," she whispered. Her litany to the tyrants and bullies and despots. *This far, and no farther. If my life means anything after I'm gone,* she thought, *I hope it meant that.*

"What's that, boss?" Jillian asked. Her number two was strapped into the crash couch directly across the pod from her.

"Just talking to myself," Bobbie said. Then she started to sing. "Anything you can do I can do better. I can do anything better than you."

"Never heard that one," Jillian said, then sang along, trying to catch the tune. "That new? Sounds Belter."

Bobbie laughed. "No idea. My mother used to sing it. My brothers were older, and I hated losing to them at anything. I'd burst into tears when they'd win, and she'd sing that song to me. Just one of those things you pick up when you're a kid and never put back down."

"I like it," Jillian said, then closed her eyes and started mumbling to herself. It looked like she was praying. Bobbie knew she wasn't. She was running through the mission in her mind, over and over. *Two meters through the breached hull to the first junction. Turn left. Twelve meters to the engineering hatch. Breach and clear. Three meters to the right is the master console.* The other warrior's litany.

There are people I love. There are people who have loved me. I fought for what I believed, protected those I could, and stood my ground against the encroaching darkness.

Good enough.

The pod screeched a short-lived collision alarm at them. The *Storm* had sent her pair of rail-gun shots past the hull close enough that Bobbie could have reached out and swatted them as they went by.

"Brace for impact," she said, using her sergeant voice. As forceful as it could be without quite being a shout. This was her job now. To seem an immutable fact of nature. The avatar of Olympus Mons come to life and striding through the battlefield. God of war now. Shriveled husk later. Maybe. If she wasn't lucky.

All around her, her squad of six handpicked strike team members locked and inflated their couches. All of them wore Laconian Marine power armor, though the blue color scheme had been repainted black. They were, as her father would have said, the pick of the litter. Jillian from Freehold and five of the Belters.

The Belters were old-school OPA, grizzled veterans of the endless insurgent war with the inner planets before Laconia came and made that irrelevant. Old men and women well practiced in conflict. Her total force on the *Storm* numbered forty, and included warriors from nearly every one of the old factions. But for a high-speed snatch-and-grab boarding action, you couldn't find better fighters than Belters.

"Battle mode," Bobbie said, and her armor woke up, humming with impatience for the fight. The HUD flashed an ammunition inventory at her, then minimized it into one corner of her field of view. A wireframe layout of the interior of the freighter they were about to board appeared and moved to a different corner. The list of six names and the green dot showing they were alive and undamaged scrolled down the left side of her view and remained. Getting everyone back with a green dot instead of a black one was always a mission priority, even if it was never the top.

A flashing message appeared in the center of her field of view: Free Fire Authorization.

"Free fire, alpha team, Captain Roberta Draper," she said.

Through the suit radio she heard the distant clicks as six suits of armor activated their weapons. She'd never needed to do that as a fire team sergeant back in her Martian Marine Corps days. The Corps issued weapons to people and assumed they would use them correctly and according to their training. The Laconians were much more top-down. Winston Duarte had founded Laconia by betraying Mars and looting the navy. It wasn't a great surprise that distrust of the people in his chain of command was institutional.

The HUD flashed a new diagram at her. The relative position of the breaching pod and the freighter, along with a rapidly decreasing distance to target.

"Ready," she growled at her team. "Go in five!"

The breaching pod shuddered as it fired grapples and grabbed the freighter. There was a quick sideways jerk, and then the two ships slammed together. The impact with the freighter was significant, but wrapped as she was in the soft gel interior of her high-tech armor and resting on the inflated padding of her crash couch, it just felt like a sudden pressure on her chest that vanished almost instantly as the pod lost its acceleration and went into free fall. That was a good sign. It meant Alex had hit his target with the rail-gun shots, and the freighter was on the drift.

"Get ready for the burn!" she said, the last word almost lost in the sudden roar of the pod firing its massive braking thrusters to keep the freighter hidden behind Jupiter. Her couch automatically unlocked and swung the other direction, putting her back to the thrust. A new pressure mounted in her chest as the g forces piled on.

When the burn started to ease up, she yelled, "Go go go," but it wasn't really necessary. Her fire team was up and out of their couches the second the thrust stopped. Jillian hit the wall panel next to the airlock and extended the breaching sleeve. It made an airtight seal with the freighter, the deck vibrating with the impact. Two seconds later, shaped charges inside the sleeve cut a hole through both hulls of the Transport Union freighter, and the airlock door slid open.

Jillian was inside first, dropping through the glowing red hole into the freighter. She hit the bulkhead at the first corridor she reached and launched herself to the left, heading toward engineering. Hernandez and Orm followed her.

"We're on board," Bobbie said on the command channel, back to Alex on the *Storm*. Their Laconian gear was modulating the signal to match the jamming, which would hopefully let their radio cut through, but Bobbie wasn't entirely confident in the system. It didn't really matter yet. Alex would be busy fighting the two frigates no matter what her team was doing. Any messages back and forth before the *Storm* had secured the freighter's flight-space were perfunctory.

She followed into the breach, the other three members of the strike team close behind her. When Bobbie hit the corridor wall, she turned right, toward the command deck. The hallway they were in was actually the central lift of the ship, and closed hatches marked each deck they passed. Most of them would lead to cargo space. A few to the crew's living quarters. One would lead to the ops deck, and that was the only one Bobbie cared about.

Jillian and her team would take control of the drive and life support down in engineering. Bobbie would take the ops deck and cut off communication with the outside world. If the political officer wasn't in ops when she arrived, it wouldn't matter. They'd control the ship and search at their leisure. For values of *leisure* up to maybe five or ten whole minutes.

"Watch those hatches," she told her team as she skimmed along the bulkhead toward ops. It felt redundant. Their suits were scanning every square centimeter around them for heat, radiation, even the unique electromagnetic signature generated by a beating human heart. It was pretty tough to get the drop on someone wearing Laconian armor. But saying something reminded the team you were there, that you were in charge, and that keeping everyone safe was on your mind.

"Copy that," Takeshi said. "Most of these aren't warm. Guessing the cargo is in vacuum."

"Guy in a vac suit coming at us from behind is low probability," she agreed, "but low ain't zero."

Bobbie's HUD flashed an overlay over a door one deck ahead. "That one," she said, and her team fanned out and took positions around it. In the microgravity of the disabled freighter, they stood on bulkheads around the hatch, weapons ready. No matter what the orientation of the ship was under thrust, for purposes of the breach the ops deck was down.

"Remember," Bobbie said, "there are potential friendlies in there."

As she said it, a rotating 3-D profile of two women appeared on all their HUDs.

"Protect them first, take prisoners second. Copy?"

There came a rumble of assent. Bobbie slapped the wall panel next to the hatch, and her armor ran the breaching protocol that cut through the electronic security in a fraction of a second. The hatch slid open.

After that, everyone was shooting.

It was a fact of the human brain in close quarters combat that while everything was generally happening all at once, the mind insisted on trying to stitch it into a linear narrative when remembering it later.

In the moment, Bobbie threw herself through the hatch and into the ops deck, her team at her back. Incoming bullets lit up her HUD with bright trails so she'd know the direction of fire. Some of the bullets hit her, or her team. The armor thought the odds of taking real damage were trivial, and ignored it. Seven people in the compartment, wearing light protective armor. Her suit tagged one as a friendly. One of the two resistance partisans. Five with guns shooting at her. One doing his best to hide behind a crash couch. The political officer, if she had to guess.

Her arm moved without her thinking about it, and the gun mounted at her wrist spun up briefly, cutting two of the armed crew in half. The other three were turning into red spray and body parts under the barrage of fire from her team. The whole fight couldn't have lasted more than two seconds, though when she remembered it later and her brain turned it into a narrative, it would seem much longer.

Less than thirty seconds after she'd opened the hatch, two of her strike team were protectively flanking the partisan, and Takeshi had the political officer shoved up against a bulkhead and was zip-tying his hands. Bobbie examined the deck. No hull breaches, her armor assured her. The Laconian antipersonnel rounds for shipboard use were pretty good tech. Lethal against lightly armored opponents, but they just fragmented into powder when they hit bulkheads.

"Ops is ours," Bobbie said.

"Engineering is ours," Jillian immediately replied. "We have one of the two spies. You got the other?"

"Copy. Our people are secure, and we have the package."

"Oh goody," Jillian said. "Can't wait to see his face when he realizes his life just went down the recycler."

"Jillian, escort the friendly up here," Bobbie said. "Let's get everyone into emergency suits and prep them for the ride over to the *Storm*. The rest of you, fan out and get an eyeball inventory. When the *Storm* arrives we're going to want to take all the best stuff with us, and we won't have much time. Get to it."

"Copy that," Jillian said.

"I think we win," Bobbie said to Takeshi. He grinned back at her.

"Easy peas—" he started to say and then blew apart.

Bobbie knew intellectually that they must have taken a raking pass from someone's PDCs. But from inside the ship it looked like the bulkheads on either side of the compartment decided to explode in several dozen places all at once. The room was full of glowing shrapnel bouncing off walls and panels, and the gray smoke of vaporized metal. Takeshi was a tangle of technology-wrapped body parts floating in a nebula of blood globes.

It didn't look like anyone else was directly hit, but before Bobbie could even start to issue an order, the air in the room was just *gone*. Too many holes on both sides. One moment they were in a pressurized cabin, the next they were in vacuum. It happened so fast it barely ruffled the political officer's Laconian blue suit jacket.

"Get them in suits!" she yelled, but it was already too late. She was a Martian. She'd started doing vacuum drills in grade school. Fifteen seconds and you lose consciousness. Anything that you needed to do had to happen in that first fifteen seconds or it didn't happen at all. Any vacuum suit that is more than fifteen seconds away is a lifetime away.

All she could do was watch the partisan who'd helped them take the ship gasp out a cloud of mist that was her very last breath ever. The political officer, their whole reason for coming, died a moment later with a look of profound puzzlement on his face. A thousand facts and secrets that could have meant the difference between the underground thriving and all of them dying in a gulag evaporated as the man's cells gave up.

Every panel on the ops deck that still worked was flashing red. The ship was dead too.

"*Storm*, this is strike team," Bobbie said, opening the command channel. She heard only dead air and the faint hiss of background radiation. "*Storm*, come in."

Nothing.

"Shit," Jillian said. She came into the ops deck dragging their dead ally from the engineering deck with her. "Did we lose the *Storm* too?"

"Chama," Bobbie said, pointing at one of her people. "Get outside and see if you can spot the *Storm*. Maybe line-of-sight comms will work. The rest of you, mission hasn't changed. Get me that inventory. Get it ready for rapid transfer once we find the ship."

"Or," Jillian said, "get ready to fall into Jupiter and die because we're way under orbital speed now and don't have an engine."

"Or that," Bobbie agreed, surprised at how much she wanted to push across the room and punch Jillian in the face. "But until we do, we'll stay on mission. Get the fuck out of here and make yourself useful packing cargo."

On the radio, one of Jillian's squad mates said, "Lots of stuff here, boss. Ammo, fuel, it's the mother lode. Primary mission is fucked, but secondary is a win."

"A moral victory, I guess," Bobbie sighed.

"You know who talks about moral victories?" Jillian asked as she floated out of the room. "The team that lost."

Chapter Eight: Naomi

Communication was a problem.

The ring gates created interference that made trading messages across them difficult and tightbeam between systems essentially impossible. Laconia controlled the repeaters on either side of the gates, and Medina Station in the center of everything, the guard at the great crossroads of the empire. They had eyes and ears in every system and pattern-matching algorithms combing through every frequency on the spectrum. Saba had been able to carve out a few holes here and there—tightbeam antennas with outdated or compromised security code that could drop incoming records out of the logs, newsfeeds that could be altered to carry messages hidden in the flux of the image signal. The same old tricks the OPA had been using since before either she or Saba had been born, but updated for the new circumstances. The danger was twofold: first that Laconian forces would intercept and understand their messages, and second that they'd track the signal back to its origin.

The first problem wasn't trivial, but there were ways of making it difficult. Self-scrambling encryption, interference signatures, context-shifting linguistic encoding. Nothing was perfect, and even with the forensic work that Bobbie and her crew had done on the *Gathering Storm*, the full extent of Laconian military signal processing was three parts guesswork and one part hope for the underground. But Naomi was confident enough in it that she didn't lose sleep.

The second problem—not having the signal traced back—was easier because of the bottles.

Naomi had never actually seen an ocean except through a camera, but language held on to things that were long gone. Tight-beams still had "lines" even though the physical wire that *line* referred to had been light for generations. Sol was still "the sun" even though there were thirteen hundred more like it, shining down on human heads. *Message in a bottle* held a whole host of nuances and expectations for Earthers that she could only inherit thirdhand—through jokes and cartoons and entertainment feeds. The actual bottles she used were the torpedoes that she kept in her container, each of them carrying a burst transmitter and an explosive payload large enough to turn the equipment into bright dust. She'd written the code herself, and she knew it was solid.

To get information in *from* Saba and the underground, all she had to do was listen. It was all there, screaming through the void and amplified on the networks, since she knew which feeds to look at. The gossip and the newsfeeds and the empty, fluting static where the notes had been tucked in. Even Laconian propaganda. Even, sometimes, the rebroadcast messages Duarte made Jim send out to her.

No matter what ship she was on, the information came in, passive and untraceable. She fed it into the local system in her couch and her hand terminal—more raw information than she could have read in a lifetime, and updating constantly. And the system filtered out the reports and information for her to work from.

She made her analysis, her recommendations, her arguments for what the forces opposing these new inners should do and how. And when she was ready—when time was short or she felt like she'd come to a natural break point—she would transfer the information into one of the missiles and signal her shipboard contact. Once the missile was dropped out an airlock, her code would kick in.

A randomized direction, a randomized number of turn-and-burns, a randomized length and power of thrust, and a randomized time before delivery. Sometimes she'd drop it off a day or two before she left the system, or after the shell-ship she'd come in on had moved on. Sometimes she wouldn't. Patterns were the enemy, even patterns that were meant to cover her tracks.

When the time came, the bottle screamed out everything she'd told it in a single burst. Somewhere in the system, Saba would have an antenna listening just the way she did. Quietly, passively, undetectably. It was an act of cosmic ventriloquism, and it was how the underground passed information back and forth—slowly and imperfectly—while the enemy could send its own messages anywhere it chose to at the speed of light.

That was what being the underdog meant.

The hardest part was the time between sending the bottle out and when it detonated. Hours or days or, rarely, weeks of second-guessing herself. Poring over her own plans and suggestions, certain that she'd made a mistake she couldn't stop before it rippled out through the systems. Listening to all the new information coming in that would have changed one aspect or another of what she'd already said and couldn't take back.

It was what she was doing now.

Her box had left the *Mosley* for another ship, almost its twin, called the *Bhikaji Cama*. They were on a quarter-g burn for Auberon with mining equipment salvaged on the cheap from Mars. The hum of the drives was familiar enough by now that she didn't hear it unless they were making some adjustment to speed or trajectory, and then it was only when the vibrations hit a harmonic and made something ring. The rations she'd gotten as a farewell gift from the *Mosley* were Earth-made. Rice and vegetable protein and curry sauce that might almost have been Belter food, except for the added raisins. She set her system to local, not tying into the *Cama*'s computers at all unless there was something she could only get there. She had music—soft mambo cereseano like she'd danced to when she was a girl—and as many newsfeeds as she could stand. She'd arranged her space so that there was room to stretch and exercise, and she made herself keep to a schedule religiously, pushing herself to a sweat twice a day. She slept to schedule too, dimming the lights for eight hours, no more and no less, never sleeping in. Never taking naps. Routine was what kept the darkness at bay, when anything did.

And in between, she studied her data again and waited for her most recent bottle to break.

The monitor showed a schematic of Bara Gaon Complex with both the existing settlement and the newly proposed expansion. Bara Gaon was one of the most successful of the new human systems, with three planets already boasting self-sustaining cities, an independent mining cooperative surveying a particularly rich asteroid belt, and bases on two moons of the system's only gas giant. The map of humanity's presence in the system looked like the first growth of a leaf: pale, elegant, thin, and promising a greater strength still to come. The initial waves had been led by an agricultural corporation based on Ganymede and a progressive Muslim community out of the Greater Terai Shared Interest Zone. The two had managed a functional partnership that drew five more waves of settlement in under two decades.

It was a fraction of Sol system, but it wouldn't be for long. The expansion plan had been trapped in negotiations for years before Laconia had rolled through, and now Duarte's will was kicking it forward.

Five new cities had been proposed, two each on the planets nearer to their sun, one on the cooler outlier. A high-end sensor network that would be able to map the system over the course of the next six years. Eighteen new exploratory missions. An increased civil infrastructure rolled out in two-year increments, with an emphasis on scientific and cultural support. If it worked, Bara Gaon would eclipse Sol system in under a century. It was as ambitious as any plan Naomi had ever seen, and it might even be possible.

That ambition was also the underground's best hope. *Her* best hope.

She flicked through the lists of project proposals. She'd been over all of them a hundred times. Every phase had its own requirements. The sensor network alone was slated to hire a hundred and thirty engineers and subject specialists. And while the network's primary function was mapping, it didn't take a genius to see its potential as system surveillance. It would make the underground's covert operations in Bara Gaon Complex easier if between 10 and 20 percent of those engineers and specialists also answered to Saba.

She'd put together her own map of the project. Not impeding the expansion, but taking control of it from within. The Personnel Directorate of Bara Gaon was her first target. They were already putting out requests for applications, beefing up the bureaucracy that would be evaluating new hires. Naomi had identified seven critical positions and built candidate profiles that Saba could use to flood the job openings with his allies. It was important that the people not be false identities, but actual people with real histories and qualifications. If they managed to get two of the seven positions now, it would be enough to give them an edge on later ones. Three, and they'd be able to cover their own tracks well enough that prying them out would be difficult even if Laconia became suspicious. Five, and Saba would effectively control the Bara Gaon Complex expansion.

She'd also identified problem issues. The chief administrator of Zehanat province on Bara Gaon-6—the planet they called Al-Halub—was a close friend of Carrie Fisk and openly supportive of Laconian rule. It was important that the projects based there be deprioritized and his personal influence undermined. Labor unions on the gas giant's moons had ties to an old inner planets hate group and still fought against everything the Transport Union did with the zeal of the self-proclaimed oppressed. Saba would need to create other allies there. The local government had a communitarian faction that was growing more vocal about armed resistance against Laconia that would bring more scrutiny without gaining any useful ground if it wasn't reined in.

You can't fight a shooting war armed with paper clips, Bobbie said in Naomi's imagination.

"Watch me," Naomi answered. Her voice echoed with the music in the container. A pinch of annoyance bothered her. She closed down her files and pushed the monitor aside. In the time since she'd left Sol system, she'd hoped that their last conversation would have lost some of its power, but like a splinter under her skin, it bit a little every time she touched it.

When two people get in a fight, and only one has a gun and the will to use it? That's a short damned fight.

Only it wasn't Bobbie's voice that said it this time. It was Amos'. A few decades flying the same ship together had built little versions of her family in her head. Made some part of them a part of her, even when she didn't particularly want them to be. Even when the little mirrors of them only told her that their conversation wasn't finished.

She hauled herself up out of the couch, the gimbals hissing as she shifted. She turned the music to a brighter selection with a clearer, faster beat. Something to push her. It was early in her day for a workout, but she needed to move. As if working the long muscles of her arms and legs and back could relieve a tension between her and people not present.

"It's never a short fight," she said as she hooked resistance bands to the top of her container. The fasteners had been painted gray when she'd first stepped into her little box. They were bright raw steel now. "Last time I fought it, it was generations old before I even stepped in the ring. We can't shoot our way to peace."

Peace isn't the only good victory condition. How about just shooting our way to freedom or justice?

Naomi sank her feet into the floor loops, braced herself, locked the bands in place, and pulled. It was hard work. It hurt a little, but hurting a little was the point. The voice in her imagination wasn't Amos' now, but Jim's.

That's the thing about autocracy. It looks pretty decent while it still looks pretty decent. Survivable, anyway. And it keeps looking like that right up until it doesn't. That's how you find out it's too late.

"I am fighting," she said, then grunted and pulled down hard again. "The quiet work's still a fight. It's a better one. It's one we can win."

Not in our lifetimes, Bobbie said. And that was the point, really. That was the deep, true thought that Naomi was working her own way through with all the beloved voices in her head.

Sweat was pooling at her hairline, the quarter g not quite enough to pull it down her face. Her arms were trembling with every pull. She made herself go slowly, watching her form. It made the work harder, which she liked. And it made her less likely to injure herself, which was critical. Slow, careful, focused. Avoiding damage.

Feels like it ought to be a metaphor for something, Jim's voice said, and she laughed at his joke.

Growing older was a falling away of everything that didn't matter. And a deepening appreciation of all the parts that were important enough to stay.

She had unhooked the bands and started repositioning them to work her back when the alert came, chirping on her couch monitor and her hand terminal at the same moment. She wound the bands up and put them away. She'd finish later. The monitor had a single notification up. The *Cama* had picked up an encrypted message that matched her confirmation signature. Out in the depths below Auberon's ecliptic, the bottle had broken and its data had all spilled out. She grabbed a copy out of the ship buffer and had her system run a comparison. There would be some degradation. There always was. But there was also repetition in the signal and checksums along the way. It would take terrible luck or a very high-radiation event to swamp her work past the point of recovery. She only made sure because it was the right thing.

All the files and reports opened from the copy as they had from the original files. The system's final verdict popped up with a click like someone snapping their fingers. No UNRECOVERABLE LOSS.

So that was done. Another round of analysis, a new set of orders and recommendations released to the wild. She had, of course, already started on the next one. She enjoyed the sense of accomplishment all the same.

She shifted to the newsfeeds, purging the unflagged copies local to her couch and replacing them again like dipping a cup into a fountain that never ran dry. Tapping her finger against the screen, she paged through the items the system thought most likely to pertain to her. A minor election on Sanaang had gone unexpectedly to the second-ranked candidate, a move she had recommended in her bottle before last. A code farm on Mars had partnered with Medina Station to build a new security infrastructure, which wasn't what she'd wanted, but had been on her list of acceptable fallbacks. A security alert had gone out in Sol system. A red flag, but without the details to say what it was.

Except that whatever it turned out to be, she knew what it was. Bobbie's war. The one with guns.

Somewhere out there, far enough away that even lightspeed meant hours, Bobbie and Alex were risking their lives. Maybe losing them. There was nothing she could do. Frustration washed over her. Or maybe she just became aware of what was always there.

She'd chosen her role. She'd picked her place, helped with designing the little dried shell-game pea that she lived in. There had been a dozen other ways she could have worked with the underground. Thousands of ways she could have made a new life without them. She was here because she had chosen to be here. The container had felt like solitude, not isolation. A refuge where she could wait for the mud in her heart to settle and her mind to become clear.

It had seemed like a good plan at the time. It had seemed to work. Now, her fingertips hovering over the security alert, she wasn't sure it did anymore.

With a tap like she was killing an insect, she shut the newsfeeds. Her data analysis was still up behind it, cheerfully reporting No UNRECOVERABLE LOSS.

"Seems like that should be a metaphor for something," she said, and imagined Jim's laughter beside her. Trading the same joke back and forth between them like they had in better days.

Then, a moment later, "God damn, but I have to get out of this fucking box."

Chapter Nine: Teresa

Carrie Fisk was the president of the Association of Worlds. It was, Teresa knew, a measure of how important she was that President Fisk was allowed to meet with her father over breakfast. Teresa sat at her father's right at the little table, and Fisk sat opposite him, so Teresa felt a little like she was watching table tennis listening to them talk.

"A trade compact between Auberon and the five-world group does have some real advantages," Fisk said. "By picking a handful of systems to really focus on, we can make progress quickly. Auberon or Bara Gaon can bring another three to five systems up to self-sufficiency in seven to ten years, then each of those systems can take on clients. The geometric growth model brings all the systems up much faster than having every individual colony be an equal priority."

Her father nodded slowly. It was a gesture she recognized. He glanced over to her and raised an eyebrow. A little gesture of complicity. Teresa could feel Fisk squirming a little. The woman was so anxious for her father's approval it was a little embarrassing. Teresa shrugged. Just a few millimeters of movement that meant *Do you want me to ask?* Her father nodded.

"What about corruption?" Teresa said.

Fisk laughed. "Auberon's reputation precedes it. Governor Rittenaur assures me that it's under control. There were a few bad apples, but that's to be expected in an unregulated colony. Now that it's under Laconian supervision, the problem is being addressed."

Teresa nodded, then leaned back to see how her father responded. He was slower. Teresa took another bite of her eggs. The yolk was runny, the way she liked, and she sopped it up with a bit of toast. Kelly—her father's personal valet—brought Fisk another coffee. When her father sighed, the defeat was clear in Fisk's eyes. Just for a moment, and then covered over, but Teresa had seen it.

"The architecture is good," he said. "I'm not certain these five are the right worlds to lead with. Let me review this and get back to you next week."

"Yes, sir," Fisk said. "Of course."

After the breakfast meeting was done, Fisk left and Teresa stayed. As Kelly cleared away the dishes, her father stood, stretched, and turned to her.

"What did you notice?" he asked.

"She was nervous," Teresa said.

"She always is," her father said. "That's part of why I chose her. When people get too comfortable, they get loose. Sloppy. What else?"

"She knew that the corruption question was coming. And she focused it on Auberon instead of how the five worlds were selected."

"Was she trying to cover something up?"

"I don't think so," Teresa said. "It looked to me more like she knew Auberon had a bad reputation, and she was just reaching for the obvious thing. When you focused on the world selection she seemed...relieved?"

"I agree. All right. That was interesting. I have a military briefing from Trejo in Sol system. Any interest in reviewing it?"

The answer was no. It was peer class day, which meant seeing Connor. More than sneaking out to see Timothy, more than playing with Muskrat, more even than being with her father, she wanted to go to class. But she also felt guilty about her desires. She didn't want to make her father feel like he wasn't important to her, especially when it was a little bit true...

"If you want," she said, making her voice bright and carefree.

He chuckled and tousled her hair. "I don't need it. You can go work with Colonel Ilich. If Trejo has something critical, I'll let you know."

"All right," she said. And then, because she could tell he knew what she'd been thinking, "Thank you."

"Always," he said, and waved her on.

She knew as soon as she stepped into the classroom that something was wrong. Usually the others were spread in clumps, lounging on the sofas and chairs of the common area, with half a dozen conversations going on among them. They would notice when she walked into the room, but they didn't make an effort not to stare at her. Today, they had scattered to the edges of the room, leaning against walls or against the pillars like little prey animals that knew a predator was close. Connor was by himself, frowning at a handheld like it had insulted him and he was trying to keep his temper. The others all glanced at her and then away again, but Connor didn't see her with an energy and focus that felt deliberate.

"I'll be right back," Colonel Ilich said, touching her on the shoulder. "I just need to get one thing before we start."

She nodded, dismissing him. Her attention was on Muriel

Cowper. She was a year older than Teresa, with dusty brown hair, a chipped front tooth, and a talent for drawing that meant she did all the face painting at the large-group events. She approached Teresa now, and it looked like she was trembling. It reminded Teresa of Carrie Fisk.

"Teresa," the other girl said. "Can I...could we talk for a minute?"

Teresa felt a little prick of dread, but she nodded. Muriel took a couple steps toward the door to the courtyard, then stopped and looked back the way Muskrat did sometimes, to be sure Teresa was following. In the courtyard, Muriel held her hands in front of her belly like a child being disciplined. Teresa wanted to take them, push them back down to her sides, make her act normal. Muriel's anxiety was like heat from a fire, and it made Teresa feel anxious too.

"What's going on?" Teresa asked.

Muriel licked her lips, took a deep breath, and looked up, her eyes locked on Teresa's. "There was a camping trip with the school last week, and all of us went, and it was overnight so a bunch of us snuck out to the water when we were supposed to be asleep and Connor kissed me."

Teresa felt something. She didn't know what it was, but it lived in her abdomen, just below her navel, and in deep enough that she knew it couldn't be muscular. The implications clicked over in her mind like dominoes. Connor had kissed Muriel. Not just that, but Connor had *wanted* to kiss Muriel. Not just that, but Muriel had known that Teresa would care. And so had everyone else.

Oh God, and so had Connor.

"I can break up with him," Muriel said softly. "If you want me to."

"I don't care what either of you do," Teresa said. "If you and Connor want to go into the woods and kiss, it doesn't mean anything to me."

"Thank you," Muriel said, and went back into the common room, almost skipping. Teresa followed her, trying not to let anything that was happening in her body show on her face. Colonel Ilich arrived as she did, smiling warmly. He had a round black-and-white ball the size of a decapitated head under his arm.

"Today," he said to all of them, "we're going to be learning some new football drills. The rain's made the east lawn a little damp for the process, so if you fine ladies and gentlemen will please follow me to the gymnasium, you can change into more appropriate clothes…"

The middle of the day was filled with echoing shouts and the burn of her legs and back. She kicked too hard and missed more of the shots than she made, and through all of it, she felt the attention of the class on her. Of Muriel. Of Connor. Even Colonel Ilich noticed that she was off her game, but apart from a gentle question about how she was feeling, he didn't follow up on it. When the time came to shower and change back into her regular clothes, she didn't go to the locker rooms with the others. She had her own apartments. She didn't need to be with them anymore. Not any of them.

As she left, she looked to see if Connor was with Muriel. If they were holding hands. If they were kissing. As it happened, they weren't—Connor was at a brushed steel drinking fountain with Khalid Marks and Muriel was pretending that she'd died and had to be carried off the floor by Anneke Douby and Michael Li. Teresa thought it should make her feel better, but it didn't.

In the privacy of her rooms, she let herself cry. She felt stupid for having to. Connor wasn't anything to her but the boy she'd thought about more than other boys. She'd never kissed him or tried to hold his hand. Until today, she'd have said that he didn't even know that she felt different about him. That no one knew. Except now he was sneaking out of his tent with Muriel fucking Cowper in the middle of the night. Who was even in charge of the camping trips that they let things like that happen? Someone could have been drowned or mistaken for prey by a local animal. They were incompetent. That was the problem. That—improbable as it was—was why she was sobbing.

Muskrat forced a thick, prickly nose under her arm, pushing

up. The concern in the old dog's eyes was unmistakable. Her thick tail wagged uncertainly.

"I'm stupid," Teresa said, and her voice sounded exhausted even to her. "I'm just really stupid."

Muskrat coughed out something less than a bark and hopped on her front legs. An unambiguous invitation. *Let's forget this and go play.* Teresa threw herself down on her bed, hoping that sleep would come or that the bed would open up like in the movies and let her escape to a different dimension where no one had ever heard of her. Muskrat huffed again. Then barked.

"Fine," Teresa said. "Just let me put some clothes on that don't stink like sweat. Idiotic dog."

Muskrat wagged harder. More sincerely.

The morning clouds had gone, but the landscape was still soaking from the rain. The water cycle was something that all the worlds in the empire shared. Any world with life had rainstorms and mud puddles. She walked down the colonnaded paths, tending away from the more inhabited parts of the State Building. She didn't want to have any company but her dog and her self-pity.

She wondered what she could have done differently. If she'd told Muriel no, that she had to break things off with Connor. She could have done that. She still could, a little. If she went to Colonel Ilich and said she didn't feel comfortable with Muriel anymore, she could have the girl kicked out of the peer interaction activities. Even request that Connor spend more time at the State Building if she wanted to, and it would just happen.

But everyone would know why she was doing it, and so she couldn't. Instead, she walked across the gray-green of the back gardens, looked out at the low, green rise of the mountain beyond the State Building's grounds, and wished she could leave or die or turn time backward.

Muskrat alerted, dark, floppy ears pointing forward with excitement. The dog barked once in what sounded like excitement and then bounded away faster than an animal on old worn-out hips should have been able to. Despite herself, Teresa laughed.

"Muskrat!" she shouted, but the dog was onto something and wouldn't be turned away. The thick, wagging tail disappeared behind a hedge of lilacs imported from Earth, and Teresa trotted after.

She half expected to find Muskrat worrying a skitter or ash-cat or other local animal that had wandered onto the grounds. The dog did that sometimes, even though the local animals made her sick when she ate them. Teresa always worried that one of the larger native predators would sneak in someday. But when she made her way around the hedge, the only thing besides Muskrat was a human figure, sitting on the grass and looking out toward the horizon. Graying, close-cropped hair. Laconian uniform without an insignia of rank. An amiable, empty smile.

James Holden, and Muskrat sprawling on the grass beside him, wriggling to scratch her back. Teresa stopped short. Holden reached out idly and rubbed her dog's belly. Muskrat hopped to her feet and barked to Teresa. *Come on!* Almost against her will, Teresa found herself walking toward the most famous prisoner in the empire.

She didn't like Holden. Didn't trust him. But whenever they spoke, he was polite and unthreatening. Even a little amused by everything in a vague, philosophical kind of way that made it easy to be polite back.

"Hey," he said, not looking up at her.

"Hello."

"You know what's weird?" he said. "The rain smells the same, but the wet ground doesn't."

Teresa didn't say anything. Muskrat looked from the prisoner to her and back again, as if she expected something she was looking forward to. After a moment, Holden went on.

"I grew up on Earth. When I was your age—you're fourteen, right? When I was your age, I was living on a ranch in Montana with eight parents and a lot of animals. Rain smelled like this. I think it's the ozone. You know, from the electrical charges? But the ground after a storm had this deep smell. It was like...I don't know. It smelled good. Here, it smells minty. It's weird."

"I've been around wet soil before," she said, almost defensive. "That smell's called petrichor. It's actinomycete spores."

"I didn't know that," Holden said. "It's a good smell. I miss it."

"That's my dog." The implied *so get away from her* was lost on him.

"Muskrat," Holden said, and Muskrat thumped her tail, pleased to be included in the conversation. "That's an interesting name. Did you pick it?"

"Yes," Teresa said.

"Ever seen a real muskrat?"

"Of course not."

"So why the name?" The way he asked seemed weirdly open. Almost innocent. Like she was the grown-up and he was the kid.

"There was a character named that in a picture book my father used to read to me."

"And was the character a muskrat?"

"I guess so," Teresa said.

"Well, there you have it," Holden said. "Mystery solved. You don't have to be afraid of me, you know. She's not."

Teresa shifted her weight. The ground under her was still soft from the rain, and he was right. It smelled like mint. A half dozen possible responses came to mind, from turning and walking away to telling him that she wasn't scared of him and he was stupid to think she was. If she hadn't already been feeling humiliated and angry, she probably would have laughed it off. But it turned out she was spoiling for a fight, and he'd handed her one. He was one of the few people it was perfectly safe to bite at.

"You're a terrorist," she said. "You killed people."

An expression crossed his face almost too quickly to see, then he smiled again. "I guess I was. But I'm not anymore."

"I don't know why my father doesn't keep you in prison," she said.

"Oh, I know the answer to that one. I'm his dancing bear," Holden said, and lay back on the grass and looked up at the sky. High white clouds against the blue, and the glittering lights of the construction platforms beyond them. Teresa understood the game. He was pulling her into conversation. The thing about the rain and the soil. How Muskrat got her name. Now this mysterious dancing bear comment. All of them were invitations, but it was up to her whether to play along.

"Dancing bear?" she said.

"Old kings used to have dangerous animals in their courts. Lions. Panthers. Bears. They'd teach them to do tricks or at least not to eat too many of the guests. It's a way to show power. Everyone knows a bear is a killer, but the king is so powerful that a bear's just a plaything for him. If Duarte kept me in a cell, people might think he was afraid of me. Or that I might be a threat if I got out. If he lets me out, lets me roam around with what sort of looks like freedom, it tells everyone that comes to the palace that he's cut my nuts off." He didn't sound angry at all. Or resigned. If anything, he was almost amused by it.

"You're getting your back wet, lying down like that."

"I know."

The moment stretched, and she felt the silence pushing at her. "How many people did you kill?"

"Depends on how you count it. I tried not to get anyone killed when I could help it. The thing is? I *am* in prison. Right now, I'm pretty sure there are at least two very well-trained snipers ready to open up my brainpan if I try to hurt you. So not only am I not inclined to hurt you, I literally couldn't, even if I thought it was a good idea. That's the point of a dancing bear. It's the least dangerous thing at the court, because everyone's aware of it. The ones you trust are always the most dangerous. A lot more kings and princesses got poisoned by their friends than eaten by bears."

Her handheld chimed. Colonel Ilich asking to speak with her. She sent an acknowledgment, but didn't open a connection. Holden grinned up at her.

"Duty calls?" he asked.

Teresa didn't answer him except to tap her leg. Muskrat hauled herself up to her feet and trundled over, as pleased to leave as to stay. Teresa turned back toward the State Building. When Holden called back after her, there was a buzz in his voice. Like he was trying to fit more meaning into the words than the syllables could hold.

"If you're worried, you should keep an eye on me."

She looked back. He was sitting up. As she'd warned, his back was dark with wet, but he didn't seem to care.

"They're watching me all the time," he said. "Even when it seems like they aren't. *You should keep an eye on me.*"

She frowned. "All right," she said, then walked away.

As she headed back toward her rooms and the colonel, Muskrat huffing contentedly at her side, Teresa tried to decide what she was feeling. The sting of Connor and Muriel was still there, and the shame at feeling stung. But they weren't as immediate as they had been. And along with them was an uneasiness she couldn't quite fit her mind around, only that it had to do with the fact that Muskrat liked stumbling across James Holden and she didn't.

She found Colonel Ilich in the common area. The couches and sofas felt very different with all the other students gone. The walls themselves felt like they'd taken a step back and left a fraction more room for the emptiness. Her footsteps echoed, and so did Muskrat's claws tapping against the tile. Ilich was going through something on his handheld, but he stood up as soon as she came near.

"Thank you," he said. "I hope I wasn't interrupting anything?"

"Nothing important," she said. "I was just walking."

"That's excellent. Your father asked me to see whether you were available."

"An incident?"

"Piracy in Sol system," Ilich said. Then, a moment later, "Piracy with some unfortunate security implications. There may need to be an escalated response."

"Did something important go missing?"

"Yes. But before we go to your father?" Ilich's expression softened. For a moment, he had the same expression she'd just seen on James Holden. It was eerie. "I don't want to intrude, but I had the feeling that there was something bothering you at the peer seminar today."

This was her moment. All she had to say was that she didn't feel comfortable with Muriel anymore, and the girl would never be welcome at the State Building again. Or that she wanted to go on the next camping overnight that the school took. Then she could sneak out at night and kiss a boy down by the water. She could feel the words in her mouth, solid and hard as candy. But then Ilich would know. He knew already.

The ones you trust are always the most dangerous.

"Teresa?" Ilich said. "Is something wrong?"

"No," she said. "Everything's fine."

Chapter Ten: Elvi

Something was wrong. She didn't know what it was, only that she had an overwhelming sense of threat and dislocation. She was coughing and vomiting breathable liquid, and Fayez was already gone. His couch looked empty and dry. He'd been out of it awhile. Her mind slowly came back. She was on the *Falcon*. They'd been burning hard to the Tecoma system. She'd been in a high-g crash couch. And something had gone wrong.

She tried to say *What happened?*, but all that came out was, "Wa appa."

"Don't try to speak yet," her med tech said. A likable young ensign named Calvin with dark skin and features that made Elvi think his ancestors might have come from the same region of West Africa as her own. She'd never asked, because he almost certainly wouldn't know. Laconians did not share the Earther interest in ethnic origins. His face seemed to swim in and out of focus, and her mind felt weirdly disconnected from her body.

"Wa—" she said, ignoring his advice, and then she vomited again.

"Stop it," Calvin said more forcefully. "You had a reaction to the sedative mix while you were under. We had to run some tests and a procedure before we revived you to make sure we didn't do any damage."

Calvin pulled a medical cuff off her arm that she hadn't even noticed was there. The needles stung as they retracted. Several tubes ran from the cuff to a drug-dispensing monitor nearby. Elvi tried to read the screen to see what they'd been pumping into her, but her eyes couldn't focus. The words remained a mysterious blur.

"What—" she managed to get out without vomiting, but before she could finish, Fayez burst into the room.

"You woke her? Why didn't anyone call me!" he yelled at Calvin. "Let me see her chart!"

Fayez grabbed her hand and squeezed a little too hard. Up close, she could see that his eyes were a little red and puffy. Had he been crying?

"Sir," Calvin said. "She woke because the procedure had finished. All her scans are clean. No brain damage. There should be no loss of function."

"Brain damage?" Elvi croaked out. "Were we thinking brain damage?"

Her throat felt raw. Fayez grabbed a plastic bottle of water with a straw and held it up to her lips. She drank greedily. Apparently she was thirsty. Good to know.

"There was some concern that your breathing had been depressed," Fayez said as she gulped down the water. "We just wanted to be sure."

"It was unlikely," Calvin added. "But we wanted to take every precaution."

"What happened?" Elvi finally managed to say once her thirst was quenched.

"You didn't tell her?" Fayez shot at Calvin. "Els, honey, you had a reaction to—"

"No," she cut him off. "I know that. Where are we? I feel gravity. Are we through the transit?"

As she spoke, Calvin began putting his instruments away. It looked like whatever had happened to her, the treatment for it was over.

"Yes," Fayez said. "We're in Tecoma right now. We're finishing our deceleration burn."

"I've been out that long?"

"I was scared to death, Els. I'm getting a full battery of tests run to make sure this doesn't happen again."

"Sagale's schedule won't—"

"Sagale agreed with me. I was surprised too. I think the prospect of losing Duarte's pet biologist had him pissing his uniform."

Calvin snorted at that. "I'm done here. Do you need anything else?"

"No," Elvi said. "Yes. When can I go back to work?"

"Now, if you feel up to it."

"Thank you, Calvin," Elvi said.

Calvin gave her a salute and a smile. "My pleasure, Major," he said, then left the compartment.

"Maybe you should rest," Fayez said. He was frowning at her. Elvi laughed. He almost never frowned, and with his baby face it made him look like a petulant child.

"I'm fine," she said. And then, "Okay, I'm not fine. I'll be fine. It's just travel."

"I don't like it," Fayez said. She took his hand. Her skin felt sticky. She was going to need a real shower.

"So, Tecoma system," she said. "The probes said it was a neutron star?" She tried sitting up. Her head swam a little, so she stopped there.

"It is," Fayez agreed, putting a hand on her back to help steady her. "But, you know, weirder."

The dizziness passed, and her eyes were focusing better as

well. The text on the screens around her became actual letters and numbers.

"Help me up," she said, then dropped her feet to the floor. Fayez put an arm around her waist as she tried standing. Her legs were a little weak, but the gravity felt like they were only burning at a quarter g or so, so it was easy to stay upright. Fayez gave her a look, then took his arm away, waiting close by to grab her if she fell. She didn't.

"I'll need some clothes," she said. Fayez nodded and opened a nearby storage locker. "Weirder how?"

"Emptied," Fayez said, then tossed her uniform and some clean underclothes on the couch. "Massive rapidly spinning neutron star, no planets, planetoids, asteroids, nothing."

Elvi pulled off the thin smock she wore in the submersion couch and headed to the shower. Fayez followed her in, carrying a towel. The blast of hot water made her dizzy again, but one hand on the wall and some deep-breathing exercises cleared it up in a few seconds. Fayez watched closely, but once he was sure she was all right, he relaxed. As she washed the last of the goop off her body, Elvi said, "They cleared everything out to make a diamond backup drive too."

"This is more than that. I don't mean no planetary bodies. I mean no nothing. No micrometeors. No dust. No spare protons floating around. The vacuum here is as hard as it can get."

"That's…Okay. Weirder." Elvi turned the water off, and Fayez tossed her the towel. "I mean, is that even possible?"

"No. Not unless there's something keeping it clean. We're still in the Milky Way. There should be some spare crap floating through now and then. So not only is the system cleaned out, something's actively keeping it cleaned out. And—get this—the gate is five times farther out from the star than any of the other gates. And it's above the plane of the ecliptic. Ninety degrees. Don't even get me started on the star."

"What's going on with the star?"

"It's massive. I mean, like, spit-on-it-and-it'll-start-to-collapse-into-a-black-hole-level massive."

"Good that there's no spit around, then."

"Right? It turns out neutron stars aren't much to look at. Unless you can see magnetic fields, they're just…underwhelming. I mean the densest matter possible, forces so powerful as to break space-time? Sure. Bright as hell, you bet. But I was expecting a light show or something. It just looks like another sun, but smaller and kind of angry about it. This one is spinning fast enough to land in the pulsar range. We're far enough away to avoid the worst of the magnetic disturbance."

She took a deep breath. She could hear the anxiety in his words. She knew what they meant.

"I'm *fine*," she said.

"You aren't. You could have died."

"I didn't, though. And now, I'll be fine."

"Okay."

Elvi finished drying off and stuffed the towel into the recycler. Fayez pulled a jar of scalp cream out of a cabinet and began rubbing it into her short, tight curls with his fingertips. It felt wonderful to have him massaging her head. When you find a man who takes pleasure in helping you avoid dry scalp, Elvi thought, you keep him.

"You can do that all day if you want," she said.

"If we had all day, my attentions would begin moving south," he replied with a grin. "But we're killing our burn in about two hours, and I don't believe that you're going to wait one more second to start working."

He closed up the cream jar and put it away while she started pulling on her clothes.

"So what were they thinking?" Elvi said.

"Hmm?"

"Making a neutron star so big it's hovering on the edge of collapse, and then clearing everything out of the system so that it doesn't. Moving the ring out of the ecliptic."

"You think they made a neutron star? Seems more likely they just built a gate to a dud system."

"How? There had to be life here for them to hijack, or the gate wouldn't have been built. This was a living system like Sol that got turned into..." She waved her hand.

"Yeah," Fayez agreed. "I don't know. Honestly, this miracles-and-wonders thing feels like drinking from a fire hose sometimes."

Elvi finished with her uniform, then brushed her teeth as Fayez waited and watched her. She gave herself one last critical look in the mirror, then said, "Let's go see the boss."

Fayez grabbed her and undid her careful uniform straightening with a hug. "Thanks for not dying, Els."

Forty-eight hours later, they'd gone through the drill. The ship's system had analyzed the telescopic data. Elvi had gone to pay her respects to the catalyst the way she always did, and then performed the experiment. The protomolecule reached out, and the data streamed in. The *Falcon* searching for any change, any effect. This time, Elvi actually let herself sleep in between. Near-death experiences wore her out, apparently, even if she hadn't been aware of them at the time. In addition to which, this time, there wasn't much to see.

When they'd finished their analysis, Sagale came to the bridge and braced himself on one hand-hold and one foot-hold. His eyes shifted from one screen to the next, taking in the data streams with an air of pleasure.

"Mehmet," Elvi said.

"Major Okoye," Sagale said, and nodded toward the main monitor. Magnified so that it filled the screen, the tiny but massive star was the only object within nearly two light-years of the Tecoma gate. "Tell me that *this* system is the most important scientific discovery of all time."

"No," Elvi replied. "Pretty sure the big green diamond still wins that prize. But it is amazing."

The neutron star on the screen was too hot to radiate much

energy as visible light, but the screen still had to dim it down to keep it from blinding everyone in the room.

"More than three stellar masses stuffed into a ball half the size of Rhode Island," Jen said.

"What's a road island?" Travon asked. He'd been a Martian, back before they were all Laconians.

"Major Okoye," Sagale said, ignoring the banter. "Am I correct that this is exactly what it looks like? A single unusable star in a system devoid of other artifacts or exploitable planets?"

Something in his tone caught Elvi's attention. It had a stiff formality to it. As though he were asking her questions under oath. She felt like they were engaging in some sort of ritual that he understood and she didn't.

"That's what it looks like," she said carefully. "Yes."

Sagale nodded his massive head at her. The pleasure seemed to radiate from him. "Come to my office in five minutes."

He pulled himself away, disappearing down the corridor. Fayez met her gaze and lifted an eyebrow.

"Makes me nervous too," she said.

She checked the data one last time like she was going over her class notes before a test. She had a sense that there was something in it she'd overlooked. It wasn't a feeling she liked.

"Coffee?" Sagale asked when she arrived. He was floating next to the beverage machine inset in one of the bulkheads of his office. Two drinking bulbs drifted next to him. It was the first time he'd ever offered her anything in hospitality. It made her nervous.

"Sure," she said so that he wouldn't notice.

The machine hissed as it injected cups of coffee into the bulbs, one at a time. "Sweetener? Whitener?" Sagale asked, still fussing with the machine.

"No."

Sagale turned to her and gently pushed one of the bulbs in her direction. She caught it and depressed the bubble on the lid that opened the flow to the drinking tube, then took a sip. The coffee was just right, hot but not scalding, bitter and strong and vaguely nutty.

"Thank you," she said, waiting for the other shoe to drop.

"I want to extend the thanks of the Laconian Empire for your work on this project. Now that we have identified a system of no utility, we are moving to the military phase of the operation," Sagale said after a short pause while he sipped at his coffee.

"The what?"

"Two ships are entering this system as we speak," he said. "They are both uncrewed, and controlled remotely from this vessel. Both are large freighters. One is empty. The other has a payload."

"A payload?"

"The high consul has been able to use the construction platforms over Laconia to isolate and contain antimatter. The second ship is carrying slightly over twenty kilograms in a magnetic containment device."

Elvi felt light-headed again. Maybe she was still recovering from her near-death experience. Maybe it was her superior officer telling her that he had enough explosive power to glass the surface of a planet. Probably it was both. She took a moment to get her breath back.

"And why?" she asked.

"The high consul's directive for this expedition was twofold," Sagale said. "The first was the mission you were briefed about. You and your team have done all that could be asked in this effort, and my reports back to naval command reflect this."

"Okay. Thanks. What was the second thing?" Elvi asked.

"The second aspect of this mission is outside your expertise, which is why it was kept on a need-to-know basis. We were to find a gate-connected system with minimal value. Such as this one."

She let go of the coffee bulb, and it began gently floating away. "Am I allowed to know what phase two is? Because if I don't need to know, it seems sort of mean to have this conversation."

"You are. In fact you are essential to it, and I have every confidence that you will continue to excel as our mission changes, though you will no longer have operational command," Sagale said. There was something like sympathy in his eyes. For the very first time, Elvi got the sense that Sagale liked her. Or at least respected her. "The high consul's first priority is to find a way to defend humanity against whatever destroyed the gate builders." He paused for a moment like he didn't quite believe what he was about to say. Like he'd been waiting for a long time to say it. "The test we are about to perform is the beginning of that process."

He tapped at his desk, and a map of the Tecoma system appeared above it. The neutron star at its center, the distant gate, the *Falcon* floating at the midway point, and the two new freighters drifting near the entry point.

"We are going to monitor this system with every instrument at our disposal, just as we always have," Sagale said. "But this time, out in the hub network, traffic control is running ships through the gates until the energy transfer load reaches the critical state. When the critical level is reached, we are going to transit the empty freighter from this system."

"You're going to deliberately dutchman a ship?"

"We are. When it vanishes, and while the energy transfer load is still high enough to make transits impossible, I will set the trigger on the antimatter containment field and transit the second ship. It too should vanish, but it will have a timer set to detonate the load."

Elvi felt her stomach cramp up like he'd punched her in the solar plexus. It was suddenly hard to breathe.

"Why would you—"

"Because one of two things is true," Sagale said. "Either there is an intelligence that lies beyond those gates that is making the choice to destroy our ships, or there is some natural effect of the gate system itself that does it. This is how we will determine that."

Elvi reached for a handhold in the bulkhead behind her, and pulled herself to the wall. Her heart was going faster.

"You think you can kill them?"

"That isn't the issue. Whether something on the other side dies or doesn't die, what matters is that it is punished. After this experiment, some time later we will run the energy up to the point of another dutchman and see if the ship is taken. If the ship survives transit, we will know the bomb convinced our opponent to change their stance toward us."

"That's a terrible plan."

"If it does change, we'll know the enemy is capable of change. That it's intentional, and possibly intelligent. If not, we'll repeat the test until we're reasonably certain that no change will be forthcoming. I take it from your expression that you have some thoughts on the mission you'd like to share."

Elvi's voice sounded outraged, even to her. "The last time we made them angry, they turned off every consciousness in the Sol system and there was a massive surge in virtual particle activity. They fired a bullet that broke spooky interactions in ways we're still trying to make sense of. Every one of those things defies our understanding of how reality works. So we're going to throw a *bomb* at them?"

Sagale nodded, agreeing and dismissing her at the same time. "If we could send a sternly worded letter, we'd try that. But this is how you negotiate with something that you can't speak to. When it does something we don't like, we hurt it. Every time it does something we don't like, we hurt it again. Only once. If it can understand cause and effect, it will get our message."

"Jesus."

"We aren't the aggressor here. We didn't hit anyone first. We just haven't hit anyone back until now."

She could hear Winston Duarte in the word choices. Even in the cadence Sagale delivered them with. It made Elvi want to throw her coffee bulb at his face. Fortunately, it had drifted several meters away, saving her from a court-martial.

"Thanks to you, we've found a sample system. This is the safest place in the empire for humanity to conduct these tests."

"This is a bad, bad idea. I don't think you're hearing what I'm saying."

"When humans first began experimenting with fission bombs," Sagale said, as if she hadn't spoken, "they used empty islands for their tests. Consider this our Bikini Atoll."

Elvi laughed at him, but there was no humor in it.

"My God, you people really are this dumb," she said. Sagale frowned at that, but she powered on anyway. "First of all, the Bikini Atoll *wasn't* empty. The people that lived there had their homes stolen and were sent away. And the islands were filled with plant and animal life that was annihilated."

"We have established that this system has nothing that—"

Elvi didn't let him finish. "But putting that aside for a moment, I just said whatever lives inside those gates has a very different understanding of physics than we do. Is it limited to taking its anger out on only one solar system? *You don't know that.* You *can't* know that."

"Passivity didn't save the gate builders. It won't save us. The high consul has considered the risks and judged a proactive, direct path to be the best option available."

He spread his hands. *What can be done?* As if Duarte's word were a force of nature, inescapable and unquestionable. It was like talking to a recording.

"You are about to run an n-equals-one experiment where one is the number of universes we can break trying to satisfy Duarte's curiosity."

Chapter Eleven: Alex

The shipyards on Callisto were a perfect example of the old idea that ships and buildings keep learning even after they're built. History took whatever it found and used it for what was happening at the time, remaking the spaces into whatever worked well enough to get by at the moment, until history itself became a kind of architect.

Callisto had been a divided base once. Pretty much the same way medieval villages had been built just outside castle walls, civilian shipyards had grown up around the older MCRN base until the military and commercial concerns were almost the same size. The Free Navy had raided the Martian side even before the Free Navy really existed, pounding that half of the base into dust and bodies. Then, in the aftermath of the great defection that became the seeds of Laconia, the rebuilding of the Martian shipyards had been left incomplete. During the starving years, it had been abandoned. But the real estate was there, and as the need grew again, what had been military structures were taken over again. Nothing died without becoming the foundation for what came after.

They had been on Callisto for eight days so far, and it wasn't certain when they'd ship back out. There were several of the big cargo ships in Sol system that might be able to smuggle the *Storm*, if that was what the underground decided to do next. Or maybe they'd stay in Sol. For all Laconia's ambitions, there were still more people, stations, and ships in the Sol system than outside it. That was changing, though. Someday within Alex's lifetime, they'd cross the threshold, and Sol really would be just one system among many. The oldest, most human system in the empire, sure. But not home. There would be a thousand homes, and if history was a guide, in a generation or two, everyone would think wherever they were was the most important one.

The restaurant Caspar had taken him to, for example, was in a reinforced dome that had clearly been Martian military construction. A supply depot, probably. Now all the fail-closed locks were gone, and the reinforced walls were hung with batiked cloth and the kind of tapestry that interior decorators churned out by the square meter. The menu billed itself as Moroccan, but the couscous was made with mushrooms and the beef all had the overly consistent grain that meant it had grown in a vat. The recipes might have had their roots on Earth, but Alex knew Belter food when he tasted it.

He and Caspar and the rest of the crew wore printed flight suits with a triangle-and-curve logo that implied they worked for a gas-mining cooperative called Három Állam that worked the Jovian moons. The *Gathering Storm* was hidden in a generations-old mine that was marked on the surveys as having been lost to collapse fifteen years before. It had been an OPA smuggling base, and the plan was to leave it there for a few weeks while the Laconian security forces were on high alert. Which meant, in the meantime, the crew could take a little time off the ship, drink, visit brothels, play golgo and handball and two-court football. Or fold up their legs on soft, woven cushions, listen to flute and drum music from hidden speakers, and scoop up little bits of fungus pretending to be wheat flour and cubes of spiced beef that had never been a cow.

Another advantage was that a little time on Callisto with civilians meant they could take the temperature of the system. See how everyone was reacting to the news of the underground's attack. It turned out the response wasn't what Alex had expected.

"Nothing?" Caspar said.

Alex cycled through the newsfeeds again. Food production on Earth and Ganymede were up this quarter, easily matching the established projections. A group in the Krasnoyarsk-Sakha Shared Interest Zone was petitioning for trade autonomy. The settlement on Navnan Ghar was reporting the discovery of a massive underground crystal network, and a special scientific commission was being assembled to determine whether it was another alien artifact or something that had occurred naturally on the planet. The lead singer of Tuva T.U.V.A. had sent nude photos of himself to an underage fan, and the authorities were investigating. The Laconian Science Directorate was reporting a potential breakthrough in the survey of dead systems: a massive green diamond that experts suspected might contain records that, if decoded, would spell out the history of the species that had created the ring gates.

That two Laconian frigates and a freighter carrying a critically important political officer had been destroyed in Sol system was listed precisely nowhere.

Or at least nowhere he could see without searching the newsfeed indexes. And since Saba had it on good authority that Laconia was keeping a close eye on search terms, Alex was stuck browsing and hoping for something. Anything. But...

"Nope," he agreed. "Nothing."

Caspar took bit of bread and scooped up a bite of his tagine. "I don't know if that's a good thing or a bad one."

"When I was your age," Alex said, "it would have been on every feed. Earth and Mars would have had official responses, and there would've been eighteen different mainline feeds analyzing every word they said from different perspectives. The Belt would have had a thousand different pirate broadcasts with at least a dozen of them taking credit for it personally, and at least one saying it was all a Jesuit conspiracy."

Caspar grinned. One of his eyeteeth was a little yellowed. Alex had never noticed that before. "Sounds like you miss it, grandpa."

Alex looked up, questioning. Caspar put on a comic frown and an exaggerated drawl. "When I was your age, we had to make our own water from scratch every morning and dinosaurs roamed Mariner Valley."

Alex felt a little stab of annoyance, but he pushed it back and laughed. "There was some variety at least." He gestured toward the feeds spooling through on the tabletop monitor. "Everything on this feels like it's been vetted by the same bureaucrat on Luna. It's all got the same voice."

"Probably was."

"Yeah," Alex said, shutting it off. "It probably was."

Caspar stretched like a cat waking up from a nap, then tapped the monitor. The newsfeeds vanished and the restaurant's interface popped up.

"We can split this," Alex said.

"You buy next time," Caspar said. "Anyway. Not like it's real money, right?"

All the *Storm* crew on Callisto had false identities generated by the underground and slipped into the systems. Including biometrics and bank accounts. It was an uncomfortable way to live, knowing that everything was brittle. Alex's fake records could all be exposed if the Laconian security system raised a red flag. He could spend tonight and then the rest of his life in a jail cell. Everything could fall apart at any moment.

Which, to be fair, had always been true. It was just harder to forget now.

"I'm meeting some of the engineering crew down on the third

level. There's a bar that has open mic comedy and half-price whiskey. Enough karaoke, and a pretty boy like me might even find someone to take him home tonight."

"Drink one for me, and don't make any mistakes you can't regret the next morning," Alex said, rising from his cushion. "I've got some things of my own to do."

"Fair enough," Caspar said. "See you when I see you."

They parted in the corridor. Caspar headed for the passage leading deeper below the moon's surface, Alex off to the left and toward the docks and the coffin apartments for people on shore leave. People like him. He walked with his hands stuck deep in the flight suit pockets, his eyes on the ground ahead of him. Avoiding eye contact with the people walking in the same halls. The passage came to a Y intersection with a brushed steel sculpture that didn't seem to know if it was a human or a transport shuttle. Above it, the ships and their berths were all listed. All but his.

When Alex had been a boy back on Mars, his great-uncle Narendra had come to stay with his family for a week once while his group home in Innis Shallows had been renovated. Alex still remembered his great-uncle walking through the corridors of Bunker Hill with a calm, bemused expression while he and Johnny Zhou explained the fine points of the game they had been playing. Alex felt the same expression on his own face now.

Maybe it was something that happened with every generation, this sense of displacement. It might be an artifact of the way human minds seemed to peg "normal" to whatever they'd experienced first and then bristled at everything afterward that failed to match it closely enough. Or maybe the change that Laconia's conquest was ushering in was different in kind from what had come before. Either way, the Callisto shipyard didn't feel like Sol system anymore, or at least not the one Alex knew. It felt like the first days of Laconian rule. The sense of fear and fragility like a ringing in his ears that never went away. Amos used to say that everywhere was Baltimore. That wasn't true anymore. Now everywhere was Medina.

His coffin apartment was near the docks. It was one of the larger models, a little over a meter high so that he could sit up in it. The mattress was old, recycled crash couch gel, and the walls and ceiling were layered glass and mesh with lights embedded in them to create the illusion of space going out beyond the surface. Alex crawled in, closed the access door, and made himself comfortable. He had a couple new entertainment feeds he'd been thinking about checking out. Over the years, he'd made himself an expert on neo-noir crime thrillers, and there had been work coming out of Ceres even before the Laconian takeover that used Pilkey montage to do some interesting things. He wondered, though, if signing in through the coffin's system would compromise him. If Laconia knew enough about Alex Kamal to put together the kind of movies he liked, the kind of food he ate, the way he walked, and whatever other data he'd left behind him to pierce the mask that Saba had given him. If he was too much himself, would it send security officers to his door? Did it make more sense to watch something popular and generic and stay at the center of the herd?

He pulled up his profile on the coffin system. A red icon showed a private connection from the *Storm*. There was a certain irony in the fact that he was more worried that Laconia would catch him out because he watched a certain kind of entertainment feed than he was that actual encrypted communications from the underground would give him away. But there it was. He'd made the decision to trust Saba's old OPA techs when he got into this business. Didn't make sense to start second-guessing them now. He opened the message, and his son looked back at him from the screen.

"Hey, Da," Kit said with a grin that reminded him of Giselle. Kit looked more like his mother than like him. Thank God. "Weird to hear from you again so soon. Are you in-system? I mean, don't tell me. I know we're all hush-hush. But hey. Things are great this semester. I'm pulling top marks in three of my sections, and"—the smile turned rueful—"I've got a good tutor for the other two. And…ah…yeah. So I'm dating this girl, and I think it's starting to look kind of serious. Her name's Rohani. I haven't told her about...um...*you*. But if there ever gets to be a chance for you to come meet her? Mom is talking to her family, and I think she may be your daughter-in-law pretty soon here. So it would be good, yeah?"

There was more to the message, and Alex listened to it with a warmth in his chest, and a sorrow. He wasn't going to meet the girl. He wasn't going to attend the wedding if there was one. Rohani would go on the list with Amos and Holden and Clarissa. Another loss. It was just another loss. He'd live with it. He had to.

His hand terminal chimed, and an alert popped up from the false ID that Saba used for high-priority messages. With dread in his gut, he opened it.

BE ADVISED THAT THE TEMPEST HAS BROKEN ORBIT AND IS MOVING TOWARD JUPITER.

"Well," Alex said to himself. "Shit."

"My little man's getting married?" Bobbie said, but she kept looking at the supply crates while she said it. "Girl will be lucky if I don't swoop in and carry him off first."

The warehouse was on the edge of the complex. It didn't use the station's power grid, and the environmental system was a retrofit from an old rock hopper. It left condensation on the walls and ceilings, water discoloration like leopard spots. The larger gear, like torpedoes, was still on the *Storm*. But the smaller salvage from the Laconian freighter had been transferred onto four wide rows of pallets and moved to the warehouse. Bobbie had unpacked them, scattering the storage crates through the space as she did her own private inventory. Scorch marks darkened some of the boxes. The chalky smell of ceramic that had been heated until it flaked hung in the air.

"You're taking the news that the largest battleship in the empire is heading toward us very calmly," Alex said.

She took a deep breath, and kept her voice patient. "Jillian's getting word to everyone. The *Tempest* is days out, and this work needs to be done one way or the other. I'm hoping by the time I'm done with it, I'll have a plan."

"How's that working for you?"

"Nothing so far. I'll let you know."

Alex sat on one of the boxes. He felt heavier than the gentle gravity of the moon could explain. "Bobbie, what are we doing here?"

She paused, looked over at him. She had a lot of different expressions, and he'd come to know most of them. He knew when he was talking to his friend and when she was the captain. Right now, she was listening to him as the woman he'd been on the *Roci* with, back in the day. The one who had known him since before Io.

"Fighting the enemy," she said. "Degrading their ability to bring force and influence to bear. Denying them the use of resources."

"Sure," Alex said. "But to what end? I mean, are we trying to get back to the Transport Union running things? Or are we trying to make it so that every planet is calling its own shots, and then seeing if it all works out?"

Bobbie crossed her arms and leaned against a stack of boxes. The work lights were harsh, and Alex could see all the roughness in her face and arms that decades of hard work and radiation had left. Age looked good on her. It looked right.

"I'm hearing you ask whether authoritarianism is necessarily bad," she said. "Did I get that right? Because yeah, it is."

"That's not what I mean. It's just...I don't know what it is. I'm feeling overwhelmed. And maybe a little demoralized."

"Yes," Bobbie said. "Yes, we are."

"You too?"

"We lost the target. That political officer might have given us something that could break these fuckers back to the Stone Age. I mean maybe not, but I'm not going to know now. So yeah, I'm a little grumpy. But I'm guessing that's not exactly what's biting you?"

"I don't know what the win looks like."

"Well, for me, it looks like dying with the knowledge that humanity's a little bit better off than it would have been if I'd never been born. A little freer. A little kinder. A little smarter. That the bullies and bastards and sadists got their teeth into a few less people because of me. That's got to be enough."

"Yeah," Alex said, but she kept going.

"I'm not a grand strategy girl. That's for the eggheads. I'm a ground pounder, and I always will be. These people want every planet to be a prison where they get to pick who's the guard and who's the inmate."

"And we're against that," Alex said. He heard the exhaustion and agreement in his own voice. "You ever think Naomi's right? Maybe it's better to try getting inside the system. Changing it that way?"

"She is right," Bobbie said, turning back to her inventory. "It's just I'm right too. Naomi wants there to be one way to fix this, and she wants it to be the one where there's no blood."

"But there's two ways," Alex said, thinking that he was agreeing.

"There's no way," Bobbie said. "There's just pushing back with everything we've got and hoping we can outlast the bastards."

"You know we're on the clock here," Alex said. "I'm thinking about Takeshi."

"I sent a message to his people," Bobbie said. "It's always hard losing someone, and we'd been very lucky up to that point. It couldn't last."

"I'm thinking that he was one of your best, and he was damn near sixty. Jillian, Caspar, and a few others aside, our resistance is made up of old Belters. Old OPA."

"Agreed," Bobbie said. "And thank God for that. Most of them have a clue what they're doing."

"Behind them is a whole new generation who were never in the OPA. Never fought the inner planets for independence. Who grew up fat and rich on Transport Union freighters, with respect and important jobs. Kids like Kit. How are you going to convince them to give up everything they've got and join this fight?"

Bobbie stopped and turned to look at him.

"Alex, where is this coming from?"

"I think we have a resistance right now because we have a lot of old guys who grew up resisting an enemy too strong to ever beat. They've been inoculated against fear of failure. But when they're gone, I think we're done. As a movement. As a force in history. Because we're not going to convince anyone born after the Transport Union was formed to fight an unwinnable fight. And maybe, in the long run, Naomi's plan to win politically is all we'll have left."

He saw Bobbie's eyes go flat. "Unwinnable fight?" she said.

"Well," Alex said. "Isn't it?"

Chapter Twelve: Bobbie

An unwinnable fight.

Alex was gone, heading back to the *Storm* to figure what exactly their evac options looked like. If they had any. What he'd said stayed after him.

The temporary warehouse their OPA friends had found for them smelled like burnt ceramics and old ice. Bobbie had been working in it long enough now that the smell didn't trigger a gag reflex, so that was sort of a win.

She ticked off an entry on her supply list: twelve crates of Laconian fuel pellets. They'd been intended for the *Tempest*, but they'd work in the *Storm* too. And because the Laconian reactors seemed to want to use only their own brand of pellet, it meant her ship would get to keep flying for a while. Unless the *Tempest* shot them all into atoms. But the *Storm* didn't have a lot of storage space. They'd need to make some decisions soon about how much of their stolen loot to carry with them and how much to hide or sell. Fuel, bullets, or food. The hierarchy of needs, wartime edition. And now, with a *Magnetar*-class dreadnought heading in their direction, the importance of every decision was even greater.

An unwinnable fight.

Bobbie had been at Medina Station when the *Tempest* came through the Laconia gate for the very first time. She'd watched it use its primary weapon on the rail-gun defenses, and turn them into spaghettified atoms in a single shot. And while she hadn't been part of the defense of Sol system when the *Magnetar*-class battle cruiser made its attack, she'd read the reports. The combined might of the Earth-Mars Coalition hadn't even been able to slow the *Tempest* down. She had no illusions that their one destroyer stood a chance. Run and hide was their only option now.

Alex had been a navy boy for twenty years before he'd become the pilot of the *Rocinante*. He'd always been reliable under pressure. But something had happened when they met with Naomi this last time. Or maybe it was the idea of his kid getting married. Or maybe it was that he was a little smarter than she was, or a little less angry, or a little more realistic. Maybe it was that he'd seen a little sooner than she had why the fight was unwinnable. The underground was held together with spit and baling wire even at the best of times. Saba did what he could to help the old OPA fighters keep the Laconians uncomfortable where they could, but the simple truth was that the *Storm* was their only meaningful asset. The ship, and by extension her strike team, were the resistance's only real weapon against Laconia. The Transport Union didn't have gunships, and the void cities had been disarmed as part of the treaty negotiations. The Earth-Mars Coalition fleets couldn't help even if they wanted to now that they all had Laconian flag officers on them reporting directly to Admiral Trejo.

If Alex was losing heart, Bobbie didn't believe for a second he was alone. The failure to capture the political officer combined with the looming threat of the battleship might be enough to get her crew wondering why they were still risking their necks fighting an unbeatable foe.

And as much as she disliked it, Alex was right.

The old-guard OPA attitude of resistance for resistance's sake would only keep them going so long. Part of what she should be doing was training up the next generation of fighters. Only so far, they weren't waiting in the wings to step in. Duarte and his people were smart. They kept things from getting bad too quickly. They made the right speeches about respect and autonomy. They let people believe that government by a king would never go wrong. And by the time it did, and things got bad enough to inspire a younger resistance, she and Alex and the old-school OPA would be off the board. Then who would be left to fight? Why would they think there was any hope in it?

Recruitment wasn't her job. It belonged to Saba or Naomi or one of the other secret leaders of the underground, but she couldn't stop thinking about it. Alex had opened the issue. Now it itched.

Bobbie finished her check of the fuel cell crates and moved on to something the manifest listed as sensor components. The team had grabbed it off the freighter because any repairs the *Storm* needed were done in-house and on the fly. Spare parts were always at a premium.

Inside the crate was a sealed gray ceramic box about the size of a toaster with seven input ports on its side. Bobbie used her terminal to look up the serial number on the case. It was listed as an active sensor array control node—the little processing station that coordinated data coming in from the radar and ladar sensors, did first-level analysis, and acted as the hindbrain between the main computer and the sensors themselves. An expert pattern-matching system about as smart as a pigeon. If they were sending a new one to the *Tempest*, it might mean that they'd lost one in the fight for Sol. It was a nice idea, anyway. That the big dreadnought had taken some damage in the fight it couldn't just heal for itself. And it made sense. The weird hulls and reactors and engines of the ships might heal like the ship was a living thing, but they were protomolecule technology. The sensors and computers on the Laconian ships were human tech. Anything built by humans had to be hand repaired or replaced. It was one of the few weaknesses of the hybrid ships.

And if she had the replacement parts, it might mean there was a hole in the *Tempest*'s sensor package. If they could figure out where it existed, maybe they could get close to the big ship before detection. They could...fire one meaningless torpedo before the big bastard swung around and ripped them into atoms. Paint something rude on the hull. Pee on it. Jillian's crack about moral victories was annoying, but that didn't make her wrong.

Bobbie put the sensor node back into its case and marked the box as one to definitely keep for themselves. An hour later, she'd finished going through the pallet of spare parts and tagged them all as keepers. Her terminal was playing a little three-dimensional game of "fit all the loot." Every time she marked a crate, the program shuffled everything in the *Storm*'s storage compartments looking for a place to put it. At some point, they'd have to start storing things in the staterooms and hallways, and that point wasn't far off.

She opened a crate of protein flavorings for the galley food processor and marked it Do NOT KEEP. She started to close it, then sighed and changed it to KEEP. The terminal played its little space-shuffling game. An army marches on its stomach, the ancient saying went, and people who were risking their lives for the cause should probably be able to have a tasty meal every now and then.

It was interesting, though, that the *Tempest* was coming after them. It felt good to know she'd hit the enemy hard enough to sting. Maybe it was just pride. Admiral Trejo angry that a pirate would dare act in his solar system. Or maybe the political officer had been close enough to someone high in command that this was a personal vendetta now. Or maybe they just really wanted their protein flavoring back. Whatever it was about the raid that made Laconia jump, she hoped they were as bothered and itchy as she was.

She reached the end of her row of pallets, which meant her work was half-done. A few more hours digging through boxes, and she could sneak off to one of those old bars at the port and drink her troubles away. Or at least distill them down to nausea and a hangover. And maybe she'd get a steak. She felt like Saba and the resistance could afford to buy her a steak. Her stomach rumbled at the thought. So maybe she called it a day now, and came back to finish tomorrow.

A small pile of high-impact crates had been set off to the side, away from the main rows of pallets. They had a variety of warning labels on them, so her crew had put some space between them and the rest of the supplies. All right. Go through the dangerous stuff now, *then* call it a day.

The top crate in the pile had a caustic chemical warning, and was filled with spray cans of degreaser. Not exactly a threat to life and limb. She moved the crate over to the regular supplies. Beneath it was a crate marked HIGH EXPLOSIVE that had reloads for the rocket launchers the Laconian power armor could attach. She marked that one as definitely keep and set it aside.

Under that was a large metal crate. The label said MAGNETIC CONTAINMENT EXPLOSIVE DANGER. That was odd. None of those words seemed to go together in a way that made sense to her. She checked the serial number on the side of the crate with her terminal, and it came back ID not found.

Curiouser and curiouser.

Nothing on the crate indicated that opening the latches was hazardous, so Bobbie popped them and lifted the lid. It was much heavier than it looked. Lead lined, maybe. Inside, cradled by enough foam to keep a robin's egg intact during high-g maneuvers, were four metallic spheres about the size of Bobbie's two fists held together. All four had cables running to a massive power cell that gave off a low hum of high electricity. The power cell's indicator showed that it was at 83 percent charge. Each sphere had its own indicator where a cable from the power cell connected to it. They all showed 100 percent.

Bobbie very carefully lifted her hands away from the box and took a step back. Nothing in the box itself looked all that dangerous. Just four big metal balls and a high-capacity battery. But every hair on her body was standing straight up. It was all she could do to stop herself from running away.

Bobbie knelt back down next to the crate and very gingerly lifted one of the metal balls out, making sure to keep the cable connected to the power supply. Once it was out of its foam cradle, warning text could be seen. ENSURE MAGNETIC CONTAINMENT SYSTEM REMAINS CHARGED—DANGER OF EXPLOSION, it said. Another, smaller warning read, DO NOT RUN ON INTERNAL POWER SUPPLY FOR MORE THAN TWENTY MINUTES. The labels on it were from the Laconian Science Directorate. Not military, except in that everything Laconian was military. Not usual ordnance, anyway. Nothing familiar.

Bobbie returned the sphere to its place in the foam. And sat back. Something in the spheres exploded when it wasn't magnetically restrained. Fusion reactors worked that way. The magnetic bottle held the fusion reaction suspended because nothing material could handle the heat of the core. These little spheres weren't reactors, though. A fusion reactor was huge. It required extensive support mechanisms to inject fuel pellets, compress and fuse those pellets, and turn the fusion reaction into electricity. The Laconians were advanced, but it didn't seem plausible that they were so advanced that they'd created fusion reactors a little bigger than a softball. And these things were using power, not generating it.

She pulled out her terminal and called Rini Glaudin. She was an old Belter on the *Storm*. A high-energy physics PhD from way back in the day at Ceres Polytech who'd gotten radicalized in college and spent a couple of decades in a UN prison after she started helping the Voltaire Collective build bombs. Now she was the chief engineer and resident gearhead on the *Storm*.

"Boss," Rini said after a couple moments. She sounded sleepy, or drunk.

"Catch you at a bad time?"

"You can leave now," Rini said, but her voice was muffled, like she'd covered the mic with her hand. A minute later, "What is it?"

"I have a weird question, but if you had company," Bobbie said.

"He's gone. He was pretty enough, but postcoital conversation was not his strong suit. What's going on?"

"I'm going through the loot we pulled off that freighter," Bobbie said. "And I found this crate of stuff I'm having a hard time identifying. Thought maybe you could help."

"You're at that warehouse by the surface? Let me pull on some clothes and I'll get right down there."

"No," Bobbie said. "Don't do that. I think this might be dangerous and I don't want anyone in here until I figure it out. Hold on, let me send you some video."

Bobbie passed her terminal across the crate, giving Rini a good look at the power cell and the spheres. Then she propped the terminal up against the edge so she could use both hands to pick up a sphere and show the warning text to the camera. When she was done, she said, "Any ideas?"

There was a long pause. Bobbie felt the unease rising in her like an illness.

"Fuck me," Rini said at last.

"What do you think it is?"

"So the big question about the *Magnetar*-class ships has always been power," Rini said. There was a lot of background noise as she spoke, drawers opening and closing. Clothes being pulled on. She was dressing in a hurry. "The stars the ships are named after have incredible magnetic fields, but they're rapidly rotating neutron stars, so how do you get that beam effect the ships have without, you know, spinning up a neutron star?"

"Okay," Bobbie said. Her knowledge of astrophysics was pretty thin. "How do they?"

"No one knows!" Rini said. "But it would take way more power than a typical fusion reactor puts out. Everyone just sort of assumed that meant the Laconians had much better reactors than us. But we have the *Storm*, and our reactor is good, but its design is nothing paradigm shifting."

"I'm sitting right next to this thing while you talk," Bobbie said, "so go faster maybe."

"Antimatter results in a one hundred percent conversion of matter into energy. Nothing else even comes close. If the Laconians power their beam with antimatter, that actually makes sense."

Bobbie laughed. There was only a little mirth in it. "Am I sitting next to four bottles of antimatter, Rini?"

"Maybe? I mean, the only way to contain it would be a magnetic field. If it touched anything, boom. So, sure? Maybe."

"How much of that stuff do you think is in here?"

"I don't know. A kilo? A gram of it would be a bomb big enough to level a city. Based on the size of those orbs, you've probably got enough there to punch a hole in this moon. I mean, if that's what's in there."

"All right," Bobbie said. "Thanks. I'll be in touch."

"Fuck that, I'm on my way down there," Rini said, then killed the connection. At least Bobbie understood now why the *Tempest* was treating this as high priority. Looking at the metal balls in their case was making Bobbie's scalp crawl.

And then, all at once, it wasn't.

The fight had just changed. And she knew how to win.

Chapter Thirteen: Naomi

The question is," Saba said on Naomi's monitor, "why did they have a political officer in the first place, que no?"

The *Bhikaji Cama* was on the float, and still half a week from a gentle quarter-g braking burn that would take weeks before they reached the transfer station at Auberon. With the drives on the ship, they could have done a full g the whole way, but efficiency and speed weren't always the same thing. Carrying the reaction mass to accelerate and brake that hard would have meant giving up more of the cargo space. Maybe someday the Laconian technology would overcome the constraints of inertia—the protomolecule had been doing so since Eros—but for now that mystery was still a mystery, like so many others. Where did the ships that went dutchman end up? What would draw the attention and anger of the thing that had destroyed the protomolecule engineers?

Or, on a smaller level, why had a Laconian political officer been riding on a Transport Union freighter?

News of the failure had been slow coming to her. The first report had been sketchy and brief, and said little more than that the raid had gone pear-shaped. Political officer, the informants on the freighter, and one member of the assault team lost. The next thirty-four hours had been a thin slice of hell as she waited for the full after-action report, certain beyond doubt that Bobbie had been the one who'd died.

Only it hadn't been her. One of her crew was dead, and her mission objective had slipped through her fingers, but Bobbie and Alex and the *Gathering Storm* lived to fight another day. The death of the political officer was just one of the stupid, random tragedies that happened anywhere, anytime, but significantly more often during battle. If he'd lived, they'd know much more about what he'd been doing. As it was, they were down to educated guesses.

"We have confirmation that he was on his way to the Transport Union's transfer station at Earth," Saba said. "But whether that was a permanent placement or a stop along a longer path..." He shrugged eloquently.

Naomi stretched. She liked the freedom of free fall even though it meant doubling up her exercise routine. Or maybe because it meant that. More hours in the resistance band meant at least doing something physical. Feeling her body. And also there was a sense of being where she belonged. From the recording, she could tell that Saba was someplace with a steady gravity. The last four communications from him had all been the same, so a spin station or a mass large enough to hold him down. No one was on a steady burn for that long.

It wasn't really a surprise that something was happening on Earth important enough to warrant a dedicated representative at the transfer station. Apart from Sol's permanent role as humanity's original home, it was still the largest population center in the gate network. And Earth had the largest population of any planet. Even with settlements like Auberon and Bara Gaon Complex growing, there would never be enough ships or shipping to make a dent in the billions still left on Earth. But what exactly was on Winston Duarte's mind about Sol system was an important question. And one that they could have answered, if luck had broken their way just a little bit more.

She considered, rubbed her eyes, and hit Record. She'd edit her response down before she committed it to a torpedo, but just saying the words helped her think. And she could pretend she wasn't quite as isolated and alone as she was.

"The loss of our informants on the ship is going to be important," she said. "Without them, we wouldn't have known that the political officer was there in the first place. And if they hadn't spoken up, they'd still be alive. Not the best argument for working with us. Their families need to be taken care of, and by us. Not Duarte's people. Otherwise we'll see fewer of these tips in the future."

It's always about relationships, Jim said in her imagination.

"It's always about relationships," she said. "And we have to hold up our end of the bargain. Take care of our own. To the other point, if we're going to find what Duarte's doing there, we need to get one of ours on the transfer station. Either find someone already on staff sympathetic enough to feed us information or someone who can be inserted into the administration. Trying to get the *Storm* to intercept another freighter is too high a risk."

But she thought it was possible that someone from the *Storm* could act as an agent of the underground on TSL-5. She wondered if Bobbie would go. Part of her thought she would. It was the dangerous assignment, after all. But Naomi also couldn't quite imagine her giving up command of the *Storm*, even for something important.

But she was getting ahead of herself.

"Before we take any direct action, we should finish a full inventory of what was on the freighter. If there were any supplies or equipment on it that were out of the ordinary, that might—"

Her system threw out an alert, and Naomi's heart leaped despite her better judgment.

It was a new message from Jim.

Duarte had been doing this almost since Jim had been taken to Laconia. Not quite public announcements, though there had been some of those too. Broadcasts sent out and picked up on passive with an old, compromised encryption scheme. Someone would have to want to know what was in them, anyway. The security wasn't the issue so much as a signature. An address. Here was a message that Laconia could spread through every system in the gate network, but only she could watch it. Or only she and the *Roci*. Or someone else who'd taken the time to crack the *Roci*'s old codes.

It was a private message, then, between Jim and her and every high-end government censor on Laconia. She had a vague memory about nobility on old Earth having witnesses on important wedding nights to watch the newlyweds fuck. This felt about as dignified.

And still, there was nothing under any sun that would keep her from playing it.

The message began with the blue wing-shaped crest of the Laconian Empire, a test tone, and then there he was. Jim looking into the camera with a mild amusement that most people wouldn't recognize as a variety of rage. He had on a collarless shirt, and his hair was combed enough to show where his hairline was starting to pull back a little. Anti-aging regimens had pushed human life from the three- to four-decade range of prehistory to four times that, but wear and tear still counted for something. Jim had suffered more than his fair share of punishing life experiences. And then the fake grin ended and he really smiled, and the decades fell away. Even before he spoke, she heard him. The mix of sorrow and amusement in his eyes, like a guest at a party that had gone so wrong that the travesty had lapped itself and become a little bit fun again.

She stopped the playback as he opened his lips and took the moment with him. Even just the picture of him. Then, steeling herself, she started the message.

"Hey there, Knuckles. Sorry it's been so long this time, but things got a little busy over here. I'm guessing you heard about Avasarala? The funeral brought in a lot of other guests to the palace."

Using the nickname Knuckles, which he never had when they were together, was the signal that he knew they were still hunting her. She also heard the ghost of sarcasm in the way he said *guests*, but the censors hadn't. There were real challenges to controlling communication between two people who'd been intimate for as long as she and Jim had been. The private language between them couldn't be perceived by bureaucrats, and what couldn't be seen couldn't be stopped. The story of her life, these days.

"There's still not much I can say. You know how it is. Uh. I met the guys who actually review this before it goes out. So hey, Mark. Hey, Kahno. Hope you guys are having a good day too. But yeah, things are fine here. Some rain in the afternoon, and Laconia's getting on toward what passes for midsummer. They're letting me have a lot of access to the grounds and I'm catching up on my reading. Mark and Kahno say I can't talk about what I'm reading in particular, but it's nice to have access. I'm also watching the newsfeeds, and the things that Duarte…They want me to call him High Consul Duarte, but really it seems pretentious. Anyway, the work he's doing about figuring out the gates and what happened to the protomolecule engineers is actually pretty impressive. We disagree on other things, but he's on the job with that. Which, you know. Hopefully…

"But I hope you're okay. Give the kids my fond regards, and I'll send you another message as soon as Mark and Kahno have an open slot in their schedule. They're good guys. You'd like them. I love you."

The image cut to blue, and Naomi let out her breath. It always hurt to see him. And *the kids* meant Alex and Bobbie and Amos. He had no way to know Amos was lost to them, probably killed on the same planet where Jim was being held prisoner. Or that Bobbie and Alex were off leading the fight on the front lines as pirates and revolutionaries. But even with all of that, hearing him always made her feel a little better too. It was as near to proof of life as she'd get. He didn't look sick. He didn't sound like he was under duress—

The image changed again, and a new face appeared. A man with dark eyes, acne-scarred skin, and a calm in his expression that landed him directly in the uncanny valley. Naomi found herself pulling back from the screen even before she realized who she was looking at. High Consul Winston Duarte, emperor of thirteen hundred worlds, smiled as if he'd seen her reaction and sympathized with it.

"Naomi Nagata," he said, and his voice was pleasant and reedy. "I know I don't usually insert myself in these messages, and I hope you'll forgive me this rudeness. I don't mean to intrude, but I think we should talk, you and I. I want to extend an invitation to you. Contact any of my security people on any station or base or city, and I will have you brought safely here. I understand that you and your fellow partisans don't see eye to eye with me about the shape that humanity should take moving forward. Come talk to me. Convince me. I'm not an unreasonable man, and I'm not a cruel one. The truth is, over the last few years Captain Holden and I've found we have much in common."

Naomi chuckled despite herself. *Sure you did.*

"You've seen how Holden is treated. If you come as my guest, you'll have all the same courtesies and comforts, and you'll have access that will let you advocate for the changes you want without the violence and death. I know we haven't met, but everything Holden has told me says you're more than some old-fashioned anti-government extremist. He believes in you, and he has convinced me to believe in you too. Accept my offer, and you and Holden can be eating breakfast together before you know it. He'll tell you himself I'm a decent host."

He made a self-deprecating smile. *Carrot done*, Naomi thought. *Now stick.*

"If you choose not to, that is your right. But as an enemy of the state, the consequences will be less pleasant. It's going to be better for you and for me and—excuse me if this sounds grandiose—for the whole of humanity if you come as a guest. Please at least consider the option. Thank you."

The message ended. Naomi shook her head once, tightly, and

held on to her anger like it was a vaccine against something worse. Whether Duarte said it or not, the offer included trading all she knew of Saba and the underground. In return, she would be waking up next to Jim, living in a prison a thousand times larger than the one she'd imposed on herself. That was all obvious. The poison was the rest of it—access, influence, the emperor's ear. It was exactly the path she'd argued for. Working within the system to make a revolution without starvation and hatred and dead kids. He was offering it to her on a plate, and it was possible—just possible—that he was even sincere.

Everything Saba had learned through his sources said that Jim really was being treated well. A guest as much as a prisoner. That was the cheese in the mousetrap. It was cunning almost to the point of wisdom. If she believed in her heart that Duarte would break his word, it would have been a thousand times easier to reject him. But all the stories about the devil making a deal and then cheating missed the point. The real horror was that once the bargain was struck, the devil didn't cheat. He gave you exactly and explicitly all that had been promised.

And the price was your soul.

The knock startled her. It was like something from a different world. A moment ago, she'd been on Laconia. Eden, complete with a snake. And now she was back in her box, floating a few centimeters above the gel of her couch, the straps drifting around her like seaweed wrapping the drowned. She shifted her monitor to show the exterior of the container, half-afraid to see the *Bhikaji Cama*'s security chief ready to take her in, half-hoping.

The woman outside gripped a handhold and looked straight into the hidden camera. A black zippered duffel floated beside her. She was heavyset, with gray-streaked hair pulled back into a harsh bun and dark skin that got darker around her eye sockets like she'd cried too long and it had stained her. Naomi recognized her as Saba's agent on the ship, but didn't know her name.

Naomi pushed off from the crash couch, drifting fast toward the far end. She landed feetfirst, absorbing her momentum with her knees, and tapped her security code into the mechanism. The mag bolts clacked. In the silence, they sounded like gunshots. Before Naomi could open the door, the other woman did. She slid through, pulling the black bag with her, then shut the door behind her and glanced around the container as if there might be something unexpected in it.

"What's the matter?" Naomi asked.

"Captain got a call middle of last shift," the woman said in a clipped accent that sounded Europan to Naomi. "Took me longer than it should have to get a copy. That's on me."

She shoved the bag at Naomi. Even without opening it, the shape of mag boots and the hiss of a flight suit were unmistakable. Naomi didn't wait. She slid the zipper open and started pulling the uniform on over her own clothes while the woman talked.

"Laconian destroyer burning in for a rendezvous. Should be here in eighteen hours. Say they're going to make a full inspection, so alles la—" She gestured at Naomi's things. The home she'd made for herself. "Yeah, we're going to have to get clever about making that match the manifest."

"Inspection?"

"Full," the woman said. "This is all supposed to be bacterial samples. They see this..."

If they saw the false container, they'd know how the underground was staying hidden. And that some fraction of the Transport Union was in on the scheme. It might not be the end of the shell game, but it would be a data point too clear for Laconia to overlook for long. And it would be the end for her.

"Is it only us?" Naomi asked.

"Does it need to be more? Us is our problem. Focus on—"

"No," Naomi snapped. "I got an offer of amnesty if I turned myself in. This just after that? Are they coming for other ships, or do they already know I'm here?"

The woman's face went gray. "Don't know. I can find out."

"Do it fast. And get me a loader. I'll try to find a way to cover this over."

"Yeah," the woman said. "And crew manifest. I got to put you in somehow—"

"Not the priority," Naomi said.

"But...," the woman said. Then, "Right. All right."

Naomi looked around her container. It seemed sadder now that she had to leave it. She'd have to wipe the system, just in case she was taken. All her belongings would have to go too. She'd be starting over from nothing again.

Or she could go to the security office, announce herself, and spend the rest of her life waking up next to Jim. Eating real food. Maybe even talking Duarte into a better, kinder, less authoritarian future for all of humanity. If it was a trap, it was a good one. Offer her an out, make the threat, and then tighten the screws. If she'd been younger, it might have been enough to panic her. Convince her to announce herself. Sign the deal. It would be easy, and she could even tell herself that she was protecting the underground and the people like the woman before her. She'd only tell Duarte things that wouldn't compromise Saba and their network. That wouldn't threaten Bobbie and Alex and the *Storm*.

She could imagine the version of herself that would have been able to do it. Not so different from who she was now. Younger. That was all.

"Emma," the other woman said. "We're going to pass you for crew, you'll need to know names. I'm Emma Zomorodi."

"You can call me Naomi."

"I know who you are," Emma said. "Find me someone who doesn't."

The woman—Emma—looked at her again, more closely, then turned away, shaking her head. The fear in her expression was thick enough to see. *It's okay*, Naomi wanted to say. *I know what to do. It'll be all right.* It would have been a lie.

"Come on," Naomi said. "We don't have time."

Chapter Fourteen: Teresa

Yes," Teresa said. "I know. Okay. Let me get ready."

Muskrat barked once as if she'd understood the words. Probably she had. Dogs could have broad functional vocabularies. It was a point Dr. Cortázar often made. The fact that humans were not the only conscious animals seemed very important to him. It had always seemed obvious to her.

Teresa set her room to high privacy and sleep, dimming the lights and locking her doors. No one would disturb her now unless they were evacuating the State Building. Muskrat wagged hard enough that her back legs looked unsteady as Teresa changed into the same simple tunic and pants she normally used for gardening. They had no technology, so they weren't connected to the palace network. She started up an entertainment feed on her system on low volume as if she were dozing and watching an old Caz Pratihari adventure.

Her window had a sensor in the frame that alerted a security officer when it was opened. So Teresa had opened it every now and then over the course of weeks, trying different ways to get around it. Was it electronic? She tried keeping the window and frame touching with a copper wire. Security still got their alert. Optical? She searched everywhere for anything resembling a pinhole camera or light sensor, but never found one. Motion activated? She tried opening the window very slowly over the course of days, but on the fifth day security got their alert. Not motion sensing, and it only went off when there was an eleven-millimeter gap between window and frame. Interesting.

It had turned out to be magnetic. A low-strength magnet in the window, when moved too far from a sensor in the frame, set off the alert. She'd solved this by using a plastic letter with a tiny magnet in it from her preschool alphabet set. Moving it a little bit every time she tried to open the window, until one time she opened it and no one showed up outside to make sure she was okay.

Now she slid her magnet to the correct spot, manually undid the window, and lifted Muskrat carefully out. She climbed out after, pulling the frame closed behind her. Muskrat chuffed and started off along the path to the edge of the palace, and Teresa followed behind.

It had been too long. It was time to go see Timothy.

She'd found the secret tunnel almost a year before. It was hidden by a rock in a group of ornamental trees. She'd initially thought it might have been dug out by some local animal. There was a kind of underground wasp that left holes that looked similar to it when they died and their hives collapsed. It had turned out to be part of a flood relief system to make sure the gardens never drowned in heavy rain. It led under the walls of the State Building compound and into a small field beyond. Intellectually, she knew that a normal girl might not have gone down the tunnel with the spearmint smell of broken ground and the thin coat of slime. She had pushed through easily, joyfully even, and a few dark moments later had found herself on the far side of the perimeter and free for literally the first time in her life.

She'd gone walking. Exploring. Discovering. Engaging in developmentally appropriate rebellion. And, most importantly, she'd made her first real friend.

Animals had made the path she and Muskrat followed through the forest. Bone-elk and ground pigs and pale, shovel-faced horses, none of which had any relationship to Sol system elk or pigs or horses. She walked down the path, her hands in her pockets. Muskrat bounded through the dappled shade, barking at sunbirds and smiling a wide tongue-lolling grin when they hissed back. It had been too long since she'd been to see Timothy, and she had too much she wanted to talk with him about. It wouldn't all fit in her head at the same time.

The forest at the edge of the State Building thickened at first, the gloom growing around her, and then the land began to rise. She started feeling her breath get deeper, and it felt good. Before long, the path led out of the trees entirely and into a clearing at the skirt of the mountain. She knew from her studies that the mountain wasn't natural but a kind of artifact of some long-forgotten alien project. Like a sandcastle, but tall enough that the top seemed to touch the clouds. Not that she'd ever been to the summit. Timothy's cave was much closer than that.

The entrance was in a little canyon not far from the clearing where she'd first come upon him. Muskrat knew the way better than she did. She walked down the pale sand along the path carved by water that had long since dried. Wide, fresh Labrador paw prints marked her way. By the time Teresa left the last scraggly trees behind, the dog was already at the bend that led there, barking and wagging her tail.

"I'm coming," Teresa said. "You're such a pain."

Muskrat shrugged off the insult, turned, and bounded ahead like a puppy. Teresa didn't see her again until she stepped under what looked like an overhanging shelf of sandstone and into the deeps of the cave. The natural stone gave way almost immediately to the soft glow of the cavern. Stalactites hung from the ceiling like bright icicles, and the walls were built with swirls and shapes in them like a seashell and a Euclidian proof had joined together and become an architect. Teresa always had the feeling that the walls changed to greet her, but of course she was only there when she was there, so she couldn't be certain.

A flock of tiny, glowing gnats flowed past her like a wave. Like she was underwater. The air smelled thick and astringent, and a coolness radiated from the walls.

Soft padding sounds came from ahead. Not human sounds, and not Muskrat either. The footsteps weren't even animal, not really. The repair drones were a little smaller than Muskrat, with dark, apologetic-looking eyes and multiply jointed legs. Totally alien, but they were the closest things to canine friends that Muskrat had, and the real dog ran around them, yipping excitedly and sniffing their rears as if there were anything doglike to smell back there. Teresa shook her head and moved forward. The repair drones made their query tone, trying to intuit whether Muskrat wanted something. The drones were surprisingly good at judging at least the rough intentions of humans. Real dogs still seemed to baffle them.

The repair drones, the light gnats, the slow, creeping, wormlike stone diggers were all in the weird space between life and not-life. Designed by an intelligence that evolutionary forces had taken in a direction very different from humanity. They weren't exotic to her at all. As far as Teresa was concerned, they'd always been there, just like that.

"Hello!" Teresa called. "Are you here?"

The words echoed weirdly out of the deepness. "Hey, Tiny. I wondered when you were coming back."

Timothy's part of the cave was like another phase change. Nature to alien to human, if not exactly the kind of human residence she was used to. A backpack reactor leaned against the wall, thick yellow power cords going to a wooden rack of neat, well-maintained machines. She recognized the yeast incubator and the emergency recycler from her tours of the early settlements. Other decks she didn't know. All together, it was enough that Timothy could live like a monk and a wise man in his mountain for more than a human lifetime. His bed was a cot against one wall with a blanket of woven polycarbonate that seemed never to show wear. He didn't have a pillow.

The man himself sat next to a length of wood, a knife in his thick, callused hand. A pile of thin, curled slivers rested between his feet where they fell as he carved. He was bald and pale, with a thick, bushy white beard, wide shoulders, and arms with muscles like ropes.

She'd come across him months ago during one of her first excursions. She'd been trying to get high enough on the mountain to see the State Building, and there he'd been, eating his lunch and drinking from a scarred ceramic water purifier. He'd looked like nothing so much as an old cartoon of an enlightened guru meditating on a mountaintop. If there had been any threat in his smile, she might have been scared of him. But there wasn't, and she wasn't. And anyway Muskrat had liked him immediately.

"Sorry," she said, sitting on the edge of his cot. "I've been busy. I have a bunch of new things I'm studying. What are you working on?"

Timothy considered the half-carved wood. "I was going for a marking gauge. I've got one already, but it's a little big for the fine work."

"And you can't have too many tools," Teresa said. The phrase was something of a joke between them, and Timothy grinned.

"Damned straight. So what's up?"

Teresa leaned forward. Timothy frowned and put down the wood and the knife. She didn't know where to start, so she started with her father's plan to train her up.

He had a way of shifting his attention so that she felt like he was actually listening, not just preparing a reply in his head and waiting for her to stop talking. He focused on her the way he did on the wood he carved or the food he cooked. He didn't judge her. He didn't quiz her. She never worried that he would be disappointed with what she said.

It was the way she imagined her father would listen to her if he weren't her father.

She wandered from topic to topic, telling Timothy about Connor and Muriel, the briefings and meetings her father was adding to her schedule, and all the day-to-day worries and thoughts that had built up without her even knowing, and ending with the unnerving conversation with Holden the dancing bear and the weird way he'd said *You should keep an eye on me* like it meant something more than it seemed...

When she ran out of words, Timothy leaned back and scratched his beard. Muskrat had curled up on the floor between the two of them. The dog snored softly, and one leg twitched as she dreamed. Two repair drones queried each other, their voices clicking in descending musical tones. Just telling the story left her feeling better.

"Yeah," he said after a while, "well, for what it's worth, you're not the first person that felt like the captain was a splinter they couldn't dig out. He has that effect on people. But if he says you ought to keep an eye on him, maybe you ought to keep an eye on him."

Teresa leaned back against the wall and pulled her knees up. "I just wish I knew why he bothers me so much."

"He don't treat you like you're special."

"You don't treat me like I'm special. We're friends."

He considered that. "Maybe it's because he thinks your dad's an asshole."

"My dad's not an asshole. And Holden's a killer. He doesn't get to judge other people."

"Your dad's kind of an asshole," Timothy said, his expression philosophical, his voice matter-of-fact. "And he's killed a lot more people than Holden ever did."

"That's different. That's war. He had to do it or else no one would have been able to organize everyone. We'd just have stumbled into the next conflict unprepared. My dad's trying to save us."

Timothy held up a finger like she'd made his point for him. "Now you're telling me why it's *okay* he's an asshole."

"I don't—" Teresa started, then stopped. Timothy's comment made her think of a philosophy lesson, and Ilich talking about consequentialism. *Intention is irrelevant. Only outcomes matter.*

"I don't tell anyone how to live," Timothy was saying. "But if you're looking for moral perfection in your family? Prepare for disappointment."

Teresa chuckled. If anyone else had said the same thing to her, she would have bristled, but it was Timothy. That made it okay. She was glad she'd made the time to come out to see him.

"Why did you call him captain?"

"That's who he is. Captain Holden."

"He's not *your* captain."

A flash of surprise passed over Timothy, like it was a thought he'd never had. "I guess he ain't," Timothy said, and then a moment later, and more slowly, "I guess he ain't."

"Dad says he's afraid," Teresa said. "Holden is, I mean. Not Dad."

"They both are," Timothy said, picking his knife back up. "Guys like them always are. It's people like you and me that aren't scared."

"You're never scared?"

"I haven't been scared since I was younger than you, Tiny. I had a rough start."

"Me too. My mom died when I was a baby. I think my father doesn't like having women around me because it feels like replacing her. All my teachers have been men."

"I never knew mine either," Timothy said. "But I put something together later that I could sort of pretend was family. It wasn't bad for someone that grew up on my street. While it lasted. I'll tell you what, though, as fucked up as my childhood was? It's got nothing on yours."

"My life's perfect," Teresa said. "I can have anything I want. Anytime I want it. Everyone treats me well. My father's making sure I have the training and education to govern billions of people on thousands of planets. No one has ever had the advantages and opportunities I have." She paused, surprised by the hint of bitterness that had crept into her voice.

"Uh-huh," Timothy said. "That's why you're always looking over your shoulder when you sneak out to see me, I guess."

That night, back in her room, she couldn't sleep. The small nighttime noises of the State Building took on a weird power to distract and startle her. Even the gentle ticking of the walls as they radiated away the day's heat felt like someone knocking for her attention. She tried turning her pillow to press her cheek against the cool side and playing gentle, soothing music. It didn't help. Every time she closed her eyes and willed herself down toward dream, she found herself five minutes later with her eyes open, halfway through an imaginary debate with Timothy or Holden or Ilich or Connor. It was past midnight when she gave up.

Muskrat rose with her, following her from bedroom to office, and then, when Teresa sat on one of her workbench stools, curled up at her feet and fell immediately to snoring. Nothing bothered her dog, or at least not for long. Teresa pulled up an old movie about a family living in a haunted apartment on Luna, but her mind slid off the entertainment as quickly as it had off the pillow. She thought about going out and walking around the gardens, but that annoyed her too. When she realized what she actually wanted to do, she'd already known it for a while. Admitting it to herself felt like a surrender.

"Security log access," she said, and her room's system shifted from the haunted corridors of Luna to a businesslike user interface. Even as honored and important as she was, there were logs that she didn't have access to. No one except maybe her father and Dr. Cortázar could have access to the recordings from the pens, for instance. That was normal. And it didn't matter for what she needed. No one was worried about preserving Holden's privacy. She could have watched him sleep if she'd wanted to.

She set the system to generate a full track for Holden over the past week, then scrubbed through it. She knew that the State Building had ubiquitous surveillance built into it, but it was interesting to see where exactly the microlenses were and how much they could capture while staying invisible themselves. As she scrubbed through Holden's passage in the buildings and the gardens, she thought about all the other things she could watch on the feeds. Connor and Muriel, for instance.

On one of her screens, Holden sat on the grass, looking out at the same mountain where Timothy lived. The accelerated scrubbing made his casual gestures and adjustments seem spasmodic. Like he was vibrating. Then Muskrat was there with him. Then she was. She didn't like looking at herself on camera. She didn't look the way she felt like she did. In her mind, her hair was smoother and her posture was better. Without meaning to, she shifted on her stool to sit up straighter. Holden flopped to the grass and sat up with his back wet, and then she and Muskrat zipped out of the frame. She forgot her posture again and leaned forward.

Holden fidgeted on the screen, then rose and sped off. Her scrub was at twenty times faster than base. In under an hour, she could take in the shape of his whole day. Holden at his dinner reading something on a handheld. Holden walking through the same common area her class had been in, pausing to talk to a guard. Holden in the gymnasium, exercising on the old-style machines that they used to use on ships. Holden sitting at a table on a veranda overlooking the city with Dr. Cortázar and a bottle of wine—

She tapped the feed, dropping back to normal speed, and found an audio track.

"—also jellyfish," Cortázar said. "*Turritopsis dohrnii* is the classic example, but there are half a dozen more. An adult reverts to a polyp colony form under stress. Like an elderly man turning into a fetus. That's not the model we're using, but it means the organism has no set maximum life span." He took a long sip from his wineglass.

"What model *are* you using?" Holden asked.

"The original inspirations for the work were corpses that the repair drones got hold of. Not really immortality at all, but the new organisms had some improvements. That's where the breakthrough comes. That's what we should really be focusing on, sacrifice or no. Healthy subject with a well-recorded baseline instead of this..."—his voice rang with contempt—"this *fieldwork*. How to achieve a more robust homeostasis. Just because it's difficult to do doesn't make the principal science unsolvable."

"So not unnatural at all," Holden said, tipping a little more wine from the bottle into the doctor's glass.

"Meaningless term," Cortázar said. "Humans arose inside nature. We're natural. Everything we do is natural. The whole idea that we are different in category is either sentimental or religious. Irrelevant from a scientific perspective."

"So if we get to a place that we can all live forever, that's not unnatural?" Holden sounded genuinely curious.

Cortázar leaned in toward the prisoner, gesturing with his left hand while he swirled his glass in his right. "The only limits on us are what we can do. It's perfectly natural to seek personal benefit. It's perfectly natural to give advantages to your own offspring and withhold them from others. It's perfectly natural to kill your enemies. That's not even outlier behavior. That's all in the middle of the bell curve all the time."

Teresa rested her head in her hands. She was pretty sure Cortázar was drunk. She'd never been herself, but she'd seen some adults at state functions get the same vague focus and sense of being a little off their own points.

"You're right, though," Cortázar said, "You're exactly right. The foundation needs to be broad. That's true."

"Immortality is a high-stakes game," Holden said, like he was agreeing.

"Yes. Plumbing the depths of the protomolecule and all the artifacts it opens up is the work of a hundred lifetimes. Making the researchers die and be replaced by other people with a less advanced understanding is clearly—*clearly*—a bad idea. But that's policy. This is the way forward. So this is the way forward."

"Because Duarte made it policy," Holden said.

"Because we're primates who hold valuable things for our own bloodlines at the expense of everyone else," Cortázar said. "Only one person can ever be immortal. That was what he said. But then he changed the rules. She can be too because he's found a justification for her. That she's really just an extension of him. I'm not mad about that. That's just the organism we are. I'm not mad. But it doesn't matter."

"That's good," Holden said.

"The important thing is that we get good data. One person. Lots of people. All the same. But bad experimental design? That's what sin really is," Cortázar slurred. "That's not me either. Nature eats babies all the time."

Holden shifted, looking directly up into the surveillance camera as if he knew exactly where the hidden lens was. As if he knew she would be watching. *You should keep an eye on me.* Teresa felt a crawling sensation coming up her neck and the feeling, even after he looked away, that he saw her as clearly as she saw him.

She shut down the feed, closed the logs, and went back to bed, but she still didn't sleep.

Chapter Fifteen: Naomi

Getting what you want fucks you up. Naomi pushed the thought aside as she had a dozen times before.

The first part of breaking down her shelter was the easiest. She'd spent years on the float, sometimes running cargo herself, sometimes fighting smugglers for the OPA and the Transport Union. She knew all the tricks. Disassembling her crash couch and system into parts was the work of two hours. Everything she had was modular. Easy to take apart, easy to put into rotation as spare. Everything she'd had could dissolve back into the larger ship and not appear as anything more than a handful of off-by-one inventory miscounts.

The empty container was a little harder, but only a little. According to the manifest, her container was supposed to be filled with the same payload of Earth-farmed bacteria and microbes and starter soil as seventy other containers in the ship. Shifting the contents of just a dozen or so to a slightly less dense configuration left plenty of overage to fill the space that had been hers. By the time the supplies reached their destination, she'd be elsewhere. And even if Laconia backtracked the discrepancies, there wouldn't be much to suggest anything more than run-of-the-mill theft.

The real problem was time. Well, the *first* real problem.

The Laconian ship was already on a braking burn. Eighteen hours to rendezvous didn't leave her much time for everything she had to do. Emma was a help. The woman had more years working transport than Naomi did, and she could drive a loading mech like it was part of her body. Even so, they were cutting it close. And every hour of the mechs hissing and clacking, the smell of industrial lubricant, and the bone-deep ache of effort was another chance for the regular crew to notice that something strange was happening. Toward the end, Naomi sent Emma away to see whether there was any information about the larger picture. If other ships were being stopped. If this was a coincidence, or if the destroyer knew that Naomi was there.

Until she knew, she had to assume there was hope. Another motto for her life these days.

Naomi moved the last pallets into the steel and ceramic that had been her home for months, closed the doors, sealed them, and slapped a customs inspection sticker over the seam. She still had to stow the loader mech and replace the stickers on all the containers she'd cracked, but that wouldn't take more than another few minutes. She had almost half a shift before the inspection. A little over four hours to reinvent herself and blend in with the ship's crew. That was the second real problem...

Getting what you want fucks you up.

They'd been in a bar on Pallas-Tycho not long after the two stations had become a single object. Clarissa had been in relatively good health then. Strong enough she could go drinking, anyway. Naomi didn't remember which bar they'd been in, except that it had gravity, so it had to have been in Tycho's old habitation ring. She did remember that Jim had been there. They'd been talking about how to address Alex's upcoming change in marital status. Whether he'd be bringing his new wife on the ship or taking a leave of absence to be with her or what. Every option had advantages, every one had drawbacks. Looking back, Naomi thought that on some level all of them knew that the relationship was doomed. Clarissa had leaned back in her chair, a glass of whiskey in her hand. Her voice was thoughtful. "Getting what you want fucks you up," she'd said. "When I was in jail, there was nothing I wanted more than to be anywhere else. Then I got out."

"Into an apocalyptic hellscape," Naomi said.

"But even after that. When we got up to Luna and when we got on the *Roci*. It was hard. I knew what I was when I was in prison. It took me years to figure out who I was outside."

"We're talking about marriage, aren't we?"

"Getting what you want fucks you up," Clarissa had said.

Naomi put her hand on the transport container. She'd put herself in prison in order to be safe, and her safety had turned her captive. All she wanted was to wake up next to Jim again. To have something like a pleasant, day-to-day life with him. And now that she couldn't have it, all she wanted was her hermitage back.

Her hand terminal chimed. There was only one person it could be.

"Where do we stand?" she asked.

"I've got a plan," Emma said. "Meet me in med bay three."

"I don't know where that is. Does the ship have a directory function? Because I don't really think asking for directions is our best plan."

"Shit. All right. Wait there. I'll be down in ten. I can take you there."

"Copy that," Naomi said, and dropped the connection. It gave her time to reseal the containers.

Emma, on the float beside her, held the hypodermic needle between her finger and thumb like she was playing darts. Her technique aside, though, the plan was about as solid as Naomi could hope for at short notice. She stretched her chin up and Emma stabbed again, a quick pinch at her jawline at the right to match her already-swelling left.

"How's that feel?" Emma asked.

"Itches," Naomi said.

"Still up for the eyes?"

"Yeah."

Inserting her into the ship's roster wasn't possible. Even if they could backdate all the paperwork to the *Bhikaji Cama*'s last port, Emma didn't have the authorizations she'd need. And messing with the system immediately before an inspection was an invitation to disaster. Fail to shut down one logging system, and the last-minute change was a flashing pointer to whatever you most wanted hidden. So making Naomi into a regular crewman wasn't possible, but making her not immediately match the biometrics for Naomi Nagata was in reach. All it took was a few well-placed needle sticks and some fluid that caused mild swelling. The only trick was changing the shape of her face in ways that made her look like someone else and not just herself, only puffy.

The med bay was old, but well put together. Nothing had the shine of the new. Everything was worn. But it was only worn, not neglected. Naomi had been around long enough to know the difference. She considered her new face in the hand terminal's camera. Emma's first move had been to shave her hair into an unflattering topiary that made her forehead seem wider and her eyes closer together. The swelling in her brow and jaw had thickened her features already. The system's match to her normal appearance was only 80 percent. Enough that even if they identified her, it could be written off as a false positive.

Unless they already knew she was there.

"I'm putting you in with the crew working the heat sink," Emma said. "Chief has them swapping out coolant exchanges."

"Joy," Naomi said.

"The stink'll give you a reason to be wearing a mask," Emma

said. "And it's a mixed-shift crew. Any luck, everyone will think you're from the other one."

Emma drove the needle into the flesh under Naomi's eye. It only hurt a little. "How long do we have?"

Emma checked her terminal and spat out a low, grunting curse.

"We should go," she said, dropping the needle into Naomi's skin one last time. "They're already positioning for transfer."

"If they take me," Naomi said, "I will try to hold out until you can get away. But go quickly, and make sure Saba knows what happened."

Emma didn't meet her eyes, but she nodded. This had always been a risk. It was what they'd signed up for. As Emma gave her a mask and led her down to the engineering decks, Naomi wondered how Bobbie and Alex would find out about it if she was captured. And what Jim would hear. The temptation was still there. If she did it—if she jumped instead of waiting for the push—she could control the fall.

The coolant lines on the *Bhikaji Cama* were an old design but in decent condition. She'd flushed lines like them back in her water hauler days, and the process wasn't that hard. Punishing and foul, but not hard. There were four others on the team. Five people on a three-shift boat. It wasn't much of a disguise.

The full process would run about four hours if nothing went wrong. She had to hope it was long enough for the Laconians to come, make their inspection and move on. All she would have to do was stay quiet and small until the danger passed. She fell into the work, taking orders from the foreman, doing her part with as little fuss as she could manage. She'd almost forgotten there was anything to worry about more pressing than not getting too much coolant in the air filters, when the interruption came.

"Make safe! Make safe! All you fucking bastards hold the work and make safe, yeah?"

The others all closed down the lines. Naomi did too. There wasn't much choice.

The man who pulled himself past the yellow work barrier was

dressed in a chief engineer's uniform. Behind him, three soldiers in Laconian blues, one with a captain's bars. Naomi hooked her foot into a wall handhold. Her heart was going fast, and a hint of nausea plucked at her that had nothing to do with the stink of coolant. The chief engineer motioned for them to take off their masks. The others started to comply. If she hesitated now, it would only call attention where she didn't want it.

Naomi pulled off her mask.

"Was that discussed with senior staff?" the Laconian captain demanded, continuing whatever conversation they'd been having before they came in the room.

"No," the chief engineer said. He was a younger man, but with a rough, scarred face that made him ageless. "Why would it be? Captain says it. We do it. That's how it is. That a problem?"

One of the other Laconians held a hand terminal up to the face of her team foreman. The terminal chimed. Naomi felt a sick kind of peace descend over her.

"It's an irregularity," the Laconian captain said. "The political officer will want a full report when you reach the transfer station."

"Political officer?" the chief engineer asked. Despite herself, Naomi's ears pricked up. If this was related somehow to the mission in Sol—if Laconia was making a broad crackdown—maybe they weren't here looking just for her. It was a thin hope, but it was something.

"New oversight regulations," the Laconian captain said as the hand terminal tracked over Naomi's face.

"Never heard of them."

"You're hearing about them right now," the captain said.

The soldier frowned. "Sir? This one's not on the crew list."

I am Naomi Nagata. I would like to accept the invitation of High Consul Duarte. Please let him know. It was all she had to say. It would even be a relief, knowing that she'd done all that she could first. The chief engineer looked at her and shrugged. "Course she's not. She's on the apprentice program."

The Laconian captain looked at her, uncertain. She kept the

confusion off her face. No one on the ship but Emma was supposed to know she was there. *Play along*, she thought. *Just play along.*

"She's old to be an apprentice," the captain said.

"Had some trouble back home," she said. "Trying to make something new." The lie was easy.

"She needs to be on the crew rolls," the Laconian captain said, turning away.

"Why?" the chief engineer asked. "She's not crew. She's an apprentice."

"Apprentices are part of the crew," the captain said, a note of exasperation in his voice.

"First I've heard of it," the chief engineer said. "If I put her in, it starts counting her hours toward a benefits package like she was crew. That's not how it works."

"You can take that up with the political officer too," the Laconian captain said. The last of the work crew was scanned and cleared.

As they left, the chief engineer looked back. His eyes met hers. There was a subterranean joy in them. "As you all were. Shit's not going to maintain itself."

"Yes, chief," Naomi said, and put her mask back on.

They fell back into the familiar rhythms of labor, but Naomi's mind was working on more than the lines. The others on the team didn't seem to have noticed anything odd in the conversation. One of them—a thick-faced man called Kip—treated her a little worse, but that was probably just because he thought she was lower status now. Nothing odd about that. When the new exchange was in, the old one sealed, and the diagnostics all in optimal range, Naomi wanted nothing more than a shower and a meal. She didn't have a cabin of her own, she didn't know where the gang showers were, and she wouldn't have a locker there. Even if she got to the right place, after she cleaned up, she'd have to put the same coolant-stinking jumpsuit back on. That seemed worse than not cleaning up in the first place.

She followed the others as they headed back to the crew decks. Lagging behind. She wanted to go to her container. The urge to check her incoming feeds itched as badly as her jawline where the swelling was just starting to go down. But it was gone. Months of habit had just become irrelevant, and she pulled herself along the off-white halls, moving from handhold to handhold with the feeling of having woken from a long dream to find herself in some foreign station where she didn't belong.

The mess hall had six people in it, but it was built for thirty or more. She pulled herself to a dispenser, but couldn't get food. It wanted an access code or ID match that she didn't have. She went to a corner by herself, bracing on a wall-mounted foothold, and waited without knowing what exactly she was waiting for.

Her thoughts moved in the silence of other people's conversations. When, after an hour or so, Emma appeared, Naomi was almost surprised to see her. The woman pulled a double share of food and brought it over.

"They've moved on," Emma said quietly. "Docked, ran down the whole fucking ship stem to stern, told the captain that he'd need to talk to someone at the transfer station, and gone."

"Political officer," Naomi said. "I heard. We got word of one heading for the transfer station in Sol system too. Earth."

"Well, looks like we have political officers now," Emma said sourly.

Naomi nodded with one fist. The crackdown was broad, then. A tightening of control over the whole Transport Union. More than that, it might be a sign that Duarte and his machinery were starting to suspect the Transport Union's role in smuggling the underground from system to system. Or had other plans that wanted loyal and trusted eyes beyond the governors and their staffs.

If they found the shell game, it could mean a serious retooling of their methods at best. At worst, the end of the underground. With Medina in control of the slow zone and their methods of transportation exposed, they were in real danger of becoming thirteen hundred fragmented, isolated movements, unable to support or help each other.

"No one checked you, though?" Emma said.

"Oh, they checked her," a voice said behind them. The chief engineer floated over and took position beside them. "They caught her."

Emma blanched. So apparently she hadn't been behind that.

"I appreciate you covering for me," Naomi said. "It might be better for you if we just kept it at that. I don't want to get you in trouble."

"Are you kidding?" the chief engineer said. "That was the best thing that's happened to me since I signed up for this haul. Seriously, it was my pleasure."

"I appreciate your enthusiasm, but—"

He handed her a card. "Override access to a private cabin and a commissary account," he said. "It's off the books, so even if there's an audit, it'll just come back as unused and overages."

Naomi looked at it, then at him. Never look a gift horse in the mouth, they said. But it was bad advice. "I'm guessing there's something you'll want in return? Because I think we're going to need to be very, very clear what that is."

"No," the chief engineer said. "Nothing. You've already paid me out. I'm just glad I get the chance to hand some back."

"Excuse me for being rude," Naomi said, "but I've never really trusted the whole kindness-of-strangers bit."

"You're not a stranger," the chief engineer said. "You're the reason I'm an engineer. My dad was a kid on Ceres when the Free Navy stripped it. You and your crew? You put your hands out in peace in the middle of a civil war. You built the Transport Union. As far as I'm concerned, we should kick the captain out of his quarters and give them to you. You more than earned them."

Naomi reached for her hair, trying to pluck it down over her face, but Emma's haircut didn't leave enough for that. "You know who I am, then."

The chief engineer coughed out a laugh. "Of course I do.

Anyone in the Belt's going to know Naomi fucking Nagata. It's just these Laconian fucks who can't see what they're looking at. And again, it's a real honor."

"Chuck," Emma said, and her tone made the word a warning.

"I won't say it again," the chief engineer—Chuck—said, lifting a hand. "But don't either one of you worry. I'll get you shuttle access as soon as we're close to port. You're safe with me."

Naomi nodded her thanks, and Chuck beamed. She saw now how young he was. His delight with himself made her heart ache a little. He'd gotten away with something, and his pride was bright enough to read by. She even had a sense of what she must look like through his eyes—a demigod. A figure from myth appearing in his life. A celebrity. God knew she'd seen enough people look at Jim with that expression. This must be what it had been like for him all those times.

It was a feeling she could easily learn to hate.

Chapter Sixteen: Elvi

The ships were old transports that had been hauling people and supplies around Sol system's asteroid belt for a generation before the first gate opened. Elvi watched them being positioned near the surface of the Tecoma ring gate with the *Falcon*'s highest-power optical telescopes, and the images were still fuzzy. Both vessels were at most a few dozen meters top to bottom, and they were almost a billion kilometers away. If the *Falcon*'s sensor arrays hadn't been orders of magnitude more sensitive than her eyes, they wouldn't have been anything close to visible. But she could make out the mechs and drones crawling over them, making the automated checks and last-minute verifications. Maneuvering thrusters bloomed and vanished as they shifted along the plating and drive cones, checking and double-checking that nothing would go wrong. There was deep irony in that, but if she thought about it too much, she just got angry.

"Hey, sweetie," Fayez said from the doorway. "Can I get you anything?

"Still no. Just like three minutes ago," she snapped. She grunted, regret jumping into her throat just behind the words. "Sorry. That was shitty."

"No, I see where you're coming from," her husband and intellectual companion of decades said. "I'm hovering. Look."

He let go of the handhold and floated free for a moment, grinning at his own physical pun. She laughed more at the grin than the joke.

"I'm fine," she said. "Really. Perfectly fine."

"Good. That's good. Because some people, when they almost die from being semidrowned in half-alien goo while under a sustained high-g burn, get a little rash. Or zits. Near death can really do terrible things for acne."

"I'm sorry I scared you," she said. "I didn't mean to. Really. But I'm fine now."

Fayez pulled himself into the room, twisting ungracefully to hook his ankles around the wall footholds and absorb the momentum with his knees. He stood on the wall beside her, looking down at the images on her screen.

"I'm sorry," he said, "that my deep existential panic at the prospect of your death hasn't faded as quickly as yours."

"It's okay. I probably wouldn't be as calm about it if it had been you. By the time I found out about it, I already wasn't dead. Doesn't really have the same punch when you miss all the will-she-or-won't-she clinging-to-life thing."

"Yeah," Fayez said. "I didn't love that part. I mean, in fairness, I don't love this part either."

She put up her hand, and he wrapped his fingers in hers. It was how they always were. Decades of habit shrouded what they meant in humor and wit, but she knew his distress was real. And that her resentment of it wasn't really about him as much as the raw idiocy playing out near the transit ring. She took a long, deep breath and let it out slowly between her teeth.

"I feel stupid," she said. "I really thought we were a scientific mission."

"Aren't we?"

She pointed one thumb toward the monitor. "That's not science. 'Light shit on fire and see what happens' isn't science. This is throwing dynamite into a pond to see if any fish float to the top."

"So...natural philosophy?"

"Military bullshit. Solving every problem by trying to blow it up."

"Yeah," Fayez said. "Almost makes you wish you could quit, doesn't it?"

Elvi pushed back from the monitor. In free fall, it was only a gesture that she was disengaging. Fayez's dark eyes didn't leave hers. "It wouldn't be the first thing that made me think that."

"But."

"I know. If it wasn't us," she said, "it would be someone else. Someone who didn't know as much as we do. It's just..."

"You think whatever's on the other side will hit back?"

"Yes. Maybe," she said. "I don't know. I don't like things that can only happen once. You can't make sense of something when there's no pattern. One data point is the same as none."

"Would you feel better if the big man committed to doing this again a few dozen times?"

A couple billion kilometers away, the drive lit up for a moment, flickered, and went out.

"I think he did."

Elvi wasn't sure what the atmosphere on the science deck really was. She wanted to think that everyone else was just as uncomfortable with Sagale's plan and, like her, staying as quiet about it. But the truth was that Jen and Travon looked excited. Their screens showed the inputs from a dozen probes and arrays scattered through the local void and three countdown timers. The first timer showed the time—down to minutes now—when the first ship would pass through the gate and, hopefully, into oblivion. Trailing that by only a few seconds, the timer for the second ship—the bomb ship—that would follow it. And then with three full minutes more, the detonation clock.

They were too far away to disarm the antimatter bomb. Making sure the experiment failed safe if it failed would be up to Medina Station. If the bomb ship somehow actually made the transit into the gate network, Medina would shut it down without detonation. The *Falcon*, almost a light-hour away, was watching literal nothingness for signs that the thing beyond the gates—the thing *inside* them—had even noticed what they'd done.

"You know what would be funny?" Fayez said. "If this whole blowing-things-up plan broke the gate and we were all trapped here on this ship for the rest of our lives with no way home."

Sagale glowered and cleared his throat.

"You're right," Fayez said. "Too soon."

The first counter fell to zero, turned from blue time-to-transit to red time-since-transit. In an hour they would see it happen, hear the tech ship's report. In the vast emptiness, all they had was the assumption that the plan had actually gone forward.

"Everyone strap in," Sagale said. "If the enemy fires another of those void bullets at the system, we may lose consciousness for a time."

Jen and Travon put on their restraints. Elvi already had hers on. Twice before, she'd lived through the consciousness-breaking backlash of pissing off whatever had murdered the protomolecule. Once on Ilus with an army of alien bug-robots ready to cut her down, once sitting on a couch in a waiting room on Luna watching the newsfeeds as the *Tempest* prepared to annihilate Pallas Station. She was almost used to it at this point, or that was what she told herself. Still, she wasn't looking forward to doing it again. The second timer zeroed. The bomb ship was through the gate. Presumably it had gone dutchman too.

The seconds seemed to go slower as the last timer fell. On the screen two ships waited outside the gate, preparing to begin the first transit. It was like looking into the past, waiting for something to happen that had already happened. The light bouncing off those ships and streaking toward her was almost an hour old, from her frame of reference, anyway.

The last timer hit zero. Somewhere farther away than a mere normal light-hour, something very violent happened in whatever non-space the gates passed through. Elvi held her breath.

"Are we seeing anything?" Sagale asked, his voice tight and tense.

"Nothing yet," Jen said.

Elvi waited for the weird dilation of perception. The sense of being able to see atoms and waves, of experiencing herself and her environment in such detail that the border between them vanished, her body and the universe smearing together like a watercolor painting under a faucet. One breath, then another. It kept not happening.

"All right," Sagale said. "Protocol says we will hold position and remain in safety restraints until—"

"Holy shit," Travon said. "Are you guys seeing this?"

On the screens, the space around them boiled. As Elvi watched, confirmation started rolling in from the outlying probes. One after the other, they all reported the same thing. An uptick in quantum particle annihilation. The underlying hum of the vacuum cranking up to a shriek.

"That," Travon said, his voice low and breathy, "is beautiful. Just look at it."

"Report," Sagale said.

"It's like what we saw in Sol system, sir," Jen said. "Virtual particle activity has increased massively. I'd have to say they noticed us."

"Check the time stamp," Sagale said. "Have we lost consciousness? Did we stay awake the whole time?"

"We did," Elvi said even before she checked the data. "I mean the second one. We didn't lose consciousness. We stayed awake."

"Yeah, our entanglement experiment didn't break either," Jen said. "They all failed in Sol system. Ours looks fine. Whatever this is, it's different."

Sagale chuckled, and a broad smile grew on his lips. Elvi thought it was the first time she'd seen the man showing anything like real pleasure. "Well now," he said. "*That* is interesting."

"God *damn*," Travon said, "look at this. This is incredible."

The rates of virtual particle creation and annihilation were swamping the sensors. All the readings pegged at shit-if-I-know-but-more-than-I-can-keep-track-of. Elvi pressed her fingertips to her lips. She'd been braced for the weird dive into broken consciousness. That it hadn't come was somehow worse.

"Continue monitoring," Sagale said. "High Consul Duarte will be pleased with this."

"Why?" Elvi asked.

Sagale looked at her as if she'd made a joke he didn't quite understand. "The behavior changed. It suggests the enemy can be negotiated with."

"It doesn't show change at all. You fired the magnetic field projector in Sol system and whatever this is responded with the bullet on the *Tempest*. Then you came here and did something completely different, and it responded differently. There's literally no data we can take from that."

"We know now that when we send a punishment ship through, the enemy feels it," Sagale said. "All this? It isn't because a couple of ships vanished. Ships have been vanishing since we started using the gates. This tells us that the tool we've made can hurt them. That's *very* important. We won't know if it can teach them until we repeat the experiment."

And there it was. *Repeat the experiment.*

"Jen?" Travon said. He hadn't heard anything Sagale said. All his attention was on his screens. "Are you seeing this? There's precipitate."

Sagale's attention turned. "There's what? What are you seeing?"

"The virtual particles aren't all annihilating. It's generating some...looks like hydrogen ions? Basically just raw protons."

"Does it pose a threat?"

"No, this is trivial. Even in normal interstellar space, you have an atom or two per cubic centimeter. This is still way below that. If this system hadn't already been weirdly empty, I wouldn't have noticed this at all. I mean, I guess if it goes on for a few decades, it could get to be a problem? Maybe?"

Sagale looked over at Elvi. His plate-flat face was expressionless. It made him seem smug.

"Still," Jen said, "if it's the whole solar bubble, that is a shit-ton of energy. Not rigorously speaking, of course, but just a lot."

"Energy?" Fayez asked.

"Energy. Matter," Jen said. "Same thing. If they're creating actual matter, they're throwing a lot of energy at us to do it."

"Is it evenly distributed?" Fayez asked. Elvi heard something in his voice. A deep rasp that spoke of growing fear.

"Oh," Jen said. And then a breath later, "Oh shit."

"Kind of early to know that," Travon said, clearly behind the curve. "We've only got a couple dozen probes out there. Why?"

"So I know I'm just the geology guy here," Fayez said. "But aren't we a little less than two light-hours away from a neutron star? One that we were all really impressed at how something had designed it to be right on the edge of collapse? And now something's putting more energy and mass into the system? Because that sounds like it could be a problem."

Elvi's gut tightened.

"Hold on," Jen said, her fingers dancing fast over her controls. The screen flickered as she generated energy curves against time and mass. A few seconds later, she made a little grunt like she'd been punched. "Well, shit."

"Let's not get ahead of ourselves," Sagale said. "Nothing has happened yet. The star looks stable."

"The star was stable two hours ago," Jen said. "But when a rapidly spinning neutron star collapses into a black hole, a gamma ray burst comes out of the poles. A few seconds of it releases as much energy as Sol would in its whole ten billion years. They're very rare."

Travon's face had gone ashy. Elvi felt a shifting sensation deep in her gut, pulling her between fear and awe.

"Commander Lively, are we about to experience one?" Sagale asked, but Jen was elbows deep in calculations before he said it.

"It won't have gone critical," Jen said. "Not yet. Assuming the precipitate generation rate is uniform, which I don't actually know. But we should get out of here as quickly as we can."

"As quickly as we can without killing Elvi," Fayez said. "We almost lost her once. We can't do a max burn."

"All of us dying isn't better," Sagale said. Despite everything, Elvi felt a bleak tug of amusement at how fast the man could change his opinions in the face of evidence.

The admiral pursed his lips. His eyes focused on something internal as he thought. Then, "Commander Lively, please send out your analysis to the tech ship and the team on Medina." He tapped his control board, and his voice echoed through the ship. "All hands make ready. Expect an extended high-g burn."

"We can't just shoot the ring gate, sir," Travon said. "We've got about a billion kilometers to get to the ring, and a million to slow down in on the other side. Less if we go at an angle, and we still need to miss Medina and the central station so..."

"I'm aware of the issues," Sagale said. "Please make ready. Major Okoye, I'm going to ask that you report to the med bay. My understanding is that we may be able to make this safer for you if we forgo sedation in the submersion couch. It will be unpleasant."

"That's okay," Fayez said. "She's okay with that. We'll both go without. I will too." He turned to her. "I'm sorry, sweetie. I just really need you not to die."

"I understand, Admiral," Elvi said. "I'll go now."

Sagale nodded once, tightly. Elvi undid the restraints, pushed gently off, floating in the cool air. Fayez had already launched himself down the corridor toward the couches. Elvi grabbed a handhold, stopping herself. She didn't know if the feeling in her chest was rage or fear or a bitter kind of amusement. Whatever it was felt cold.

"Admiral…"

"Yes, Major Okoye?"

I told you so hovered in the air between them. She didn't have to say it. She could see that he'd heard.

On the screen behind him, the first ship's drive came to life, moving the ship toward the ring gate. The illusion that it could still stop—that they could undo what had already happened—was as powerful as it was wrong. The bomb ship's drive cone flared a moment later as it moved to follow.

In a smaller window in the same screen, the neutron star at the heart of the dead system glowed tiny and bright.

Chapter Seventeen: Alex

Hiding a ship in space wasn't all that different from hiding on a school playground. Find something bigger than you, and put it between you and the person looking. Even without something to hide behind it wasn't impossible. Space was vast, and the things that floated through it were mostly cold and dark. If you could find a way not to radiate heat and light, it was possible to get lost in the mix.

Alex ran a map of the Jovian system forward in time, then back again. The moons spun around the gas giant, then reversed and spun back to their starting places. Possible paths shot through the imaginary space like threads of copper, tracing the complex interactions of thrust and temperature and the ever-changing invisible clockwork of interacting gravity. And as he manipulated the variables—what paths became open if they could add another half a degree to the ship, what closed down if they shortened the burn time—the paths blinked in and out of existence. A plan slowly began to form.

Finding an escape route to get the *Storm* off Callisto before the Laconian battleship came in range meant plotting a course off the moon that only included engine burns when the massive bulk of Jupiter was between them and the inner system, and then floating cold and dark when they were in the open. That narrowed the range down. But it was still a little more complicated than that.

Io, Europa, and Ganymede all had observation stations that might be in Laconian control and could pick up their launch and flag it as suspicious. He also needed to plan the launch for a time when Callisto had Jupiter between it, the sun, and the other three Galilean moons. Alex ran the orbital simulation forward again. A solution existed. There was a window where Callisto was alone on the antisunward side of Jupiter, caught in its shadow long enough to get the *Storm* off the ground. It made for a tight window. Maybe too tight.

They did have a few advantages. The *Storm*'s skin returned an extremely low radar profile compared to other ships. Her internal heat sinks could store days of waste heat. And when necessary, capillary-like microtubules in the ship's skin could be flushed with liquid hydrogen to ensure that the hull's outer temperature remained only a few degrees warmer than space. It was a very stealthy ship when it was flying dark. If the Laconians were looking for a standard rock hopper or salvaged military ship, the *Storm* could look too small to fit the profile. He checked the hydrogen supply, adjusted the temperature variables in his search, and looked again. The window opened a crack wider.

They could take off from Callisto when the moon was behind Jupiter, then do one very hard burn with the planet blocking line of sight to the *Tempest* and any other inner-planet observation posts. It wouldn't keep other ships and minor posts from picking up the drive plume—there were just too many eyes in the system to evade all of them, no matter how complex his flight path. But between running cold and keeping the main observers blocked, he could get a decent delta-v for a few hours. Then they could kill the burn and float dark for as long as the heat sinks held up. Once they'd put a little distance between themselves and the Jovian system, cozied up to the gravitational low-energy paths that the Belters and salvage miners used, they could fade in their fake transponder, start a very gentle burn toward the ring, and hope they looked like just one of dozens of ships headed that way.

Once they were far enough away, put in a call to Saba and see if any of the union ships had room to scoop them up and get them the hell out of Sol system.

It was pretty damn thin, as escape plans went. But they were living in thin times.

Alex ran the simulation back and forth, adding in various launch and escape burn projections until he'd come up with a plan that the computer agreed gave them the best chance of success. If he hadn't overlooked anything. If the variables were weighted correctly. If the gods didn't just hate them that day.

He leaned back, and his skull throbbed like his brain had an appointment elsewhere. He stretched his neck. The muscles felt like he'd been punched. There had been a time he could go for hours fine-tuning a flight plan. And he still could, but the price was higher. He swatted the desk to shut down the holographic map display. The room lights came up on the small and dingy working space he was occupying during their stay on Callisto. A desk that fed directly to the *Storm*'s system so that none of his queries would leak out to Callisto's larger data environment. A wall screen with access to a couple thousand different information and entertainment streams. A combination sink, toilet, and shower alcove in the corner that included a rank mildew smell free of charge. It even had a cot with a flat pillow and threadbare blanket if he decided not to head back to his coffin hotel. All the discomforts of a naval base bachelor pad. It didn't make him nostalgic.

He was stirring a chalky analgesic powder into a glass of water, the grains of medicine swirling like stars, when his terminal began playing the first few bars of his favorite Dust Runners song. "Accept connection," he yelled at it, then gulped down his medicine. The bitterness crawled up his tongue like a living thing, and he shuddered. "Yo, Bobbie, what's up?"

"Meet me at the dining room in twenty," she said, then closed the connection before he could ask a question.

Dining room was just a code phrase for a small storage compartment off a seldom-used side tunnel. It was one of half a dozen rooms they'd designated for secret meetings. They were swept every couple of days for listening devices, and members of Bobbie's strike team dressed in civilian clothes kept an eye on them to see if anyone else was going in or out.

Alex's time in the military had all been on board ships or on naval bases waiting for a shipboard assignment. He'd never been a spy or special forces operator like Bobbie. He found the built-in paranoia that came with a secret mission lifestyle exhausting.

"I should probably pick up some food," he said to his terminal. It beeped a recognition at him, then sent an order to a noodle shop in the lower medina. The owner of the shop was a resistance member who would send a pickup notification to Caspar. It was another code. He wasn't even vaguely hungry, but if someone heard him or got a copy of the signal, it sounded innocuous. Nothing about his life was what it looked like anymore.

Ten minutes later Alex walked into the back room of the noodle shop and found Caspar waiting for him. When they weren't using the space for secret meetings, it was the noodle shop's dry goods pantry, and boxes of supplies were stacked up against most walls. The station's heating ducts had been closed off, so the room stayed about ten degrees cooler than the shop itself, and Alex could just see his breath in the air.

"How long do you need?" the kid asked without preamble.

"Dunno. Give me two hours, then we'll meet up at the casino. Blackjack. I'll be at the five-dollar table."

"Copy that," Caspar said. He pulled off the heavy hooded jacket he was wearing and handed it to Alex. Alex put the jacket on and passed his terminal to Caspar. The kid would wander the station for a couple hours. Anyone who was tracking Alex by terminal location would be sent on a merry chase. It was unlikely that anyone was tracking any of them. The terminals were as stripped down and anonymized as it was possible to make them. If their false identities had been cracked, they would probably already have been picked up by security and interrogated by Laconian operatives. But Bobbie had laid down the operational security law, and they all followed her rules to the letter.

Caspar took the terminal and stuffed it into his jumpsuit pocket, then gave Alex a cheery little wave and headed for the door. "Wait," Alex said.

"Everything okay?" Something in Alex's tone had put a little worry line between the younger man's eyes. *Nothing is okay*, Alex wanted to reply, but didn't.

"Just be careful. Something happens to you, it doubles my workload." He tried to make it a joke, but it fell flat. The line between Caspar's eyes deepened.

"I don't need you to daddy me, Alex. I know my job."

"Yeah, sorry about that," Alex said, then leaned against the wall and rubbed his eyes. His headache made him want to press his face against it. Only a thin layer of composites and insulation separated him from the natural tunnel. Maybe some ice that was as old as the solar system itself would be cool enough to numb the throb in his temples.

"It's no big deal," Caspar said. "But my father pulled up stakes when I was seven. I didn't need one then, and I don't now."

"Fair enough. Truth is..."

Caspar waited. Alex heaved a sigh.

"Truth is I'm worried shitless about my own kid, and I'm just projecting onto you. Don't take it as anything else, okay?"

Alex waited for Caspar to leave, but he didn't. Instead he sat down on a stack of boxes labeled Soy Noodles and crossed his arms. "You think the Laconians know it was us?"

"What? No, I didn't mean—"

"Don't fuck around, Alex. I have family too."

"It's not that," Alex said. He spotted a small bag of dehydrated onion flakes and picked it up. It felt cold in his hand, and heavenly when he pressed it to his temple. Caspar sat on his boxes, staring and bouncing one knee impatiently.

"Then what is it?"

"He's getting serious," Alex said. "Maybe even married. Probably married. It's just making me think about how much I don't want to mess things up for him. You always think you're going to leave things better for your kid than you found them for yourself. That's not working out for me."

Alex moved his bag of onions to the other side of his head, but it had started to warm up.

"Worrying feels like you're at least doing something," Caspar said. "I get it. When I started flying for the union, I worried about my mom so that I wouldn't feel guilty for leaving her behind."

"You're too smart for your age," Alex said. "But yeah, that's probably it. Or close enough. I was a shit father long before I left my family to play revolutionary."

"I dunno," Caspar said, then stood up. "My father took off because my mother asked him to stop spending the rent money on pixie dust. You'd win father of the year if it was down to a two-man race."

"Thanks," Alex said, and surprised himself by laughing. "That's a hell of a compliment."

Alex's terminal buzzed in Caspar's pocket. The kid pulled it out, then said, "Cap wants to know where the fuck you are."

"On my way."

The dining room was an abandoned storage space about six meters square with spray foam insulation walls and a carbon fiber door that didn't even have a latch. Piping that entered through the walls and then just ended hinted at a past as a machine room, though what infrastructure used to occupy the space was lost to history. A tiny green chalk X had been placed on the lower left-hand corner of the door and was surrounded by other graffiti. The graffiti was mostly gang boasts and assertions of sexual prowess. The green X meant the room had been swept for surveillance less than thirty hours ago and found to be clean. If it had been red, the underground would have left the devices in place and abandoned the room.

Bobbie was waiting for him when he arrived. Impatience in the former Marine eluded most people. She didn't pace. She never bounced a knee or a foot. The only time he'd ever heard her crack her knuckles was before they sparred in the gym. But Alex knew something was up the moment he walked into the room. She was standing perfectly still, but she was stiff, as though she was half flexing every muscle in her body.

"You're late," she said.

"I got caught up talking to Caspar at the drop, and now you're kind of scaring me."

"We have the battleship that shrugged off the combined fleets of Earth, Mars, and the Transport Union cruising toward us because we killed a high-ranking Laconian officer. If you weren't already scared, you're fucking stupid, and I know you're not fucking stupid, Alex," Bobbie said.

"Copy that, Gunny. It's a fair point," Alex said, and raised his hands in mock surrender. The dining room was his least favorite place to meet, mostly because there was nothing in it to sit on. Instead he found a patch of wall without any pipes sticking out of it and leaned into the foam of the insulation. "Why don't you get me up to speed?"

"Sorry," Bobbie said. She clenched her hands into fists and jammed them into her pockets. "I'm pissed at you right now and it's not your fault."

"What can I stop not doin' so it ain't not my fault anymore?"

Bobbie chuckled at that and shot him a thin smile. It wasn't a very funny joke, but he knew she appreciated his not taking her anger personally.

"Something's been bothering me. You're right. And Naomi's right," she said. "The timer's running out on our little resistance, and what have we accomplished? We've annoyed the empire. Snatched a few ships, some supplies. Killed a few Laconians. And maybe I used to think it was enough to spit in my enemy's eye while he strangles me. But I've been thinking about Jillian's assessment of the objective value of moral victories, and she wasn't wrong either."

Bobbie went silent, like she was listening to the words she'd said. She probably hadn't spoken these thoughts out loud until just now.

"Are we talking about what I think we're talking about?"

"I don't know what you think we're talking about, Alex."

"Because," Alex said, "if we're talking about packing it in, it's a lot easier to get off Callisto if we're not trying to take the *Storm* with us. I mean, I've got a plan either way, but—"

"No," Bobbie said, "we're not talking about that."

Anger roughened her voice. He wanted to pull back from her. Retreat, but he'd known her long enough to see it was the wrong way with her. Whatever she was thinking through, she needed someone to slam it up against. Placating her wasn't going to make either of them happy. Or safe. Even if she did scare him a little, she was still Bobbie Draper, his old friend and compatriot.

But she was also a creature of violence whose frustrations were coming out sideways.

"Copy that, Gunny," Alex said, trying not to sound like a hostage negotiator.

"I'm not giving up," Bobbie said. "I'm figuring out how to *win*. How can we take our present circumstance and find the orthogonal move, the surprise attack that snatches victory from defeat. How do we do more than just *survive*?"

"*Survive* is a pretty good start," Alex said. "I've worked up a launch plan to get the *Storm* off of Callisto, if that helps."

"Yeah, it does. But running away isn't going to solve our larger problem."

"Cap...Bobbie," Alex said. "There are three *Magnetar*-class ships in the universe, and the one that kicked the whole combined fleet's ass is steaming toward us right now. Pickin' a fight with her is like me pickin' a fight with you. Not being scared is fucking stupid, to use your own words."

Bobbie didn't answer. She pulled a terminal out of her pocket. It was one of the cheap ones that kiosks in the markets would spit out for a few bucks. Enough battery charge for a few hours, and then you just threw it away and bought another one. She tossed it to him. On the screen was a picture of a small metal ball with text printed on it, and some sort of cable running out of the top.

"The fuck is this?" Alex said.

"The report's linked."

Alex flicked the screen with his index finger, and it changed to an article about the theoretical uses of antimatter for high-energy reactors. Even so, it took him a minute to understand what she meant.

"No," he said.

"Oh yes," Bobbie replied. "Rini is ninety-nine percent sure. She's been looking them over and doing the research. We've been able to produce trace amounts of antimatter since the dark ages, but it's never been practical. Now it is. The Laconians know how to produce and store it. I will bet you a week's wages that it's coming from the same construction platforms that made the *Storm* and the *Tempest*, and it's part of the resupply for the battleship. That big cannon of theirs must burn it like crazy when it fires."

"Laconia's a hard target, but if you're right and we could figure a way to knock out those platforms—"

"Yeah, taking out their resupply is great," Bobbie said. "But that's just a tactical victory. That's my kind of target. It's not yours. Or Naomi's."

"My kind of target?"

"If we blew out the Laconian construction platforms, Duarte

and his admirals would know why it mattered. But Kit's friends at university? They're the ones we need to inspire, for them it has to be something they can see. We have to do something that shows Laconia's not invincible. That there's a chance for us to get a new generation on board."

"You want to drop these on Laconia?" Alex asked, aghast. Sure, they were enemies, but the idea of killing a planet full of people was horrifying. Even in war, there were lines no one should cross. "If we start carpet-bombing civilians, we're worse than the enemy."

Alex felt a rush of relief. He was still fighting for the good guys. "Okay, good. I didn't think you'd—"

"I want to kill the *Tempest*," she said. "We show Earth and Mars and everyone in the Belt and every other colony out past the gates that Laconia's battleship isn't invincible. Show them that we can win. We'll create a whole new generation of people willing to fight by lighting the biggest god damn signal fire the human race has ever seen."

"Bobbie," Alex said. Something in her eyes was more frightening than her fists had been. A fervor he wasn't used to seeing there. All the fear and desperation suddenly transformed into something verging on fanaticism. "This is crazy."

"We're fucked, and we've been playing not to lose. I'm going to start playing to *win*."

"No, you're not."

Bobbie stared at him. Her jaw slid forward a fraction of a centimeter. Every fiber of his body told him to back off, except for the one little part of his brain that knew showing weakness now was a path to disaster.

"You aren't," he said. "You're stung because we had a win in our hands and we lost it. And then Jillian twisted the knife because she was frustrated too, and she's kind of an asshole. And we found this"—he held up the hand terminal with the antimatter information—"so it feels like the universe handed you a way to redeem the loss. But what you're really doing is trying to win back what you've lost by going all in. It's shitty poker, and even worse as a battle strategy."

"Fuck you, Alex. I do this for a living."

"And you're really good at it. And you're smart. And I'm just a glorified bus driver who takes you where you need to be so you can kill people. But you're wrong about this one, and you know you're wrong."

"That's not what I meant."

"You want the big symbolic victory," Alex said. "When has that ever been the smart move?"

For the first time, a shadow of doubt crossed Bobbie's eyes. She crossed her arms, but she looked away from him. He leaned forward.

"You're frustrated. And you feel trapped. And hitting back hard is what you do when you feel frustrated and trapped. But let me get us out of here. We'll get these little balls of hell to Saba. And yeah, maybe he'll send us back and we can take the *Tempest* down. Or maybe he'll do something else. But let's get more voices weighing in on this plan before we go all damn-the-torpedoes. Okay?"

"You think it's an unwinnable fight. That's what you just said."

"I do," Alex admitted. "But I've been divorced twice now. I wouldn't take my word as gospel. I could be wrong about a lot of things. Yeah, your best soldiers are old shoe leather like you and me. But kids like Caspar are here too. Not as many as I want. Not as many as I think we're going to need. But some. I just don't think we should throw them away without a lot of consideration. Let's get out of Sol system. Let the big brains have a crack at the new info, and see what they think is the right strategy."

Bobbie took in a long slow breath and let it out through her teeth. "How long before dust-off? *If* we run?"

"We've got some time."

"All right," she said. "I'll think about it."

"Good," he said, and stood up, ready to give her the room. "Alex?"

"Yeah, Gunny?"

"Don't take this wrong."

"All right?"

"If you really believe we can't win, you should think about whether you're coming with me if I go."

Chapter Eighteen: Naomi

It wasn't the first time Naomi had found herself the new addition to a crew. Even under the best circumstances, there was an unsettled period. Anyone coming into the webwork of established relationships, enmities, and personal loyalties that was a ship's crew needed time to find or create their own place. A time of isolation in the midst of a crowd.

In that sense, her appearance on the *Bhikaji Cama* was no different from other times. In the sense that she had appeared on the ship halfway through a run without stopping at a station or transferring over from another ship, it was a little weirder. And while they'd kept her identity hidden from Laconia, the small town's worth of crew on the ship was corrosive to secrets. Even as the command staff made a point of not noticing her existence, everyone knew who she was.

Her presence was equal parts embarrassment to the Transport Union, threat to the crew, and the most interesting thing that had happened in the long weeks of transit. Pulling herself down the corridors or getting meals from the commissary, she felt the attention in the way people didn't meet her eyes and the killing effect she had on conversations.

When they reached Auberon, she would need to vanish for a while and hope that her mysterious appearance was put down to rumor and myth. *I was serving on a ship last year, and when the ship was searched, Naomi Nagata just showed up in with the crew. Stayed with us for the rest of the run.* It was implausible enough that it might pass. Or it might be a problem. Either way, she had to touch base with Saba and see what her options were. The advantage of keeping the underground firewalled was that any single accident couldn't bring down everything. The disadvantage was that she could never know what the big picture looked like. Even as one of Saba's top-tier strategists, she only knew what he asked her to know. And it was possible—likely even—that he chose to be ignorant of some operations himself.

The commissary was wide enough to seat fifty at a time, but she tried to come at off-hours when the three rotating shifts were in the middle of work or sleep cycles. The tables were bolted to the floor, but on the float, no one used them anyway. The food dispensers were old, gray machines that decanted a nutritive slurry in eight different flavors directly into recyclable bulbs. Even the worst rock hopper in the Belt was more pleasant. Someone had painted bright flowers—daisies in yellow and pink and pastel blue—on the walls to make the place seem welcoming. Oddly, the effort halfway worked. Naomi ate the yellow curry flavored gruel with her feet hooked into footholds in the wall. But afterward, there was coffee that was a thousand times better.

Three environment technicians floated in a clump on the far side of the room, talking through a problem with the water purification system. The temptation to insert herself into the conversation was huge, but she held back. Hearing normal human conversation but not being part of it was like a starving woman smelling fresh food but not able to put it on her tongue. She hadn't realized how badly she missed humans until she was among them again. And so when Emma pulled herself into the commissary, it was a relief to see her.

In the days of Naomi's internal exile, she'd learned that Emma's last name had been Pankara before she'd taken Zomorodi as a contract name with four other people. She had siblings on Europa in Sol system and Saraswati, one of the three habitable planets in Tridevi system. She'd been in private security before she joined up with the Transport Union. And she had a hookah designed to function anywhere between five gs and the float. She was also willing to talk to Naomi directly, which made her company more precious than gold. Now she pulled herself to a stop at the machines, took a bulb of something, and launched out to stop herself at Naomi's side and in her orientation.

"All well?" Naomi asked.

Emma shook a flat hand in a gesture that meant *yes and no.* "Captain Burnham won't talk to me and Chuck won't stop."

"I made things hard for you," Naomi said.

"I made things hard for myself," Emma said, cracking the seal on her food bulb. "You're just when it blew up on me."

"Fair," Naomi said. It was astounding how good it felt to speak to someone in person and without light delay. Even when the conversation was banal. Maybe especially when it was. "Chuck seems like a decent person. He's underground?"

Emma chuckled. "He's not cut out for it. He worries too much. The only reason he's not sucking down euphorics now is that he figures that no one will say anything to this political officer at the transfer station. Half of the people on the ship have something they'd rather not be looked at too close, and the other half have to work with them."

"Seems tenuous."

"Because it is," Emma said. "But we work with what we have. Besides, that's what the fight's all about, isn't it?"

"How do you figure?" Naomi asked.

Emma took a long, thick pull on the bulb, then shrugged as she swallowed. "The first ship I served on after I ditched Pinkwater, the XO had a thing for one of the mechanics. They were both babies. More hormones than blood. The company had a no-fraternization policy, but what can you do about it? The XO, she started being where the mechanic was. Started using the ship system to keep track of where people were, on shift and off. Mechanic didn't love that. Got to where they had a screaming fight in the middle of the med bay. XO started crying. Didn't come out of her cabin for two days. Good XO otherwise. Mechanic knew his job too. But both of them got fired. Rules, you know."

"That's how you see the underground?" Naomi said through a real smile. "Making the union safe for romantic drama?"

"Easy to make rules," Emma said. "Easy to make systems with a perfect logic and rigor. All you need to do is leave out the mercy, yeah? Then when you put people into it and they get chewed to nothing, it's the person's fault. Not the rules. Everything we do that's worth shit, we've done with people. Flawed, stupid, lying, rules-breaking people. Laconians making the same mistake as ever. Our rules are good, and they'd work perfectly if it were only a different species."

"You sound like someone I know," Naomi said.

"I'll die for that," Emma said. "I'll die so that people can be fuckups and still find mercy. Not why you're here?"

Naomi considered the other woman. The anger in her jaw and the pain in her voice. She wondered whether Emma had been the XO. It probably didn't matter.

"We're all here for our own reasons," Naomi said. "What they are isn't as important as the fact that we came."

"True," Emma said.

Naomi laughed, and it was a hard, bitter sound. "Anyway, I spent too much time already with people telling me they'd shoot me if I didn't do what they said. That tank's empty for this lifetime."

"May it never refill," Emma said.

A flat-faced man in a command uniform pulled himself into the commissary, glanced at them, and did a fast double take. The environmental techs looked from him to Naomi, then pushed off, shoving their spent bulbs in the recycler as they left. The officer went to the dispenser, pulled a drink of some sort—coffee, tea, maté—and left again without looking back at them. His disapproval made the air feel cooler.

"You've got what you need?" Emma asked, as if the man hadn't been there at all.

The question had more weight than the words deserved. "I'm good," Naomi said. "When we get to port, though—"

"We'll get you out safe," Emma said. "After that..."

"I know," Naomi said. After that, she was still a criminal. Still a fugitive. Still a mouse looking for a safe hole. That would come. "Saba may have something for me."

"I'll light you a candle. Meantime, if you need something, better me than Chuck, maybe," Emma said, then sucked the last of the paste out of the bulb, smacked her lips, and launched for the door. Naomi floated alone in the commissary for a few minutes more. She felt a little guilty taking a bulb of tea back to her cabin, but only a little.

The *Bhikaji Cama* was a massive ship. Three quarters of a kilometer long and wide enough to look squat in the schematics. It had been built decades earlier to ferry enough people and supplies to one of the outlying worlds that a self-sustaining colony could arrive all at once. Buildings and recyclers and soil and reactors and fuel. Everything that humanity needed to make a toehold in an unfriendly alien ecosphere except a sense of fashion and guidelines on how to woo your mechanics. The halls were a drab green with hand- and footholds that hadn't been scrubbed in a few too many weeks. The ship conserved water jealously, using passive radiators to shed heat instead of evaporative feeds, and it left the air hotter than she liked.

Her cabin was tiny. Not just smaller than her storage container had been, but smaller than some supply closets she'd had on the *Roci*. The crash couch was cheap, with gel that stank a little, and there wasn't enough room for her to stretch her arms in it. The design was called *albuepartir* back in the Belt, because if your arm drifted off the edge in your sleep, a sudden deceleration could break it. Some previous tenant had illustrated the anti-spalling cloth with a complex and violent firefight between two sets of stick figures, one with colored-in circles for heads, and the other pale and empty. Naomi strapped herself into the couch, pulled up the system and the false record Chuck had given her, and got back to work.

The ironic thing was that, with the access she had now, she could actually reach more information than with the passive feeds she'd relied on before. She tried to be careful about it, not abuse her access in a way that would raise any more red flags than were already flying. But she had requests out to the union database mirror about political officers and changes to Laconian transfer point regulation. It was the sort of thing that anyone on a ship like the *Cama* might be—and probably was—looking into. It was only her perspective on the information coming back that made it different.

Thinking that the political officer in Sol system had meant something specifically about Sol was the mistake she'd made. That they'd all made. There was also one on Auberon, and that changed the scope. Now that she knew to look for the pattern, it was there. Freighters diverted to Medina on their transits or held. Environmental audits on ships that were running close to their theoretical maximum load.

It still wasn't confirmation. Nothing so overt as that. But if there had been a massive wave of Laconian bureaucrats being quietly repositioned throughout the colony worlds—a new level of infra-structure being put in place without fanfare or warning—this was what it would look like. One political officer going to Earth was an opportunity. Two political officers being set in place in Sol and Auberon were a threat. A new Laconian mandarinate covertly set to keep eyes on the transfer points was an escalation. If Laconia continued the trend and put officers on the ships themselves, it was the end of the shell game.

She flicked through the data, looking for places where she might have been wrong. Where her interpretations could have been mistaken or where another interpretation could have fit the same data. She was reaching for hope the way a patient might by holding a doctor's hand and saying, *But it might not be terminal, right?*

Emma accepted her connection almost as soon as she requested it.

"I need to send a message," Naomi said.

"Where to?" Emma asked over the gabble of other voices.

"Upstairs," Naomi said. "Do you want me to say the name?"

Emma was silent for a moment. Then, "Can you find your way to ops?"

"I'll meet you there," Naomi said, and dropped the call.

She moved through the ship faster when her mind was on something else. As if her body, freed from thinking about her place in the rhythms of the ship, found them automatically. She composed the message as the decks passed by her, what she could say to make the situation clear to Saba but obscure to anyone intercepting the tightbeam either here or at the repeaters that bridged the interference through the gates.

She heard Emma's voice before she reached the ops deck. Her tone was high and rough as a decking saw. Naomi pulled herself onto the deck and grabbed a handhold to stop. Emma was on the float by the comms station, her arms folded and her jaw jutting out. A man with a salt-and-pepper beard longer than his close-cropped hair looked away from her long enough to recognize Naomi, then back at Emma in disgust. His uniform identified him as Captain Burnham. The comms tech was between them like a mouse at a catfight.

"The answer was no before," Burnham said, then pointed toward Naomi with his chin. "Now that *this* one is on my deck, the answer's go fuck yourself."

"It's nothing," Emma said. "Five-minute tightbeam to Medina? No one would even blink at it. It's trivial."

"It's already too much." He turned to look at Naomi. "Don't say anything, you. I know who you are, and I know what you are, and I have extended my unrequested hospitality to you out of grandmotherly fucking kindness."

"You have as much to hide as she does," Emma said. "Everyone knows about the sealed cabins."

The comms tech pulled himself down into the gel of his crash couch like he could disappear into it. Naomi considered the captain of the *Bhikaji Cama* with all the calm and dignity she could manage. "I appreciate that my presence puts you and yours at greater risk. I wouldn't have chosen this if there were a better way, but there isn't. If things had gone the way I hoped, you'd never have known I was here. That's not the way it happened, though. And now I need five minutes with your tightbeam."

Burnham lifted his hands to her, palms out. *Stop.* "Ma'am, I am not a partisan, but I know a lot of my crew are. I'm the kind of man that kens when to shut up and mind my own business. I'm not turning you over to the political officer, but don't mistake that for loyalty. I'm trying to get my ass out of a crack, and I'm getting more and more convinced that locking you in a cabin and welding the door shut might be an easier path than the one I've chosen."

"It's important," Naomi said.

"It's my ship. The answer is no." His eyes were hard, but it was as much fear as anger. Naomi waited a moment, seeing what her gut said. Push or back down. Emma sighed, and the captain's beard shifted as his jaw went tighter.

"I understand," Naomi said. She met Emma's eyes for a fraction of a second, and then they moved to the bulkhead together. Emma fumed silently until they made the turn into the lift shaft.

"Sorry about that," Emma said. "He's an asshole."

"I did stow away on his ship and put him at risk of a Laconian interrogation room," Naomi said. "Expecting him to take orders from me along with it might be too much to ask. I'll find another way."

"I can help unbox some of those communication torpedoes," Emma said. Her tone made it an apology.

"I'd rather find another way to use the tightbeam. Time may be important. But Emma, you have to be more careful."

"He's not going to fold," Emma said. "I've shipped with that man long enough to tell when he's at his edge. There's a thing he does with his lips. I can clean him out playing poker too."

"That's not what I mean," Naomi said. "You said five minutes talking to Medina."

"They were going to know where the message was going anyway," Emma said. "They had to."

"I didn't know Saba was on Medina Station, and I do now," Naomi said. "Now if they catch me, it compromises him."

Emma pressed her lips tight. "Sorry. I assumed that...Sorry."

"We'll tell him. I'm sure he has plans to shift locations if he needs to."

Emma nodded, then muttered *fuck* under her breath. Even as she thought about other ways to get comm access, Naomi spared a moment to feel sympathy for her.

Emma's hand terminal sounded at the same moment that hers did. Another chime sounded from down a corridor. A ship-wide alert. Or something bigger. Naomi thumbed the notification open.

ALL UNION SHIPS: TOP PRIORITY. ALL TRAFFIC THROUGH ALL GATES IS SUSPENDED BY ORDER OF LACONIAN MILITARY COMMAND. NO SHIPS PERMITTED THROUGH ANY GATE UNTIL FURTHER NOTICE. ALL TRANSITS ARE ON HOLD. ALL SHIPS ON APPROACH ARE TO EVACUATE THE LANE TO .8 AU IMMEDIATELY.

Emma was moving through data fast, flipping from one interface to another, and so intent on her hand terminal that she didn't notice she was drifting. Naomi caught her elbow and pulled her to the wall.

"What happened?" Naomi asked.

"Don't know," Emma said, shaking her head. "Something big."

Chapter Nineteen: Elvi

The hard burn out of Tecoma system without sedation was a slice of hell. The crash couch felt close as a coffin around her. The breathable support fluid was thick in her throat. She tried to tell herself that it was like being in a dream where she could never drown, but every few minutes, she felt an animal panic in the back of her head. Throughout most of human evolutionary history, the watery inside-a-pipe-with-no-way-out view she had would have been the last thing someone saw before they died in pain. It was hard to convince her hindbrain that this time was different.

The monitor, weirdly, was crisper and easier to see than normal. Something about how the fluid did or didn't scatter light. Or evidence that she needed to look into vision correction, she didn't know which. But she could track the ship's progress on its mad dash for the ring and the data still streaming in from the probes. The fizz of miraculous protons kept coming into the system, and the spin of the Tecoma star and the magnetic fields it generated were pulling some of the new matter into a glowing accretion disk. It was almost beautiful except for the part where it could collapse into a black hole and generate the gamma ray burst that killed them as fast as a neuron could fire.

With the adjustable buoyancy in the tank, she felt the burn less as being pressed down and more as being squeezed in a massive and invisible fist. Red flight information data kept her aware of how tenuous her position was. Surviving a sustained thirty-g burn in a conventional crash couch would have been about as likely as living through a free fall drop from orbit onto a pile of knives.

When they hit the midpoint of the flight, the *Falcon* kicked off its drive, flipped the ship, and started its deceleration in less than a minute. All Elvi experienced was a moment's vertigo and a bloom of black spots in her vision that cleared away again quickly. The animal panic rose in her again, and she fought to keep it back.

I AM NOT LOVING THIS EXPERIENCE, she sent to Fayez. She hated that she couldn't say it or hear his voice.

A moment later, a message came back. I KNOW. I CAN'T DECIDE IF I'M PANICKED OR BORED. V. CONFUSING. BEEN READING THE SAFETY GUIDELINES. TURNS OUT MALES ARE SPECIFICALLY DIS-COURAGED FROM MASTURBATING IN THE GEL WHILE UNDER BURN. WONDER WHAT THAT TEST PROTOCOL LOOKED LIKE.

The fluid made it hard to laugh. Her husband might not have been a good match for anyone but her. But for her, he was perfect.

Hours later, they passed through the ring gate into what everyone still called the slow zone. The *Falcon* jounced as maneuvering thrusters took them off the mathematical line defined by the gate and the star. Under perfect circumstances, the couch would have cycled through three sets of progressively thinner fluid before it finally drained, but Elvi was done. She selected IMMEDIATE RELEASE from the system menu, approved the override, and heard the deep chunk-chunk-chunk of the pump as it drew the fluid away and injected oxygen-rich air in its place. She might choke and cough and feel like she was getting over bronchitis for a few hours, but she genuinely didn't care.

Admiral Sagale hadn't either, because the first thing she heard when her crash couch popped its seals and slid open was his phlegmy voice.

"—for immediate evacuation. We have data that the high consul specifically mandated."

Elvi pulled herself up. Her muscles ached like someone had beaten her with a hammer. She floated to the bridge. Stopping herself on a handhold felt like it was going to bend the joints in her hand the wrong way. Sagale's couch was in its open configuration, but a film of fluid still clung to his hair and arm. The smell of it was too complex for her mind. Her brain kept reaching for comparisons and then abandoning them—grape jelly, cinnamon, acetate, nutmeg—over and over. Behind her, Fayez groaned. Sagale looked over at them, scowling.

"You shouldn't be out of your couch, Major Okoye," he said, and before she could respond, the comm channel did.

"Your request is noted," a familiar voice said. Elvi knew she should recognize it. The sustained high gs might have compromised her more than she'd thought. "I'll do what I can."

"Governor Song," Sagale said. "The *Falcon* is on a scientific mission critical to the empire. If we busted our asses to get here so we can die waiting in line—"

The penny dropped for Elvi. Jae-Eun Song. Governor of Medina Station. She'd heard of the woman often, though they had never met.

"Admiral Sagale," the woman said. It was strange to be close enough to another ship that the light delay made interrupting him possible. "I had no warning about this. I had sixty-four ships in the zone, including Medina Station and the *Typhoon*. I've gotten it down to twenty-eight, even with you screaming through my gate and screwing up my queue. You can give my team a minute to run the numbers."

Sagale's expression landed somewhere between annoyance and rage, but his voice was professional. "Understood, Governor. Didn't mean to step on your toes." He turned off his microphone with a gesture like a punch.

"What's—" Elvi said, then braced herself and coughed up a thick wad of breathable fluid. Fayez appeared at her side with a towel. She spat into it. "What's going on?"

Sagale put a volumetric display on the main monitor. The alien station hung exactly in the center of 1,373 gates evenly distributed around the surface of a sphere that had nothing outside it. Icons marked the repurposed generation ship that was the oldest station in the space between worlds and the *Magnetar*-class Laconian warship that was the newest. Along with them, a scattering of ships in a space barely smaller than the Earth's sun. If the icons had been to scale, they'd have been less than motes of dust. Fewer than a hundred bubbles of air in a space the volume of a million Earths.

"Governor Song is trying to evacuate the ring space per my recommendation," Sagale said. "She is also trying to move Medina Station further out of harm's way in case a gamma burst does come through Tecoma gate. But preparing the station is proving difficult, as it means stopping the spin drum and turning on drives that haven't been used in several decades. In that context, I have asked for a priority transit to Laconia."

"And?" Fayez asked.

"And her team is crunching the numbers," Sagale said, biting each word off individually. He was scared. He was right to be. She was too.

"Where's Jen?" she asked. There was a sharp pain in her chest. More fluid coming loose.

"The others are sedated," Sagale said. "There was no reason to keep them awake."

"She could have monitored the data coming in from Tecoma," Fayez said. "I mean, I can look at it, but Jen's the one that understands."

"I'd rather focus on keeping her alive so she can make sense of it later," Sagale said.

"It's going to hit the station, isn't it?" Elvi said. "The star, the gate, and that alien station that runs the ring space. They're all in a line."

"Yes," Sagale said.

Fayez raised a hand over his head like a kid in a classroom. "Um. Point of clarification? Do we really want to make a transit right before that happens? Because if I recall correctly, the whole reason that we have a *Magnetar*-class ship here at all is because hitting that little ball there with a massive energy burst makes an exponentially larger plume of gamma radiation pop out of all the gates."

"We have been able to use that effect to guard all the gates simultaneously, yes," Sagale said. "The cannons-on-the-cliffs strategy."

"And don't we want to be on this side of those cannons when they go off?" Fayez was talking too fast. Elvi took his hand, squeezing his fingers, hoping it would calm him. "I'm just asking, because the thing where we rush through to safety just in time to get cooked by the aftermath seems unpleasant."

"It's a calculated risk," Sagale said. "We aren't certain that the station will survive the blast. Or what will happen if it doesn't."

She watched new vistas of catastrophe unfold in her husband's eyes. The station might break. The slow zone might collapse. It had been unthinkable right up to the moment he thought it.

"Okay, yeah," Fayez said. "That's a fair point."

Governor Song's voice came over the comm channel. "Admiral Sagale?"

"Yes?" Sagale said, then remembered he'd turned off the mic. He enabled it again. "Yes, Governor. I'm here."

"We have slotted the *Falcon* for priority transit through Laconia gate. I am sending you the traffic control data now. Do not rush your transit. We're cutting it as close to the limit as we can here. I don't want anyone going dutchman."

Sagale's head came back a degree, as if the thought had surprised him. His voice when he spoke was clear. "Understood. Thank you for this, Jae-Eun."

"If we live through this, you owe me a drink," the governor of Medina Station said. "The ship ahead of you is the *Plain of Jordan* through Castila gate. Please monitor that and match to your plan. Godspeed, Mehmet."

Sagale turned his attention to the controls, and a moment later the gravity warning sounded. Not that anyone else on the ship would hear it. Elvi had to fight the urge to shout the emergency evacuation command and let all the other ships figure out how to be safe about it.

"How long do we have?" Elvi asked, and then laughed. It sounded like she was asking how long they had to live, and since she kind of was, it seemed funny. Sagale didn't join in.

"We're going to be at a quarter g for a while if you want to stretch your legs," he said. "Then you have to be back in the couch. Once we make the transit, I'm making a hard turn and burning perpendicular to the ring to get us away from it."

"In case of overspill," Fayez said.

"From an abundance of caution," Sagale said. He passed the back of his hand over his eyes, and Elvi realized that for all his stoic reserve, he was weeping. The drive kicked on, and she drifted to the deck. Fayez put a hand on her shoulder and drew her away.

"This is bad," he said softly.

"I know."

He nodded. "I just felt like I needed to say it out loud."

She took his hand and kissed it. It still smelled like breathable fluid. "If this is all we get...Well, then shit."

"With you on that one, sweetheart," he said, and folded his arms around her. "This whole thing really was a terrible idea, wasn't it?"

"Couldn't have seen it coming," she said. "I mean, unless..."

Something moved in the back of her head. Something about

the *Magnetar*-class ships and the way the *Heart of the Tempest* had annihilated the rail guns on the alien station during Laconia's first incursion. The way it had killed Pallas Station. The way the enemy had reacted differently.

"You're thinking something," Fayez said. "I can hear the gears turning."

"I don't know what yet," she said. "But yeah. I am."

A new voice came from the bridge. The comm channel still open on Sagale's controls. *This is* Plain of Jordan *confirming transit in two minutes. We are go, no-go in ten seconds.*

Another voice answered. *Medina control here. You are go for transit.* Sagale was muttering something under his breath. It might have been profanity. It might have been prayer. The volumetric display showed a single red dot in the vastness moving toward the pinpoint white of a gate.

"We better get back in our cans," Fayez said.

"Yes," Elvi said, but she didn't move. Not yet. "It was designed, right? Tecoma system was designed. To...to do this?"

Fayez smoothed a hand across her head. The fluid was dry enough now to be tacky, but the touch felt good anyway. "Elvi, you are the light of my heart. The woman I love and know better than I know anyone, and I can't get through the day without being dead wrong about what you're going to say or want. The protomolecule engineers were some kind of quantum-entangled high-energy physics hive mind thing. I don't know what they were thinking."

"No," Elvi said, shuffling back toward her couch in the gentle quarter g. "It was designed. There was an *intention*."

"Does that help us?" he asked. "Because that would be great, but I don't know that I see how that helps us."

This is the Plain of Jordan *transferring our status now. We are on approach to—*

The display stuttered and threw up an error readout. The lights went out and the gravity dropped away.

"Brace!" Sagale called out from the blackness.

Elvi reached out in the blackness, trying to find a wall and a handhold. "What happened?"

An emergency light stuttered on. "Sensor arrays overloaded," Sagale said. His voice was shaking. "They're resetting now. I have to get us stopped until we can..."

He didn't finish the thought. The handhold buzzed gently with the vibration of maneuvering thrusters, and the *Falcon* swung up around her, lifting her feet off the deck. Fayez helped her reorient as the gravity alert sounded again and up and down returned. The volumetric display came back up with a warning at the edge that said NO INPUT—ESTIMATED POSITIONS ONLY. Sagale gunned the drive for a few seconds, and the *Falcon* felt like an elevator lurching toward some upper floor. Then he killed it and Elvi drifted up again.

The three of them were silent for a long moment while the backup sensor arrays lurched to life. The comms clicked once, rattled with strange, fluting static, and filled with the gabble of panicked human voices. Sagale killed the channel and opened a private one.

"Medina Station, this is Admiral Sagale of the *Falcon*. Please report status."

Elvi pulled herself to Travon's station. She didn't know if it took the ship a fraction of a second longer than usual to recognize her and put her data on the monitor, or if it was just the adrenaline throwing her perceptions off. The main sensor arrays were dead. Burned out in a fraction of a second. Backup systems slowly hauled themselves to life. Cameras and telescopes all around the *Falcon* unpacked themselves from hardened compartments and deployed. More of them were damaged than she'd expected. But not all. She opened a window and fed the data from the *Falcon*'s skin to her screen, and in the darkness, there was light.

"This is Governor Song, *Falcon*," the woman's voice came, trembling like a violin. "We have sustained some damage to the ship and crew. We are still assessing."

The space between the rings was filled with whiteness. The station at the center—the alien control station that seemed to carry the rings with it like the center of a dandelion surrounded by seeds—was brighter than a sun. And some nebula-thin gas or dust cloud caught that light and shimmered. It was everywhere. It was beautiful. It was terrifying.

"It's going to be all right, Governor," Sagale said in a tone that almost made it plausible. "I need to know the status of the *Plain of Jordan*. Did it make transit?"

"Mehmet, I don't—"

"It's important. Did the ship make it through?"

Since the first time she'd seen it—the first time anyone had seen it—the boundary of the ring space had been a dark and featureless sphere, like a black bubble seen from inside. Now there was a twisting rainbow of energy or matter on it, like an oil slick on water. The darkness of it had always let Elvi imagine it to be infinite before. A vast and starless sky. Now it felt close and finite. It made everything seem more fragile. A wave of nausea passed across the edge of her awareness like it belonged to some other body.

"No," Governor Song said. "They were too close to the gate to shift back when the blast came. The energy through Tecoma gate would have... They didn't make the transit."

"Please confirm, Medina. You're saying the *Plain of Jordan* went dutchman."

"Yes. We lost them."

"Thank you, Medina. Please advise traffic control that all transits are suspended until further orders. No one comes into this space, and no one goes out. Not until I say so."

To her left, Fayez was at Jen's station, seeing—she assumed—all the same things. Feeling some version of the awe and terror and wonder that she felt.

"Understood," Governor Song said. "I'll see to it."

"Thank you, Jae-Eun," Sagale said. "We have some work to do. We'll need reports from the other systems. I'm guessing that there's been some damage from the far sides of the gates too. It may take some time to—"

"Gates moved," Fayez said in the same tone he used for trivial information. Laundry's dry. Dinner's ready. Gates moved.

"What?" Sagale said.

"Yeah," Fayez said. "Not much, but a little. And all of them. Look for yourself."

Sagale shifted the main screen. The slow zone bloomed. And with it corrections on each of the gates. The ships were all in place, all matching their expected vectors and positions. But a little yellow error code hung at the gates to show where they were expected to be, and where they were instead. Sagale's face was ashen. Elvi felt herself wondering how many more shocks the man could take. Or, for that matter, many how many she could.

"Yeah, so," Fayez said. "Pretty sure I see what's going on. They just reordered. Because there's not as many of them now. Equal distance between them got a little bigger. Tecoma gate's gone. And...Oh yeah. Look at that. Thanjavur gate was pretty much straight across from it. And it's gone too. We just lost two gates, Admiral. And one of them had an entire world filled with people behind it."

Chapter Twenty: Teresa

The science exposition was held in one of the public halls and on the grounds outside it. The vaulted ceiling gave the hall a sense of something that had been grown more than built, and the acoustic controls kept what could have been an overwhelming din of voices and noise calm and reassuring. A thousand children from five years old to sixteen ran and talked and made groups, associating for the most part with people they already knew and who attended the same schools they'd come from.

The open schools all had their own stations in the hall, each one showing what the students had been studying in the last year and how it would add to the overall work of the empire. Some, like the water cycle demonstration, were basic, meant for the youngest children. Others, like the forest of life that compared the different ecosystems of the new worlds, and the programmable matter station that showcased the most recent materials science from Bara Gaon, were sophisticated enough to be interesting for her.

And Connor was there.

As the days passed, she found the sting of remembering Connor and Muriel being involved with each other grew a little less raw for her. Not painless. The image of them kissing—which she had very clearly in her mind for something she'd never actually seen—still bothered her. So when Connor nodded to her when she walked by and tried a little smile, she didn't know what to make of it. Did he still like her? Was he trying to tell her that his connection with Muriel had been a mistake, or that he was glad that he and Teresa were still friends? She wasn't sure which option she was hoping for. Or if she was hoping for any of them. Connor was confusing. Muriel and the others from her school had a booth about soil science and how to design microbes that could pass nutrients between organisms from different biomes, and Teresa was technically supposed to be with them. She didn't want to be there. And really, she could go wherever she wanted. It wasn't like someone was going to tell her she couldn't.

Instead, she went to the puzzle station where younger children worked with blocks trying to re-create shapes or argued over how to fit circles into a square or build a complex structure with only gravity and friction to hold it together. She'd done all the puzzles a thousand times over when she was younger. She moved through, giving encouragement and hints to the frustrated, and wondered if Connor would follow her there.

A young girl—maybe six years old—sat at one of the tables by herself, scowling. Teresa sat across from her because she could see the place where Connor would be from there.

The girl looked up at Teresa and seemed to gather herself. When she spoke, it was with the stilted formality of someone who had been coached in what to say and how to say it.

"Hello. My name is Elsa Singh. I'm pleased to meet you."

"I'm Teresa Duarte," Teresa said.

"Are you a teacher?" Elsa asked.

"No, I live here."

"No one will play with me," Elsa said, scowling at her.

"I could teach you something, if you want."

"All right," Elsa said, and seemed to settle deeper into her little wooden chair. Teresa glanced over toward the school display. Muriel and Connor were talking, but Muriel was doing most of it, her lips moving fast like she was fighting to keep his attention. To her surprise, she felt a little pang of sympathy for the girl. If Connor had convinced Muriel to alienate Teresa Duarte, daughter of the high consul and maybe someday ruler of the Laconian Empire, and then gone cold on her? That would be a shitty thing to do. Effective too, because the pang passed as quickly as it had come. Muriel could deal with her mistakes on her own.

"All right, Elsa," she said, refocusing. She pulled up her handheld. "This is called the prisoner's dilemma. Look at this…"

Teresa built a table like the one Ilich had built with her, explained the rules—each player would decide to cooperate or defect, and they'd each be better off if they defected, but it would be better in the long term to cooperate. Elsa seemed only mildly interested, but willing to follow along.

Connor started moving away from his group just as a new bunch of presenters arrived, washing through the hall with delight and gabbling. He seemed to disappear behind the flood, but she caught a glimpse of his brown hair. She thought he was coming toward her. Her heart started beating a little faster. She wasn't sure she was more worried that he would find her or that he wouldn't.

She played the game with the little girl, pretending to care about it more deeply than the stream of humanity over Elsa's shoulder. They both cooperated for a few rounds, and then, when Teresa felt like it was time for the rest of the tit-for-tat lesson, she defected. Elsa looked at the handheld with the results as if it didn't make sense.

"Now," Teresa said. "The thing is, once someone defects like that, you have to decide what—"

"You cheated!" The little girl's voice was more than just loud. It was a shriek of rage. Her face was twisted in a vicious scowl and dark with blood just under the skin. "You said we should be *nice!*"

"No," Teresa said. "It's part of the lesson…"

"Fuck your *fucking* lesson," Elsa said. Out of a child that young, the profanity was like a slap. Elsa grabbed the handheld and threw it into the crowd, standing up so fast her chair toppled, clattering on the ground. Before Teresa could do anything, Elsa collapsed and started weeping on the floor.

Security personnel were already moving through the crowd toward them, but Teresa waved them off. She felt trapped between wanting to comfort Elsa or get her handheld back or leave in humiliation and shame. Elsa's mouth was square and gaping as her sobs turned into screams again. Someone nearby shouted, *Monster!* and Teresa thought for a second they meant her. Then the woman was there. Older, with eyes the same shape as Elsa's, the same skin tone. Elsa's mother scooped the girl up in her arms, rocking her.

"It's okay, Monster," the mother said, and hushed her gently. "It's all right. Mama's here. I'm right here. It's okay."

Elsa clamped her hands over her ears, closed her eyes, and buried her head in her mother's embrace. The mother rocked her, gently making cooing sounds to soothe her. Teresa took a step forward.

"I'm so sorry," the mother said. "Elsa gets overstimulated. It won't happen again."

"No," Teresa said. "It was my fault. She's fine. It was me. I didn't explain the game well enough."

The mother smiled and turned her attention back to Elsa. Teresa waited for the mother to start asking questions of the little girl. *What just happened?* and *What mistake did you make?* and *What would you do differently next time?* All the things her father would have asked her to make the moment meaningful. But Elsa's mother did none of that. She only calmed her daughter and told her that everything would be all right. That she was loved. Teresa watched with a sensation she couldn't quite recognize.

She didn't notice Colonel Ilich coming up to her until he touched her shoulder.

"I'm sorry to interrupt," he said. "Your father is asking to see you. Now, if you can."

"Of course," she said, and followed, only pausing to retrieve her handheld.

Her father's private office was small. A small desk with a monitor built into the surface that could display flat on the surface or volumetrically over it. As she came in, it was showing a schematic of the slow zone—the gates, the alien station at their center, Medina Station, and a few dozen ships scattered through 750 trillion cubic kilometers. A space smaller than the interior of a star. Her father was still as stone, looking at it. It was like he didn't need to breathe anymore. "Is everything okay?" she asked.

"What do you remember about the experiment in Tecoma system?"

Teresa sat on the little couch, folding her legs up under her. She tried to recall everything she could of the science briefings she'd been in, but all she could think of was the crying little girl and her mother.

"It's where we were doing the first tit-for-tat experiment," she finally said. "To see if the enemy can be negotiated with." It seemed ominous that she'd just been reviewing the prisoner's dilemma, and that it had gone badly.

"To see if we can make it change its behavior, yes," her father said, then gave a small, rueful chuckle. "There's good news and bad there." He gestured at his monitor, throwing a report to her handheld. "Look this over. Tell me what you make of it."

Teresa opened the report like it was a test from Colonel Ilich. Her father watched her while she read through it, looked at the datasets, tried to make it all make sense. She tried not to read Admiral Sagale's summary at the end, because that felt like cheating. She should be able to draw the conclusions herself.

Then she reached a part of the report that she had to read three times to be sure she'd understood. She felt the blood draining from her face.

"It collapsed into...it collapsed into a black hole? They collapsed the neutron star into a *black hole*?"

"We believe so," her father said. "It was precariously balanced, and apparently maintained at that balance point in a way we don't understand. When more mass was added to the star, it was enough to push it over." He put a hand over the report and looked into her eyes. "Dr. Okoye and her team saw that there was a danger from that. Do you know what it was?"

"The gamma burst," Teresa said. "It's the most energetic event that there is. We've seen gamma bursts from other *galaxies*."

"That's correct," he said, but she couldn't get her mind around it. "And what do you remember about Tecoma system?"

She drew a blank. She should have known. Should have remembered.

"The star's rotation put the poles in line with the gate," he said, gently. "No other system we've ever seen has been like that."

"What happened?" Teresa asked. He took his hand away, letting her read the rest of the report. "We lost two gates?"

"We did," her father said as if it were a normal thing. "And we saw plumes of gamma radiation coming out on the solar system side of every other ring gate, much the way they did when the *Tempest* hit the alien station in the ring hub with its magnetic field generator. And..."

It was like hearing that sometimes you woke up in the morning and didn't have a color anymore. That red could die. Or that three could be shot off the number line. Learning that a gate could be destroyed was like learning that a rule of her universe so basic that she'd never even thought of it as a rule had been violated. If he'd said *You actually have two bodies* or *Sometimes you can walk through walls* or *You can also breathe rock*, it wouldn't have felt stranger. More displacing.

He raised his eyebrows. What else? She looked at the report.

She felt like she was shaking, but her hands looked steady. It only took her a few seconds.

"And the *Plain of Jordan* failed its transit," she said. "We lost a ship."

"Yes," he said. "That, it turns out, is the critical issue. Here is the decision we have to make. What do we do about it?"

Teresa shook her head, not disagreeing but reaching for some kind of clarity. The scale of the damage was overwhelming. Her father leaned back in his chair, steepling his fingers.

"This is a policy decision. And policy decisions are difficult," he said, "because there may not be a right answer. Put yourself in my place. Think about the larger picture. Not just now, not just here, but everywhere that humanity is going to spread. And forever. What is the wise course of action for me now?"

"I don't know," she said, and her voice sounded small, even to her.

He nodded. "That's fair. Let me narrow the options. The rules of game theory are that when a ship fails to transit, we punish our opponents. That's the basis of the policy I put in place. So in light of what happened, do we follow that now, or do we stop?"

"We stop," Teresa said without hesitation. She saw the disappointment in her father's eyes, but she didn't understand it. It was the obvious answer. He took a deep breath and tapped his fingers against his lips for a moment before he said anything.

"Let me give you some context. There was an incident when you were young," he said. "This was when your mother was still with us, so you were very young. Barely able to speak. You had a favorite toy. A carved wooden horse."

"I don't remember it."

"That's all right. There was a day when you needed to nap. You were very, very tired and very cranky. Your mother was trying to feed you, the way she did before you slept, but you were chewing on your horse. Your mouth was full. So your mother took the horse away, and you threw a tantrum. In that case, we had two options. We could keep the toy away from you so that you could do what needed to be done. Or we could hand it back, and teach you that throwing tantrums worked."

The image of Elsa in her mother's arms came to her like it was being projected on her brain. Had all that been a mistake? Had Elsa's mother, by comforting her child, told her that it was okay to shout and flip over tables? It hadn't seemed like that at the time.

"You think we should . . . You're sending through a bomb ship?"

"Tit for tat," he said. "It means keeping traffic out of the ring space for a time. It means not evacuating any more ships until we can make the experiment. But we can show the enemy that we are disciplined. Or we can show it that we aren't."

"Oh," Teresa said. She didn't know what else there was to say.

Her father tilted his head. His voice was still gentle. Almost coaxing. "This is why I want you with me. These are the decisions people like you and I have to make. Normal people don't. This is the logic and the vision we have to apply. And we have to be ruthless about it. The stakes are too high for anything else."

"It's the only way we can win," she said.

"I don't know that we'll win," he said. "I've never known that. I've always known that we'd fight. From the moment the gates opened, I knew we'd go through them. That, and the chances were good that we would encounter whatever had killed the civilization that came before us."

"Goths," she said. "Goths and lead-lined water pipes."

He chuckled. "Ilich has been talking about ancient Rome again. Yes, well. We can call them Goths if you like. As soon as we knew that there was something out there, we knew that we would come in conflict with it. The war was inevitable from the second we had an opponent. I don't know whether we'll defeat them. But I know that *if* we defeat them, it will be like this. With intelligence and ruthlessness and an unwavering purpose. Those are the only tools we have that matter."

Teresa nodded. "I'm sorry," she said. "I had the wrong answer."

"I knew you might," he said. "It's why I asked you here. You will learn, over time, how to think the way I think. How to be the kind of leader that I've taught myself to be. Some of it will take effort. Some of it will happen naturally just because you get older. And some of it, I think, will happen as you...change."

"Change?"

"Transform. Become immortal. I've spoken to Dr. Cortázar about beginning the process with you. It will take time, of course, but since I began the treatments, I've learned so much. Things I couldn't know when I was just...just human, I suppose."

He took her hand. The opalescence in his eyes and skin seemed to brighten for a moment. When he spoke, there was a depth to his voice like the room had gained an echo.

"There's so much that I see now that I never saw before. You'll see it too."

Chapter Twenty-One: Elvi

Elvi could see Sagale steeling himself for her reaction. It was in the way he tightened his jaw and the flatness of his eyes. She had one foot tucked into a hold on the wall, her hand on another. She waited for the outrage or the vertigo or some physical sign in herself to match his expectations. What she found was a bleak disappointment.

When he'd called her to his office, she'd suspected it was bad news. Now that the rest of the crew had been decanted and brought up to speed, anything said on the bridge, no matter how softly, was common knowledge in minutes. Fear did that to people. Made them fast to share and gossip.

"If I object to this plan?" she said. "Because we both know I object to this plan."

"I will pass it directly to High Consul Duarte," Sagale said.

"It is as important to him as it is to me that you understand how seriously we take your concerns."

"Will it change anything?"

"Candidly?" Sagale said.

"For fuck's sake. Another bomb ship? After..." She gestured toward the deck with her free hand, meaning the ring space, the missing gates, all of it. She'd had almost three days to process the enormity of it, and she couldn't. It was too big.

Three days was long enough for Sagale to report in and for Duarte to deliberate and respond. It probably wasn't long enough for Sagale to have pushed back and been shut down. He hadn't even tried. That was the disappointing part.

"We have protocol. It is that when a ship fails to transit, send a bomb ship through the same gate. It's the only way to keep our message clear."

"And then see if we can lose another gate or two?"

"The losses that we have suffered are...significant," Sagale said. "But it is the considered opinion of the high consul that they do not represent an escalation on the part of the enemy."

"How do you even get there?"

Sagale lifted a hand, palm out, but the softening in his eyes made it a request to hear him out more than an order that she be silent. Elvi crossed her arms and nodded him on.

"The attacks the enemy made on us have been ineffective in that—*in that*—they did insignificant primary damage. The loss of consciousness that we experienced in Sol system when Pallas died might have been deadly for the protomolecule's designers, but it was largely ineffective against us. The response in Tecoma system would have been trivial in any other system. The effect was...unfortunate only because of features of the landscape, so to speak, that are not in play elsewhere in the empire."

"So I just picked a bad Bikini Atoll?" Elvi said.

"No one holds you responsible for what happened, Doctor. You couldn't have known any more than we could. If anything, the strategic error was mine. I saw the inhospitable nature of the system as an advantage and overlooked the possible consequences."

He spread his hands.

"Or," Elvi said, "it was a trap."

"I don't see how—"

"No. Be quiet. It's my turn now. What we saw in Tecoma wasn't even similar to the previous interactions. We were awake the whole time. It didn't change our perceptions of anything. That was something different. And if you look at the logic of it? It's not even hard to see."

"Walk me through it."

"That star wasn't natural, it was created. And it was created from a system that looked like Sol. It was manufactured and it was pointed at the ring gate. They *aimed* it like tying a shotgun trigger to a doorknob. Our bomb ship did something to activate it. Maybe it got something to come look at us, and that's what set it off. I don't know. But it was built to be a booby trap."

Sagale's scowl looked like he'd bitten into a bad date. "That is an interesting interpretation," he said.

"It fired off the largest gun that it's possible to make given the physical laws of the universe. And what's more? The station was built to withstand it. It took a gamma burst from a collapsing neutron star, and *it's not dead.*"

"You find that significant."

"I find that pretty clear evidence that we're way out of our weight class here and we should stop throwing punches!"

"You don't have to shout, Doctor."

Elvi unballed her fists and tried to relax her jaw. Her blood felt hot in her face, and she didn't know if it was from fear or anger or if any normal emotions actually fit into a situation like this. Sagale's system chimed an alert, and he muted it.

"I don't disagree with you," he said. "But what does not throwing punches look like?"

"Not sending bomb ships through would be a start."

"It would. But so would abandoning the gates entirely. Would you recommend doing that? There are colonies that will collapse if we choose that, and maybe those are acceptable losses. But once the trouble began last time, shutting down the gate network didn't save the beings that used it. They were dead when we turned the system back on."

"Not starting trouble was my argument."

"Trouble started long before Laconia existed. Ships have been disappearing for decades. Whatever this is, it began before we recognized it. The fastest way to undermine a strategic plan is to abandon it before there's sufficient reason to do so. The high consul has been briefed. He believes that the tit-for-tat plan still has merit."

"And so you're going to do it."

"I do as I'm told, Doctor. I am an officer of the Laconian military," Sagale said. "As are you."

The mood on the *Falcon* showed in small ways. Instead of wandering to and from the commissary while she thought, Jen remained rooted at her station. Travon moved through the ship tapping his thumb and middle finger together in a fluttering beat every time a new status update came from the *Typhoon* or Medina. Sagale stayed in his office for the most part, avoiding Elvi and Fayez and the rest of the science team as if their disapproval bothered him.

Out near Medina, a captain drew a short straw, and the *Myron's Folly* was chosen as the bomb vessel. On the main screen, a swarm of loading mechs and drones hauled the cargo out of its hold. The little flares of their thrusters reminded Elvi of termite swarms.

The antimatter had been stored on Medina for a moment just like this. Governor Song's engineers would set the ship's reactor as close to critical as they could and disable the fail-safes, so that when the bombs went off, the reactor failure would add its own destructive punch to the mix. But there was the problem of making the ship go dutchman in the absence of other traffic.

The safety curve was based on the amount of matter and energy making transits though the gate network. Usually that meant keeping the flow down to safe levels. Now it meant driving it up past the threshold without sending another ship through. Protocol demanded, Sagale kept pointing out, that the bomb ship be the next thing to go. If they started pushing a dozen other ships through, the enemy might not understand the high consul's point.

To do that, they had to pour a massive amount of energy through the gate. The *Typhoon*'s ultrahigh magnetic field projector could do it, but they were making sure there was nothing that would be damaged on the far side of the gate. The combination of caution and recklessness took her breath away.

"I should go talk to him again," Elvi said.

"Tell him that he's wrong more forcefully?" Fayez said. "See if he changes his mind because you disagree at him harder?"

"He's not that bad," she said. And then, because she knew that he was, "There has to be something."

"There doesn't, sweetheart."

Jen looked up from her station monitor. Her lips were thin, her gaze restless. "Eighty thousand people in Thanjavur system," she said. "One habitable planet with three cities, and a moon base on its major satellite. And they're…I just can't get my head around it. They're just gone."

"They might be fine," Elvi said. "Just…out of contact. They may be better off than all of us at this rate."

"Unless their sun exploded. There are stories about that, aren't there? The protomolecule engineers burning whole systems?"

Travon fluttered his finger and thumb together again as he worked his station's monitor. "Thanjavur's only eight and a half light-years from Gedara. If there's a big flash in eight and a half years, we'll know what happened."

"I don't like this," Jen said.

"None of us do," Fayez said. "Honestly, I think old Sagale would skip this part if he could."

"What?" Jen said. "No, not that. I mean yes, I don't like that. But this too."

She threw a dataset Elvi didn't recognize onto the main monitor. The *Myron's Folly* blinked away and a series of energy graphs took its place. Jen turned to look at them as if the significance were obvious.

"I'm a biologist," Elvi said.

"We're seeing radiation coming from in between the rings. We've never seen that before. There hasn't been anything there to radiate. This little pocket universe just ends at the rings. Anything that went out was gone like it passed an event horizon. Now, since... well, since us? Something's coming through."

"Something's knocking around in the attic," Fayez said. "That's not reassuring. I'm not reassured."

"What do you make of it?" Elvi asked.

"I don't know. I just have data, and it says something's happening that didn't happen before. And it's not calming down."

A voice in her memory said the words as clearly and distinctly as if they had been spoken: *Distributed responsibility is the problem. One person gives the order, another carries it out. One can say they didn't pull the trigger, the other that they were just doing what they were told, and everyone lets themselves off the hook.* She let her breath out slowly from between her teeth.

Elvi opened a connection request to Sagale's office. To his credit, he accepted it immediately. "Dr. Okoye."

"Admiral, could you join us on the bridge? There's some incoming data I'd like you to look at."

She heard the hesitation while he decided whether it was a ploy to stop the bomb ship plan. Just because the data was real didn't mean it wasn't a ploy.

"I'm on my way," Sagale said, and cut the connection.

"We could always mutiny," Fayez said brightly.

"We wouldn't stand a chance," Travon said. "I did the nav analysis. Even if we took control of the ship, the *Typhoon* could blow us to dust before we got out a gate."

"*Jesus*, Travon," Fayez said. "I was joking."

"Oh," Travon said. "Sorry."

"I remember when I was just a scientist," Elvi said. "I liked that. It was nice."

Five minutes later Sagale came on the bridge, floating toward his station like none of them were there. Elvi remembered seeing him in the same place, still damp from the crash couch and weeping. He was a different man now. For a moment, against her will, she admired him. Sagale considered the display in silence. The loudest sounds were the hush of the air recyclers and the flutter of Travon's right thumb and middle finger.

He considered the energy graphs as Jen explained them again. Sagale took it in impassively. When Jen had finished, he floated quietly in his crash couch restraints. His gaze flickered to Elvi's, and she thought there was something in them. Gratitude, maybe.

With a gesture, he opened a comm channel.

"Admiral Sagale," Governor Song's voice came. "How can I help you?" It had a hint of Mariner Valley drawl. Elvi wondered if it was the mark of a Martian working for Laconia or a Laconian who'd carried her accent out into the alien worlds and back again. Whether this obedience was peculiar to Duarte's people or if it had been part of the Martian character all along.

"My eggheads came up with an analysis I'd like your eggheads to take a peek at, Governor. It may be nothing, but I'd recommend we hold action on the bomb ship until we know what we're looking at."

There was a long pause. "You have my curiosity, Admiral. Send over what you have."

"Thank you," Sagale said, and the governor cut the connection. "Share that with the *Typhoon* and Medina, Dr. Lively. Let's see if they share your concerns."

"Yes, sir," Jen said, and started packaging her information like she'd been given an extra five minutes on her final exams.

Fayez touched Elvi's shoulder and said, almost too softly to hear, "Do you think we just got away with—"

The universe exploded.

If it had been a sound, it would have been deafening. Elvi put her hands over her ears just the same. A reflex. An approximation. Jen was screaming. Elvi tried to sink to the deck, but only managed to pull her legs up so that she was floating in a fetal position. The curve of the handhold before her was ornate and beautiful. The smudge of darkness where the oil from the crew's skin hadn't been cleaned away was like a map of a vast coastline, fractal and complex. She was aware of Fayez beside her, of the waves of pressure passing between them, touching, and reflecting away as they both screamed. The air was a fog of atoms. Sagale was a cloud of atoms. She was a cloud.

You've been here, she thought. *You've been here before. Don't get distracted by it. Don't lose yourself.*

The cloud that was her hand, vibrations in emptiness, slipped through the void and clatter to the cloud that was the handhold. Fields of energy between her atoms and the bulkhead's atoms turned into a dance of pressure, and the surge sent lightning up her arm, so complicated it was hard to keep track of. She was aware that she felt it, but there was so much happening it was hard to keep the sensation in mind.

Elvi found that she could see right through the suddenly vaporous ship, and right through the other ship clouds around it. Medina was a vast but wispy thunderhead at the center of them all.

Something was moving through the clouds, dark and sinuous as a dancer slipping between raindrops. And then another. And then more. They were everywhere, sliding through the gas and liquid and solid, scattering the clouds with their passage. They were solid. Real in a way the clouds of matter were not. They were more real than anything she'd ever seen. Tendrils of darkness that had never known light. That *could* never know light. *You've seen this absence of light before. A darkness like the eye of an angry god... You said that to someone.*

One darted and swirled, off to her left if left meant anything now. It furled like a question mark, and the pattern of atoms and vibrations swirled around it and into it. The beauty of it, the grace, were hard to look away from. Clouds mixed and swirled together in its wake, colors so pure they were only colors. It took effort to recognize they were blood.

She'd been here before. It had been overwhelming the first time. It was overwhelming again now, but at least she knew what it was. That made holding her mind together possible. At least for a moment.

You're doing great, kid. You're doing great. You can do this. Just a little more. But do it now...

She tried to remember what her throat was. Tried to imagine that the dots of matter and emptiness had said words before. That they still could. They were her body, the air she breathed. She tried to make it all work together long enough to scream.

Emergency evacuation. Major Okoye authorization delta-eight. A tendril of darkness darted toward her...

...and dropped away. All of them slid away, falling like black snowflakes through the cloud of vibrations that was the deck. Everything swirled, one form folding into another. If she unfocused her eyes, she could just recognize them. Jen's body, rolling as maneuvering thrusters made the deck into a hillside. Someone's arm from fingers to elbow, and even a few centimeters of flesh beyond. The glow of the main display, too much itself to hold any meaning beyond the simple elegance of photons caught in air. She was aware of her own pain like it was the sound of a distant water-fall. She fell through it and into something like sleep.

And a blink later, she was back. Thrust that could have been a third of a g or five gs pulled her down. When she forced herself to sit up, blood glued her cheek to the deck. The air stank, but with too many different volatiles to make sense of. Alarms were sounding, echoing off each other in a meaningless cacophony. Everything had gone wrong at once. She hauled herself up to standing.

The bridge was a thing from a nightmare. Swaths of the bulkheads, decks, equipment were gone. Like an artist had come in with an eraser and taken away bits of it at random. And the others too.

Sagale was still at his post, a long loop of his head and right shoulder simply vanished. Jen lay in a still pile where the deck met the wall, covered in blood that might have been her own. Travon's arm lay beside his station, but where his crash couch had been, there was a soft-edged hole down to the next deck and the one below that. It was like seeing a coral reef made from her ship and her friends and—

"Fayez!" she screamed. "Fayez!"

"Here," his voice said behind her. "I'm here. I'm okay."

He was in two-thirds of a crash couch. The fluid in the reservoir had all poured out and down and away.

"I'm okay," he said again.

"Your foot's gone," she said.

"I know. But I'm okay," he said, and closed his eyes. Elvi stumbled to the console that looked most nearly intact. It was hard to walk, and she didn't know why until she looked down and saw that a scoop of her thigh the size of a softball was missing. As soon as she saw it, she felt the pain.

A lesser ship would have been dead a hundred times over, but the *Falcon* was hardy. Its skin had been cut a hundred times, and it had regrown fast enough to keep in air. The reactor was throwing errors and emergency corrections, the log spooling so fast she couldn't keep track. She pulled up the sensor arrays, and stars appeared on her screen. The ship was out of the slow zone. Free of the rings. The system identified Laconia's sky. She turned the ship's attention back to the ring gate falling away behind them. It looked calm. As if nothing at all odd had just happened. She felt laughter burbling up in her throat and tried to keep it down, uncertain whether it would stop once it got started.

She opened a broadcast channel and prayed that enough of the *Falcon* still existed to get the signal out. For a moment, the system didn't respond and her heart sank. Then the transmitter hauled itself to life.

"Thank you," she told the ship. "Oh, thank you, thank you, thank you."

She gathered her strength, wondering how much blood she'd lost. How much she had left.

"To any ship in range. This is Major Elvi Okoye of the Laconian Science Directorate. I am in need of immediate aid. We have mass casualties—"

Chapter Twenty-Two: Teresa

I've never seen anyone that angry before," she said. She was telling the story of little Monster Singh and her mother. "I mean, I've probably been mad, but this was different. This girl was…"

"Seriously? You're one of the angriest people I know, Tiny," Timothy said.

His food recycler was in pieces laid out on a blanket, everything carefully in place like an exploded drawing of itself. Only the built-in power supply was still inside the frame. Timothy was going through the components now, cleaning and polishing each one. Looking for the signs of wear. Teresa sat on his cot with her back against the cave wall, her legs pulled up in front of her and Muskrat snoring contentedly at her side. A repair drone lurked at the edge of the light, its bulbous black eyes looking vaguely hurt that Timothy wasn't letting it take care of the equipment.

"I'm not an angry person," she said. Then, a moment later, "I don't think I'm angry."

Timothy tossed her a pair of dark goggles and motioned for her to put them on. She did, and put a hand over Muskrat's eyes so that she wouldn't be blinded. After a few seconds, the light of a welding torch burst in her vision like a tiny green star. The smoke was acrid and metallic and she liked it.

"Thing is," Timothy said, loud over the roar of the torch, "there's only a couple kinds of anger. You get angry because you're afraid of something or you get angry because you're frustrated." The torch turned off with a pop.

"Safe?" Teresa asked.

"Sure, you can take 'em off." When she did, the cave seemed brighter than when she'd put them on before. Even with the intensity of the light, her eyes had adapted to darkness. She scratched Muskrat's ears as Timothy went on. "If you're...I don't know. If you're scared maybe your dad isn't the kind of guy you thought he was, you might get angry. Or you're afraid no one's got your back. Like Nutless."

"His name's Connor," Teresa said, but she smiled when she said it.

"Yeah, him," Timothy agreed. "Or maybe you're afraid he made you look stupid in front of your crew. So you get angry. If you didn't give a shit whether your old man lived or died? If Nutless and your crew didn't matter to you? Then you're not angry. Or the other way? You're trying to get something to work. A conduit to fit. Been working at it for hours, and just when it's looking about right, the metal bends on you and you gotta start over. That's angry too, but it ain't scared-angry. It's the other one."

"So you look at me," Teresa said, derision in her voice, "and you think I'm scared and frustrated?"

"Yep."

Teresa's mockery died, and she hugged her knees. It didn't fit at all with who and what she thought she was, but something in her leaped toward his word. It felt like recognizing someone.

Like catching a glimpse of herself from an angle she'd never seen before. It was fascinating.

"How do you deal with it?"

"Fucked if I know, Tiny. I don't do those."

"You don't get angry?"

"Not out of fear, anyway. I don't remember the last time I was afraid of something. Frustration was more my thing. But I had this friend, and I watched her die slow. I couldn't do anything about it. That was frustrating, and I got angry. Started looking for a fight. But I had another friend who straightened me out."

"How?"

"She beat the living shit out of me," Timothy said. "That helped. And ever since then, nothing has seemed like it was worth getting too bent out of shape over."

He rolled a bright silver cone about the size of a thumb in his palm and scowled.

"What is it?" she asked.

"Injector's getting a little ragged at the mouth is all," Timothy said. "I can touch it up. Just means I'll be drinking my yeast patties more than eating them."

"You spend a lot of time with that thing."

"You take care of your tools, your tools take care of you."

Teresa leaned against the wall. The stone was cool against her back. Deep cave temperatures were the measure of the underlying climate average. Mass and depth smoothed out the daily highs and lows—even the annual fluctuations of summer and winter. She knew it intellectually, but she hadn't understood it until Timothy's cave. The way it always felt cool in the heat and warm in the chill.

"You know, the wise man living alone on the mountain is really cliché," she said, smiling when she said it so he wouldn't think she was being mean. "Anyway, I don't have anything to be scared of."

"Assassins with pocket nukes for one," Timothy said, slotting the injector back into its housing.

Teresa laughed, and after a second, Timothy smiled too.

"If anyone's going to kill me, it'll probably be Dr. Cortázar," she said.

"Yeah? Why's that?"

"It's just a joke. I was watching Holden, like we talked about? And I heard this conversation he and Dr. Cortázar were having."

"What about?" Timothy asked, idly.

Teresa thought back. What had they been talking about exactly? Mostly she remembered Cortázar talking about how nature ate babies and Holden looking into the camera. But it had been about her father too.

She took in a breath, ready to speak, and the air rattled against the back of her throat and down into her lungs like a billion little molecule-sized marbles banging against the soft tissue. Her respiration system was a cave inside Timothy's cave, and she was acutely aware of the complexity of her own body and the answering complexity of the caverns around her. Veins and chips in the wall before her fragmented and smoothed together. Gravity trying to tug her down into the floor, and the astonishingly complex dance of the electrons in the stone and her flesh pushing back. She managed to wonder if she'd been drugged before her awareness was overwhelmed by the immediacy and complexity of the air and her body and the increasingly invisible boundary that failed to really divide her from the world...

Muskrat barked anxiously. She'd slumped down on the cot at some point without knowing she was doing it. Timothy stood up, his expression perfectly focused and his recycler forgotten. The repair drone made a weird yipping sound as it tried to stand up, staggering drunkenly.

"That wasn't just me, right?" Timothy said.

"I don't think so," Teresa said.

"Yeah, all right. It's been fun, Tiny, but you need to head home now."

"What was that? Is there something wrong with the air in here? Are there fumes?"

"Nope," Timothy said, taking her by the arm and lifting her to her feet. "Air's fine. That was something else. And it probably happened to a lot of people, so they're gonna be scared, and they're going to want to find where everyone important to them is, and that's you. So you need to be not here."

"I don't understand," she said, but Timothy was pulling her forward, toward the mouth of the cave. His grip on her arm was like a vise. His expression was blank. It made him frightening. Muskrat followed behind, barking like she was trying to warn them of something.

In the open air, the world was normal. The strange sensations she'd had before already seemed like a bad dream or an accident. Timothy's reaction was the only thing that made it frightening. He looked up, scanning the sky, then nodded to himself.

"Okay, Tiny. You and the furball head back home."

"I'll come back as soon as I can," she said. She didn't know why she wanted to reassure him.

"Okay."

It was the way he said it. Like his mind was already someplace else. She'd had adults treat her like that before—polite and agreeable, but elsewhere. Never Timothy, though. He was different. He was supposed to be different.

"Will you be here when I do?"

"I'll have to, I guess. I'm not done yet, so—"

She hugged him. It was like hugging a tree. He pulled back, and when he looked at her, she thought there was something like regret in his expression. It couldn't have been pity.

"Good luck, Tiny," he said, then turned back toward his cave and was gone. Muskrat barked once and looked after him, as worried as Teresa was.

"Come on," she said, and started for her secret passage back into the State Building and home. The afternoon was cool. The leaves were starting to retreat back into their winter sheaths, leaving the trees looking stubbly. A sunbird hanging on a low branch opened its leathery wings at her and hissed, but she ignored it. At the horizon, wide clouds bunched and trailed gray veils of storm. If they came this way, the drainage tunnel would be impassable and she'd be stuck outside the walls. She picked up her pace...

The sound of the flier started as a high and distant whine, but it grew louder quickly. Less than a minute after she first noticed it, the sound was a roar. The black laminate body and three cold thrusters appeared over the treetops and fell into a thin meadow, hardly more than a break between trees. When the door popped open, she expected to see the light-blue uniforms of security. She prepared to identify herself and explain that she'd decided to go for a hike. It was only partly a lie.

But while there were two armed guards, the first person out of the flier was Colonel Ilich. He trotted toward her, and his face was dark. The thrusters didn't cycle all the way down, so when he reached her, he had to shout.

"Get in the flier."

"What?"

"You need to get in the flier now. You have to get back to the State Building."

"I don't understand."

Ilich's jaw clenched and he pointed at the open door. "You. There. Now. This isn't difficult."

Teresa stepped back like she'd been slapped. In all the years Ilich had been her tutor, he had never been mean to her. Never been anything but patient and supportive and amused. Even when she didn't do her work or did something inappropriate, the punishment was just a long talk about why she'd made the choices she did and what the goals of her education were. It was like seeing a different man in an Ilich suit. She felt tears welling up in her eyes. She saw *Oh, for fuck's sake* on his lips, but she couldn't hear it.

He made a little bow and gestured her forward like a servant making way for his master, but she felt the impatience in it. The contempt. The anger.

Oh, she thought as she walked to the flier. *He's frightened.*

At the flier, Muskrat balked, and before Teresa could coax her in, Ilich assigned one of the guards to go back on foot with the dog. The flier's door closed with a deep clank, and they lurched up over the trees. Even though the body of the flier had looked opaque from the outside, it was no darker than tinted glass from her seat. She could see the State Building clearly as soon as they cleared the top branches.

"How did you know where I was?" Teresa asked.

Ilich shook his head, and for a moment she thought he wasn't going to answer. When he did, his voice had more like its usual tone: patient and gentle. The difference was that now she knew it was a mask.

"You had a locator implanted in your jawbone when you were born. There is never a moment when security doesn't know how to find you, and your safety is part of my sacred duty."

It was like hearing a language she almost understood. She could pick out the meaning of each word, but she couldn't quite make sense of the whole. The idea was too foreign. Too wrong.

"Your father felt it was important for you to have some experience of rebellion and autonomy, so he permitted your excursions so long as they didn't take you too far from the State Building. He said he was solo free-climbing on the surface of Mars at your age, and that he learned things about himself that way. He hoped you would find use in the same independence and solitude."

Solitude. He didn't know about Timothy, then. There was nothing on any world that would make her tell him either. She felt the buzz of outrage in her throat. "So you just let me *think*..."

The flier passed over the outer wall of the State Building and curved around to the east. They weren't heading for the landing pad but the lawn outside the residence. A single figure stood in the gardens, watching them pass. She thought it was Holden.

"I respected your autonomy and your privacy to the extent that security protocols permitted," Ilich said. "But I needed to be able to find you in case there was an emergency."

"There's an emergency?"

"Yes," he said. "There is."

Her father smiled at her, the wrinkles at the edges of his eyes deeper than she remembered them. The opalescence in his iris was more pronounced, and something seemed to glow from under his skin. His study had been a bedroom, back when he'd still slept. That hadn't been for years. Now it had a desk hand carved from Laconian wood with a grain like sedimentary rock, a wide table, a shelf with half a dozen physical books, and the divan where he was sitting. Where he had been sitting when the change came.

"Father?" Teresa said. "Can you hear me?"

His mouth changed into a little o, like he was a child seeing something marvelous. He reached out, patting at the air beside her head. She took his hand, and it was hot.

"Has he said anything?" she asked.

Kelly, her father's personal valet, shook his head. "A few things, but none of it made sense. After it happened, I came to see him, and he was like this. Just like this." He nodded to Cortázar, sitting on the edge of the table. "I got Dr. Cortázar as quickly as I could."

"Your opinion?" Ilich asked. His voice was cool, and her father didn't react to it at all. "What's wrong with him?"

Cortázar spread his hands. "I could only speculate."

"Then do," Ilich said.

"The…event. The lost consciousness? It seems to match what Admiral Trejo reported from Sol system. The theory I always heard was that it's the weapon that killed the protomolecule engineers. However their minds were organized, this…effect broke it. Well, the high consul has been making himself more and more like the builders for years now. It might—*might*—leave him more vulnerable to the attack than the rest of us."

Teresa's chest hurt like someone had punched her sternum. She sank to her knees at her father's side, but he was frowning at something behind her. Or nothing.

"How long before he gets better?" Kelly asked.

"If I had been permitted to have more than one test subject, I might be able to guess," Cortázar said. It was the same tone of voice he'd used to say *Nature eats babies all the time*. It made Teresa's skin crawl. "As things are? He could come back to himself in a moment. He could be like this for the rest of his life, which in his case could be a very long time indeed. If I can take him to the lab and run some tests, I might get more insight into the question."

"No," Kelly said, and it was clear from his tone it wasn't the first time he'd said it. "The high consul stays in his rooms until..."

"Until what?" Cortázar said.

"Until we have this situation under control," Ilich said, firmly. "Does anyone outside this room know about his condition?"

The high consul's terminal chimed, a high-priority connection request. The three men looked at each other in alarm. Her father scowled, then farted like the blare of a trumpet. The perversity and indignity of it cut Teresa like a blade. This was her father. The man who ruled all humanity through his vision and audacity. Who knew how everything was and was supposed to be. The body in front of her was only a crippled man, too broken to be embarrassed. The chime came again, and Kelly grabbed it with his hand terminal.

"I'm afraid the high consul can't be disturbed," he said as he walked out of the room. "I can accept a message for him."

The door closed behind him.

"I can bring some equipment here," Cortázar said. "It won't be as good as having him in the pens where the real equipment is, but I could do...something."

Ilich ran a hand over his scalp, his gaze flickering from her father to Cortázar to the window that looked out over a bamboo garden in some different universe where the sun still shone and life wasn't broken. Teresa shifted, and Ilich looked at her. For a long moment, their eyes were locked on each other's.

She felt a wave of panic. "Am I supposed to be in charge now?"

"No," Ilich said, as if her fear had resolved something. "No, High Consul Winston Duarte is in charge. He is deep in consultation with Dr. Cortázar on matters critical to the state of the empire, and cannot be disturbed under any circumstances. It's easy to remember, because it's true. He specifically ordered Kelly to keep anyone but the doctor here and you, because you're his daughter, away from the residences until further notice. Do you remember him saying that?"

"I don't—" Teresa began.

"You need to remember him saying it. He was sitting right here. It was just after the event. We all came back to ourselves, and he told Kelly in front of you that he needed Dr. Cortázar, and that he couldn't be disturbed. Do you remember?"

Teresa pictured it. Her father's voice, calm and sturdy as stone.

"I remember," she said.

Kelly came back in the room. "Something happened at the ring. The *Falcon* made an unscheduled transit. Now it's putting out a distress call. A relief ship is on the way, but it won't be there for hours. Maybe as much as a day."

"All right," Ilich said. "We need a secure channel to Governor Song and Admiral Trejo. Someone will have to take over coordinating the military. Apart from them, no one can know anything.

"Until we get the high consul back to himself, our little conspiracy here *is* the empire."

Chapter Twenty-Three: Naomi

The plume of energy that came from the ring gate was invisible to the naked eye. An optical telescope would have seen at most a few flares of brightness where bits of matter caught in it glowed for a moment as they were ripped apart. Moving at the speed of light, it flared into the space where ships coming into Auberon or preparing to leave it were most likely to be, widening like a wave with distance, hundred thousand kilometers after hundred thousand kilometers, spreading out like a cone. If it became less powerful as it spread, it wasn't enough to help the *San Salvador*. The Transport Union ship had been slow moving out of the restricted zone, and almost instantaneously, it and everyone aboard it became a cinder.

Naomi sat in the commissary and played the newsfeed of its loss in a loop, watching the ship flare white and die so quickly the frame rate couldn't quite make sense of it. She had spent very nearly her whole life on ships and stations. She'd been on six ships that had suffered micrometeorite hits, two that had lost atmosphere from them. Once, she'd had to drop core to keep her reactor from blooming out like a tiny, brief sun. She'd jumped between ships without a suit, and the feeling of breathing vacuum still came to her in nightmares decades after the fact. She would have said she was intimately aware of all the dangers life outside an atmosphere could hold.

This one was new.

"Did *they* do this, you think?" Emma asked, hunched over her bulb of morning tea. The *Bhikaji Cama* was in its braking burn now. The one-third g had felt strange until Naomi realized she'd never been in the crewed parts of the ship when there was up and down before. After that it still felt strange, but she knew why.

"*They* Laconia or *they* Saba's people?"

Emma lifted her eyebrows. "I meant the first, but either."

The crew clumped around the commissary in quiet groups of two or three, and they treated each other with the brittle courtesy of a funeral. Some of them had likely known the crew of the *San Salvador*, but even if they didn't it had been a ship like theirs. Its death reminded them of their own, still somewhere down the line, but coming.

"I don't know," Naomi said. "The point of having the *Typhoon* in with Medina was always that they could defend every gate at once. Hit the station with its magnetic field projector and all the gates bake anyone that's too close, but..."

"I saw the data from when they did that. It wasn't this big."

"It wasn't even close," Naomi agreed.

Emma sipped from her bulb, hunched in a degree more, and lowered her voice. "Did we make a play? Did we try to take the slow zone?"

"If there was an attack planned, I didn't know about it," she said, but with a knot in her gut. She didn't think Saba would have put together something that audacious without her, but maybe he would. She had been arguing for restraint and less violent, longer-term

strategies. If all she'd managed was to cut herself out of the loop...
She imagined Bobbie and Alex and the *Gathering Storm* burning in
toward the gate with a ragged and improvised fleet. They *couldn't*
have been that stupid. But even if they had, the gamma burst from
the gate had been so much more powerful...

"Can you find where we put my system?" Naomi asked. "If I
can rebuild it, I might be able to find Saba's signals. Get a report."

"Could hunt it down, maybe," Emma said. "But we're putting
you on a shuttle for Big Moon in four hours, get you out before
we're in range of the transfer station. Doesn't leave much time."

"So we hurry."

Finding all the spare parts of her former cell was harder now
that thrust had changed the nature of the architectural space,
but Naomi didn't need all of it. The physical hardware had some
built-in security that made finding the hidden messages easier, but
without the keys and information that she kept only in her own
memory, they'd have been useless. Her records from the long passages in the storage container were wiped. Even if the Laconians
had found the devices, they wouldn't have been able to pull the
secrets of the underground from them. But neither could Naomi.

Emma drove a loading mech, shifting the heavy pallets that
they'd moved before, and Naomi found the pieces she needed—
the signal processor from her crash couch, a monitor different
from the one she'd had but close enough, a hand terminal interface. They set up in a workroom by the machine shop. Neither of
them had said it, but they both knew that everything would be
broken down again and hidden away when they were done.

The workroom was small and grimy, with long, discolored
patches on the fabric walls. The tool racks had been used for so
many years that the ceramic was wearing through and the titanium bones glittering under it. It smelled like oil and sweat, and
Naomi liked it better than anyplace she'd been on the *Cama*
before.

She looked through all the usual places where Saba hid communications for the underground, but most of them weren't there

at all. Not just empty of hidden messages, but whole channels missing. The Transport Union's coordination feed—the running record of ship locations and vectors—was just a repeating standby message. The entertainment feed from Medina of a young man talking breathlessly about the three-factor philosophy of design for hours on end wasn't transmitting at all. Medina's communications channels were closed for business, covert or otherwise.

"That a good thing, or bad?" Emma asked.

"I don't know what it is," Naomi said.

"Got to get you to a shuttle soon."

"Just another few minutes."

Emma shifted her weight, trying not to show her impatience. It wasn't just the time pressure on the shuttle. Everything about the situation itched.

Naomi was almost ready to resign herself to failure when she found the message. It was hidden in false-static fluctuations under a navigation beacon for the repeaters that ferried comm signals across the interference of the gate. The encryption was key based, and it took her six tries to find the right one. When it popped onto the monitor, it was text. No voice, no picture. Nothing to show that it had come from Saba apart from the fact of its existence.

MAJOR INCIDENT IN THE SLOW ZONE. SUSPEND ALL OPERATIONS AND SHELTER DOWN. NO IMMEDIATE THREAT TO THE ORGANIZATION, BUT ENEMY SURVEILLANCE HIGH. NO TRANSITS IN OR OUT OF ANY GATE BY ORDER OF LACONIA. TWO GATES LOST. UPDATE TO FOLLOW.

" 'Two gates lost'?" Emma said. "What the hell does that mean?"

"Be patient and find out, sounds like," Naomi said. She shut down her system, the words blinking into darkness.

The shuttle was a two-couch model. No Epstein drive, but an efficient teakettle good enough for orbital transits that didn't take more than a month or two. She wasn't going to be on it for more than a couple of days. It was the kind of thing a new prospector would rent for claim surveys or an old couple for a long, slightly adventurous vacation. Naomi felt Jim's absence even though he'd never been on board it. As the *Bhikaji Cama* dropped away behind her and she did her first sustained burn toward Auberon's lunar outpost, she checked the transponder output. A day ago, the shuttle had been a maintenance and safety vehicle for the Transport Union. Today, it was a rental craft registered to Whimsy Enterprises and had been for the last year and a half. The ship didn't care what story they told about it. It worked just as well either way.

She set the local censored newsfeed to play for a while, using the thin-faced, cheerful man spouting the Laconian official positions as a kind of white noise while she thought. In the hours she let it play, neither he nor the dour and serious woman who took his place mentioned Medina or the *Typhoon* or the gamma radiation burst. Or how someone could *lose* two ring gates. She tried to reassure herself that, whatever was going on, it at least wasn't Bobbie and Alex charging into the teeth of a *Magnetar*-class battleship and dying. There was even the chance that the crisis, whatever it was, would open some opportunities for the underground. With her bottles gone, she'd have to find another way to get messages back to Saba.

Auberon was one of the success stories of the new systems. A wide, lush planet with clean water, hundreds of viable microclimates, and a tree of life that coexisted with Earth's biochemistry in a kind of mutual indulgent neglect. The story was that a farm on Auberon could grow native plant analogs and Terran crops side by side, with each acting as fertilizer for the other. It sounded like an exaggeration, but there was a seed of truth there. Food and water weren't a struggle on Auberon the way they had been on so many of the other worlds. It had twelve cities with populations over a million and a wide scattering of smaller towns, farms, and research stations. A lunar station that fed cargo and supplies through the near asteroids and a handful of dwarf planets big enough to have civilian populations. It had almost one-tenth of a percent of

Earth's population at its height, and it had been self-sustaining for over two decades.

Naomi found the place a little creepy.

The docks, when she reached them, were cleaner than any she'd seen in a lifetime traveling through Sol system. It wasn't just the eerie perfection she disliked, though. The void cities that had been, for a time, the dream of Belter culture made real had been as new and shining and optimistic as Auberon's lunar base. But they had been rooted in history. Everything in Sol system, from the great port of Ceres to the rock hoppers digging ore and water from asteroids that were hardly more than a hold's volume of gravel, had come from a shared past. Yes, the expansion into the void had been bloody and cruel and filled with as much violence as cooperation, but it had been real. Authentic.

There were no old levels in the station, because there was no old. On Ceres, there were neighborhoods built in the excavations where the great engines that had spun the asteroid up had been housed. On Ganymede, there were levels of tunnels that had been abandoned in the war and never recovered. On Earth, there were cities built on the ruins of the cities before them, layer after layer back through millennia. Auberon was a theme park version of itself. A prefabricated culture that could have been assembled anywhere with equal cheerfulness. It didn't feel human.

The Whimsy Enterprises office was a closet-sized door between an ice cream shop and a land claims lawyer. Inside, the air smelled like hydroponics tanks and fresh plastic. A woman her own age with close-cut hair stood at the kind of desk Naomi expected to get takeaway food from.

"Hello," the woman said with a barely repressed grin.

"I have a ship I've brought back," Naomi said.

"You don't remember me, do you?" the woman said. "Not your fault. It was a long time ago. I crewed your ship."

"My ship?"

"The *Rocinante*, under Captain Holden. Back in the bad old days, when the rocks fell. You were busy at the time, sa sa que?

With that fucker Inaros. Looked like you'd been through a recycler when we pulled you off that racing pinnace."

Naomi's brain stripped away the years, filled in the woman's cheeks, undid the gray of age. She was a pilot. She'd worked for Fred Johnson on Tycho. "Chava Lombaugh?"

"Welcome to Auberon," Chava said. "You can talk freely in here. I sweep for surveillance every other day, and I made a special pass when I heard you were coming."

Naomi walked to the desk and leaned against it. "Thank you for that. Do you know what's going on?"

"Not in specific," Chava said, "but I can say that the Laconian security forces have been shitting themselves boneless since that first no-transit alert came. We haven't been able to decrypt their feeds, but the volume of traffic has been huge. Governor Song was pushing like hell to get every ship she could out of the slow zone before the gamma bursts, and now she's not letting anyone in or out."

"Do you have a way to reach Saba?" Naomi asked.

"The Laconians have been updating the security on the repeaters," Chava said. "I still have a couple back doors, though."

"Are you sure they're secure?" Naomi asked, and her voice echoed strangely, like she was hearing more of it than usual. Undertones and overtones rippling against each other as the vibrations touched the hard surfaces of desk and floor and wall and rebounded to make new complexities. She stepped back as Chava's eyes widened. She could see the wetness in them, the tiny dark dot of her tear duct, the river pattern of blood in the whites of her eyes like a map of an unknown world.

"Fuck," Chava said, and it was a symphony. Overwhelming and complex. Naomi felt herself falling into the sound and the wide, full, complicated air—

When she came back to herself, her head was pressed against the abrasive industrial carpeting. Chava was still at the desk, her face bloodless. She looked around the room, trying to focus, trying to find Naomi. It took a few seconds.

"What...," Chava said. "What was..."

"It's the same thing that happened in Sol system when they killed Pallas. How long have we been unconscious?"

"I...don't..."

"Do you keep logs? Security tapes?"

Chava nodded, working up from barely a tremor until she was bobbing her head so much it seemed like it would be hard to stop. She opened a screen on her desk display. Nothing inside the room, but a view of the front door from outside. As she rolled it back until Naomi appeared, an alert tone came over the station's public speaker loud enough to hear even inside the office. *This is a public security announcement. Please remain where you are. If you are in need of assistance, use the emergency alert on your hand terminal, and government responders will come to you. Do not seek help on your own. Do not leave your homes or places of business.*

"Three minutes," Chava said. "It's like time just blinked out."

"Is there a *Magnetar*-class battleship in Auberon? That's the only thing I know that does that...or almost the only thing."

"No, nothing like that."

"We have to risk your back doors on the repeater. We have to get a message to Saba. Something's going on here, and if it's related to whatever happened that got Laconia worried, he may need to know about it."

Chava gestured for Naomi to come around the desk. "Follow me," she said.

Chava's office was small, with white, generic furniture of ceramic and steel, but it was well equipped. Naomi sat at the other woman's desk and built a short message, typing fast and not worrying about errors. The Auberon gate had a fifty-five-minute light delay from the planet. Even if Saba wrote back at once, it would be two hours before she heard, and it might take him longer.

In the long wait, Chava made them chamomile tea from the office supplies. The sweetness cloyed, but Naomi drank it anyway. It was something to do. The security alert came off an hour and thirty-five minutes after it started. *The station is safe and secure. Please return to your normal activities.* It seemed optimistic to the point of being naive.

Chava Lombaugh's system chirped ten minutes shy of the two-hour mark, and she slapped open the new message like it had stung her. As she read it, she bared her teeth.

"What is it?"

"It's nothing," she said, and shifted the monitor for Naomi to see. TRANSMISSION ERROR. REPEATER NOT RESPONDING. MESSAGE QUEUED FOR LATER DELIVERY.

"The repeater's down?" Naomi said.

"Theirs is," Chava said. "The one inside the ring. The Auberon-side repeater generated this message, but the two aren't talking to each other. We might be able to do something else, though. Ring gate interference is a bitch, but it's not impossible to punch through. I have some ships in the rental fleet with tightbeams, and if I got one close…"

Naomi shook her head. "No. Nothing obvious. I want him briefed, but not at the risk of exposing the organization. Saba can get the message when he can get the message. He knows how to find us once he does."

Chava made a frustrated sound at the back of her throat and slammed down the last of her tea. "Let me take you to the safe house, then. At least we can chew our nails someplace comfortable. Laconia takes the repeaters seriously. Whatever the issue is, getting the communications network back up will be high on their to-do list."

"Thank God for the efficiency of the enemy," Naomi said, making it a joke. Chava even laughed at it a little.

But a day later, the repeater was still down. And the day after that. It was almost a week before a high-speed probe made the long journey to the ring gate and through it, and sent back the images that even the censor's office couldn't keep a lid on.

Auberon system—Naomi and Chava and the crew of the *Bhikaji Cama* included—saw the swirling colors that had replaced the darkness between the ring gates. They found out why the repeater on the slow zone side of the gate wasn't responding. It was gone, and so were all the other repeaters like it. And the *Eye of the Typhoon*. And Medina Station and all the ships that had been quarantined inside the ring space. Only the alien station at the center remained, glowing bright as a tiny sun.

Naomi looked at it all until she was on the edge of vertigo, then looked away and had to go back to check that it was real. Over and over again, locked in a cycle of disbelief.

All human existence in the small artificial universe between the gates had been wiped away as if it had never been there at all, leaving no sign of what had killed it.

Chapter Twenty-Four: Bobbie

The bar was worse than shitty. Shitty had character. The place was generic. Fake stone meant to echo a tunnel on Ceres or Pallas marked with graffiti to make it look edgy until you noticed that the pattern of it repeated every couple meters. The appearance of counterculture as churned out by a corporate designer. The food wasn't bad. Vat-grown ribs in a hot marinade and vegetable kibble that hadn't been cooked to a mush. The beer was decent, if a little hoppy for her taste. A screen at the back usually played highlights from football games around the system. Now it was playing a newsfeed. And while most of the time the screen was a background for the conversations and drinking, today everyone was watching it.

"The event mirrors the one experienced when the *Tempest* was forced to employ its magnetic field generator against separatist forces on Pallas Station," the woman on the screen said. She was pale skinned, with long, dark hair and a serious expression. Bobbie thought the broadcast was out of Luna, but it could as easily have been Ceres or Mars. They all looked the same these days. "But while the previous effect had a clear trigger and was restricted to Sol system, the few ships that have made the transit into Sol since the event report that this was much more widespread, possibly affecting all known systems.

"The loss of Medina Station and the *Typhoon* along with all civilian ships in the ring space is assumed to be related, but no official report has been released at this time to confirm that."

Caspar made a low sound, something between a cough and a chuckle. Jillian, across from him, lifted her chin as a question.

"More critical than their pet journalists usually are," Caspar said.

"You can still see the censor's arm up her ass working her lips," Jillian said. "If we had a free press, they'd be tearing these bastards eight new assholes an hour until we got an explanation."

An old man in a collarless shirt appeared on the screen with the dark-haired newsfeed host. He was smiling as anxiously as if the camera were mugging him. There was a chyron identifying him and his credentials, but the screen was too far away and the print too small for Bobbie to make them out, except she thought his first name was Robert. She leaned forward, trying to hear better.

"What can you tell us about these events, Professor?" the host asked.

"Well, yes. Yes. The first thing, of course, is that it's a mistake to use the plural, yes? *Events* plural. What we're seeing is better understood as a single, nonlocal event. Which fits with everything we've learned about the...I don't like to say alien life. Too many presumptions. Call it the previous tenants and their enemies." The old man's smile grew a little warmer, amused by his own joke. Bobbie thanked the good angels that she'd never taken a university course from him.

Jillian sneered. "They just lost one of their battleships, the central traffic control for the ring gates, a shitload of ships, and two whole fucking gates, and they want to talk about the limits of locality?" She pointed to the screen with a pale bone that had recently been wrapped in rib meat. "These people are idiots."

Caspar shrugged. "We just lost the underground coordination from Medina and we're having beer and barbecue."

"We're idiots too," Jillian said.

"You are, anyway," Caspar said, but he smiled when he said it.

The announcement that the Sol gate was closed for business until further notice had been bad. No one on her crew had said anything to her directly, but they hadn't had to. No ships in or out of the system didn't make the shell game impossible. They might still be able to escape. Sneak off Callisto and find a Transport Union ship to hide in. But even if they did, that ship wouldn't be going anywhere until the quarantine was lifted. Any hope of slipping out to a different system, hiding on some undeveloped moon until the attack in Sol system blew over was lost. Instead, they'd be trying to hide from the tiger without leaving its cage.

Then things got worse.

Bobbie was asleep when it happened. It had been getting harder and harder to get any rest. She'd pull herself onto her cot in what had been a warehouse office, kill the lights, and her mind would launch into scenarios of escape or capture or violence, running through every combination of circumstances she could invent. She felt lucky to get five full hours in a cycle, so when she woke up groggy and confused, she'd thought it was just exhaustion finally catching up. It wasn't until her hand terminal chirped to let her know that everyone from her crew to the Callistan emergency service to the top newsfeeds in the system had been trying to get her attention that she understood something deeper had happened.

"The important thing to understand," the old man said, looking into the camera like he was everyone's kind uncle, "is that while

these incidents can be very upsetting and certainly they have
caused some accidents when people were in the middle of sensitive
or dangerous activities when they came, they pose no real threat
in and of themselves."

"Can you explain that?" the host asked.

"These spells have not been shown to have any long-term
effects. There is no indication that they are more than an incon-
venience, really. It's important, of course, to keep in mind they
may happen, at least until the Science Directorate understands the
cause and…ah…*control* of them. Until then, we should all make
sure fail-safes are engaged on our vehicles and equipment. But
that's good advice in any case, yes?"

Caspar roughened his voice, mimicking the old man. "And
don't concern yourself with the fact that it destroyed gates and
battleships. Oh my, no. Don't worry your pretty little heads about
that."

"Where's Alex?" Bobbie asked.

"He was heading home last time I saw him," Jillian said.

Home meant the *Gathering Storm*. The window for their
escape was coming soon. That might have been the reason he'd
gone to the ship. Or he might have been avoiding her. She'd
pushed him harder than usual last time they'd talked, and she
knew he avoided conflict when he could. She'd never have said
it aloud, but she wished Amos or Naomi were still with them.
Or even Holden. She was always a little worried that she'd break
Alex without meaning to.

"I'm out," she said, then left the shitty bar and the Laconian
propaganda channel behind. Everyone else stayed behind to finish their beer and gossip. They could sense she wasn't looking for
company.

She walked through the public corridors of the station, her
hands deep in her pockets, her eye on the floor ahead of her.
Between her physical size and training almost from the cradle to
control the space she occupied, it wasn't easy for her to back down
and look unremarkable. But it was important. They'd already

been on Callisto longer than she liked, and she saw that the crew was getting used to it. They were developing favorite shitty bars, favorite brothels, barbers and coffee shops and pachinko parlors. It was normal to fit in after a while. Normal to make a life wherever you found yourself. But it was dangerous for them, because it was also how you became known, and being known too well meant they were all in prison or the pens or the grave.

At the turnoff, she used her hand terminal to unlock the service passage and ducked down into the infrastructure of the shipyard. It was a long walk through poorly heated hallways to the old OPA smugglers' den. Her footsteps echoed along with the unsteady drip of condensate and the hum of the air recyclers. The graffiti on the walls here was ancient, much of it written in Belter creole or cipher. What little she could make out was wishing ill on the UN and the MCR. The hatreds of the past seemed almost quaint now. Just being authentic made it better than Laconia.

What are my victories? Will I leave the universe a better place than I found it?

When she was a girl, she'd thought she understood what the future would be. Improvement. Progress. She expected to serve her nation, protect the terraforming effort from the resentful Earth and the feral Belt. She knew from the time she could speak that she wouldn't live to see humanity walking freely on the surface of Mars, but she believed she would die on a world with the spreading green of engineered moss and the aurora of a magnetosphere. The life she'd actually lived was unrecognizably different from the dream she'd had. More astounding, and more disappointing. And her sense of having a place in it was gone. She had her role, first on the *Rocinante*, now on the *Storm*. She had her people and her duty. It was Mars that had changed and darkened. It had metastasized into an empire and a grand project she wanted no part of.

She still had decades in her, if she kept her treatments and exercise regimen up. The universe she died in might still be better than the one she lived in now, but she had a hard time believing it would be better than the one she'd been born into. Too much had been lost, and what wasn't lost was changed beyond her ability to understand it.

Her hand terminal chimed. A message from Jillian, still back at the bar. Bobbie looked at it with distrust. Jillian was a smart woman and a good fighter. Another couple decades of life might eventually convince her to build up her team instead of undermining them. The way she felt at the moment, Bobbie wasn't sure she was in the mood to hear whatever Jillian was about to say. But she was captain, and Jillian was her XO. She thumbed the connection open. The recording had a tag that read THOUGHT YOU'D WANT TO SEE THIS. Bobbie started playing it.

The screen from the bar jumped to life. The refresh rate of the image there and the recording made a moiré pattern over the newsfeed host's face, but not so badly that Bobbie couldn't make her out. Or the man in the window beside her. The old man was gone, and a familiar face had replaced him. Admiral Anton Trejo of the *Tempest*, de facto governor of Sol system.

Bobbie stopped walking.

"—planned for months," Trejo said.

"So your return to Laconia isn't related to the events in the ring space?" the host asked.

"Not at all," Trejo said with a smile. He was about a thousand times better at lying than the host. "But I see how people would come to that conclusion. What happened with Medina was a tragedy, and I mourn the loss of life as deeply as anyone. But I have been assured by the Science Directorate and the high consul himself that the situation is under control. I'm just an old sailor heading for his next post. Nothing more dramatic than that. Vice Admiral Hogan is a good man and ready to take command. I have absolute faith in him."

A third window opened on the screen, pushing Trejo and the host a little smaller and more masked by the interference. Vice Admiral Hogan was a serious-faced young man in Laconian blue. He could have been Caspar's older brother.

"Well, speaking for the citizens of Sol system, I'd like to thank you for—"

The recording ended. Bobbie typed up a response with one thumb. THAT'S INTERESTING. She leaned against the wall. Trejo was leaving Sol system. Maybe was already on his way. A new officer—a Laconian officer, not an MCRN veteran—was taking command of the *Tempest*. It might have been enough to convince her, if she hadn't already decided.

The *Storm* sat on a mobile landing platform wide enough to fit three more like her. The platform's treads were taller than Bobbie, and designed to roll it through the massive cavern it was hiding in. Half a klick into the darkness, the passage angled up to a concealed hangar on the moon's surface. For the moment, the ship stood tall as a tower in its gantry crane, the drive cones almost resting on the platform and the top of the ship lost in the shadows above her.

She made her way up the crane to the airlock, climbing the metal ladder hand over hand rather than calling the powered lift. When the airlock cycled open and she stepped in, she disconnected her hand terminal from the Callisto system before she synced up with the *Storm*. It wasn't likely that a dual connection would give them away, but it wasn't impossible, and every unnecessary risk was unnecessary.

The ship told her Alex was in the machine shop, and that four of her crew besides him were in various parts of the ship. All that mattered to her at the moment was that Alex was alone. This wasn't a conversation she needed the others to hear. Not yet, anyway.

The machine shop looked less like the manufacturing workshop that the *Rocinante* had and more like a showroom or a spa. The cabinets were set into gently curving walls, the seams too fine to see. The light came from the walls themselves, the skin of the ship glowing softly and uniformly to make the space gentle and shadowless. Alex stood at one of the benches with a manufacturing printer that looked like it had been grown from a seed more than built. He was thinner about the middle than he'd been when he was married. What was left of his hair had gone white, and a stubble of pale whiskers marked his dark cheeks. He reminded her of the man who'd run the ice cream shop by her school when she'd been a child. He looked up at her and nodded, and the memory faded. He was only Alex again.

"Something broken?" she asked, and pointed to the printer with her chin.

"The center brace on my crash couch was showing some wear. I broke down the old piece and I'm printing up a replacement," he said. "What brings you back to the ship?"

"I was looking for you," she said. "We need to have a conversation."

"I thought we might."

"The things you said before? About why I was...reaching for something. You may have been right."

"Thank you."

"But you aren't now," she said. "The situation's changed on us. The calculus shifted when they closed the gates."

"There are still Transport Union ships we could meet with. The gates will open at some point. I mean, they can't keep them closed forever, I don't care what happened out there."

"But until they do, we're stuck in Sol system. But that's not the big point. They lost the *Typhoon*. They only had three of these monsters. The *Heart of the Tempest* controlling Sol system because that's the place with the power and the resources. The population."

"The history," Alex said. "It has the story of a time when Laconia wasn't in charge."

"That too," Bobbie said. "The *Eye of the Typhoon* to control the gates. The *Voice of the Whirlwind* back in Laconia protecting their home system. Now they're down one because of whatever this disaster was. And they're scrambling. Trejo's been called back to Laconia. No one's in control of the ring space. Everything

I said before about showing people that the fight is winnable is still true, and if it works we'll be taking their fleet down to a single battleship. Maybe they'll keep it in Laconia. Maybe they'll take it to the ring space if they think whatever that was won't happen again. They won't bring it here. Sol system will get a lot easier for the underground to navigate. It's still the most important system, and we can go a long way toward taking it back. It's not just a symbolic win anymore. It's tactical and strategic too. I can't let the opportunity go."

"I hear what you're saying," Alex said.

The printer ticked to itself for a few seconds.

"I know you have reservations," Bobbie said. "I respect them. Seriously."

"No, it's not that," Alex began. "I just—"

"I don't want you in on this if you aren't certain. No, listen to me. It's a long shot. The *Tempest* is the deadliest machine humans have ever built. We both know what it stood up to in the war. Even if we do manage to deliver the package, I don't know for certain that the antimatter will be enough to kill it. You have a kid. And before long, he's probably going to have a kid. Holden's gone. Amos is gone. Naomi's doing her hermit thing. The *Roci*'s mothballed. And...if this doesn't work, the *Storm*'s gone too. If you want out, that's not a wrong thing."

"If I want out?"

"If you want to retire. We can get you a fresh name, or do more background for the one you've got. Set you up with a job on Ceres or Ganymede or here. Whatever. You could actually get to know Kit and his wife. No one will think less of you for wanting that."

"I might," Alex said.

"I need you a hundred percent or nothing."

Alex scratched his chin. The printer chimed that its run was finished, but Alex didn't open it to take out the new brace.

"You're speaking as the captain of this ship," he said. "You actually pronounce things a little differently when you're being in charge. You know that? It's subtle, but it's there. Anyway, as the captain, I know what you're saying. And I know why you're saying it. But as my friend, I need a favor from you."

No favors, no compromises, either you're in or you're out popped to her lips.

"What do you need?" she asked.

"Run it by Naomi. If she says it's the wrong thing, listen to her. Hear her out."

Bobbie felt herself pushing back against the idea. The old fight was like a knot in her gut, hard as stone. But...

"If she agrees?"

Alex squared his shoulders, lowered his center of gravity, and smiled amiably. No one else on the ship would have recognized the imitation of Amos, but she did.

"Then we go fuck some motherfuckers permanently up," he said.

Interlude: The Dancing Bear

Holden woke up with the light of dawn streaming through the high window and casting shadows across the ceiling. The last trails of a dream—something about crocodiles getting into a water recycler and him and Naomi trying to lure them out with a salt shaker—slipped away. He stretched, yawned, and pulled himself up out of the wide bed with its soft pillows and plush blanket. He took a moment at the foot of the bed to take everything in. The flowers in the vase by the window. The subtle pattern woven into the sheets. He worked his toes against the soft, warm rug. And he recited silently what he always did, every morning since the beginning.

This is your cell. You are in prison. Don't forget.

He smiled contentedly because someone was watching.

His shower was tiled with river stones, smooth and beautiful. The water was always warm, and the soap was scented with sandalwood and lilac. The towels were soft and thick and white as fresh-fallen snow. He shaved in a mirror that was heated to keep condensation from forming on it. His Laconian uniform—real cloth, not recycled paper—was pressed and clean in his footlocker. He dressed himself, humming a light melody he remembered from his childhood because someone was listening.

He had come to Laconia in a much less pleasant cell. He had been questioned in a box. He'd been beaten. And in the early days, threatened with worse things than that. In the later days, tempted with the promise of freedom. Even power. It could have been much, much worse. He had, after all, been part of an attack that had crippled Medina Station and ended with the agents of the underground scattering to systems all around the empire. Some-one had even managed to steal one of Laconia's early destroyers out from under them. Holden had known a lot about how the underground on Medina functioned, who was involved with it, and where they could be found. He was alive and had all his fin-gers with the nails still attached because he'd also known about the dead space that had appeared on the *Tempest* when it used its magnetic field generator in normal space. And the dead spaces like it in all the systems besides Sol. He was the one person in the whole of humanity who had—escorted by the enslaved rem-nants of Detective Miller—been inside the alien station and seen the fate of the protomolecule's builders firsthand. And from the first moment they'd allowed it, he'd been shoveling everything he knew about that at them. Calling him cooperative on the subject would have been a vast understatement, and with every passing week, his knowledge of the underground was more out of date. Less useful. They didn't even bother asking him about that stuff anymore.

Duarte was a thoughtful, educated, civilized man and a mur-derer. He was charming and funny and a little melancholy and, as far as Holden could tell, completely unaware of his own mon-strous ambition. Like a religious fanatic, the man really believed that everything he'd done was justified by his goal in doing it. Even when it was the push for his own personal immortality—and then his daughter's—before slamming the door behind them, Duarte managed to cast it as a necessary burden for the good of the species. He was above all else a charming little ratfuck. As Holden grew to respect the man, even to like him, he was careful never to lose sight of the fact that Duarte was a monster.

There was a lock on his door, but he didn't control it. He put the handheld he'd been issued in a pocket, walked out into the courtyard, and closed the door behind him. Anyone who wanted in could go in. If they wanted for some reason to lock him out—or in—they could. He put his hands in his pockets and strolled down a colonnaded walkway. The ferns in the planter came from Earth. Maybe the soil did too. Some minor functionary of the state came out of a doorway before him, turned and breezed by him as if he hadn't been there. He was like a fern that way. Decorative.

The commissary was larger than a whole deck of the *Rocinante*. Pale, vaulted ceilings and an open kitchen with three cooks on duty any time of the day or night. A few tables by the windows, a dozen scattered in another courtyard at the back. Fresh fruit. Fresh eggs. Fresh meats and cheeses and rice. Not too much of any one thing. The elegance came from the labor and deference of the people, not from conspicuous waste. Loyalty valued over wealth. It was amazing what you could learn about someone by sitting quietly for a few months with what they'd built.

He got a carved wooden tray and a plate of rice and fish, the way he usually did. A smaller plate of melon and berries. A light-roast coffee in a white ceramic cup the size of a small soup bowl. Cortázar was sitting alone in an alcove at the back, looking at something on a hand terminal. Out of discipline, Holden grinned and went to sit across from the sociopathic professional vivisectionist.

"Good morning, Doc," he said. "Haven't seen you in a while. Universe treating you gently?"

Cortázar closed whatever file he'd been reading over, but not before Holden caught the phrase *indefinite homeostasis*. He didn't know what it meant exactly, and he couldn't look it up without someone knowing he had.

"Things are fine," Cortázar said, and the glimmer in his eyes meant that was true. Which probably meant they were terrible for someone who wasn't Paolo Cortázar. "Very good."

"Yeah?" Holden said. "What's the good word?"

For a second, Cortázar teetered on the edge of saying something, but he pulled back. It was a confirmation of his good mood. The doctor liked knowing more than the people around him. It gave him a sense of power. The times he was most likely to let his guard down were when he was angry or annoyed. Or drunk. Drunk and complaining Cortázar was the best version of the man.

"Nothing I can talk about," he said, and rose from his place even though his food was only half-eaten. "I'm sorry I can't stay. Schedule."

"If you get time later, track me down and we can play some more chess," Holden said. He lost a lot of chess to Cortázar. He didn't even have to throw the games. The guy was good. "You will always find me at home."

Left alone, Holden ate his breakfast in silence and let the atmosphere of the room wash over him. Another of the things he'd learned during his time as a dancing bear was not to search for clues to anything. The effort of the search actually made him overlook things. It was better to be passive and notice what was there. Like the way the cooks spoke to each other, scowling. Like the speed of the dignitaries walking into and out of the commissary, the way their shoulders were tight.

Ever since the most recent event—the weird shift in his perception, the lost time and consciousness—the atmosphere in the State Building had been like this. Something was going on, but Holden didn't know what. No one had even mentioned it to him. And he didn't ask. Because someone was always listening.

When he was done, he left his plate to be cleared away, got his usual two cups of fresh coffee in takeaway mugs, and tucked a half link of sausage into his pocket. He walked out toward the gardens. It was a little cool. Seasons were longer on Laconia, but the autumn was definitely starting to get its roots into things. High above, one of the weird jellyfish-looking cloud things sailed through the air, the blue of the sky showing through its transparent flesh. The guard post was little more than a bench with a square-jawed young man who looked like he might have been one of Alex's cousins.

"Good morning, Fernand," Holden said. "Brought you a little something."

The guard smiled and shook his head. "I still can't accept that from you, sir."

"I understand," Holden said. "It's a shame, you know, because the coffee they serve at the VIP commissary is really good. Fresh beans that they didn't roast like they were hiding evidence. Water with a little bit of minerals, but not so much that it tastes like you're drinking a quarry. It's excellent stuff, but…"

"It sounds wonderful, sir."

Holden put one of the takeaway mugs on the bench. "I'll just put this here so you can dispose of it safely. And this one that Lieutenant Yao can dispose of too. It has a little sugar in it."

"I'll let her know to get rid of it," the guard said with a smile. It had taken weeks to get that far with the kid. It wasn't much, but it wasn't nothing. Every person in the State Building who saw humanity in Holden, who shared a joke with him, or who had a pattern in their day that he could be a part of, made him that tiny bit harder to kill. No one thing he did made a difference. All of it together might decide between mercy or a bullet in the back of his skull somewhere not too far down the line. So Holden chuckled like the guard was a friend and ambled out into the gardens.

There were patterns in the life of the State Building. Everyone had routines, whether they knew it or not. Here at the heart of the empire, with thousands of people making their way into and out of and through the buildings at the source of authority and power, he could have spent lifetimes tracking them all. It was like sitting and watching a termite hive until each insect stopped being itself and turned into an organ in a much larger, older consciousness. If he lived as long as Duarte intended to, he still wouldn't understand all the subtleties of it. For his present purposes, the smaller patterns were enough. Things like Cortázar enjoyed winning at chess and the guard lieutenant liked sugar in her coffee and Duarte's daughter went out into the gardens in the late morning, especially when she was upset.

Not that she always did. Some days, Holden put himself in what he hoped would be her path and wound up spending hours reading old adventure novels or watching censor-approved entertainment feeds. Not news. He had access to the state propaganda feeds, but he couldn't bring himself to watch them. Either they'd make him angry, and he couldn't afford to be angry, or through simple repetition they'd start to seem true. He couldn't afford that either.

Today, he picked a little pagoda set by an artificial stream. The plants there were local varieties. The leaflike structures were darker than the plants he'd known growing up. Blue black with whatever chlorophyll analog Laconia's evolutionary history had come up with. Still wide, to catch the energy of the sun. Still tall to get above everything they were competing with. Similar pressures yielded similar solutions, just the way flight had evolved five different times on Earth. *Good moves in design space.* That's what Elvi Okoye had called it.

He took out his handheld, and for almost two hours let himself sink into an old murder mystery set on an ice hauler in the Belt before the gates opened, and written by someone who had clearly never been on an ice hauler in their life. The first sign that he wasn't alone was the barking. He put down his reading just as the old Labrador came galloping around the hedge, grinning the way only dogs could. Holden took the sausage out of his pocket and let the dog eat it from his palm while he scratched the old girl's ears. There was no better way to seem trustworthy than to be liked by a dog, and there was no better way to convince a dog to like you than bribery.

"Who's a good dog?" he said. The dog huffed once just as the girl came around. Teresa, the heir apparent. Princess of the empire. She was fourteen, and in the phase of adolescence where every emotion spilled down her face. He barely had to glance at her to know that something had wrecked her.

"Hey," he said, the way he always did. Every time the same, so that the pattern of it became familiar. So that *he* became familiar. Because things that are familiar aren't a threat.

Normally she answered with *Hello*, but today she broke the pattern. She didn't say anything at all, just looked at her dog and avoided Holden's gaze. Her eyes were bloodshot, with dark smudges under them. Her skin was paler than usual. Whatever was going on, it was personal to her. That narrowed the options down.

"You know what's weird," he said. "I saw Dr. Cortázar at breakfast, and he was in a big rush. Normally he'll stop, chew the fat for a little while. Today, he skinned right out of there. Didn't even bother to whip my ass on the chessboard."

"He's busy right now," Teresa said. Her voice was as ruined as she was. "He has a patient. Dr. Okoye. The one from the Science Directorate. Her husband too. She got hurt, and she's here at the State Building so she and Father can talk. She isn't hurt badly. She'll be fine, but Dr. Cortázar is helping to take care of her."

At the end of the speech, she nodded, like she was reviewing what she'd said and approved of it. It was a small gesture. The kind that would lose her a lot of money if she ever started playing cards.

"I'm sorry to hear that," Holden said. "I hope she gets better."

He didn't ask what had happened. He didn't dig for information. He should have left it at that. From a tactical point of view, anything more was a mistake.

"Hey," he said. "I may not be the guy you want to hear this from, but whatever it is? It's going to be okay."

The girl's eyes went wide, and then they went hard. It didn't take a second.

"I don't know what you're talking about," she said, then turned and stalked away, slapping her palm against her leg to call the dog. The dog looked from her to Holden, regret in the dark-brown eyes. The hope of more sausage weighed against the distress of her person.

"Go," Holden said, nodding at Teresa's retreating back. The dog barked once, a friendly sound, and galloped away again.

Holden tried to go back to his book, but his attention kept wandering. He waited for almost an hour, then put the handheld away and walked. A cool breeze was starting up. He thought about going back to his cell and getting a jacket, but decided not to. Something about being a little uncomfortable was right for the day. Instead, he made his way to the mausoleums.

Garlands of flowers rested in the corner where the stone met the ground. Red and white and a lavish purple. Some were native Laconian plants, some were out of a hydroponics tank. They'd be replaced until the order came to stop replacing them. If the people in authority forgot, there might be fresh flowers at Avasarala's grave forever.

The woman herself looked down at him from where she was etched in stone. It was probably just his imagination, but she seemed amused. Like now that she was dead and not actually responsible for fixing any of the vast and secret shit show that was human history, she finally got the joke. He looked up at her, remembering her voice, the way she'd moved. Her eyes, bright and intelligent and pitiless as a crow's.

"What is going on here?" he asked, softly. "What am I looking at?"

It didn't matter if they heard that. Without the context of his thoughts, it wouldn't mean anything.

He was seeing Teresa, devastated. The State Building vibrating with banked anxiety. Cortázar—entitled, narcissistic, protomolecule-obsessed Cortázar—quietly gleeful. Another bout of strange consciousness and lost time, this one at least in Laconia system, and maybe beyond. Elvi Okoye's return being used as a cover story for Cortázar's presence at the State Building. Because he needed to be there, was happy to be there, and someone wanted to hide the real reasons why.

Put like that, something had happened to Duarte.

If it was true, Cortázar's hands were freer. Which meant his plans to vivisect and kill Duarte's daughter would probably kick into high gear. And also Elvi was back from her missions in the other system, so Holden's plans could move forward too. It was a race now, and he had a strong suspicion that he was behind. That was too bad. He had hoped to have more time.

Don't be a whiny little cunt, Avasarala said in his imagination. *Hope in one hand and shit in the other. See which one fills up first. Get to work.*

First he chuckled, and then he sighed. "Fair point," he said to the dead woman. This time she didn't answer. He turned and walked back toward the buildings as the first genuinely cold rush of air came and stirred the ground cover that wasn't quite grass. There would be a storm by nightfall, he was sure of it. Maybe snow. Snow was the same everywhere.

He had to find his next step. Maybe Elvi. Maybe her husband, Fayez. He'd always liked Fayez. Maybe Teresa. Maybe it was time to go to Duarte, if it wasn't already too late. If only there had been more time…

This was the problem with thousand-year Reichs. They came and they went like fireflies.

Chapter Twenty-Five: Naomi

Naomi had lived long enough to see history change more than once now. In the reality where she'd been born, Earth and Mars had maintained an alliance built to keep their boot permanently on the neck of Belters like her. The idea of alien life had been something for scientific speculations and thrillers on entertainment feeds. Some changes had been so slow it was almost possible to miss that they were happening. The change of Belter identity from underclass to the de facto governing party at the height of the Transport Union's power had spanned decades. The rebuilding of Ganymede after its collapse also. The others had been sudden, or had seemed that way. When Eros moved. When the gates opened. When the rocks fell on Earth. When Laconia came back.

The sudden changes, as different as they were, all followed the same pattern. After it happened—whatever it was—humanity went into a kind of shock. Not just her and the people around her, but the whole vast and varied tribe of people. For a moment, it was as if they were all still primates on the fields of Africa going silent at a lion's roar. All the rules they'd lived by were suddenly open to question. *The inner planets have always been my enemy, but are they still? The far reaches of the solar system are as distant as humanity will ever be, but can we go farther? Earth will endure, won't it?*

Naomi didn't like the feeling, but she recognized it. And more than that, she saw the power in it. Moments like these were opportunities. They could bring new alliances, new empathy, a new and broader sense of being together in a single human tribe. Or they could be the poison that ran through human minds for decades to come and welcomed ancient wars onto new and bloody battlefields.

Auberon held its breath and waited to see if the predators were coming for it. She saw it on the in-system newsfeeds that were the only newsfeeds now. It was in the wideness of the Laconian governor's eyes. And, Naomi had to admit, it was in her own heart too.

The *Typhoon* was the absolute symbol of Laconian dominance. After the *Tempest's* inexorable conquest of Sol system, Laconian rule was a given. It wasn't just that Laconia had found a way to defend the ring space against simultaneous attacks from any or all gates, though that was part of it. It was also the clear knowledge that by being in the slow zone, the *Typhoon* was already halfway to anyone's home. That once it started coming, nothing could stop it but the whim of the empire.

And now it was gone.

Medina Station had been a feature of the ring space from the start. It had been one of the first ships through the Sol ring, and taken up its place even before the other gates had opened. Medina had been the farthest trading post of the new land rush and then the traffic cop at the center of the colony worlds. Its history as a religious generation ship and then as a battleship for the OPA had made it as rich and complicated as the people who lived on it. It was a permanent fact of how humanity moved through the rings, as constant and permanent as the rings themselves.

It was gone too.

If it had been just one or the other, maybe it would have been simpler. But having the hammer that had threatened every head in the empire and the longest-standing human presence at the gates both wiped away at once pulled Naomi's heart in two directions. She was rejoicing and mourning at the same time. And also feeling the deep unease that came from the reminder that that being familiar wasn't the same as being understood.

"How do you take your eggs?" Chava asked.

Naomi, sitting at the breakfast bar, rubbed the sleep from her eyes. "Usually reconstituted and from a nozzle."

"So...scrambled?"

"That would be great."

Chava's rooms were in a fashionable part of the station, assuming there was an unfashionable part. Auberon hadn't existed long enough to have history built in its bones yet. Nothing there had been reappropriated or reused or reimagined yet. The hard industrial white of Chava's kitchen was exactly as the designer had imagined it. The ferns in the hydroponic vases that showed the white of their roots and the green of their fronds were placed exactly where they would photograph best. The windows looking out over the common space three levels below as if it were a city apartment on Earth, except cleaner, had the intended effect. In a generation or four, it would develop its own style and character, but it hadn't yet.

Or maybe Naomi just needed to get some coffee and work out. That was possible too.

"Did you sleep well?" Chava asked over the sizzle and pop of eggs on their hot pan. "I don't usually have visitors. You're the first one to be in the guest room for more than a night."

"It's lovely," Naomi said. "Is there any news?"

Chava put a white ceramic coffee cup on the bar next to Naomi's elbow and then a small glass French press already filled with black coffee beside it. "The political officer at the transfer station is saying all traffic out of the gate is prohibited until we've had instructions from Laconia. Which is tricky because the repeaters are still down. There's a freighter that was on its way out when the shit hit the fan, and the Transport Union is saying that if it doesn't get its cargo to Farhome system, there'll be a lot of starving people a year from now."

Naomi poured the coffee into the cup. Black welled up in the overwhelming white, steam rising up from it. The smell was lighter than she was used to. She wondered if Jim would have liked it.

"Any word from the governor?"

"Radio silence," Chava said. "There are stories that the governor's been taking payoffs for a long time. His loyalties aren't perfectly clear."

"That's weirdly refreshing," Naomi said. The coffee tasted better than it smelled. Another layer of sleep that she hadn't recognized slipped away. The smell of the eggs started to seem very interesting.

Chava saw it and smiled. "Hungry?"

"I think I am," Naomi said. "The local underground. How does it look? What kind of resources does it have?"

Chava shrugged. "I don't entirely know. Saba keeps us compartmentalized. I'm not even sure how much he knows, except that he knows who to ask if something's possible." She realized the error in what she'd said, and her lips pressed thin. "Knew, I mean. I can't quite believe he's…"

"I know," Naomi said. "Without coordination, we're not really an underground anymore. We're thirteen hundred different undergrounds that can't talk to each other." Communication, she thought as she sipped her coffee, was always a problem.

Chava swirled the pan of eggs and decanted the fluffy yellow clouds onto a white plate. "On the upside, there are thirteen hundred different Laconias now. Less than that, really. A lot of the smaller colonies don't have governors on-site yet. They're essentially free."

"And in danger of collapsing without support. I'm not sure dying free is as attractive when it stops being rhetorical."

"Truth," Chava said.

The eggs tasted strange. Thicker and more substantial than the approximation that the *Roci* had put out, and with a different aftertaste that Naomi couldn't decide at first whether she liked or not. Having food in her stomach felt wonderful, though. And it went well with the coffee.

Chava hadn't brought up the subject of Naomi's future. They both knew that there were too many unknowns now for any plan to mean much. Even if there was a ship that could take in the shell game, there was no Saba to send her information to analyze or consider her recommendations. Naomi's role in the underground, the underground's ability to survive, everything was radically uncertain. They papered over the gaps with hospitality and kindness. Naomi was Chava's guest. Slept in her spare room. Ate her food and drank her coffee as if they were sisters.

It was strange to think that people lived like this. Not just citizens either. People in the underground had nice apartments and windows with carefully sculpted views, fresh fruit, and coffee. It was so exaggeratedly normal that it felt like the bait in a trap. Would Chava be able to walk away from it all the way Naomi had left the *Roci* and Alex and Bobbie? Or would the comfort keep her here too long if something went wrong? If something had already gone wrong?

"Problem?" Chava asked, and Naomi realized she'd been scowling.

"I was thinking about..."—she reached for something less rude than *my instinctive disapproval of your lifestyle*—"traffic control in the ring space. If that freighter does make the transit, it'll be going through blind. They all will be." Now that she was saying it out loud, it actually did worry her. "And there's going to be pressure. All of those colonies that aren't quite self-sustaining yet? They may wait for a while. Hold back, but sooner or later, the risk of making the transit is going to be better than the certainty of having their colony fail."

"That's true," Chava said as she cracked another egg into the pan. "But I can't see rebuilding in the ring space either. Not before we know what happened and whether there's a way to keep it from happening again. Can you? I mean, maybe Laconia will send another one of its system-killer ships through and park it there again, but only if they're up for the risk of losing it."

"It does start looking like hazard pay," Naomi said, trying levity. It didn't feel right, though. Not yet.

"Once could mean anything," Chava said as the new egg started to bubble and pulse from the heat. "Maybe it was just the one time. Or maybe it's every thousand years. Or every third Thursday from now on. We don't even know what triggered it this time."

"By the time we have enough points to make a good scatter plot, it's a lot of dead ships."

"If there's even a way to know when a ship went dutchman. There's no one watching, so who'd be keeping track? The whole communications grid is down at this point. If someone did know, they'd have to build some way to tell us. No one's in charge. Do you want some more coffee?"

"No, thank you," Naomi said, her mind already racing along somewhere new.

She and Chava weren't the only ones having this conversation. Thousands of other people in Auberon were thinking about these same things in restaurants and bars and on ships traveling though the vast emptiness between this sun and gate. It was how the shock started to wear off. How the moment after the moment created itself.

And it wasn't only Auberon either. Every system with a ring gate was looking at the same questions, fearing the same possible futures. Every system including Laconia.

The thought landed with a weight. Her grief at the loss of Saba and Medina and her unexpected hope in seeing the *Typhoon* destroyed. The dread of the mysterious enemy and its escalating body count. They all led to the same conclusion.

It was like a nightmare where you spent the whole night running from something and ended up in its lap all the same. *No one's in charge.*

"Sorry?" Chava said as she slid her own egg with its golden yolk onto a plate. "Did you say something?"

"We're going to need to break some protocols," Naomi said. "And I'll need access to a machine shop. You wouldn't know how I could get my hands on some torpedoes, do you? I don't need warheads. Just the drives and the frames. Long-range designs, if we can find them."

"I can look," Chava said. "How many do you need?"

"Ideally about thirteen or fourteen hundred."

Chava laughed, saw Naomi's expression, and sobered.

"And," Naomi said, "if the offer's still open, I might take the coffee after all."

The yard that Chava found would have been small back in Sol system. There were thousands like it scattered through the Belt. Improvised shipyards that catered to rock hoppers and independents who couldn't afford docking fees at Callisto or Ceres or any of the other centers. Apart from the fact that this one didn't have anything manufactured over fifteen years ago, it could have been anywhere.

The man who ran it was called Zep, and he had a faded split-circle tattoo on his neck. He spoke English, Mandarin, Portuguese, and a dialect of Belter creole that put his background in the Martian trojans. He gave her the tour of the yard. It was a high, pale bubble of ceramic and steel with harsh white work lights overhead and a misting of oil every morning to trap the lunar fines. Everything there was a little sticky to the touch and stank of gunpowder. It was the first place in Auberon system she felt even slightly at home.

Even with the oil, the fines—tiny bits of stone smaller than dust that erosion had never smoothed—were dangerous enough that she wore a mask and eye protection. She went through the rows of decommissioned ships that had been repossessed or damaged by misadventure or malice to the point that it made more sense to sell them as scrap. They were mostly orbital shuttles and semiautomated prospectors. The shuttles were no use to her, but some of the prospectors had probes. They didn't have the range or speed of real torpedoes, but she could start with them. Over the course of a long, sweat-soaked morning, she'd assembled half a dozen that seemed worth closer examination.

The idea wasn't that different from the bottles she'd used before. It was only the scale that was different. And the stakes. She could load transmitters and explosives into the probes and then send them out through the different gates. No one would be exposed to danger by coming through the newly haunted slow zone, and the messages would be untraceable. Anyone listening as she had been would hear them just like the ones she'd dropped off before. She needed to work on the exact wording. It would be the first voice from the underground since Medina. Getting it right mattered. Getting it done quickly mattered more.

There had been a moment in the neo-noir films that Alex always watched that happened so often it became a cliché. She had to have seen it a dozen times over the years, and she hadn't been paying much attention. A firefight would start with operatic choreography and impossibly high-capacity magazines. The hero and the villain would play through the scenario with whatever peculiar flourishes the director had invented to make this one different from all the ones before. Then, at the climactic ending, the two enemies faced each other, and both would run out of ammunition. The resolution of all the heroic violence came down to which of them could reload faster.

That was where the underground and the empire stood. They were both disrupted. Whichever of them was able to organize again first would survive. Laconia still had the firepower. It still had the technological edge. But if the underground could rebuild a communication grid faster, she could change the story of their inevitability. Laconia's advantages wouldn't be enough.

Speed mattered. If Saba were still alive, if Medina had survived, it would have been time for him to stand up, announce himself, and become the public face of the opposition. To forge the thirteen hundred different undergrounds that were out there now in the cut off systems back into one thing, and exploit the confusion of the enemy before Duarte could find his feet. Take the crisis and make it a turning point, even if it meant more pressure on Drummer and the Union. Naomi would have told him it had to be done. She'd have been right.

Her hand terminal chimed. She pulled off her goggles and air filter and accepted the connection. There was only one person it could be. Chava was in her office, her hair perfectly in place, her blouse unsmeared and her demeanor as polite and professional as if she did work like this every day.

"I have the secure connection you asked for," she said. "The light delay won't make it a conversation."

"How far?" Naomi asked.

"About fifty minutes, one way."

Naomi pictured the Auberon system. Its three gas giants the greater and lesser belts. The *Bhikaji Cama* was still a fair distance from the ring. She had time.

"Thank you," she said.

"Not a problem," Chava said. "I'm sending you the route and encryption. I'll see you for dinner tonight?"

"I don't want to impose."

"It isn't an imposition," Chava said. "And it's safer than anyplace else."

"Then yes, thank you," Naomi said. Chava smiled and killed the connection. Naomi thumbed up the data packet configuration and slotted in the information she'd been given. If it worked, it would slide unnoticed through the Transport Union's system and appear to Emma Zomorodi in particular.

Naomi considered herself in the preview display. Dust and sweat-smeared skin. Hair more pale than black. Wrinkles at her eyes and mouth. This was the woman who turned down High

Consul Winston Duarte's invitation to live the rest of her life in a palace with the man she loved in order to take on the one job she never wanted. She smiled, and the woman on the screen looked happy. Exhausted, yes. Well bruised by life, yes. But happy. She started the recording.

"Emma, I need to ask you to break protocol for me. I want you to send me everything you know about the status and function of the underground. Contacts. Ship names. Procedures. Anything you have, tell me. And if you can get messages to your operatives, tell them to expect a message like this from me in the near future.

"I know it's exactly what I told you never to do before, but the situation has changed. Medina is off the board, and we've lost Saba. We have to regroup, reorganize. And someone has to take initiative."

A thick trickle of sweat broke free from her temple and began its slow fall down toward her eyebrow. She wiped it away, pulling her hair back from her eyes.

"Until you hear otherwise from me, I will be running the underground."

Chapter Twenty-Six: Elvi

Elvi woke herself trying to scream. She didn't remember the dream, just the sense of overwhelming fear and paralysis. The effort to make herself heard that seemed to go on for hours, even though all it managed was a little groan, loud enough to bring her back to consciousness. It left her in the darkness, drenched in sweat and grateful for another few sleepless hours.

The suite was courtesy of the Laconian state. Two beds, both with autodocs built into them. One for her, the other for Fayez, who, fortunately, was still breathing deeply and heavily. She knew without looking that she hadn't woken him up. She was grateful for that too. She didn't turn the light on. Her cane was at her bedside, and she found it easily enough. She levered herself to the edge of the mattress, steeled herself, and swung her legs over. It hurt like hell, but only for a few seconds. Standing up was actually better, and she was leaning on the cane less than she had been.

The night terrors were looking pretty robust, though.

Trying hard not to make enough noise to wake her husband, she went through the darkness to the closet. The servants had left robes for them both, thick, textured cotton with a lining of something that might have been silk. She pulled it on one sleeve at a time, cinched it closed, and made her way out to the courtyard and a stone bench carved with complex mathematical patterns like something out of a mosque.

Her memory of the rescue was spotty at best. She remembered giving the emergency evacuation order to the *Falcon*. She remembered coming back to consciousness in normal space and calling for help. Crawling through blood and crash couch gel to Fayez. That part was pretty clear. After that, a few lucid moments of trying to cinch a belt around Fayez's calf as a tourniquet. At some point, she'd decided that she was losing too much blood, slipped her hand into the hole in her leg, and made a fist in there to apply pressure all around. That probably should have been the worst part—her wrist vanishing into the skin of her own leg like a graphics processing failure. What she actually felt at the time was pride at having come up with a graceful solution. The tourniquet had been hard.

They told her she had been conscious when the rescue ship came, but she didn't remember it. She knew because she'd read the reports that Jen had lived and was being treated somewhere else in the city. That Admiral Sagale had died, half his head ripped away. That Travon was technically listed as missing, since it was possible he could have survived someplace without the arm he left behind.

The casualties among the rest of the crew were similar. About half had survived. No one had come through uninjured. The *Falcon* had been stabilized too and brought home to be healed. And studied.

Some local animal was making its call. Four distinct notes, repeated again and again, at different speeds. Mating call. Warning. Alerting the hive to a food source. She had no way to know, but it was pretty. The night air was cool almost to the point of discomfort, but she didn't want to go back inside for a coat. She'd just wait until she got tired and head back to bed or else find some other lobby in the palatial buildings to sit in until dawn broke. If anyone wondered why there was a lady with a bathrobe and a cane wandering around, she'd just tell them it was classified.

Exobiology wasn't medicine. She knew more about predictive parallel evolution models than she did about wound care. If she hadn't had a rank in the Science Directorate, she wouldn't have been able to see her medical records, and mostly for good reasons. It was dangerous for someone with one expertise to try to interpret something in a different but similar field. Laypeople didn't understand how much scientific literature was about nuance and shared understanding. Even with expert systems to help, she was more likely to avoid errors with one of Jen Lively's physics analyses than her own medical records, if only because she knew that she didn't know physics.

But she'd looked anyway.

The medical team had fought hard to keep her and Fayez alive. The cuts where their flesh had gone missing were strange. Something about the wounds had made clotting weird too, which of course immediately left her thinking of vampire bats and leeches. Organisms that fed on blood and produced anticoagulants. Which there was no reason to think these attackers had. The incisions in the decking had the same too-perfect margins.

A more comprehensive report was still in draft form, but she was able to access that too. Sagale appeared to have died instantly. Others in the crew had lived long enough for the wounded *Falcon* to haul them through the gate and out of danger, only to bleed out or succumb to shock. The missing matter was just that. Missing. The scoop of her leg, Fayez's foot. Most of one lobe of Sagale's brain. All of Travon but his arm. It wasn't that they had been torn away. They'd been excised and taken...elsewhere. All told, the *Falcon* had lost 12 percent of its mass, apparently at random. The dark things that moved between the spaces hadn't been targeting the crew. They'd meant to take everything. The human parts they'd removed were just points along a path. It almost made them worse. At least murderers had motives.

She pulled aside the robe and looked at the wound. The medical gel that filled in the missing flesh was pale, but getting pinker. She could already trace the lines where blood vessels were starting to form. Muscle and skin would follow over the next few weeks and months. In the end, she'd probably have a slightly discolored patch on her leg where the skin was younger than she was. Sagale, on the other hand... She shuddered. It was still hard to accept that he was gone.

She didn't notice the dawn starting. The courtyard didn't open to the east, so it was just a slow, subtle graying of the Laconian sky. The retreat of the stars and glowing construction platforms. Even then, what she noticed was the local organisms getting louder and the gentle vinegary smell that one of the local bird analogs made when it was waking up during mating season. She was cold and stiff and uncomfortable, but she didn't move until Kelly, Duarte's personal attendant, appeared.

"Major Okoye," Kelly said. "You're up early."

"Or late," Elvi said, trying on a smile. It didn't really fit.

"Admiral Trejo arrived from Sol system last night."

"That was fast."

"I understand the burn was punishing. Still, he asked if you could join us after breakfast."

"I can," Elvi said. "But the one I need to talk to is the high consul."

Kelly's smile revealed nothing. "That's worth discussing with the admiral."

Elvi had had only ever seen Anton Trejo on screens. In person, he was a little underwhelming at first, and then, after a few minutes, she understood how he'd become the most decorated man in the Laconian military. He was stocky. His hair was dark and thin enough she could see pretty much all of his scalp through it. His eyes were a vivid green. A few years back, he'd conquered all of human civilization in less than a month. His manner was gentle, like everyone but him was a little fragile and he didn't want to break them unintentionally.

He didn't come across as having much to prove.

The meeting room was casual. Tapestry-upholstered couches and a low, long table of polished stone. The others were all men. Colonel Ilich, who Elvi had met a few times when she'd first been pressed into the Laconian military, Kelly who had brought her, and her immediate superior, Paolo Cortázar, who headed the Science Directorate and coordinated pretty much all the research Laconia did. Winston Duarte wasn't there.

"Thank you for joining us, Doctor," Trejo said as she took a seat across from him. "I read the reports on the incident in the ring space. That's some hairy shit there."

She took the casual profanity as a sign of his respect. He was treating her as a peer.

"It was," she said. "I'm hoping not to do that again."

"We'll try to keep it that way. I was a little anxious making the transit myself. I mean, I wasn't awake for it. I heard you were awake in one of these new full immersion couches? I don't think I'd enjoy that. I don't like going over twenty g asleep, much less watching it happen."

"I'm glad you made it," Elvi said. Cortázar shrugged and looked at his fingernails. Performative boredom. He wasn't happy she was there. With a little taste of spite, she found a way to draw the pleasantries out a little more. "I hope there wasn't any trouble for you?"

"No, no," Trejo said. "I was fine. There are problems, though. People are starting to make their own transits. One poor bastard out of Bellerophon tried to speed through. Transit into ring space and transit back out in the same burn. He hadn't heard about how the gates all shifted position a little. His ship hit the edge of the gate hub about three hundred klicks to the left of the gate he was aiming for."

"Ouch," Elvi said.

"People are getting desperate. For every system that can sustain itself, there's dozens that aren't there yet. Trade isn't optional for them. It's life and death. And without a traffic authority, death comes a lot more often."

"I'm sorry about Medina and the *Typhoon*," Elvi said.

"Admiral Song was a good sailor," Trejo said. "Died with her boots on. That's as much as any of us can ask. But there'll be time enough to toast the dead later. I have a problem, Doctor. And I have chosen to make part of my problem your problem too."

Cortázar sighed and looked away. Trejo explained what had happened to the high consul, then asked Kelly to bring them some tea while Elvi got over the shock. It was green tea, poured from a cast-iron kettle into black ceramic mugs. She'd had two servings before she felt like she'd found her feet again.

"So there's no one running the empire," she said.

"We are running the empire on the high consul's behalf until such time as he is sufficiently recovered to take over the duties himself," Trejo said, then paused and added, "or his daughter has reached an age sufficient to take over in his place."

"She's very bright," Colonel Ilich said. "And she's controllable. The high consul believed, and I agree, that the narrative of succession had to be familiar and reassuring. Primogeniture is a common model across a wide band of cultures and backgrounds. Of course, she won't be expected to actually wield power until she has shown an aptitude and willingness."

"How old is she?" Elvi asked.

"Duarte hoped he'd have a couple centuries to train her up," Trejo said. "Hell, he hoped she could stay on the bench forever. But these are the cards we have, and so we're going to play them. I'm not going to sugarcoat this. We've got a lot to carry, and most of that is going to fall on the Science Directorate."

"How can I help?" Elvi asked. It sounded better than *What the fuck do you want me to do about this?*

"Your top mission is to get the high consul back," Trejo said.

"Dr. Cortázar will walk you through everything he's done so far. We're hoping a pair of fresh eyes will find something he hasn't."

Elvi looked over at Cortázar. He wasn't looking at her. So this was why he was pouting. Trejo had called his competence into question. That was going to be unpleasant.

"While you do that, I'm going be getting things back under control," Trejo said. "The *Voice of the Whirlwind*'s still a few weeks shy of her shakedown, but we're not stationing any crewed vessel in the ring space, and we're keeping the transits short. *Whirlwind*'s going to be protecting Laconia. *Tempest* is staying in Sol. There's a situation there that needs an eye on it, and Sol's the most unruly system we have to worry about."

"And the traffic control?" Elvi asked.

"We can't hold the inside of gates," Trejo said. "So we're going to have to take the outsides. We have two hundred and eighty *Pulsar*-class destroyers to police thirteen hundred and seventy-one gates."

For a moment, Elvi saw the enormity of what Trejo was facing press down on him. The bright-green eyes focused on nothing, and the cheerful, confident face only looked tired. But a moment later, he was back.

"I'll be deploying those to systems most likely to have high traffic. We'll get the comms network back. And after the *Whirlwind*'s ready, we're turning all the construction platforms over to generating more antimatter charges. That brings us to your number two priority. I think we can all agree this tit-for-tat see-if-we-can-be-reasonable plan hasn't gone so well. We're going to gear up to fight this war for real. Anything you can find that will give us an—"

Adrenaline flooded Elvi's bloodstream. Her heart hit her ribs like a hammer. "Are you fucking crazy?"

Ilich and Kelly shared a look as if she'd confirmed something. Cortázar sneered.

"I'm sorry," Elvi said. "Wait. No. I'm actually not. Are you fucking crazy? Did you not see what just happened?"

Trejo bowed his head. His scalp glimmered at her through his sparse hair.

"I understand that this is a hard conversation for you right now, Doctor. You've been through a lot. But I'm a military man, and the fact is that we are at war. We have been at war since the first time a ship failed a transit."

"Those things killed—"

"I know what they did." Trejo's voice was harsh. It pushed her back into her seat. "And I know *why* they did it. Because they got hurt. That means they can *be* hurt, and unless they find some way to sue for peace, I intend to prepare our forces to hurt them again. Candidly, I don't like it. We're going up against something we don't understand with unfamiliar tools on a battlefield whose constraints we're working out as we go along. It's a stupid war, but it's ours. If it can be won, I intend to win it. You're going to help me."

A hundred objections rose in her mind, but fell back at the sight of the bright-green eyes.

"Yes, sir," she said.

"Good. Please begin your review with Dr. Cortázar and keep me apprised of any insights or progress."

I will Elvi said at the same moment that Cortázar said *We will.* Trejo accepted the answers as if they'd been the same. When he spoke, he spoke to Elvi. "If you disapprove of my plan of action, it's easy to stop me. Just get me my boss back."

"I'm going to try," Elvi said.

Elvi walked back to her rooms before she left the State Building for the Science Directorate. She wanted to clear her head, but it wasn't clearing. Every thought she had seemed to fight its way to consciousness like it was swimming through gel. Her leg ached worse now, and the sleepless hours were starting to weigh on her, pulling her toward bed now that she had obligations. Or maybe she was just realizing that her time of healing after the trauma was over, and she wasn't remotely okay.

The grounds were beautiful. Better than the best luxury resort. The weird leathery fliers they called sunbirds were out, flapping high above the buildings and looking more like bats than birds. Something like a dragonfly zoomed past her, wings buzzing here both the same as and entirely differently than they would have on earth.

The scale of it all was too big. There were too many billion people in too many hundred solar systems for anyone to really understand. For any human to really understand. Maybe that was why Winston Duarte had decided not to be human anymore. Him or his daughter either. It made her wish she'd majored in mathematics instead. They hadn't sent any mathematicians to Ilus. And without Ilus, she wouldn't have been the nearest thing to an expert on the wounds in reality that those dark things left. And she wouldn't have been recruited by Laconia. And she wouldn't be here. One little change early on could have meant a whole different life.

She turned the last corner before her courtyard, and there, out in the gardens, Fayez sat. One leg ended in a bright blue pod the size of a boot where his missing foot was already starting to grow back. The other was stretched out on a bench. And leaning against the back of the bench, James Holden.

As if he had felt the pressure of her gaze, Holden looked up and waved. He seemed both older and as though he hadn't changed at all. She started toward the bench, leaning more on her cane than she'd had to before. The gel in her leg felt like it was burning. Hours more standing and walking through Cortázar's labs sounded awful.

As she approached, Holden and Fayez exchanged a few words, and Holden walked off briskly. By the time she got to her husband's side, Holden had disappeared behind a hedge.

Fayez moved his good leg and gave her room to sit. There were dark pouches under his eyes, but his smile was as amused and sardonic as the day she'd met him. Or the day she'd married him. Or that one time when they'd almost died because a terrorist had booby-trapped a landing pad.

"I think I must have lived my life wrong somehow," she said.

"I know the feeling," he said. "But then I see you, and I think something must have gone right. Even if everything else treats me like my previous incarnation killed a priest."

She took his hand, wove her fingers with his. The future looked a little less bleak.

"I just had the most interesting conversation," Fayez said.

"I could say the same," she said. "But mine's classified, so why don't you go first."

"Well, he was being awfully cagey. But I think our old friend Holden just told me Cortázar's plotting murder."

Chapter Twenty-Seven: Teresa

Nothing was the same anymore. She tried to pretend that it was. That her father was only sick, the way normal fathers were sometimes. She woke up in the morning, and Muskrat was there. She walked through the gardens and the State Building the way she always had. Everyone she saw treated her just the same, except Ilich, who knew the truth.

She assumed that everyone thought her father was in deep consultations with the best minds of the empire because of what happened to the *Typhoon*. They had faith in him. He *was* Laconia. She thought the guards stood a little taller when she walked by. That the cooks at the commissary saved the best dishes for her. It wasn't because she deserved them. It was because she was the closest thing they could get to him, and they wanted to make their offerings. They were scared by what they'd seen. She was too. But they had a story where everything would be all right, and she didn't.

The closest thing she had was Ilich, and he was gone now more than he was with her. When he did see her, the only lessons they did were the new rules. Don't tell anyone about the high consul. Don't act frightened. Don't leave the grounds of the State Building.

She tried watching her favorite films and newsfeeds, but they didn't hold her attention. She tried reading her favorite books, but the words all slid off her mind. She tried running the length of the security wall as fast as she could for as long as she could until the pain and exhaustion made it impossible to think or feel anything. It was as close as she came to peace.

And in the afternoons and early evenings, she went and sat with her father. He suffered Kelly to bathe and dress him, so whenever she came he looked trim and neat. She sat beside him at his desk and used his displays to go over simple mathematical proofs or the diagrams of ancient battles. Sometimes he would nod at the images, as if deep in thought. Sometimes he would pat at the air around her head like he saw something there.

She found herself really looking at him. Staring. His cheeks were rough from old acne scars. His hair was a little thin at the temples. The skin at his jaw was soft with age. And there were other things. The opalescence that sometimes made his skin shine like mother-of-pearl and other times nearly vanished. The darkness in his eyes, like storm clouds.

The more she looked, the less he seemed like her father—the great man who strode the universe and her personal life with the confidence of a god—and the more he seemed like...just someone. The worst times were when he looked sad. Or frightened. He didn't particularly notice when she cried.

Ilich did what he could.

"I'm sorry I haven't been as available since... Well. Since."

They were sitting at the fountain where he'd taught her about displacement. How to make something heavier than water float by making it hollow. She looked at the rippling surface of the water and wondered whether she'd float now too.

"It's all right," she said. "I understand."

His skin looked ashy. His eyes were watery with exhaustion and stress. His smile was the same as it had ever been. She'd thought before it was because he wasn't afraid of her. Now it just seemed well practiced.

"This may not help," he said, "but part of what you're feeling right now is normal. There's a moment that everyone eventually experiences when they see that their parents are just people. That these mythic figures in their lives are also struggling and guessing. Doing their best without knowing for certain what their best is."

The anger in Teresa's chest was the first warm thing she'd felt in days.

"My father is the ruler of the human race," she said.

Ilich chuckled. Had he always chuckled exactly that same way, and she was only noticing it now? "That does change some aspects of it, yes. But I don't want you to feel alone."

Have you considered not making me alone? she didn't say. *Or is it just the feeling that matters?*

"I know it's hard, having this secret," he said. "The only reason we're doing this is that your father and you are so important."

"I understand," she said, and pictured what he would look like if she drowned him in the fountain. "I'll be okay."

She didn't sleep that night. The anger that had surprised her so much in Elsa Singh had infected her. As soon as she put her head on her pillow and closed her eyes, she was in a shouting match with Ilich. Or with Cortázar. Or with James Holden. Or with her father. Or Connor. Or Muriel. Or God. Even when she drifted just a little bit away from herself, she woke up minutes later with her back teeth aching from being clenched together. *Seriously? You're one of the angriest people I know, Tiny,* Timothy said in her memory. Now it felt true.

After midnight, she gave up. Muskrat thumped her tail against the floor twice.

"What are you so fucking happy about?" Teresa snapped.

Muskrat stopped wagging, and her gray canine eyebrows rose

in an expression of concern. Teresa turned on the state news-feed and watched one of the professional voices of Laconia make reassuring mouth noises. *The repair of the gate repeaters is already underway, and the communications network should be restored in a matter of weeks. Normal trade between worlds will resume very soon after that. Until then, the high consul is determining which supply ships are critical to the empire and approving transits on a case-by-case basis. The tragedy in the ring space which claimed the lives of so many loyal to the Laconian dream has shown no signs of recurring, according to the Science Directorate.* Lies, half-truths, fictions, and bullshit.

Rage and grief fought in her heart, and behind them, looming larger than the sky, a sense of overwhelming betrayal that she couldn't put a name to.

Muskrat chuffed once in concern. Teresa bared her teeth in a grin. "I'm not allowed to tell the truth. I'm not allowed to feel anything. I'm not allowed to leave the compound," she said. "I can't do anything. You know why? Because I'm so *important*."

Teresa got up, stalked to her window, and opened it. Muskrat looked away nervously.

"Well?" Teresa said. "Are you coming or not?"

She had never been to the field outside the compound at night. In the darkness, it seemed larger. Swarms of tiny insectile animals crawling along the ground glowed in patterns of moving stripes as she walked past, like her footsteps were making dry ripples on the ground. A cold breeze hissed through the bare trees. In the distance, something called out, its voice like a flute. Two others answered, farther away. A smell like pepper and vanilla hung in the breeze. Ilich had told her once that the chemistry of Laconia was so different from the one humans had evolved with that people struggled to make sense of it, inventing smells that weren't really there out of confusion. She had grown up here, though, and it seemed perfectly normal to her.

Muskrat trotted along at her side, glancing up every few steps as if to ask, *Are you sure about this?* Teresa knew the way to the mountain like it was the back of her hand. She didn't worry at all about straying from the trail.

In her imagination, Ilich sputtered and scolded. He told her that the rules existed for good reasons. For her safety. That she couldn't just go and do whatever she wanted, whenever she wanted. He'd know she was gone. That she'd ignored his rules. That was part of what made it worth doing. What could he do? Lock her in her room? When her father came back to himself, Ilich would have to answer for everything he'd done in the meantime. Her father had known she went off the compound. If he hadn't stopped her, Ilich wouldn't dare. He'd only make rules he couldn't enforce. A law without consequences wasn't a law. It wasn't anything.

The first sign she was close was a shifting in the hedges and the bulbous false eyes of the repair drones peering apologetically out at her. They made their series of three falling clicks, an obvious query for which she didn't have time or an answer. Muskrat usually barked and tried to play with the drones, but tonight, she only paid attention to Teresa.

The drones followed them to the canyon. In the deeper darkness, it was hard to make out the path, but she moved forward all the same. Now that she'd come this far, second thoughts started to haunt her. What if she picked the wrong cave and startled some local animal in its sleep? What if Timothy wasn't there? High above, the orbital construction platforms rippled and glowed. If she looked out of the corner of her eye, she could even make out the *Whirlwind*, the third *Magnetar*-class ship. Only no. It was the second now. The flute-thing called out again, closer this time. She wished she'd brought a light with her. She hadn't thought starlight would be so dark.

She found a deeper shadow that she thought was the sandstone shelf. She ducked under, her hand stretched in front of her. It only took a few steps more before she saw the cavern's lights. The cavern was brighter than the night, and warmer too. The repair drones that walked with her had followed her in, or other ones had been there to begin with. She couldn't tell them apart.

Her heart was beating faster. She was sure that she'd turn the last corner and find Timothy gone, his camp vanished.

"Timothy?" she called, her voice trembling. "Are you here?"

A slick metallic sound came from her right, and Timothy stepped out of the shadows, a gun in his hand. He shook his head. "You got to be more careful, Tiny," he said. "My eyes ain't what they used to be."

Timothy's expression and the casual way he held the gun were so comic, Teresa had to laugh. Once she started, it was hard to stop. The laughter seemed to have a life of its own, hilarity bursting out of her in a riot unstoppable and violent. Timothy's confused expression only made it funnier. She howled, she buckled over, holding her sides, and at some point she noticed that it wasn't laughter anymore. That she was crying.

Timothy watched her like she was giving birth and he wasn't a doctor. The visible understanding that there was probably something he should be doing to help, but he didn't know what it was. In the end it was Muskrat who came and put her thick, heavy, fur-covered head against Teresa. The violence of her emotions left her spent, and she rubbed the dog's ears while the drones set up a little chorus of queries, aware that something was broken but not how it could be fixed.

"Yeah, okay," Timothy said after a while. "Rough night. I get that. Come on back. You can...I don't know what you can do, but I want to sit down, so let's go back here."

Her limbs felt heavier as she walked, but her heart felt lighter. As if she'd come all this way for someone to watch her break down, and even though nothing had changed, something was better.

The big man sat on his cot and rubbed his eyes with the knuckle of his first finger and his thumb. She sat across from him on a metal box, her hands in her lap.

"So," he said. "I don't really know how to do this part. But I think the way it goes is you tell me what's bothering you?"

"So much has happened."

"Yeah?"

And she told him. All of it. From her father's tit-for-tat plan with the things hidden at the gates to the death of the *Typhoon* to the conspiracy to hide her father's illness and the bemused absence that he'd become. The more she talked, the easier it got. Timothy barely spoke, only asking a few questions here and there along the way. He just gave her his attention and asked for nothing in return.

Eventually she ran out of words. The sorrow in her chest was still there, still as painful and heavy and hard, but bearable somehow in a way it hadn't been before. Timothy ran his palm over his scalp. It was a dry sound, like dust hissing against a window. Back toward the mouth of the cave, Muskrat barked happily.

"Yeah, that all sucks," he said. "It's like that sometimes."

"It gets better, though. Right?"

"Sometimes. Sometimes it's just one shit sandwich after another." He shrugged. "What are you gonna do? It's the only game in town."

"I just want—"

Timothy held up his hand, gesturing her to silence. Muskrat barked again, the bark she used when she saw a friend. And there were voices behind it. Timothy scooped up his gun, his eyes fixed on the entrance.

"It's okay," Teresa said. "They're probably just following me."

Timothy nodded, but he didn't seem to hear her.

"Following you?"

"I have a tracker. They planted a tracker on me, can you believe that?"

His eyes widened, just for a second. "Ah, Tiny. Didn't see it coming down like this," he said. She saw something in his face, and she couldn't tell if it was sorrow or amusement or both.

Resignation, maybe. "You should lie down on the floor there. Flat as you can. Put your hands over your ears, okay?"

Who's there? came from the entrance, sharp and hard.

"No, it's all right. They're not going to be mad at you," Teresa said, and Colonel Ilich stepped out of the gloom, a rifle in his hand. Three guards from the State Building were behind him.

Everyone went quiet. Teresa felt a sudden dread bloom in her heart, the realization that she'd misunderstood something badly. That she'd made a mistake she couldn't take back.

"You!" Ilich snapped. "Put the gun down! Get away from the girl!"

"Close your eyes, Tiny. You don't want to watch this."

"Stop," Teresa said. "He's my friend."

The roar of Timothy's gun was louder than anything she'd ever heard. It was like being punched from all directions at once. The sound alone was a kind of violence. She dropped to her knees, her palms pressed against her ears. Gunfire ripped through the cave. Ilich ran toward her, fear in his eyes, and pushed her down, shielding her with his body.

Timothy was screaming like an animal—deep and full of rage. He pushed past her, past Ilich, barreling toward the guards like he could brush them aside. The charge seemed to make the nearest man forget he had a gun in his hand. He tried to grab Timothy, but Timothy took the man's wrist like it was something that belonged to him, shifted it until it snapped. Ilich pushed her down again, and she had to fight to see. Another gun fired. Someone shouted, not Timothy. Teresa twisted under Ilich's knee, trying to find Timothy in the gloom. She got her head up enough to see him just as a wound bloomed on his leg. Redness splattered the cave behind him as he fell. Timothy lay in a fast-spreading pool of his own blood, twitching. Trying to get up as if he didn't know his leg had been turned to splinters. He bared his teeth in pain and anger, swinging his gun around toward Ilich. She screamed *No!* She felt it ripping at her throat, but couldn't even hear it herself.

Someone fired twice. The first round took the top of Timothy's head off. The second blasted a wide hole in his chest. Timothy collapsed, motionless. The silence after rang like a bell.

"What did you do?" Teresa said. She didn't know who she was saying it to. Ilich pulled her up. He bunched her shirt in his fist at the back of her neck like it was a handle, pushing her past Timothy's body.

"Fall back," Ilich said. "Fall back to the truck! We have the girl."

Teresa shifted, trying to turn back to the cave. Timothy was hurt. She needed to help him. Ilich yanked her along.

"Stevens is hit pretty bad," one of the guards said.

"Carry him. We can't wait here. We don't know if the target was alone. We have to get the girl out."

"He's my *friend*," Teresa shouted, but Ilich didn't hear her, or he didn't care.

The night air was cold now. She could see her breath in the glare of the guard transport headlights. Ilich shoved her into the backseat before pushing in beside her. They threw the wounded guard in the back. He groaned when the transport truck lurched backward. Ilich leaned against her, murmuring something fast and low. Her ears weren't right, so it wasn't until she could shift enough to see his lips that she understood it was *fuck fuck fuck fuck*...There was blood on his neck, dark and thick.

"Sir!" the driver said. "Are you okay? You've been hit."

"What?" Ilich said, and then, "Teresa, are you okay? Tell me you're okay!"

The transport truck hit a bump in the road, shaking a little, and the shock of it all fell away. She understood clearly what had just happened. She balled her fists and she shrieked.

The infirmary was quiet. She was shaking. Cortázar and Trejo and Kelly were all there, standing in the anteroom talking to each other in low, urgent voices. Ilich was in the autodoc beside hers, a thick bandage on his shoulder and neck. Dawn would be coming soon. She didn't care as much as she'd expected to. The autodoc fed something cool into her bloodstream. Another sedative, maybe. It made her feel cloudy, but she wasn't going to sleep. She half suspected she'd never sleep again.

When the door opened, Trejo stepped in. He wore gray flannel pajamas a size too small for his belly. He didn't look like the secret ruler of humanity, he looked like a sleepy uncle. He pulled a chair up to her bed, sat down, and sighed.

"Teresa," he said, sternly. "I need you to tell me everything you know about the man in the cave. What he said to you. What you said to him. Everything."

"He was my friend," Teresa said.

"He was not. We have body camera data from Ilich and the recovery team. The facial recognition data matches the...the bloodstains. We know who he was, and once we have a secure perimeter and get a cleanup team back into that beshitted cave, we may have a better idea what he was doing here. But I need to hear everything from you. Now."

"His name was Timothy. He was my best friend."

Trejo's jaw went tight.

"His name was Amos Burton. He was a terrorist and murderer and the mechanic on James Holden's ship, and apparently he's been sipping tea with the daughter of the high consul for months. Anything you told him, the underground may know. So begin at the beginning, go slow, be thorough, and tell me what you have *fucking* done to us."

Chapter Twenty-Eight: Naomi

The thing that surprised Naomi most was how quickly it hap-pened. How little convincing people needed. She had assumed that Emma and Chava would agree because they knew her per-sonally. They had a history together. And maybe their contacts would be amenable to connecting with her, since known-safe members of the underground were vouching. After that, she had expected it to be difficult—sometimes impossible—to convince Saba's network to reveal itself to her. Everyone in the under-ground was in danger of death. Maybe worse. They would all be as wary as she would have been in their place.

She'd overlooked the fact that she was Naomi Nagata, and that fear drove people to look for leaders. Emma had five contacts in the underground. Three of them were on ships in other systems, but one was a technician in Auberon's planetary transfer station, and the other was an engineer on a Transport Union ship that was presently in-system. Chava's connections were more local. A doctor at one of the major hospitals down the well. A taxation agent and forensic accountant on contract to Laconia. A manager of a fashionable brothel at the governmental center. The husband of a security specialist contracted with Laconia to maintain and protect the biometric identification systems. Some of those were single nodes in the network, but some were cell leaders with four or five other connections, some of whom knew a couple other people and so on until it felt like the underground had as many loyalists as the governor.

It was an illusion, but it was a powerful one.

"The thing is the fuckers came in like the flood, yeah?" the man across the table from her said. He was a communications engineer for an independent design collective tasked with building a tight-beam network—repeaters and relays—in the still-unexplored vastness of Auberon system. He called himself Bone, but Naomi was fairly certain it was a nickname he'd given himself. "Overwhelming force, Laconia. Unstoppable. Which, yeah, they are. But you can beat the shit out of a river and not change how it flows."

"Wouldn't know," Naomi said. If he heard her, it didn't slow him down. Some men got loquacious when they were nervous.

"They're one system, and not that populous. They've got no choice but to rely on us poor local bastards for help. And Laconia…" He chuckled. "Laconia has no local tradition of cheerful corruption. They don't expect it, and they don't know what to do about it when they find it. Besides make the kind of examples of people that piss off all their families."

"Give them time," Naomi said. "They'll catch up. If we let them."

Bone grinned. His left upper canine had been decorated to look like it was made from stone. Fashion never stopped. It was one of many things Naomi was pleased that age allowed her not to care about anymore. She smiled back.

The public park was another sign of Auberon's wealth and

success. The designers of the lunar base had built in common areas and open space. The dome above them was still under the lunar surface, but light panels made it seem as open and airy as a resort on Titan. Children skipped in the thin gravity, hopping from bar to bar of a climbing structure that rose almost half the height of the *Roci*. At a full g, a slip and fall would be fatal. Here, they might get bruised.

A drip fountain beside them filled the air with white noise as the tiny drops drifted down from the ceiling and tapped an inclined slate, flowing slowly down to a fish-filled reservoir. It was beautiful. She didn't feel like she belonged there.

"The repeaters," she said, bringing them back to the issue at hand.

"Yeah, yeah, yeah," Bone said. "We got your design out. Bottle network is on its way. Nice thing about it? Cheap. Any union ship close to a ring gate can slip something out the lock." Bone made a pushing gesture so graceful it was almost dance and then snapped his fingers. "We'll be trading fresh gossip before you know."

"Sol and Bara Gaon are the priorities."

"Already got bottles through to them. They know we're here and what we're doing. This can only spread."

"And Laconia?"

Bone shrugged. "Got to figure they're putting up new repeaters, but we don't got one yet, and Auberon has money. So..."

So they should have been a priority. Maybe they were, and other cells in the underground were breaking them. The bottle network was slow compared to the light-speed transmission they had all become accustomed to, but it was also hard to stop. Repeaters at the gates were static or nearly static targets. Easy to identify and easy to destroy. The thing that had made them safe and stable all these years had been the eyes of Medina in the slow zone, the certainty that any action against them would be identified and traced back. With no eyes left in the slow zone, impossible things were suddenly practical.

"Our local network?" Naomi said. "It's unbreakable?"

"Everything's breakable," Bone said. "But we'll make them work for it, and it fails in sections, so we can shut it down before everyone's compromised."

It was the right answer. If he'd said they were safe, she'd have trusted him less. "Bien alles," she said, and rose. Bone followed her lead, holding his hand out to shake hers with a nervousness that looked like hero worship. She took his hand. Whatever the future brought, Bone could go through it remembering that he'd shaken hands with Naomi Nagata. She didn't like this sense of wearing a mask that everyone else had put on her, but it was the price she paid to do what needed doing.

"I'll be in touch," she said, and they walked away, taking different paths out of the common space.

The corridors and passages of the base were wide and had low ceilings for someone her height. White tile glittered the same on the walls as the floor. Thirty people could have walked abreast. She put her hands in her pockets, kept her eyes down, inviting everyone she passed to overlook her. Walking helped her think.

Her problem—and her enemy's—was the scale of it all. Millennia of human history had played out on the surface of a single planet. Mere centuries in the wide void between worlds. And all of that had happened before her own birth. The universe she'd known had always had stations around Saturn and Jupiter, rock hoppers eking out livelihoods in the Belt. Almost every gate led to another system that wide and complex, but without humanity. Without history. Without the infrastructure of everything humans took for granted and relied on.

It had seemed smaller when there was a hub to the wheel. Now, anyone could transit anywhere, and there was no one to coordinate or record it. The more she thought about it, the more untenable the idea of rebuilding inside the slow zone seemed. Medina and the *Typhoon* and the fleet of Transport Union ships that had been caught there were proof that the nature of the space itself there wasn't benign. Putting a crewed base there was risking the death of everyone involved. An automated one was a statement of faith in their computer security that history didn't justify. Holding and protecting over thirteen hundred gates from their starward faces was an entirely different prospect from holding one strong position in the center. It would take the largest fleet humanity had ever built just to watch the gates, and that didn't take policing the vastness of their solar systems into account.

Duarte had come in with the strategy of permitting local governments autonomy so long as they followed his rules. It had seemed like a kind of magnanimity at the time. It looked more like necessity now.

And deeper even than that, the eerie words *two gates lost*.

There had to have been a moment when they could have refused. When she and Jim and maybe a handful of other people could have looked at the ring gates and the vastness beyond them, seen the danger, and tiptoed away. All the signs had been there. A civilization had built all this vast and unimaginable power and still been scattered like knucklebones. What had made them think it was safe for them? That it was worth the risk?

She took the tube to Chava's block as if she belonged there. The crowd on the platform was a mix. Bright-eyed, tea-drinking third-shifters on their way to work. Weary second shift just coming home or heading out to dinner. A handful of youths in outlandish fashion burning the first-shift midnight oil. Naomi stayed quiet and apart, and she appreciated the beauty of it all. And the innocence. A hundred people, more or less, waiting for a tube car on a moon above a planet that circled a sun that hadn't born them, and jockeying to be the first ones through the door so that they could get a good seat. Maybe the most human thing possible.

A young man in a brown collarless shirt scowled at her for staring, as if maybe she was mocking him. She nodded her apology and looked away.

Her life as Chava's guest was pleasant. Waking in a real bed, showering with water that didn't recycle twice while she was under it, eating food that had more than one taste. The long months Naomi had spent in her container felt more and more like a spiritual pilgrimage, a journey she had gone through and emerged from changed. It hadn't seemed like that at the time.

Their schedules had drifted, and she was awake long after Chava had gone to bed. Naomi stayed quiet while she worked, but she worked. The underground in Auberon was well developed, but until she decided it was time to throw the governor and his political officers into a hole, her options were limited. Entrench. Develop more holes in their security. Compromise the enemy further. But there was nothing of Laconia's grand strategy to be learned. They were as cut off as she was.

And then, only days after her own messages had slipped out through the rings, the bottles began to return. They came in one at a time, a trickle of data that snuck into the system. Reports, requests, and messages encrypted with the most recent ciphers. Bara Gaon was on lockdown, but the exploration sites were still autonomous. New Albion had taken the opportunity to sabotage the Laconian transfer station and were now being hunted by the local security forces. Transport Union ships had started making emergency transits to systems like Tabalta and Hope where local populations were in danger of collapse. It was like slowly beginning to recover her eyesight after being nearly blind.

The message from Sol system originated on Callisto, the data passed covertly to a datafarm on Ceres and repackaged into a bottle on a Transport Union ship near the Sol gate. It was routed to her.

On the screen, Bobbie looked tired and grim. A grayness had come into her features, and the thick muscles of her neck had begun to look wiry. A decryption artifact locked a corner of the image like part of her shoulder was frozen in time while the rest of her was free to move.

"Hey there," Bobbie said into the camera, and a loneliness Naomi hadn't known she felt swamped her for a moment. She felt the memory of that last hug before she'd left Sol, and it was more alive and real to her than the last time she'd seen Jim. "I have something. An opportunity, I think. Alex wants me to run it past you."

Naomi listened as Bobbie laid out the situation. The *Storm* trapped in Sol, first by the catastrophe in the slow zone, and now by the *Tempest's* presence. The antimatter.

She felt herself sliding into the same analytic mind-set that had been her whole life in the container. She'd hardly been out— a few weeks on the *Bhikaji Cama* and now here with Chava— and slipping back already felt cold and constraining. Her mind ticked through the implications of Bobbie's plan: the exposure of the *Storm*, the scrutiny that would fall on the Jovian moon bases, the symbolic and practical effects of Duarte's losing a second *Magnetar*-class ship.

And as she did, a quiet part of her mourned.

The day she'd gone into the container and committed herself to living as a pea in a shell game had been the day she left the *Rocinante* behind. It felt like relief at the time. Like her soul had been rubbed raw, and the container was her bandage. Her whole life, she'd survived the unsurvivable by falling back and getting small. And every time, she had come back healed. Scarred, sometimes. But healed.

All it had taken was a handful of human interactions to show her that the Naomi who had fled into the container wasn't the one who'd come out. Time had passed, and she had found what peace she was going to find.

When she'd taken up Saba's role, it had been from necessity, but it had also been because she was ready to. It was only after the fact that she was starting to see what leaders were. The price the position required.

The water started hissing, and a door opened and closed from back in Chava's bedroom. She was awake and taking a morning shower. It would be time for Naomi to go to bed soon. It was also safe to respond to Bobbie without being an impolite guest. Funny how that still seemed to matter.

She set her hand terminal up with the camera pointing to her, then used the security filter to strip out the background. If the signal was intercepted, there wouldn't be artifacts leading back to Chava. It left Naomi looking like she was floating in a featureless void. She started the recording.

"Hey, Bobbie. Your plan...looks solid. I know that's not the argument I was making the last time we spoke, but the situation's changed. Several situations have. I still maintain that working through political means to a peaceful endgame is critical. But if there is a chance to do that without a *Magnetar*-class ship keeping its boot on Sol system's throat, it'll be easier. If it was just a ship, I think I might still have some reservations, but you're right. Duarte made the *Tempest* a symbol. We don't often get the chance to kill the enemy's story about itself.

"Good hunting. I love you."

She closed the message, fed it into the local encryption, and queued it to be sent to Bone and his system network. It might take days for it to get onto a bottle and through the gates. She tapped the table with her fingertips, wanting to call it back. There was still time to stop it. Soon there wouldn't be.

"Hey," Chava said as she stepped in from her bedroom. She was already dressed for her shift. Sharp, professional clothing, hair neat. "What are you up to this fine morning?"

"Second-guessing myself," Naomi said. "And I think it's my evening. I did make you coffee, though."

"You are a kind and thoughtful woman," Chava said as she poured herself a cup. The drift of the coffee to the cup was like watching the slow fountain. "You're going to have traffic analysis problems, though."

"You mean the way that vastly more bottles come into and out of Auberon than any other system?" Naomi said. "Yes, that's an issue. Is it a hint? I know you weren't looking for a roommate."

"You can stay as long as it's the smart move. But maybe not after?" Chava's smile faded. "What's wrong?"

Naomi chuckled. "You mean apart from maybe having sent two of the people I care about most to their deaths?" She wiped her eyes. "Shit."

Chava put down her cup. She took Naomi's hand in hers. The feeling of fingers against her own was almost more than Naomi could stand, and she held on like Chava was a tether.

"I spent a lot of my life trying not to be a particular kind of person," Naomi said. "Trying not to make certain kinds of decisions. But here I am all the same."

They were silent together for a moment. When Chava spoke, her voice was light. Almost conversational. "When I was in my apprenticeship, back in the day? The hardest thing I had to do was manual docking. Every time the qualification run came, it didn't matter how much I'd practiced. I'd take the controls, override the system so I had control. The only thing in my head was *Don't fuck up, don't fuck up, don't fuck up.* And then I'd fuck up. I focused so hard on the thing I was afraid of, I ran straight into its arms every single time."

"Are you trying to make me feel better?"

"No," Chava said. "We're too old for that. I'm trying to make you feel like you aren't alone in it. That's all I've got."

Something in Naomi's chest shifted. A titanic emotion breaking free. She braced herself for sobs, but all that came out was a profound sigh. The dream had been there all along, never quite given up. She would find a way to bring her family back together. They would all survive the meat grinder of history. Everything would somehow be well.

There had been a moment. It hadn't been that long ago. All she'd had to do was announce herself, accept Duarte's invitation, and leave all the struggle behind. She couldn't remember quite how she'd decided on this path, but she saw that she had. There was no one to blame but herself. She conjured up the dream of waking up beside Jim. Drinking coffee with him. Hearing Alex and Amos joking with the subtle hum of the *Rocinante* behind them. She let it go.

She squeezed Chava's hand and let that go too.

Chapter Twenty-Nine: Elvi

Elvi sat in the back of the car. The driver was a young man with close-cut, tightly curled hair. Mostly what she saw of him was the back of his neck. As the State Building fell away behind them, the city itself spread out. She could still remember the first time she'd seen it, brought in by soldiers with the scrupulous politeness of a concierge at a luxury hotel, only with sidearms. The streets were wider than anywhere she'd ever been, with greenways along the sides. Buildings rose up, tall and beautiful, with solar collection windows and rooftop gardens like Frank Lloyd Wright had been reborn and made skyscrapers. The scale of the place was massive and boastful. She remembered being overwhelmed by it, the first time.

Now, it seemed weirdly brittle. Millions of people lived in the capital city, and almost none of them had been there longer than a decade. The traffic was stopped for her motorcade, and she saw the normal people—civilians and citizens and military with status lower than hers—craning their necks as she passed, trying to figure out who she was and whether they should be excited to see her. There were no monuments, no billboards, no old neighborhoods. She sort of hated it.

"Would you like some water, ma'am?" the driver asked.

"No," Elvi said. "Thank you."

He nodded without looking back at her. She leaned back into the plush seat and tried to straighten her leg. It didn't help the ache.

The labs were massive. Technically it was part of the University of Laconia, but it was run like a military camp. The gate guards waved them through without checking, and the car took a looping path through campus, heading toward the pens. She fidgeted with her cane. As they made the last turn, a man came into view, clearly waiting for her. The relief that flooded her when she saw that it wasn't Paolo Cortázar was telling.

"Dr. Ochida," she said as she levered herself up out of the car.

"Dr. Okoye. It's good to have you back. I heard about your fieldwork. I have to say, you aren't selling me on it over nice safe labs."

"Well, the data was interesting," she said as they started down the path to the Pen. It was a dark, windowless cube, hardened against attack even in the heart of the empire, where attack seemed impossible. They said God didn't play dice, but if He did, they'd look like the Pen. Huge, square, and inscrutable.

"I hear they're sending you into the holy of holies," Ochida said. "Paolo's very close with his senescence project."

"It wasn't my choice."

"The high consul does what the high consul does," Ochida said as they reached the guards. Elvi handed over her ID badge and submitted to the verification scan. It was just a touch on her wrist, but it felt more invasive than that.

"With the rich and powerful, always a little patience," she said. The guards stood away and let them through. There was a little pop when the door opened, and the air pushed in with them. Inside, the next set of security protocols blasted them with air and scanned every millimeter of their bodies before the inner door opened.

Inside, the Pen was almost more reassuring. It looked like the kind of lab she'd been in for decades, on and off, at half a dozen universities and research institutions. Safety procedures were posted on the wall in bright fonts and six languages. The air smelled of phenol soap and air scrubbers.

"Come on," Ochida said with a smile. "I'll walk you over."

Don't get comfortable, Elvi told herself. *This isn't your home court. You aren't safe here.*

"I just had the most interesting conversation," Fayez had said back on the day she'd first been assigned her task.

"I could say the same. But mine's classified, so why don't you go first."

"Well, he was being awfully cagey. But I think our old friend Holden just told me Cortázar's plotting murder."

Elvi had laughed because it was a statement too horrifying to match the pleasant setting, and sometimes being overwhelmed was kind of funny. "I'm not sure I can deal with that right now," she said. And then, "Did he really?"

Fayez shrugged. "No, he didn't. He very carefully and *specifically* didn't. We had a perfectly lovely conversation about the importance of teaching children about negative space as a tool of political analysis. Then we talked about everyone at the head of the science effort except Cortázar while he made significant eye contact. And then made a weird segue into the history of political power struggles on old Earth, with a focus on Richard the Third."

"That's...obscure."

"Not *that* obscure. Shakespeare wrote a play about him."

"What was it called?"

"*Richard the Third*," Fayez said. "Are you feeling all right?"

She leaned her head against his shoulder. He was warmer than usual, but it wasn't strange to run a low-grade fever when a limb was regrowing. "I wasn't a theater major, and I've had a long day. What was the point of it?"

"Richard was an asshole and killed a bunch of people, but specifically a couple of kids. Heirs to the throne or something."

"You weren't a theater major either."

"I was not."

Far above them, a thin sheet of clouds moved across the stars, blotting some and revealing others. She wanted to close her eyes and fall asleep right there and wake up in their shitty apartment back on Ceres before she'd ever heard of Laconia or Duarte at all. All the things she'd learned, all the money and status and discovery could vanish like a dream, and she'd still have been happy as long as all the rest of it went too.

"So negative space and then everyone but Cortázar, and a king who killed some kids."

"Well, technically a prince who clawed his way to power by killing some kids. I think."

"Spiffy," she said.

"Wasn't Cortázar one of the ones that worked for Protogen back before Eros?"

"Back *during* Eros," Elvi said.

"I'm just saying it wouldn't be his first time."

"He created the catalyst," Elvi said. "For me. Doesn't mean I'm a murderer."

"Yeah," Fayez said, but he knew she was thinking, *Except that it kind of does.* That was what decades of marriage were for. Intimacy and pattern matching as a kind of telepathy.

He sighed, shifted, and put an arm around her. "I may have been reading more into it than was there. It just seemed strange and kind of pointed."

"He meant something by it," Elvi said. "Maybe not what you got, exactly. But something."

"You're thinking about tracking him down and asking him?"

"I am."

"If he was being oblique because Duarte's got an eye on him, he won't be straight with you any more than he was me."

Unless I let him know that Duarte isn't watching anything right now, Elvi thought. The idea left a cold mark that could have been fear or excitement or something of both. She wondered what Trejo would think, and if Holden was even on the new, secret emperor's radar.

"Maybe I can come up with something," Elvi said.

And maybe she could have if they hadn't discovered Amos Burton and his pocket nuke that night and Holden hadn't been thrown in a cell before morning.

Cortázar smiled when he saw her like it was something he'd told himself to remember to do. Elvi felt like her answering nod was equally fake, but she didn't know if he'd notice or care.

"Anything else I can help with, Paolo?" Ochida asked.

"Thank you, no," Cortázar said. "We'll be fine."

Ochida stepped away. Everything about it was perfectly normal and polite. It all felt like a threat. Cortázar turned and started walking toward a set of metal doors. She had to trot to catch up with him.

"I'm sorry we had to push this until after lunch," he said. "I've been at the security office all morning going over the things they took from the spy."

"Amos Burton," Elvi said. "Kelly briefed me. It's a little weird. I knew him. We were both on Ilus at the same time. He saved my husband's life."

"Well, he had a pocket nuke with him in that cave, so..." Cortázar wagged his hand in a so-so gesture. "I was with the analysis team. Trejo's looking at the communication deck pretty carefully. It looks like the bastard's been out there for quite a long time."

"Do we know what he wanted?"

"Not yet, but we may still get to ask him."

"I thought he was dead."

"Oh my, yes. Very much so."

"Then how?"

He presented his lanyard to a locking mechanism, and the doors cycled open. She followed him into a darker corridor. The walls were thicker. Reinforced. It was a little sobering to think that the raw protomolecule of the Pen wasn't the most dangerous thing in the lab.

"Ilich fucked that whole thing up badly," Cortázar said. "Not his fault. He didn't know not to leave the body behind."

The doors closed behind them with a deep sound. Like a prison. The corridor acted as an airlock.

"After they shot the poor fucker in the head, Ilich pulled everyone back to protect the little princess," Cortázar said. She heard the sneer in his voice, and thought of Richard III. "He should have left someone guarding the body. Or burned it before he left. Not his fault, really. He knows the rules about the repair drones, but he doesn't know the reason behind them."

A second set of doors opened, light spilling into the hallway. "I don't understand," Elvi said.

"You will," Cortázar said lightly as he walked into the private lab. He'd been teasing her.

This lab was smaller than the Pen. She recognized some of the equipment from her own exobiology labs—array sequencers, proteome sample analyzer, NIR and low-resonance scanners. Other things were as strange as any of the alien artifacts she'd come across. Cortázar ignored them all, stepping across to a transparent polymer cage the size she'd seen used for simian and large-animal studies.

"Trejo thinks having a new set of eyes on all of this will help, but the truth is you're going to be playing catch-up for months just to get to the point you can ask intelligent questions," he said. "But to get you started? These were the original cases. The seed grit in our oyster."

Two children were in the cage, a boy maybe seven or eight years old and a girl on the edge of adolescence. Their eyes were perfectly black, like the pupils had eaten iris and sclera alike. The girl stood up and walked toward the front face of the cage. Her skin was grayish. She moved almost normally, but when she stopped, there was a terrible stillness about her.

"What...," Elvi said, and then didn't know how to finish the question. She'd heard the phrase *It made my flesh crawl*, but she'd thought it was a figure of speech until then.

"They were Alexander and Cara Bisset when they were alive," Cortázar said. "Children of the initial scientific expedition that was on Laconia before the high consul relocated his loyalists here. The boy died in an accident. The girl was poisoned trying to eat local flora in the wilderness not long after. This is what happens when you have a dead body around the repair drones. Or, well. Sometimes. They don't always take it upon themselves to fix things, but when they do..." He nodded toward the dead children. *This is what happens.*

"I don't know you," the girl said.

"My name's Elvi."

"I'm Cara. Are you going to hurt us too?"

Oh, Elvi thought. *Oh, fuck this. I don't care what it takes. As soon as I get out of here, I will find a way to never, ever come back.*

"The original bodies died twenty years ago, more or less," Cortázar said. "These artifacts that were built from them have been static since their recovery."

"So they'll always be young?"

"Well. They'll always look like immature human beings," Cortázar said. "That's not exactly the same thing. They have, for the most part, similar structures and chemistry to the original bodies, only very stable. Telomeres don't shorten. Mitosis can run indefinitely. There's no buildup of senescent cells or plaques. The immune response has a couple additional pathways and structures that are interesting. Really very nice work."

"That's amazing," Elvi said, and the words felt like dropping a stone down a well. Deep and kind of hollow.

"The high consul's interest in personal immortality came from them. He thought that if we could learn the differences in structure and function from these samples and reverse engineer them into a living body instead of a corpse, sort of the way carbon-silicate lace plating was based on long-lived architectural structures...well, that would be interesting. I tried a few animal models first, and made enough progress that I felt comfortable with a human trial."

She leaned on her cane and fought back the dizziness. "Duarte agreed to that?"

Cortázar turned to look at her. He seemed confused. "Of course he did. It was the answer to his biggest problem. How do you hold a galaxy-spanning empire together over generations? Have someone running it who doesn't die. Well, here they are. Things that have all the traits you need not to age and die."

"Wasn't he worried something might...I don't know. Go wrong?"

"He understood there was some risk, but he thought it was justified by the possible return. We went very carefully, and the high consul had a great deal of faith in my abilities."

"All right," Elvi said. "Okay."

"It was fine until you triggered that—" He gestured at her injured leg. "It was working. It may still work, with some adjustments and a new subject."

"I didn't trigger anything. That was Sagale, following orders," she said, but what she thought was: *A new subject like Teresa.* It didn't sit right. Cortázar turned his attention back to the children in the cage. *No, he wants it for himself.*

"I have complete records, of course," Cortázar said. "I have them set up for you on the system here. Take as long as you want looking over them."

"In here?"

"The project doesn't exist outside of this room. The high consul was very clear on that, and I can't imagine Admiral Trejo would want to reduce security."

The private lab was smaller all told than her office back at the

State Building. The younger one, the boy, came to stand beside what had been his sister. Elvi was going to be under their eyes the whole time she was here. She wondered whether Cortázar had set it up like that to make her uncomfortable. And whether the information he showed her would be anywhere close to complete...

"Wait," she said. "Amos Burton's body was missing."

"They're out looking for it now," Cortázar said. "It will be very useful having an adult subject to compare with. I mean, it would mean more if I had complete scans and medical records of him from before the corpse was modified. That's what we really need to move forward. But I'll enjoy this all the same. There's a restroom just outside the hall. And if you need food, you should probably have it outside. We've only ever had one unintentional protomolecule contamination, but—"

"Understood," she said, and sat at the low monitor. The chair squeaked.

"I'll come check in on you later," Cortázar said. He forgot to smile this time. The doors closed behind him, and Elvi turned to the reports and the data. Her head felt like it was full of bees. There was too much, and it left her unsettled and jumpy. She expected Cortázar's work to bounce off her brain and puddle on the floor. Actually engaging with it was too much to ask.

But once she'd started looking through it, her focus started coming back, and a familiar calm came over her. Other people might take reassurance in a lover's hand or a cup of herbal tea—really a tisane since it didn't have tea leaves, but *tea* was the term people used anyway, which Elvi had always thought interesting. Elvi only had room in her mind for learning or panicking. She couldn't do both, and she didn't like panic.

The thing that struck her first was how small the differences really were. Cortázar wasn't a biologist. His background was nanoinformatics, which had a huge overlap when it came to things like genetics, epigenetics, and heritable cytoplasmic proteins, but missed basics like anatomy. The way the kids' hearts had changed to adjust for a different viscosity in their plasma, the way that their blood had changed to a more efficient, non-cell-bound hemoglobin analog, all the other tweaks and modifications weren't really changes in kind. They were just improvements.

Evolution was a paste-and-baling-wire process that came up with half-assed solutions like pushing teeth through babies' gums and menstruation. *Survival of the fittest* was a technical term that covered a lot more close-enough-is-close-enough than actual design.

When she looked up and saw the children looking back at her, it was five hours later, her leg ached like hell, and the fear was gone. The grayness in their skin was an artifact of the oxygen transport. The blackness of their eyes was an optical structure that was better at capturing light. Whatever was going on with the new kind of neurons in their brains and the extra layer in their neocortexes, all the old, purely human structures were there too.

The process of re-creating all that using tools out of the protomolecule's toolbox was an act of hubris that took her breath away. If anyone besides Duarte and Cortázar had been part of that conversation, there would have been prosecution. Two men, each convinced of their exceptionalism, were capable of leapfrogging over vast chasms of maybe-this-isn't-a-great-idea and this-is-totally-illegal. Elvi had become convinced that Cortázar was jealous that Duarte intended to feed his own daughter into the same grinder instead of his pet scientist.

She levered herself up on her cane and walked to the transparent cage. The boy stepped back, like he was afraid of her. The girl—Cara—stood her ground.

Development into a mature form wasn't the same as aging and death. Maybe the drones hadn't understood that. So that meant something about how the protomolecule designers had functioned, didn't it? That their designs didn't take growth and maturation into account suggested that the original designers only had mature forms. Adults making adults. She tried to imagine what that would be like.

"Can I ask you something?" Elvi said.

For a moment, Cara was still as stone. When she nodded it felt like watching a statue come to life.

"Did you and your brother lose time?"

"When the thing happened, and we could see the air?"

"Yes, then."

"I don't know. He doesn't give us a clock to look at."

"You're conscious, then. You're not...You aren't just...You and your brother are sentient? Self-aware?"

The huge, black eyes changed. Glimmered. A thick tear rolled down Cara's cheek. Elvi put her palm against the cage.

"I'm sorry," she said. "I am so, so sorry."

Chapter Thirty: Bobbie

Bobbie couldn't sleep.

This was a new thing, or at least one that she didn't remember from when she was young. Back when she'd been active duty with the MMC, she'd been able to close her eyes and lose consciousness whenever a few minutes presented themselves. The idea of lying on a cot in a converted office, staring up at the ceiling, strapped lightly to keep from launching herself out of bed given Callisto's mild gravity...It wouldn't have made sense to that Bobbie Draper.

But here she was, three hours into her sleep cycle, making an inventory of her muscles and forcing each tense one to relax. A live monitor on the desk's surface threw flickers of light and darkness above her. She noticed the tension that had crept back into her shoulders and made herself release it for the fourth or fifth or twenty-fifth time. She closed her eyes and willed them to stay closed. Something in the hallway dripped. Condensation that might mean a failure in the heating system or in the air recyclers. She tried to ignore it.

Her crew was scattered through Callisto Station or on the *Storm* or in their own cots in the complex of smugglers' caves. It made her anxious to have her people diffused out into the civilian population like that. It also made her anxious to have them all together where they'd make a single target. The Laconian security forces only needed one lucky break. She needed all of them.

Her shoulders were tense again.

"Fuck."

She undid the restraint with one hand and hauled herself up. Maybe an hour in the *Storm*'s gym would get her past the worst of her insomnia. But on the way out toward the hangar, she stopped at the desk, checking again the way she did fifty times a day. The map was broken into two frames. The smaller one showed the relative positions of the major bodies in Sol system, tracking the inevitable and predictable change in cartography like an orrery. The larger showed the Jovian system in great detail with data copied from the traffic control logs. On the small screen, Jupiter and its moons looked calm and serene, passing through the vastness of space with the tranquil beauty of the inevitable. Closer up, it was like a beehive. Hundreds of ships from ancient rock hoppers and mining skiffs to the *Tempest* and everything in between.

It was the *Tempest* that drew her.

Trejo had transferred out of the system on one of the fast Laconian shuttles, burning hard back to Laconia to deal with the crisis in the slow zone. The *Tempest*, on the other hand, had been sniffing around the Jovian moons like a dog searching for its lost antimatter. It had been in a complex orbit near Ganymede most of the time, though once it had darted out to Europa. It would come to Callisto eventually and force her hand. Until then, the best she could do was take comfort in imagining the fresh new Laconian vice admiral losing sleep in his cot because a moon-killing load of antimatter had gone missing and it was his job to find it.

She tapped the red dot on the map that was the *Tempest*. "Anything you can do, I can do better."

An alert popped up. A newsfeed from Ceres Station with a breaking report. She opened it, and a young man with a Lunar accent looked earnestly up at her from the desk.

"This is Davis Myles with *Ceres Beat*, and behind me you can see station security in cooperation with Laconian state intelligence agents securing a cell of criminal separatists here at the heart of Ceres Station in what is being called the biggest bust since the coalition joined the Laconian Association of Worlds."

Bobbie felt the tightness across her back get worse. It wasn't only that every loss to the underground was more risk to her and hers. She hated the way history was being rewritten before her eyes. *Sol system joined the Association of Worlds* was a hell of a way to say, *Laconia trucked in a half-alien warship and killed the shit out of everyone until we showed them our bellies.*

The time was coming when, even if she didn't hear from Naomi, she was going to have to make the ancient human decision again: fight or flight. As the reporter enthused about how many guns and enemy soldiers had been captured, she cracked her knuckles. She had three options. Take on the *Tempest*, run for the gate, or destroy the *Storm* and let her crew dissolve into the civilian population. Every option was its own kind of bad.

"The cell was exposed by the discovery of an encryption package running on a public system," the reporter said, and the feed kicked over to a wide-faced woman with a pattern of moles on her cheeks that looked like paint spatter.

"The activity of the decryption package coincided with a data drop from known separatist elements earlier today," she said, and Bobbie killed the feed.

She made a connection to Jillian. Her second in command accepted like she'd been expecting her. Before Jillian could speak, Bobbie asked, "Did a bottle come through?"

"It did," Jillian said. "We got a full copy of the data. I was going to let you sleep until the decryption run was finished."

"We're running the decrypt on our own system, yeah?"

"You saw the thing on Ceres," Jillian said. It wasn't a question. "Those yokels were stupid and so they'll die. Good riddance. We're not stupid. We won't die."

"How long before the data's clean?"

Jillian shrugged. "Another hour, maybe."

"I'll be in the gym," she said. "The minute it's done, I know it. Understood?"

"Yeah, okay," Jillian said, and Bobbie dropped the connection. Any hope of sleep was gone now. Her nerves were as bright as stars. She pulled the tactical map back up. The red dot of the *Tempest* was still near Ganymede. She stared at it for a long moment as if the commander might be able to feel her attention, might be scared by it. She closed its display and went to the *Storm*.

The gym was bright and clean. All the equipment was Martian design strained through Laconian technology. Bobbie threw herself into the effort like it could help her forget, and it did at least a little bit. She'd been in the resistance gel for forty minutes when Jillian's message came through. The bottle had been from Auberon. From Naomi. It was the reply she'd been hoping for. Bobbie, panting and wet from exertion, opened the message file.

The background filter made Naomi look like she was in a featureless white room. Like she was an angel, delivering her message from some abstract heaven. Naomi tipped her head forward unconsciously before she spoke, the way she did when she was delivering bad news.

"Hey, Bobbie," she said. "Your plan...looks solid."

Bobbie grinned until her cheeks ached.

In his last days, her grandfather talked sometimes about how weirdly clear his early memories had become. He might not quite remember the name of his nurse or when the man had last been to check on him, but the details of his childhood were vivid and immediate. Like the past was growing stronger as his present and future wore thin. He told the story about seeing a living cat for the first time, and how strange it had felt to hold it, with the same awe in his voice every time. Bobbie's memory hadn't done that, not yet. But maybe there was something. When she called the crew back to the *Storm* for her briefing, all she could think of was when she'd been back in the service on Mars.

The leader of her first fire team had been Sergeant Huk. He'd been about half a head shorter than she was, with a terrier-thin face and a receding hairline. She'd never known anyone before or since who could command her loyalty or instill fear in her the way he had. When she'd been right out of boot and as green as they come, he'd turned her into an actual Marine. Before every mission briefing, he had found a way to acknowledge her. A nod, a touch on her shoulder or arm. Something that meant that no matter what was coming next, she wasn't going into it alone. He never humiliated her by saying it aloud, and he never left it unsaid. After he retired, she'd found out he'd done the same for everyone.

Now, as her people returned to the ship, she did something similar. She stood in the airlock, seeing each of them as they boarded. Timon Coul, with his old OPA split-circle tattoo smudged by time until it was just a bluish blotch on the back of his hand. Liese Chou, with her pale-gray hair. Caspar Asoau, looking like a teenager surrounded by his grandparents. Denise Lu. Skaldi Austin-Bey. Ian Freeman. And almost last, Alex Kamal. Alex, her oldest friend, and the man she'd traveled with for what felt like half a dozen lifetimes now.

He looked weary, like she'd woken him from his sleep. Maybe she had. He wouldn't have complained. He paused in front of her, and for a moment, it was like they were back on the *Rocinante* together. Like they were home. She touched his hand, and he nodded to her like he understood perfectly. Probably he did.

When the crew was all assembled in the galley, she pulled up her map of the system. It filled the wall. Someone in the back coughed, and she realized she'd been looking at it for several long seconds. And that she was enjoying herself.

JAMES S. A. COREY

"All right," she said. "We have word from on high. New mission. High risk. High reward." She shifted to an image of the *Tempest*. As strange as the *Storm* was in its particulars, its architecture was essentially the same design language that Martian ships had been for decades before the starving years. The *Tempest* was something else. Pale, asymmetrical, with protrusions and curves more like some monstrous vertebra. "We are going to kill that."

She waited for a moment, half expecting mutiny on the spot. The *Tempest* had put its boot on Sol system's neck without seeming to break a sweat. She could have said *We're all going to turn ourselves inside out and become seagulls* and it might have seemed about as realistic. No one objected. Looking into their faces, she saw interest. Anticipation. She saw hope, and she knew she'd been right to want this.

"We have a small payload that will do the trick," she said, nodding to Rini Glaudin at the back.

"Payload of what?" someone asked.

"The *Magnetars* run on antimatter," Bobbie said. "The *Tempest*'s resupply was on that freighter we took."

"Jesus," Caspar said.

"Correct," Bobbie replied. "But delivery will be difficult, and we're only going to get one shot. In our last mission we found, along with this antimatter, replacement parts for a sensor array very similar to what the *Storm*'s using. I've been over the battle footage, and I know the story is that the *Tempest* shook off everything the Earth-Mars Coalition threw at her. But—"

She laid out the schematic. Overlapping fields sprang out from the *Tempest* like peacock feathers on display. The range of sensor arrays. She tapped one, and it dropped out.

"From the hits she took and from how she's been flying since, I think this is the array they need a replacement for. And if the information we have is right, it means the *Tempest* has a blind spot. Here."

She pulled the display out to showcase the thin cone of black where the enemy ship's eyes couldn't go.

"And if we're right about their need for antimatter, they won't be able to use the field projector. Which means they'll be down to conventional weapons only."

"Captain?" It was Caspar. Jillian scowled at the boy like she was ready to punch him, but Bobbie nodded him on. "I don't see…I mean, even with just torpedoes and rail guns, and even if there is a data hole there—"

"They can still take us in a straight fight, and they'll still see us coming," Bobbie said. "So we let them see us. We get a Callistan shuttle. Private, small. Doesn't even have an Epstein. And we put it out"—she switched back to the image of Jupiter and its moons. A single bright-blue dot appeared—"here. And on an orbital path that looks like we're heading for Amalthea. A crew of two with a gas canister torpedo. Now those are slow, yes. But they also run cold. Basically no heat signature."

"Bist bien," Timon said. "Ran hundreds like, back on Ceres, sa sa?"

Jillian's voice was harsh. "Could we *not* interrupt the captain?"

"The hard part will be putting the *Tempest* into a flight pattern like…this."

A red arc appeared going from Ganymede. A line marked the time at each point. She zoomed in to show how the little blue shuttle fell into the blind spot, and the long seconds it would stay there.

"This is the window," Bobbie said. "It doesn't look like a trap, because we aren't trying to hide. We get there first, and we're just part of the traffic. So all we need is a lure. Something so critical that the *Tempest* will follow it where we want it to go. That will be the *Storm*."

She let it sink in. It was like she could see the implications settling in each face looking toward her. It was a sucker punch. One shot, and if it failed each and every one of them would be dead. The underground would lose its only warship with Laconian tech.

"I'll captain the shuttle with Rini as tech specialist. Jillian will be in command of the *Storm*." That made her second sit up a little straighter. Her jaw was firm. She looked like a hunting dog that had caught a scent. "The *Storm*'s mission is to hold the *Tempest* to this course so that the shuttle stays in the enemy's blind spot."

Alex, sitting to the side, leaned forward. His hands were on his knees, and his eyes were cast down toward the deck. She didn't know what he was thinking.

"If anyone doesn't want to do this," Bobbie said, "I'm not going to force you. We have four days before the shuttle is ready and the orbits are where I want them. I will be accepting resignations until that time. No sugarcoating. This is the most dangerous thing we'll have ever done. Even if we win, we may sustain losses. Potentially heavy losses. But each and every one of you has my word that if I thought this was hopeless, we wouldn't be doing it.

"I have sent detailed briefs to your team leaders. Look them over. If you have questions, for fuck's sake ask them. We're not going to screw this up because someone turned left instead of right. Understood?"

There was a ragged muttering of assent.

"I said, *Am I understood!*"

The reply was more like a cheer now. It filled the space. There was power in it.

"Outstanding. You have your orders. Dismissed."

Jillian was out of her seat in a moment, herding the crew like they were sheep. Nipping at them. It was something she'd have to get over before she had a command of her own. Bobbie let it play out, though. There was an energy in the ship that needed to work itself through. She felt it too.

Back in her cabin on the *Storm*, she put herself through the routine of cleaning and straightening her things. The cabin didn't need it, but she did. The ritual calmed her. She found herself humming. She didn't know how long it had been since she'd done that. She needed to go back to her little campsite and clear out all signs of her occupation, but she waited anyway. She'd almost decided that Alex wasn't going to come talk with her when he knocked at her cabin door.

"Hey," she said.

"Naomi said it was a good idea?"

"She didn't go that far. She might have just thought it was the right bad idea for the moment."

Alex managed a little smile. His melancholy made her feel almost ashamed of her lightness and anticipation. "If you need to step back, no one's going to think less of you. Kit's your son. Being part of his life and this too... If you've got to pick one, I'd understand."

"You left out a part of the plan. What happens after the payload hits?"

"We've never done it before. So apart from an explosion that makes a nuke look like a firecracker, I'm not sure what I'd say. The *Storm's* a tough ship, though. Even if there's some debris hits, she can take it. Probably."

"You're going to want to get that shuttle behind something, though," Alex said. "Put me on it. I'll get it to shelter."

"I need you on the *Storm*. Keeping the *Tempest* where I need it, when I need it? It's going to take a great pilot. That's you. Rini and I will be in power armor. The shuttle might get shredded, but we'll be better protected than it will. And you'll be there to come pick us up."

Alex shifted his weight. She could see him looking for objections the way old married couples could see when one wanted the other to pass the salt.

"I don't like putting us on different ships either," Bobbie said. "But this is the right way to do it."

"Yes, Captain. All right." He sighed, and then, to her surprise, grinned. "This is going to be one hell of a rodeo."

"They aren't going to know what hit them," Bobbie said. "My only regret is that Trejo won't be on the ship when we blow it into hot, fast dust."

"We can find him later," Alex said. "I'm going to go obsessively run diagnostics on systems I know are solid so I can feel like I have control of something."

"Sounds good," Bobbie said. "I'm going to stay here and see how many of my crew quit rather than go through with this."

"There won't be any. These people will still follow when you lay siege to hell. We trust you." Then, a moment later, "I trust you."

The door closed behind him, and Bobbie sat in her crash couch like she was easing down into a warm bath. When she closed her eyes, she slept.

Chapter Thirty-One: Teresa

"**W**as Timothy ever really my friend?"

Holden sat on the cot, his back against the wall. The paper gown he wore was crumpled and streaked with old blood. The sclera of his right eye was blood red and the flesh around it swollen. The cheek below puffy and dark. More than that, there was a carefulness to his movements that meant everything ached. The cell was tiny. The smallest closet in her bedroom suite was nearly twice as large. The only light came from a pencil-thin strip at the top of the wall that was too bright to look at directly but left most of the room too dark to read in.

"If he said he was your friend, then he was," Holden said. "Amos wasn't a man who felt the need to lie very often."

"Why was he here?" she heard herself ask, just the way she'd been told.

Holden swallowed like it was a difficult thing to do. He seemed sad. No, not sad. Pitying. It was worse.

"They asked me all this before. I'm sorry that they're making you do it too."

Trejo had told her to stay on script, to only say what she'd rehearsed, but she took the chance now. "Maybe they thought it would be harder to lie to someone you'd hurt."

"Maybe. I'll tell you the same thing I told them. I didn't know he was here. I hadn't been contacted by him. I don't know what his mission was or who put him onto it or how long he's been here. If he had a way to get in touch with the underground, I don't know what it was. And I don't know why he had a backpack nuke, except that I'm guessing he at least wanted to have the option of blowing something up. If I'd known he was here, I'd have told him not to."

Teresa looked up at the camera. Holden had answered her next four questions without her asking them. She didn't know if that meant she should skip that part or make him say it all again.

"How's your father?" Holden asked into her hesitation. "No one told me, but I put it together that something went wrong. Plus which, he hasn't come to question me. I feel like he and I have enough of a relationship, he would have."

My father's fine, she thought. She couldn't bring herself to say it. "Don't worry about him. Worry about yourself."

"Oh, I'm on that. Plenty worried for both of us. All of us."

"What happened to his body?" she asked, trying to get back onto the script.

"Your dad's?"

"Timothy's."

"I don't know."

She paused. Her gut was tight, and she felt a knot at the back of her throat. She felt it often these days. "He's dead. I saw it."

"So they've told me. He was a good...Well, he wasn't really exactly a good person. He cared enough to try, anyway. But he was loyal as hell." Holden paused. "He was my brother. I loved him."

"What is the underground doing?"

Holden shrugged. "Trying to make enough room under your father's boot that anyone else's opinion matters, I assume. That's what I'd be doing. Hold on. Just..." Holden levered himself up and spoke directly to the camera. "Could we cut this part short? It seems kind of shitty for her, and it's not going to change anything."

At first, there was no reply, then the hard clack of the magnetic door bolts opening. Holden sat down. Teresa felt the thrill of relief that told her how frightened she'd been, alone with this man. How glad she was that this part of the ordeal was over.

"They wouldn't have let me hurt you," Holden said. "Even if I'd wanted to. I mean, I don't, but even if."

Rage shot through her, unpredictable and vicious. "You're not much of a dancing bear anymore," she said.

Holden leaned against the wall, let it hold him up. When he smiled, she saw that one of his eyeteeth was missing. "Nice to be taken seriously, though."

The door opened, and two guards came in with Colonel Ilich. Their boots squeaked on the tile floor. The guards had their hands on their batons, but they didn't draw them. Not yet. Ilich put his hand on her shoulder, and she turned to go out. *If he said he was your friend, then he was.* She wanted to believe that, but she didn't.

"It's okay," Ilich said as the cell door closed behind them. "You did well."

The magnetic bolts shot closed again. Holden was contained. She felt a little calmer. They walked down the hallway past half a dozen more doors like it. If there were people behind them, Teresa didn't know who they were or why they were there. It seemed like every day revealed some other vast area of things she didn't know.

Ever since the bad night, she'd felt more than a little like a prisoner herself. Trejo had made her go over everything she knew about Timothy—how they'd met, what he'd said, what she'd told him, how he got along with the repair drones, why she'd never told anyone about him. After hours of it, Ilich tried to call a halt, but the interrogation had gone on until she was weeping and then well past that too.

She didn't know how long it had gone on. More than one session, but whether that had been hours or days, she couldn't say. There was a timelessness to everything now. Like it had all just started and also it had all gone on forever. She felt like a puppet of herself, controlled by someone else. Whether she was being badgered by Trejo or sitting with what was left of her father or at meals pretending that nothing was wrong, she felt like her real self had been pressed into a small, black place where her heart should have been. Ilich had talked to her about trauma and violence and promised her that with time, she would feel better. Cortázar had taken over her medical care, scanning her brain and drawing her blood, but he didn't speak to her much. That was fine. She didn't want to speak.

When she slept, her nightmares were all violent. She never slept without nightmares anymore.

The observation room was a soothing, neutral green. The air smelled of cleanser and the pepper and vanilla of Laconian flowers. Trejo and Cortázar were at a volumetric display that was spinning a complex data pattern like they were watching waves or weather formations. The guards took their places outside the door, Ilich went to stand with the two other men. Teresa thought about going to a chair, but it seemed too far, so she folded down to the floor.

"What am I looking at, Doc?" Trejo said.

Cortázar shook his head. "His response patterns are always a little off. All this noise is within error bars for him. You see something similar in people who've had extensive psychedelics, but usually women. But I'd say changing the questioner didn't affect his readings significantly at all. Given his baseline, I'd say he's telling the truth."

"You're sure about that?"

"No," Cortázar said. "But eighty percent confidence. We should try it with Dr. Okoye next. He has a much longer association with her. And they're friendly."

"If you want to pull her off her present work," Ilich said.

Trejo made an impatient sound and pressed his hands into his cheeks hard enough that his knuckles went pale. There were dark patches under his eyes where the exhaustion was settling in. *He is the only thing holding the empire together*, Teresa thought. It felt like hearing someone else say it. Someone who might be lying.

"Has there been any result on the search for the...the body?" Ilich asked.

"No," Trejo said. "I've given the shoot-on-contact order, but I have bigger fish to fry than alien zombies lurching around the landscape. If he does turn back up, he won't have access to his supplies. Maybe we'll get lucky and the drones will decide he's really a table lamp."

Something moved in Teresa's mind. Something small.

Cortázar grunted. "I think you should reconsider that. Having an additional subject would make my work with the high consul much—"

"We'll wait for Okoye's report before we change any of that," Trejo said. "The important thing is keeping the separatists under control."

"Really?" Ilich said. "I thought the important thing was that something ate our ships and broke Duarte." He meant her father, but that was fine. It applied to her too, and it made her feel like she was more included in the conversation. *Given his baseline...*

"That's our second problem," Trejo said, "and we'll get to it. But if I can't keep this together, there won't be anything for the high consul to control when he's recovered."

The hollowness in his voice seemed familiar. Teresa looked at Trejo more carefully. The hours of questioning still left a coloring of humiliation in her, but his weariness and fear weren't hard to see. She'd lost her father. He'd lost his leader. His distress almost made her like him.

Like she'd been hauled back in time, the top of Timothy's head came off. She gasped, and was back in the normal time again. Trauma memory. Ilich had talked to her about flashbacks to moments her brain was having trouble integrating. He'd told her to report if it happened. It happened, and she didn't. Trejo glanced at her, then Ilich.

"You need to get her back to the State Building in time for her peers to see her."

Ilich stiffened. "Respectfully, Admiral? There's more than enough disruption to account for some deviations in the schedule. No one is going to look twice at her being a little bit late to her class."

"That's my point, Colonel," Trejo said, leaning on the syllables of Ilich's rank a little harder to point out the difference. "When everyone thinks the flood's coming up, each little bit of normalcy is a sandbag. She may not be the thing that keeps this from getting out of hand, but she can be one part of it. And she's finished her part in the doctor's little test with the prisoner. We don't gain anything by having her here."

He meant *We don't gain anything by having you here.* Ilich kept his composure, and Teresa let herself smile.

This new dynamic had come between the men since the bad night. Teresa saw it, even thought she understood what it meant. Ilich was part of the innermost conspiracy to keep her father's condition secret. Trejo had trusted him. And then it turned out that that Ilich had been letting her sneak out of the State Building compound to spend time with an assassin for the underground. Trejo had given Ilich his trust and then found that faith hadn't been justified.

Or maybe it was just that everything looked like that to her now.

"Understood," Ilich said. Then, to her, "I'll take you to the class. It will be all right."

Teresa wanted to burst into tears or scream or drop to the floor and flail like a baby. She wanted to throw a table over and scream the way Elsa Singh had. There were too many years of training and expectation holding her in place. She nodded and rose to her feet. But when Ilich started to walk down the corridor, she didn't follow.

"Eighty percent," she said, turning to Cortázar. "You're sure of eighty percent."

Trejo's eyes flashed a sharp annoyance, but Cortázar seemed happy to answer. "Well, of course that's just an estimate. But autonomic function has been something of a passion for me these last few years, and there's a lot of very good work done on the brain activity that comes with memory as opposed to the activity associated with inventing new information. It's possible that the subject created and rehearsed a set of lies so that's what he's remembering. But since new questioners and novel questions aren't finding any areas that deviate out of recall and into the creative functions, eighty is an estimate. Maybe even a low one. Holden is very probably telling the truth as he knows it."

If he said he was your friend, then he was.

In her memory, Timothy looked up at her the way he always had and said, *You can't have too many tools.*

She didn't know which one she'd been. Friend or tool.

She didn't know, and she needed to.

Peer class was in the State Building's museum. Wide, pale walls with white lights that showed every color in the paintings and sculptures without making them fade over the years. The air was controlled here, neither warm nor cold, neither humid nor dry. Colonel Ilich shepherded them past the great works of other ages like it would be impolite to wake them. He had murdered Timothy, fought with Trejo, carried the weight of the empire on his back, and his smile and voice were exactly the way they always were. She wondered what else he'd hidden from her over the years.

Connor and Muriel were standing next to each other, looking at a canvas of a man painted almost life sized. His hands were open at his sides, his face lifted as if he were staring at something in the sky. Instead of clothes, a silver sheet was pressed to his body, concealing nothing. Teresa stood with her arms crossed. The painting was so detailed, she could see the individual hairs on the backs of the man's hands. It was too perfect to be a photograph.

"It's called *Icarus at Night*," Ilich said. "The painter was a man named Kingston Xu. He was the first great artist of Mars. When this painting came out, he was almost deported back to Earth. Can anyone tell me why?"

Teresa felt the others glance at each other and at her. She didn't know and she didn't care. Her mind felt like it had been sand-blasted. There wasn't anything there.

"The sheet?" Shan Ellison said, tentatively.

"Yes," Ilich said. "That's what old medical graft material used to look like. And the man, you'll notice, is dark skinned. The early history of Mars had a great deal of proxy conflict between the nations that had founded different colonies. This model that Xu used was from a place called Pakistan. The artist was from a place called China that was its enemy at the time. The two were at war. Showing an enemy in an explicitly healing and erotic context was very dangerous, politically speaking. Xu's work could have put him in jail. Or in forced labor."

Or the pens, Teresa thought, but that wasn't right. They didn't have pens before the protomolecule.

"Then why did he do it?" Teresa was almost surprised to hear her voice.

"He thought it was important," Ilich said. "Xu felt that all humanity was part of a single family, and that the differences that divide us are trivial compared to the deep uniting factors that bring us together. That's why your father brought this painting here. The unity of the human project is a Laconian ideal."

It was a strange thought. They were torturing Holden right now over political differences. They'd killed Timothy, and maybe Timothy had come to Laconia to kill them. And now here they were, all pretending that a long-dead man's barely concealed penis was a symbol of how much they were all in it together. This was stupid.

It was worse than stupid. It was dishonest.

Ilich, maybe sensing her mood growing dark, started moving the seminar on to a collection of sculptural abstracts that had only recently arrived from Bara Gaon. Teresa was just starting to walk toward them when Dr. Cortázar appeared, smiling, around a corner.

"Colonel!" the older man said. "Here you are. I was wondering if I could borrow Teresa for a few minutes. Routine medical scan."

It caught Ilich off balance. His carefully built demeanor shifted, and she saw the flash of annoyance in his eyes. Even anger. It made her want to side with Cortázar.

"It's okay," she said. "I can review on my own later."

Ilich's smile slid back into place. "I don't know that—"

Cortázar took her hand. "It won't be long. Right back. Everything fine."

As she let herself be led away, she felt something like joy or anger. A little ember of rebellion still red and hot in the ashes of her world. She tried to hold on to it. Cortázar was humming to himself. He seemed so pleased, he was almost skipping. She waited until they were safely out of earshot before she spoke.

"Is everything okay?"

"Perfect. Lovely. I have some ideas about what happened. You know. With the high consul. There are some tests I want to run."

"Baselines?"

Cortázar's smile widened. "Something like that, yes."

They walked together through the State Building and to the private medical wing. The guards all knew them. There was nothing that would raise an alarm with anyone. Teresa had to trot to keep up with Cortázar's long strides.

Nothing felt at all off until they walked into the medical suite— the same one she'd been going to for her annual checkups and occasional maladies for longer than she could remember—and Elvi Okoye was sitting at the doctor's station. Even then, Teresa didn't know what was wrong except that Cortázar's mood soured instantly.

"Dr. Okoye. I'm afraid this isn't a good time."

"I found some notes I need to clarify with you," she said.

"This isn't a good time," Cortázar said again, his tone of voice growing harder. The rebelliousness and warmth in Teresa's chest shifted into something more like dread. She didn't understand it, but she trusted it. *You should keep an eye on me*, Holden said sometime back in her memory. It was connected to Cortázar's voice. *Nature eats babies all the time.*

"If there's something critical going on with Teresa," Elvi Okoye said, "maybe we should let Admiral Trejo know about it."

The moment stretched. For a moment, Teresa was back in the cave. Timothy told her to put her hands over her ears. She was breathing too fast. The world started to sparkle at the edges, so bright it was just like darkness.

Cortázar looked at her. "You can go," he said. "We'll do this another time."

Teresa nodded, turned, and began the walk back toward the museum and her peer class with a sense that something important had just happened. Something dangerous. And she wasn't sure what it was.

Chapter Thirty-Two: Bobbie

Copy copy, *White Crow*. Flight path amended. You good to go, sa sa?"

"Heard and acknowledged," Bobbie said. "Thank you, Control."

The tightbeam to Callisto's traffic control center dropped, and Bobbie shifted the little skiff, feeling the gentle pressure as the thrusters fired. It wasn't even enough to move her crash couch, but it bent the trajectory of her ship just enough. The display had a hard lockout that let her overlay the path of the whole plan without fear of anything leaking back. Where the *Tempest* was, where the *Storm* would appear, and where she needed to be.

She stretched her hands, and the powered gloves of the Laconian armor shifted with her. Blue showed through gaps in the black paint job. Blue and black were the wrong colors, and always would be for her. Her armor was supposed to be *red*. She opened an encrypted tightbeam and waited the seconds as it was confirmed. Everything was happening so close in, there was hardly any light delay. This wouldn't be either strategic or close quarters, but the messy part in between.

"Captain," Jillian Houston said.

"We have approval from traffic control. Monitor our position and stand by for go."

"Copy that," Jillian said, and dropped the line. It was good discipline, not leaving the connection up longer than required. Not that it would have made much difference now. By the time the Laconian forces tracked the signal, it would all be over. Or at least too far along to stop.

The *White Crow* was a terrible little ship. Even if Bobbie hadn't been taking it into combat, she'd have wanted a vac suit buttoned up tight. The cloth covering the bulkheads was pale, with lines of white showing where age and radiation had degraded it. The crash couches were lumpy and stiff, and slow to react to changes in the ship's vector. The handholds on the walls had all been polished by generations of touching, the way stone steps were supposed to be worn away in medieval cathedrals back on Earth. It was a ship that had outlasted its time, but its drive still worked, and Bobbie didn't need much more than that out of it.

She waited through minutes that felt long as they passed and sudden when they were gone. The outward-pushing, inward-pulling dilation of time before battle. It felt good.

"How are we down there, Rini?" she asked. The response delay from the airlock wasn't much less than when she'd been talking to Callisto.

"I feel like I'm cupping the devil's balls," Rini said. "But... yeah. It all looks good."

Bobbie had looked over the torpedo before they'd taken off. It was the smallest and fastest that Bobbie could find, black and boxy and hardly longer than her own leg. Rini had stripped the already spare design down to its minimum, taking away the mass of the traditional warhead in order to win a few extra milliseconds when the burn came. Instead of blowing the little fusion core, the proximity sensor would disable the power that kept the antimatter cut off from the rest of the universe, and physics would take it from there. Bobbie just had to get it close.

She checked the flight path. The *White Crow* was just about where she wanted it to be.

"I'm about to pull the pin," Bobbie said. "If you need a potty break, now's the time."

Rini's laugh was short and humorless. "I've been pissing myself since you told me the plan, Cap. At this point, I'm amazed I don't have a prolapsed bladder."

"Only a little longer," she said, and switched back to the tight-beam. "Status?"

"At your order," Jillian said.

This was the moment. The last moment. Bobbie could pull back now. Take the *White Crow* through her planned flight path, tell her crew to scatter to the winds, drop the antimatter down Jupiter's gravity well and enjoy the fireworks. There hadn't been a lot of decisive moments in her life that she'd recognized when they were happening. Usually they only came clear after the fact.

"Take her out, *Storm*," Bobbie said.

"Done," Jillian said, the single syllable sharp and hard as a thrown rock.

Bobbie took a deep breath, let it out. Down on Callisto, the *Gathering Storm* was coming to life, breaking out of its hidden berth and leaping through the thin Callistan atmosphere toward the stars. Her crew were being pressed back into their couches like God had His palm on their chests. All she could do was sit and listen to the open channel and wait for someone to notice a drive plume where there shouldn't be one.

The emergency alert cut through the chatter of voices. Military orders to make clear. The thickly traveled Jovian system, with its dozens of moons and millions of people all smashed down into a volume smaller than the slow zone, had just become a battle-field. She fired up the *White Crow*'s drive as if she were going to head for shelter. Her body felt warm and smooth. On her tactical display, the *Tempest* shifted the way it was supposed to, took the vector she'd anticipated, leaped to the attack. When she switched to visual, it looked like a tiny bone, dark against the brightness of its own drive plume.

The display showed fast movers—torpedoes already in flight from the *Storm*. And there, tiny pinpricks of light where the *Tempest*'s PDCs were firing out through holes in its skin-like plating to knock them back. The thin cone of the enemy's blind spot swept across the tactical display. She'd be in it soon. Very soon...

"Make safe, Rini," she said. "We're about to get bumpy."

"Not soon enough for me."

The *White Crow* fell into shadow, and Bobbie spun the ship hard, throwing the drive into a hard burn. The crash couch slammed up into her back. Her armor flashed a medical alert error up as her blood pressure fluttered, then took it down when she stabilized. The tactical screen had more targets than she could track. Jillian Houston was throwing everything the *Storm* had at the *Tempest*, and the *Tempest* was opening up its own volley. But so far no sign of the magnetar field generator, so their dangerous gamble was paying off for now. Bobbie slid the *White Crow* closer in, trying to narrow the gap between her and her enemy. The burn was hard. Her armor rippled down on her legs and arms in rhythm with her heart, pushing the blood along, keeping it from pooling. Even so, darkness started to creep in at the edges of her vision. She was aware of voices on her radio like they were music coming from another room. She was hiding in the middle of the *Tempest*'s blind spot. The safest she could be in the middle of a shooting war, and still not particularly safe.

She shifted to the in-ship comms, and the rest of the universe went silent. "Prepare for launch."

She was pretty certain she heard Rini's grit-toothed acknowl-edgment. She checked her drive. Seven gs. She'd done worse than seven gs before. Getting old sucked.

She didn't just feel the impact, she heard it, transmitted up through the mass of the ship and into her armor. A deep, dull clank like someone hitting a badly made bell.

"I think we took a hit," she said. "What's your status?"

Rini didn't answer. Pushing against the thrust gravity, Bobbie shifted to the network display. Rini's power armor was still con-nected, but everything on it was in error states. A sea of red where green should have been. Bobbie shouted the woman's name again, but she already knew there wouldn't be a reply.

The airlock was one deck down and then half a dozen meters from the lift shaft. If she cut the drive, the *White Crow* would fall out of the blind spot and be cut down by the *Tempest*'s PDCs. If the torpedo had broken...

If it had broken, she'd already be a rapidly expanding cloud of glowing plasma. The antimatter at least was still intact. That meant there was hope. And if there was hope, there wasn't rest. She slaved the piloting controls to her armor, checked her seals and status—a few medical stats in the yellow, but nothing in the red—and unstrapped from the crash couch. The power armor whined under its own weight as she stood, and she felt her shoul-ders trying to dislocate. The blood in her veins slammed down into her legs, and the armor clamped against her thighs, pushing it back up. A wave of nausea almost overcame her. She took the first of eight steps to the lift. She could do it. She had to.

A low growling was coming up from the deck. The maneuvering thrusters were firing. That couldn't be good. She reached the lift, and the slight reduction in g as she went down was like one drop of water to someone dying of thirst. It stopped when the lift did.

The airlock was a mess. Both sets of doors were open, venting the ship into space. The bulkhead was folded where the PDC rounds had hit. Jagged holes gaped where the raw kinetic force had shoved the outer hull into the room. The torpedo was in the far corner where the bulkhead met the floor, and Rini's body was beside it. Bobbie went to her side and knelt, the artificial muscles running through her power armor straining under the burden.

Death had come fast for Rini. She probably hadn't even known it happened. The armor was the same mostly black as Bobbie's, and it was still working hard to preserve the life that was gone. Five holes across her back and arm poured blood too fast, the thrust gravity squeezing it out of the corpse. Bobbie shifted Rini away. There'd be time for mourning later.

Rini had protected the torpedo from the worst of the damage, but the little drive wasn't unscathed. A white impact showed where a bit of shrapnel had cracked the ceramic around the drive cone. Bobbie tried to lift it and see the extent of the damage, but she couldn't. Even with the powered armor, the burn was too much. Her spine ached, and the one rib that dislocated when she was under too much thrust had slipped out of place again. It hurt to breathe.

The *White Crow* threw up a fresh alert. The maneuvering thrusters were at a little under a third of their reaction mass, and requesting permission to start drawing from the reserve. It only took seconds to see the problem. The PDC rounds had sheared off a section of the exterior plating. In a larger ship, it wouldn't have mattered, but the *White Crow* was small enough that it had shifted the center of mass. The thrusters were firing to keep her from curving off, and would until they ran dry.

She had the ship open a tightbeam to the *Storm*.

"Need good news, Captain," Jillian said, her voice wet and phlegmy from the pressure of their burn.

"Rini's down. Ship and torpedo are both compromised. I need you to make the *Tempest* stop. I can do this, but not at high burn."

There was no response for a second. "How?" Jillian asked, but Alex's voice cut in on the channel.

"Give me a second, Bobbie. I'll get you what you need."

She closed her eyes. Her consciousness was swimming. It was only force of will that made her turn toward the payload. The four little spheres of magnetism, vacuum, and hellfire. The proximity sensor. Neither of them looked damaged. She checked her tactical display. She was still in the blind spot. She rotated the ship and eased back on the maneuvering thrusters. If she was going to fall off course, she could at least fall in the right direction. The *Tempest*'s drive plume swept past, framed in the airlock doors like a comet.

"Alex?" she said. "Give me something."

And as if in answer, the *White Crow* went on the float. Bobbie rose up, then clamped mag boots against the deck. The *Tempest*'s drive plume was gone. Her blood shifted and the nausea came and went again as she unhooked the warhead and the proximity sensor. The *White Crow* was spent. The torpedo was scrap. She wasn't done. There was still a way. She took up the warhead, cradling it to her chest, and stepped out the airlock. She didn't pause as she launched.

Bobbie fired up the thrusters on her Laconian armor and burned toward the *Tempest*. It was an asteroid, a strangely shaped rock curving through a complex orbit around the small and distant sun. She was close enough to see it without enhancement. Much closer than she'd intended. Maybe a hundred klicks away. Maybe less. A machine that had brought the solar system to its knees. The unkillable dreadnought of Laconia. And somewhere beyond it, away to her left, the *Storm*. Her ship. They weren't really stationary. Nothing in the universe was. It was only that their vectors matched for the moment. Stillness was an illusion.

Something flashed and was gone. A torpedo taken out by the *Tempest*'s PDCs. Against the constant and unwavering starlight, the little glimmer of motion stood out. She saw another. A handful more. And the arcing brightness of the *Tempest*'s torpedoes heading out. The distances were so vast, they almost looked slow.

"Hold on," she said, but she didn't turn her comms on. It wasn't a message so much as a prayer.

Bobbie checked her tactical display. She was still linked to the *White Crow*, but the comms on the little ship weren't the best. It took almost a second for the full layout to repopulate.

Going ballistic was hard. The warhead in her arms was a dart, and she was trying to drop it a kilometer and land it in a coffee cup. She checked her suit, and the thrusters were good, even if they were running through her fuel way too fast. The *Tempest* was a little larger now. She killed the burn and turned, centering it between her feet. Falling toward her enemy from a great height. She held the warhead against her belly, checked the connections and readouts one last time. Was the power cut off engaged? Yes. Was the backup battery disconnected? Yes. Was the proximity sensor set so that the ship would trigger it? It was.

Bobbie took a deep breath. Another. That rib popped back into place with a deep and painful snap, and she grinned. The *Tempest* was visibly larger now. Her velocity toward it was recklessly fast, even though she could hardly feel it. She eyeballed her path, adjusted, had the suit double-check her. An augmented line from her armored toes down to the *Tempest*. She took a solid hold on the warhead, one hand on either side, and then carefully let go. Even a tiny variance, amplified over the quickly falling distance, would be a disaster. She waited for a long moment, and it floated in place, almost touching her. No drift. Perfect.

Gently, she tapped her suit thrusters, drifting away centimeter by centimeter, careful that the little plumes didn't touch the warhead. When she was four or five meters away, she started a braking burn, and the warhead seemed to leap away. Her breath sounded very loud in her ears. Very close. Her suit was running warm, the radiators doing their best to shed waste heat. The vacuum of space was only cold after you were dead.

It was too late for her. Some part of her had known that from the moment she'd seen the white mark on the torpedo, but now that it was done, she could think about it. If things had gone right, she and Rini and the *White Crow* would have been burning hard as hell away from the *Tempest* the moment they dropped their missile, trying to outrun the blast. And that had assumed the *Storm* was still leading the enemy away, which wasn't happening either. So this was it.

She twisted at the hips, stretching. The stars of the galactic disk spread against the horizonless sky. Some of that light had been traveling for centuries. Millennia. Longer. Many of those stars would have died long before she was born. What a weird fate for a photon to be spat out of a nuclear fireball, speed through the vast emptiness between stars, and land on a Martian Marine's retina while she decided whether she still feared death, or if she was ready. She'd done this a dozen times before.

The *Tempest* was getting larger. She hadn't killed all her velocity toward it. She wondered whether the *Storm* would make it. In a straight battle, it was doomed. Jillian and Alex and the rest were doing the tactical equivalent of taking a ship like the *Rocinante* and picking a fight with a *Donnager*-class. As long as the *Tempest* didn't fire up its drive, it would be worth it. Pyrrhic victories were still victories, and this was about to cost the enemy way more than it would her.

She thought about making a connection back to the *Storm*. Saying goodbye. They didn't need the distraction. If anything, she should try to divide the enemy's attention, not her allies'. Anything else was self-indulgence. She'd taken her shot, but she wasn't done.

She checked the ammunition levels in the suit. She was topped up. The thrusters still had some juice in them, and her oxygen was good for another thirty minutes, even if she didn't start running it thin. She engaged the weapons, shifted her HUD to local/tactical, and grinned. *Who am I? Did the things I accomplished matter? Will I leave the universe a better place than I found it? If I don't come back, what are my regrets? What are my victories?*

"Thanks for everything," she said to the universe, as if it had been the host of a particularly good party that was just winding down.

She turned toward the *Tempest*. Another sparkle of light. Another volley of torpedoes speeding out into the darkness. Another threat to her ship and her people. "All right, motherfucker. You want to dance? Let's dance."

She locked her targeting system onto the Laconian battleship, shifted her suit to live fire, and started her burn. Fifty-seven seconds later, she passed out of the *Tempest*'s blind spot.

Chapter Thirty-Three: Alex

Status?" Bobbie said. Her voice on the command deck only made Alex feel her absence more. All around, the others were at their stations. The tension in the air was thick. Every glance, every breath, every nervous chuckle meant the same thing: *Holy shit, we're actually going to do this.*

"At your order," Jillian said, tugging the collar of her uniform open another centimeter. Alex remembered being young enough to care what he looked like going into a battle.

Caspar was tapping the side of his crash couch. Jillian leaned forward on hers, pulling the restraints tight against her shoulders. Alex sort of wished he'd hit the head. Everyone dealt with the anticipation and dread differently.

They'd been preparing for hours, towing the *Storm* out from its hidden mine, making the cabins and workshops secure, running every system through its diagnostics. Now the only thing between the *Gathering Storm* and open space was a set of old bay doors, and Bobbie's go order.

"Take her out, *Storm*."

"Done," Jillian said, and cut the connection. "Kamal. Take us out."

Alex tapped the release and watched on his monitor as the doors above them opened. Maneuvering thrusters gently pushed them off the moon's surface. And as soon as the *Storm* cleared the dock, he lit the Epstein up. He fell hard into the crash couch gel, feeling the coolness as it crept up around his ribs and neck. Callisto fell away behind them, the surface glowing orange and gold where the drive plume had heated it.

"All systems inside tolerance," Caspar said, even though no one had asked. The kid had to do something. "We are...Okay. I'm getting a connection request from Callisto traffic control?"

"Let 'em wonder," Jillian said. "Do we have the *Tempest*?"

"Got him," Alex said.

"Show me."

Alex threw the Jovian system onto the main display. Their position, the moons, the curving arc of the gas giant below them. The shipping patterns were complex to an untrained eye, but he could read them like text. The freight traffic in gray, Laconian security in gold. Bobbie and the *White Crow* in green. And the target—the *Tempest*—in red as bright as fresh blood.

The shifting gravity of the system made lowest-energy transit lines, and the traffic between the moons followed them like iron filings showing a magnetic field. At these distances, you wouldn't even need an Epstein drive to ignore them. A decent ship flying teakettle could get anywhere it needed to be. It was only the extra scrip that ships could save that made the pattern what it was. That was always enough.

"Come on," Jillian said, not to anyone on the bridge. "Grow some balls and come get me, you big bastard."

"Security alert's just gone out, open channel," Caspar said. "They know we're here. The *Tempest* is moving. She's coming after us."

"Punch it, Kamal," Jillian said. Her bravado was almost convincing. Alex didn't think Caspar saw through it.

Alex punched it. On his monitor, the green of the *White Crow* lined up just where he wanted it to be. The *Tempest* followed in the way he'd expected it would. His jaw ached from the thrust, and the juice running through his system made him feel like he'd had too much coffee and not enough at the same time. The *Tempest* was a massive ship, but the drive was powerful enough that inertia didn't matter much. The *Storm* was smaller, lighter, and less powerful, and while it was probably more maneuverable, that didn't help this time. If he was going to get Bobbie through the eye of that particular needle, he had no degrees of freedom.

They still had advantages, though. The main one being that they were ahead and the *Tempest* was behind. The *Storm*'s drive plume gave a little cover. The torpedoes that the *Tempest* fired would have to swing out and around to keep from getting slagged. And it also had catch up to the *Storm* as it sped away. Anything the *Storm* launched, the *Tempest* would rush forward to meet. It gave the *Storm*'s PDCs that little extra slice of reaction time, the *Tempest*'s that much less. Bobbie's flight plan for him had been to ride that gap where the difference put the *Tempest* in threat and the *Storm* just outside it. It was great in theory. Practice was more complicated, because they could still be overwhelmed.

Would be.

"Fast movers," Caspar gasped. "That's a lot of them."

Jillian coughed. It sounded painful. Alex half expected her to move to text communication, but she fought through and spoke aloud. "PDCs to auto. Return fire."

The thrum of the PDCs added itself to the noise and shudder of the pursuit. Like a kid trying to outrun a cop, the *Storm* slid past the *White Crow*, and the *Tempest* boiled up from below her. Alex couldn't tell if the vibration was engine harmonics coming from the deck or his overloaded bloodstream or both. Bobbie's little ship hit her burn too, falling into the enemy's blind spot.

Soon. It would all be over soon. He forced himself to swallow. It hurt.

The *Storm* shook. "We aren't hit," Caspar shouted. "It was close, but we got it."

"More distance, Kamal," Jillian said, but he couldn't do that without prodding the *Tempest* to match. Bobbie needed the battleship to keep its current course and heading. He was too focused on the reality of the situation to explain why it was a bad order, so he just ignored it. If the *Storm* had to take a few hits, it would just have to take them.

The incoming fire was like a vast, blooming flower. Lines looped out from the *Tempest*, curved in toward them, and vanished as the *Storm* knocked them back. Alex spared a glance at the ammunition levels. They weren't as low as he'd expected. All his habits had been formed on older technology. The Laconian design for rapid printing of new rounds still wasn't intuitive.

If they had been doing what they appeared to be doing—running like hell and hoping to get to the gate and out of the system—it would have been a desperation move. The distance between Jupiter and the ring gate was vast, and the *Storm* was constrained by both its reaction mass and the fragility of the bodies inside her. And the danger of screaming through the slow zone too fast without knowing the state of play on the inside. Alex would have had to make a braking burn before they reached the gate, and the *Tempest* would have caught them. If Bobbie didn't come through, it could still go down that way. Alex realized he was already plotting in other plans—dive into the high atmosphere of Jupiter and try to scrape the *Tempest* off, loop sunward and try to get the enemy to overheat and pull back before they had to—and stopped himself. They weren't in the last ditch yet.

"New volley coming in," Caspar shouted. "We're not going to be able to stop them all."

"Evasive, Kamal," Jillian snapped, and Alex bent their flight path away, but only a little. The *Tempest* couldn't turn or shift without exposing the *White Crow*. And where the hell was Bobbie anyway?

"Brace," Caspar said, and a second later the crash couch bucked under Alex, kicking him like a mule. Even with the gel to pad him, he fought to get his breath back. He'd lost a couple of seconds. They couldn't afford that again.

"What's the damage?" Jillian croaked out, but no one answered.

The tightbeam sprang to life. Bobbie was checking in.

"Need good news, Captain," Jillian said. Her face was shining with sweat. Alex waited with dread and hope.

"Rini's down. Ship and torpedo are both compromised," Bobbie said. Her voice was strained, but with the calm professionalism of a woman in her natural environment. She'd have had the same tone if she'd just found the way to destroy her enemy or lost both her legs. "I need you to make the *Tempest* stop. I can do this, but not at high burn."

The pause seemed to last forever. Alex plotted in the flip and burn, and waited for Jillian to give the word.

Instead, she said, "How?"

"Give me a second, Bobbie," Alex said. "I'll get you what you need."

The drive cut off, the weight of acceleration vanishing in the time it took to blink. Alex took the comm control from Caspar and turned on the do-not-approach beacon. Tactically, it didn't make any damned sense. That's what he was counting on.

"What are you doing, Kamal?" Jillian said. Her tone was halfway between outrage and hope that maybe he knew something.

"Making us look like a mutiny," he said. "Seeing whether they like the idea of getting their ship back."

As he'd hoped, the *Tempest* killed its drive. They sped through the darkness in matching orbits. Callisto was already long gone behind them. Even Jupiter was visibly smaller. It felt like being alone, but every eye in the system would be watching them.

"Leche bao," Caspar said under his breath. "They're going to kill us."

"As long as they do it without starting their drive up," Jillian said, and Alex felt a little burst of pride for the girl. She was green, but she was learning. For almost a minute, the two ships stood silent, waiting, and tense. A comm request came in from the *Tempest*. Jillian didn't accept it. Alex noticed he was holding his breath.

"Fast movers," Caspar said.

"Shoot down as many as you can and return fire," Jillian said, "but do not change course, and don't give them a reason to."

Alex could only watch as the crew fired back. It would be over already if the command staff of the *Tempest* had wanted it to be. A single massive strike, and the *Storm* would be dead. Instead, like a wrestler slowly bending back the opponent's joint, they were pushing the flow of missiles, a little faster and a little faster until the *Storm*'s defenses were overwhelmed. They wanted to disable the ship and question the crew. They hadn't met Bobbie. Or Jillian Houston. If it came to it, they would scuttle the *Storm*. He knew he was looking at his own death.

Come on, Bobbie, he thought. *I'm trusting you on this.*

"I think... Is that the captain?" Caspar said. "I think that's the captain."

He threw the feed from the external sensors onto the main display. The image was a little shaky, the edges too sharp, but there not far from the *Tempest* was a single figure in power armor falling in toward the ship. Its arms ended in the rapid-fire glitter of muzzle flash, throwing two streams of ineffectual rounds at the mass of the Laconian dreadnought. The sight of a single human-sized figure flying past the battleship gave a dramatic sense of scale to its massive bulk. Next to it, Bobbie looked like an angry insect attacking a whale.

"Keep your eye on the incoming missiles," Jillian said. "If that's Draper, she's doing it for a reason."

The tiny figure flew a jagged, unpredictable path. Streams of high-speed projectiles chased it as the *Tempest*'s PDCs tracked it. The flyswatter hunting the fly. It was impossible to imagine that something so small could stand a chance against the vastness and power of the ship, but if it was Bobbie it was also impossible to imagine she wouldn't.

Alex started laying in a burn solution. "I can get to her," he said. "It's going to mean getting damned close to that thing, but..."

The figure twitched. Something bloomed out from its back. On the display, it looked so small. The arms rose up, the legs bent. Vapor sprayed from the figure. Atmosphere. Blood.

"She caught a PDC round," Jillian said. "She's gone."

Alex didn't hear her. He heard her, but he wouldn't understand. Grief like an electrical shock ran through his body, humming and violent and damaging.

"I can get to her," Alex said, turning back to his controls. Something was wrong with the juice on his couch. He couldn't catch his breath. "It's going to be a hell of a ride, but we can...we can..."

His controls flickered as Jillian locked him out.

"Give me the *fucking* controls," he shouted. "We have to get her!"

"Alex," Caspar said, and his gentleness was unbearable. The suit of powered armor drifted. It was still heading toward the *Tempest*. Inertia carrying her toward her destination even after it didn't matter. Even after she was gone. He tapped at the controls the same way, like there was a way to roll time back just a little.

"Fuck. *Fuck*," Alex shouted. The lemony taste of vomit hit the back of his throat. He swallowed hard, forcing it back down. The plan had failed.

Bobbie was gone.

"What do we do?" Caspar said, and there was panic in his voice. Before Alex could answer, the sensor feed died with an audible click and the radiation alarms started screaming.

The *Heart of the Tempest* had stood alone against the combined forces of Earth, Mars, and the Belt and won. It had put all humanity under Laconia's yoke. It was the living symbol of why all resistance against High Consul Duarte would always be in vain.

When their sensors finished their override reset, it was gone.

Without the protection of the *Storm*'s eerie skin, the burst of X-rays and gamma radiation would have killed them all. As it was, half the crew was too sick to get out of their crash couches. The medical bay was filled with people sloughing off the lining of their gastrointestinal tracts. The ship's supply of antiradiation pharmaceuticals was already down to nothing, and if the cancer rate followed the models, their oncocidals would be going down next.

The ship itself was injured too. Not even broken. Injured. The regenerative plating that covered the *Storm* had started developing blisters and thickening like the first stages of skin cancer. The vacuum channels that routed power failed sometimes for no clear reason, becoming so unreliable that the repair crews started putting in copper wire backup circuits, the metal taped to the inside of the corridors. The drive still burned, even if it ran a little dirty.

They'd won. It hadn't been possible, but they'd done it. Coming out unscarred would have been too much to ask.

Alex cycled between numbness and grief with the regularity of a clock. When he could stand it, he watched the newsfeeds from around the system replaying the explosion he hadn't been able to see because he was too close when it happened. The best one was from Earth. A handheld camera filming a child's kite competition was pointing at the right section of sky when the light reached there, and the brightness against the blue had been like a small, brief sun, even at that distance.

Everyone in the system was tracking the *Storm* as it made its way toward the ring gate. No one had the nerve to follow it. The newsfeeds were thick with analysis. The attack had been in retaliation for the crackdown on Ceres. It had been an inside job, and stood as evidence that the Laconian Navy itself was rife with factions and dissent. It was the first step toward the underground retaking Sol system or the inciting incident that would force the high consul to glass the whole system. Nine times out of ten, the speakers were celebrating Laconia's defeat. There were other stories: Spontaneous demonstrations on Mars and Rhea calling for Laconian withdrawal. The official announcement from TSL-5 that the Laconian political officer's position was being held empty until regular communication through the gate network was reestablished. A dozen pirate feeds springing up, accusing the Laconians of taking risks in the dead systems that put the whole human race under threat.

It wasn't chaos, or if it was, it was no more than usual. It was the blossoming of hope where there had been no hope before. It was everything Bobbie had intended it to be, except for one detail.

For himself, the radiation sickness was bad, but the physical distress at least kept his mind busy. When he felt well enough to work, he threw in with the repair crews. He wasn't surprised when Jillian Houston—Captain Houston—called him into her office. He'd been expecting it.

The cabin was small and spare. Laconian officers didn't show off. Another thing they'd inherited from Mars. Alex remembered his own commanders embracing the same austerity, back when he'd been a different man and the universe had made sense. The few decorations and belongings that had been Bobbie's were on the desk. Jillian looked thinner than before, and paler too. The radiation sickness had hit her harder, but it hadn't stopped her.

"Alex," she said. Her voice was gentler than usual. Like now that she'd taken power, she didn't have to be as aggressive. "I wanted you to...I thought she'd have wanted you to take care of her things."

"Thank you," Alex said, reaching for them.

"Please sit."

He did. Jillian leaned forward, her fingers steepled. "We need repairs. We need to regroup. And we need to go to ground before Laconia gets their shit together and sends ships after us."

"All right," Alex said. His heart wasn't in it. Maybe it was because he was sick. Maybe it was grief. Where one started and the other stopped was difficult if not impossible to locate.

"I've decided to take us back to Freehold. We have the support there. And the *Storm*'s home base facility. We can get her back up to trim. Resupply from the colony. Plan our next moves."

She looked at him like she expected him to say something. He wasn't sure what that would be. He considered the things on the table. A tunic. A little glass-and-ceramic commendation she'd gotten from the UN, signed by Chrisjen Avasarala. He was surprised there wasn't more, and he was a little surprised there was even that much.

"I think that's a good plan," he said. "The risky part will be getting through the gates, but with no Medina Station, we don't have to try to sneak out in a supply ship. That makes it easier."

When Jillian spoke again, there was a thickness in her voice like passion or sorrow. Or rage. "Draper was a good captain. And a better war leader. She made this ship what it is, and no one on the *Storm* will ever forget her or the sacrifice she made for us."

"Thank you," Alex said.

"I need to make this my ship now. In her tradition and her honor, but my command. I wish it wasn't like that, but it's where we are. You understand."

"I do."

"Good. Because I need you as my XO."

Alex looked at her. He knew the answer and what he was going to do as clearly as if he'd actually been thinking about it. All his next steps laid out before him.

"Thank you," he said. "But no. This is your ship, and that's the way it should be. I've got one of my own."

Chapter Thirty-Four: Elvi

Elvi woke up gasping.

"Hey hey hey," Fayez said, shifting in the bed beside her. His hand on her back grounded her. It made the dream scatter back a little. She leaned into it. "Nightmare?" he asked.

"Worse," she said. "You know that dream where you've got the big presentation that you forgot about, and now you have to pretend you did eight months of work on something you've got no clue on?"

"That is your go-to for bad dreams."

"That, except that usually when I have it, I just have to wake up and things are better," she said, smoothing back her hair. "I'd give three fingers and an eye to only have a blown lecture to worry about."

He shifted, the familiar warmth of his body moving alongside her. "How's your gut?" he asked. And then, when she didn't answer, "You need to eat, darling."

"I do. I will. It's just…"

"I know."

She reached for her cane, but when she stood, she put more weight on her hurt leg. The pain felt right. She went to the bathroom first, then started pulling on clothes. It was still dark out, apart from the lights of the State Building, the glow of the city, and the construction platforms glittering against the stars.

"Come back to bed," Fayez said. "It's too early."

"I'm not going to sleep anyway. I'll go out to the university. Get a jump on the day."

"You have to get some rest."

"Rest for me," she said, and kissed him on the cheek, and then again on the neck. They were still for a moment.

When Fayez spoke, his voice didn't have its usual lightness. "I will find a way to get us out of this if I can."

"Out of this?"

"The part where you're surrounded by psychopaths and politicians. We'll steal a little ship, head out to some backwater colony world and spend the rest of our lives trying to get cucumbers to grow in poison soil. It'll be great."

"It would be heaven," she said. "Go back to bed. I'll come back when I can."

The State Building was almost pleasant at night. Something about the quietness made it seem like she had freedom. There were just as many guards, just as many surveillance drones. Maybe it was just millennia of evolution priming her brain to believe that what happened in the darkness was hidden, private, and peculiar. She stuffed her hands in her pockets and went to the commissary. There would be something there—coffee and sweet rice, if nothing else. She couldn't keep much more than that down anyway.

The work in Cortázar's lab was punishing. There were a couple of decent virtual context translators in the lab. They helped enough that when his notes were couched in terms of nanoinformatics—complex imaginary information loss, Deriner functions, implicit multipliers—she could understand it in exobiological terms like functional regulation site persistence across generations. How either or both of them would ever be able to make the issues clear to Admiral Trejo, she couldn't imagine. But she'd been able to explain convergent evolution to undergraduates, once upon a time. So maybe she'd come up with something.

The commissary was bright and quiet. An attendant nodded to her as she entered. Or maybe he was a guard. Same thing. Elvi got herself a cup of tea—the coffee smelled too acidic and aggressive when she got close to it—and a bagel with butter and jelly. She didn't want to go to the pens or Cortázar's private labs. She didn't want to spend another day with Cara and Xan. She also didn't want to stay here. But most of all, she didn't want to do what she knew she had to do. Tell Trejo about Cortázar.

She'd wanted to find proof. A smoking gun somewhere in his notes. She'd gone over everything she could find about Duarte's transubstantiation—her term for it, not theirs—hoping to find something that showed Cortázar didn't intend to let Teresa follow in her father's footsteps, and that he never had. There was nothing. Either he'd never put it in his written musings or he'd erased it carefully enough that she couldn't find it.

Her hand terminal had a reminder function. It was meant to alert her when meetings were about to start, and one of the options was to let her know when the other people were already together. She'd made a fake appointment with Cortázar and Teresa with an unfixed time. It meant that anytime the two of them were in close proximity, she was notified, and would be until one of them noticed it on their schedule and wiped it out. She was almost certain that her unexpected appearance at the medical wing was the only thing that had kept Cortázar's work with Teresa from moving forward already.

And by *work*, she was pretty sure she meant vivisection.

She finished the last bite of bagel and washed it down with the dregs of her tea. It was still hours before daylight. If she waited, her courage would fail her. She cleaned up her plate and teacup, stretched until her leg ached, and went to the attendant.

"Can I help you with something, ma'am?"

"I need to talk to Admiral Trejo."

Trejo was dressed when she reached his office. His bright-green eyes were puffy with lack of sleep, and his shirt had the limp look of something worn for too many days in a row. His desk held a pile of exhausted single-use displays, the detritus of a flood of highly sensitive reports from inside the system and what he had managed to glean from all the systems beyond. His smile was warm, well practiced, and probably insincere.

Elvi had been laboring hard under the strain of juggling a mad emperor, a murderous scientist, and civilization-ending monsters that had killed her crew and eaten her flesh. It was uncomfortable to think that Trejo was under more pressure than she was.

"Doctor," Trejo said. "You're up early."

"So are you."

He gestured to a chair. "I'm up late. Coordination with the other systems has been...challenging. I delegate what I can, but the high consul didn't sleep, and being both him and myself has been...strenuous."

"When was the last time you slept?"

"A full night? Honestly, I'd have to do some math."

Elvi sat, folding her hands together on her knees. The anxiety hissed and spun in her chest like a firework. Sleep seemed like something in a language she couldn't speak. Neither of them knew what the term meant anymore.

"Is there something I can do for you, Dr. Okoye?" Trejo prompted. Elvi realized she'd faded out for a moment.

"I don't have hard proof," she said, "but I believe Dr. Cortázar intends to harm the high consul's daughter. Maybe even kill her."

Trejo sighed and looked down. Elvi steeled herself. She was aware how thin her argument was. Even if Holden had come right out and made the accusation, it wouldn't have carried much weight. Her trust in him would do more to undermine her own status than to dignify his report. All she had was the bone-deep conviction that it was true. She was prepared to plant her flag there and defend her position until Trejo took her seriously.

She expected him to say *What evidence do you have?* or *What makes you think that?* or *Why would he do that?* Instead, the admiral stretched his neck to the side until it popped. "Has there been any change in the high consul's condition?"

"Not that I've seen," she said. "But—"

"What options do we have for bringing him back to himself?"

"I don't know. I honestly don't know if that's even possible."

"We did the thing in the first place," Trejo said. His voice was getting a rasp to it. Frustration or fear or anger. "Why can't we undo it?"

"The same reason we can't stir milk back out of coffee or unscramble an egg. Physics is full of things that only work in one direction. This is one."

"Can we regenerate his central nervous system the way we would after a head injury?"

Elvi felt confused. She'd imagined several versions of this conversation, but none of them had involved ignoring her fears and changing the subject. She wasn't sure what to do.

"Well, um…it's not exactly like that. The cells in his brain are all still intact. Cortázar changed the way they function. Regrowing tissue means finding areas that are compromised and encouraging new cells to build there."

"If we intentionally damaged his brain and pumped in normal cell lines, would he grow back?"

"I'm sorry?"

"Burn out his hippocampus, regenerate it. Then his occipital lobe or whatever. Go through him part by part, kill what's there and replace it with fresh tissue that works like normal human flesh, and build him back up that way. Would that work?"

"I…I don't know," Elvi said. "That's the Ship of Theseus

question. Whether, when you replace all the individual parts of something, you still have the same thing. That's philosophy. But even then, regrowing central nervous systems is tricky work. We'd want to talk to medical doctors. Physicians. I'm a biologist."

"Cortázar did it."

"Cortázar is deeply, *deeply* ethically flawed," Elvi said. "I'm pretty sure he was using Duarte as an animal model to work the kinks out for his own treatment in the future, and I think he's planning to sacrifice Teresa too. That's what I'm here telling you."

"What about the things that attacked the ring space? Can we say definitively whether they do or don't pose an ongoing threat? If I park another ship where Medina used to be, is it going to get eaten? Or are we safe as long as we don't blow up any more neutron stars?"

Elvi didn't mean to laugh. It just happened. Trejo's professional demeanor slipped for a moment, and she saw the rage and despair underneath it.

"How would I possibly know that?" she said. Her voice was louder than she'd meant it to be, but she didn't rein herself in. "I don't know what they are or how they ate the ships they did. Have we had reports? Do we have data? I can't do anything but speculate without that. And what does any of that have to do with Teresa Duarte?"

Trejo went to his desk, called up a fresh window, and shifted it to her hand terminal. She looked at the images there. She recognized the *Heart of the Tempest*. It was the most iconic Laconian ship there was. The images had the hyperreal quality of optical telescopy that had been stabilized and enhanced. A few glittering sparks appeared around it.

"Was there a battle?" she asked, and the image went so white that even coming from the small screen it hurt her eyes.

"It's already known through the Sol system. It will be known through the whole empire. The *Tempest* is dead. A separatist terror cell stole secret Laconian technology and used it against us. And now I have one *Magnetar*-class ship, thirteen-hundred-odd ring gates to keep control over, and the one place where it could actually do that is haunted by..." He gestured at her leg. *Whatever the fuck did that.*

"I see," she said.

"We haven't been able to keep signal repeaters up. Every time I send them out, some rock thrower knocks them back down. The terrorists are sending messages to each other through the gates using the technological equivalent of tin cans and chewing gum, and I can't stop them. If I can put a fleet of ships into the ring space, I control everything because it's a choke point. It's *the* choke point. If I can't do that safely, I can't control the empire."

"Except if—" she began, but Trejo couldn't be stopped. His words were like an avalanche. Once they'd started, they kept going.

"Everyone—*everyone*—on every ship and station and planet is going to be waiting to see what the high consul does. And right now he's two hallways over, waving his hands like a fucking undergraduate on his first hallucinogenic trip. Governments exist on confidence. Not on liberty. Not on righteousness. Not on force. They exist because people believe that they do. Because they don't ask questions. And Laconia is looking down the throat of a lot of questions we can't answer."

By the end of the speech, his voice had risen. Grown strident. Elvi had the sudden and vivid memory of being a girl in Karhula. The manager of the grocery she and her father went to every week had found out the rent on the property was going up, that he was going to have to move or shut down. He'd had the same tone of voice, the same sense of having been overwhelmed by events, the same anger in the face of implacable reality. There was something weirdly comforting about the idea that a humble grocer and the most powerful man in a galaxy-wide empire could have something so fundamental in common. Without thinking, she reached out and took Trejo's hand. He yanked it back like she'd burned him.

It took a couple long, shuddering breaths for him to regain his composure. When he spoke again, it was the Trejo she recognized. "Your problem, Dr. Okoye, is that you think the immediate problem before you is the most pressing one. It is not. Whatever else Paolo Cortázar may be—and I have no illusions about that man—he is also indispensable."

The silence between them stretched out longer than was comfortable. Elvi felt like she was looking over the lip of a cliff she hadn't understood she was standing on. "You're telling me it's okay with you."

"I will try to keep guards on the girl," Trejo said. "I will do what I can to make sure the two of them aren't alone together."

"But if he comes in here with her head under his arm, you'll shrug and let it slide?"

Trejo spread his hands. "If he says he can fix this clusterfuck by sacrificing her, I'll find him a knife. That is my duty. I am an officer of the Laconian Empire," he said. Then, a moment later, "As are you."

The air in the room seemed thin. Elvi was having a hard time catching her breath. Either Trejo didn't see her distress or he chose not to.

"Your focus, Dr. Okoye, is to provide a second set of eyes and experience as a help to Dr. Cortázar. You and he are partners in this. There is no daylight between you. If you find that difficult or distasteful, I don't really care. We are at a critical moment in history, and you must rise to this occasion."

"She's a kid," Elvi said.

"I agree it would be better if she lived. I'll do what I can," Trejo said. "But there can't be any misunderstanding between us about what our priorities are. The sooner you and he find a way to stir the cream back out of this coffee, the sooner she'll be safe. Anything that impedes the efforts to heal Winston Duarte is your enemy. Anything that helps is your friend. Are we clear?"

I resign floated at the back of her throat. She could feel the words like they were something physical. She knew the shape of them. And she knew Trejo wouldn't let her quit. Where she was now, there was no coming back from.

"As clear as an unmuddied lake," she said. "As clear as air."

"Thank you for your time, Doctor. My door is always open to you."

It was, she thought, an ironic way to tell her to leave.

She rose and walked out into the hall, and then the wide lobby, and then the darkness of the gardens. In the east, the first hint of dawn was turning off the dimmest stars. The air smelled like burnt cinnamon. It was the mating display of a species of ground-dwelling grub-like animal native to Laconia. On Earth, it would have been birdsong. She stood for a long moment and breathed it deeply.

She had done fieldwork for decades, traveling to new worlds with her sample bags and testing kits. She was probably the only person living who had seen as many different trees of life as she had. All the numberless different solutions that evolution had come up with under all the different stars, and all responding—more or less—to the same pressures. Eyes on every world, because things that sensed light were more likely to survive. Mouths near the sense organs, because things with feeding coordination did better than things without. She'd probably killed and dissected representatives of more individual species than anyone in history in the name of science. And still, she didn't think of herself as a killer. As complicit in murder. As monstrous.

On the horizon, a plume that looked almost like smoke but was really millions of tiny, green-bodied, screw-shaped worms rose up into the sky and then flattened. They shimmered in the rising brightness, a bioluminescent display. Nature was beautiful, wherever she found it. And it was cruel. She didn't know why she kept expecting humanity to be different. Why she pretended the same rules that applied to mountain lions and parasitic wasps didn't also constrain her. Red in tooth and claw, and at every level. In the Bible, even angels murdered humanity's babies when God asked them to.

The swarm on the horizon finished advertising its quality as a mating cluster, the light going out, their bodies going gray. The clouds took on the pink and red of any planet with enough oxygen to selectively scatter the shorter wavelengths. The cinnamon smell grew stronger.

"Good luck, little grubs," she said. "Hope it works out for you."

She headed back into the State Building and then through to the other side of the compound, where a car was waiting for her. She got in without exchanging pleasantries with the driver, and they headed out into the great city where lights were just turning off as the sun rose. High-rises and streets and warehouses and theaters, all of it reminding her of nothing so much as a huge hive.

At the university, she walked herself from the parking structure to the Pen. Cortázar was sitting on a bench outside the windowless cube, a cup of coffee in one hand and a corn muffin balanced on his knee.

He smiled to her as she came close. "Beautiful morning, isn't it?" he said.

He had dark eyes. His cheek was brown, stippled by white stubble where he hadn't shaved. He looked like someone's chemistry professor, not a monster.

"We should get to work," she said.

Chapter Thirty-Five: Naomi

For all Naomi's life, the problem had been knowing which information to believe. A few billion people with access to networks and as many newsfeeds as there were transmitters made it easy to find someone loudly declaiming every possible opinion in every corner and niche of the solar system. And once the repeaters were up, information came to and from the distant worlds beyond the gates with a light delay of only hours. To understand her new reality, she had to find models in ancient history, when the living voice or marks on physical media were the only means of storing and moving information. Ancient North America had used something called the pony express. A series of carts and animals that hauled written information across the then-vast deserts. Or that was how she understood the process, never having seen a pony or a handwritten letter on paper. Now the ponies were ships and torpedoes, the letters were compressed data bursts, and the deserts were the hard vacuum of space and the emptiness of the gate hub at its center. The effect, though, was that news of the far worlds came unreliably. The events on Auberon and in Auberon system took on an exaggerated importance because she knew about them immediately. Anything going on in Bara Gaon or Laconia or Sol, Freehold or New Cyprus or Gethen, became foreign and exotic by being rare. The discovery that "two gates lost" meant that the Thanjavur and Tecoma gates had been destroyed and the systems behind them stranded only added to the sense of vast things happening, far away. The universe had expanded again, and all the things that had been close were once again much more distant. The reports that did come through were precious as air on a leaky ship.

And so, when word came from Sol that the *Tempest* was dead, it felt like a revelation.

It didn't come from underground sources. Bobbie hadn't sent a report, or if she had, the bottle had been lost in transit or slowed to the point that the civilian news outpaced it. The first Naomi heard of it was on Laconian state feeds run by the governor. The tone of the report was outraged and meant to inspire fear. Terrorists had murdered a Laconian diplomat and stolen military technology which they'd then used to slaughter the protector of Sol system. The danger of chaos and riot in Sol system were, to listen to the feed, apocalyptic. Laconian forces were gearing up to protect innocent civilians from the waves of reprisals and violence that were sure to follow.

Probably it had sounded persuasive to Laconian ears. The bone-deep assumption that all things Laconian were good and all opposition evil made for a hell of a blind spot when it came to writing propaganda. For Naomi and Chava it was the resolution of an uncertainty they'd been carrying. They knew now how Bobbie's plan had worked out. For all the others in between—the normal citizens of Auberon—the message was that the unstoppable Laconian machine could, in fact, be stopped. *Had been* stopped. The certainty that had come with imperial rule had a crack in it wide enough to drive a ship through. And like all good news, it brought a list of new problems with it. Good problems, the problems Bobbie and Naomi had been hoping for, but problems all the same.

"Five years of shipping records deleted," Chava said. "Wiped out."

"And it wasn't us?"

"It wasn't anyone I'm aware of," she said, pouring out a cup of coffee. "You know the network better than I do, but..."

"It just means that they'll load it from backups," Naomi said, taking the cup. She'd gotten used to Chava's French press coffee. It was strong and bitter and occasionally carried a bit of the coffee grounds in it. She found she was starting to prefer it to the normal ship-dispensed kind. "So it sounds like someone managed to get access to the backup. Put in whatever they want history to have been, and now it's the official record."

"That's what I was thinking. Might be one of our cells acting independently. Or civilians taking initiative. Or criminals. Hell, it could be Laconians using the opportunity to hide something they did and blame it on us. No matter who it is, though, they weren't confident enough to risk it before, and now they are. And what's happening here? Some variety of it is going on everyplace else too."

Decentralized authority was what Belters had done since the start, generations ago, when the power to communicate orders outdistanced the power to enforce them. Old Rokku, back in her radical days, had talked about the inners being like a sword that hit in one place hard enough to destroy. The Belt was like water, able to push in from all places at once. The death of the *Tempest* hadn't actually changed anything for the systems outside of Sol. It wasn't like Duarte had been willing to send his planet-killer warship to follow up on suspicious data loss. What had changed was the confidence people had in the system, and that uncertainty created new holes, cracks, and opportunities.

Laconia was powerful because it had a single vision, and one brilliant mind behind it all. The underground, like the OPA before it, probably had as many visions as there were people in it, and even as the titular leader, Naomi's was only one of many voices. Duarte's machine was limited. With enough going on at any given time, his attention could be flooded. That was his weakness and their power.

"New contacts are coming in too," Naomi said. "I've had reports on almost a dozen since the first report came in."

"That's a good sign. People feel the tide turning."

"Some of them do," Naomi agreed. "And some of them have other agendas. I've spent months figuring out how to get our people hired on by their managers. They're capable of doing the same thing to us."

"I'll be careful," Chava said. "Background checks, surveillance on new recruits, test assignments. The whole show. I won't let anybody sneak in the aft airlock."

"You will, though," Naomi said. "Test the people you trust too. Make it random. And make it so that someone can keep eyes on you. It's like checking the seals on your suit. Everyone checking everyone should just be normal. And be ready for the crackdown. Because it's coming."

Chava sipped her own coffee and nodded. "I wish you were staying. I mean, it will be nice to be able to invite my friends over to my place again, but... I've enjoyed having you here."

"Even though it risked getting you killed?"

Chava was one of those people who could frown with just her forehead. "Maybe because of that. I think I'm too much of an adrenaline junkie to survive as a ship rental manager. If it wasn't this, I'd be slingshotting on my vacations."

Naomi finished her coffee, put down the white porcelain cup for the last time, and hugged Chava goodbye. Naomi's belongings were in a tight-wrapped bag by the door. They fit easily under her arm. She looked around Chava's rooms one last time. The kitchen, the common area, the passage to the bedroom that had been hers for really not so long a time. Still, long enough for everything to change at least twice.

The knot she felt in her chest wasn't sorrow at leaving here. She liked Chava, and it was a pleasant space to be in, but it wasn't home. What she missed was the idea of a home of her own. People she knew for more than a few weeks at a time. It was worse, because she'd had a place once. And a family with it. She would never stop missing that.

The transport tubes on Auberon's lunar base ran cars every seven minutes, and the signs and directions were clear and well designed. It wasn't hard getting from Chava's place to the docks, or from the docks to the skiff taken out in a false name tied to an imaginary corporation and insured with a policy that would never be used.

Auberon was a target, and not only because it was a successful colony. Any Laconian traffic analysis of the bottles the underground used was going to show high throughput on the Auberon gate. With the *Tempest* dead, there would be a response, and neither she nor Chava nor any of her other high-level contacts doubted that part of that response would come to Auberon. And the best way to survive an asteroid strike was not to be on the planet.

While she waited for the traffic control queue to reach her, she opened a window and called up the visual telescopy on the planet below her. Another blue marble in the void. The wide whirl of a hurricane covered part of an ocean she'd never see. The scattering of continents across the visible hemisphere below her was like dice thrown in a backroom craps game. A vast, beautiful sphere with so few people on it. Cities with universities full of students who'd never known a different sky. She doubted she'd ever see it again, and so she watched and told herself to remember. There were so many last times that passed unrecognized. Knowing in the moment what was ending and wouldn't come again was precious.

The connection to traffic control went live. "Skiff eighteen forty-two, your transit to Bara Gaon is approved. You are clear to exit."

"Acknowledged, Control. Releasing the clamps now."

The little ship, light as an empty food can, shuddered when the docking clamps let go, and Naomi opened the throttle on the drive. The image of Auberon grew a little smaller, and a little smaller, and a little smaller until she closed it down. The moment was over.

The skiff was a tiny little thing, too small and undistinguished for a name. A transponder code, a number, and a perfunctory paper trail. It was as cramped as a racing ship, but without the maneuverability or high-end crash couch. It was intended for in-system trips, usually between planets in similar orbits. Taking it into the depths of the system, through the ring, and then back down some stellar gravity well meant traveling well outside its intended use. Naomi didn't find it intimidating. She'd gone much farther in much worse in her life. After a few days' hard burn, she went on the float.

She spent the hours double-checking the system, such as it was. Making sure the air mix was where it should be, the reactor bottle, the water tanks. Knowing everything about her little bubble of air and life was comforting. If she caught a micrometeorite, it would be too late to learn, so she did it now. Prepare for the worst and be pleasantly surprised. The skiff didn't have a gym, but she still had her resistance bands from her life in the shell game. She could adapt. She always did.

She also found herself imagining conversations with Saba and with Jim and Bobbie and Alex. There were strategic decisions she was going to have to make. Bobbie's victory put Duarte on his back foot.

With only a single *Magnetar*-class ship left, there was a chance for the underground to drive Laconia into a purely defensive posture. Even restrict it to its own system. It would mean making a real and credible threat on Laconia itself, but it was possible. But it wasn't enough.

There had been a time when the Transport Union and the governments of Mars and Earth had expected Laconia to be like any other colony world: struggling for base survival and aiming for self-sustaining agriculture sometime in a generation or so. But Duarte had taken the protomolecule with him along with the expertise to use it, and he'd found the construction platforms that could build ships like the *Tempest* and the *Storm*. And apparently a way to create and bottle antimatter. A threat wasn't enough. She had to find a way to break that manufacturing capacity. If Laconia fell, it had to fall hard. It had to know that its dream was over, that it wasn't exceptional. Once it was broken down to the same level as other worlds, it could be brought back. Reintegrated. Because that was the trick. That was the deep lesson of the Belters and the inner planets. The OPA and the Transport Union.

It was the single central argument that the universe had made to her through her whole life, and she was only now seeing it clearly: Wars never ended because one side was defeated. They ended because the enemies were reconciled. Anything else was just a postponement of the next round of violence. That was her strategy now. The synthesis of her arguments with Bobbie. The answer she wished they'd found together, when they were both alive.

Once she reached Bara Gaon—the other major success among the colony worlds—she'd have to get a sense of what warships she could muster and the transit times. If there was a way to lure Duarte's forces out away from Laconia system and then push in when their home fleet was spread thin, there might be a way.

She was still thinking about that, imagining what Saba or Bobbie or Jim might think, when she started the braking burn. The bottle from Sol system passed through the Auberon gate just a few hours after that. The skiff captured the encrypted data, just the way Chava's system would do back on the planet's moon. It took half a day to finish unpacking, so hours passed before she heard Alex's voice again and knew what they'd lost in order to win.

He looked...not older. He didn't look old. Or tired. She'd seen him look tired before. He looked diminished. Like the grief had taken some of the color from his eyes.

"So it turns out I'm done here," he said in his private message to her. "I got this young guy I been training up should be able to take over. We're headin' for...our little dry dock. You know the one." Even in three layers of encryption, Alex wouldn't say the word *Freehold*. "When we get there, I'm stepping out. I thought I might go check on the old girl. Make sure nothing's been makin' a nest in her. After that, I don't know. I guess that's your call, since you're running the show now. I don't want to take her out unless you're good with it. You and me are the only ones left now. So. Yeah. I'm sorry. I didn't mean to let Bobbie go."

"Don't apologize to me," Naomi said to the screen. Her tears made lenses over her eyes. "Oh, sweet man, don't apologize for this."

But the message was done, and the passage through the ring gate was almost upon her. She passed into the slow zone with a heaviness that didn't have anything to do with the rate of her change of velocity.

It was her first transit since they'd lost Medina. And Saba. And the model of human civilization that she'd understood. The station at the center of the ring was glowing bright as a little star, still shedding the energy it had absorbed from the gamma burst. The surface of the ring space, which had been a featureless blackness, danced with twisting auroras that were weirder and more threatening than the dark had been. What scared her more, though, were the ships.

She had expected the space to be empty. After everything that had happened, she'd thought traffic between the gates would be close to nothing. She'd been wrong. Her little skiff picked up transponder signals for almost two dozen ships, and drive signatures for more than that. The Laconian directive that the ring space be kept clear was being ignored on a scale she hadn't understood, and the raw danger of it took her breath away. With no Medina Station to control the passages, the chances of going dutchman were much worse than they should have been.

She'd made her transit in distraction and ignorance, and she could have vanished and never known why. And that was assuming that the event that killed Medina and the *Typhoon*, that had destroyed two of the gates in the network, hadn't changed the rules. If the threshold for vanishing was different now, they wouldn't know. Not without testing it.

Maybe it was the need for supplies on the vulnerable colonies or the chance to deliver goods without paying the union. Maybe it was that humanity, given freedom, forgot about the prospect of consequences. Whatever the drive, it took her breath away. It was such a shock that she didn't notice at first that two of the ships were Laconian warships like the *Gathering Storm*, or that they were burning toward her. In the mess of the traffic and her own internal chaos, she didn't see that until the skiff got the connection request from the *Monsoon*.

Her system had the software to disguise her voice and appearance, and she checked five different times that it was running before she accepted the request.

"This is Chief Petty Officer Norman of the *Monsoon*," the man on the screen said. "You are in violation of quarantine. Please leave the ring space immediately." His voice had the irritated singsong of someone reciting a hated ritual.

"I'm sorry," she said. "I didn't mean to. It's just that my brother's sick. I was supposed to be back to him weeks ago. I don't have any contraband, I swear."

"I don't care where you go," the Laconian said. "Just get out of here and stay out. There will a permanent force in here soon, and this kind of thing will get people shot. Be somewhere else when that happens."

"Yes, sir," she said. "I'll transit out right away, sir."

The connection dropped. They were swamped. More than that, they had ships in the slow zone that weren't stopping to control the space. That meant they either understood the risks and were keeping their exposure to a repeat of the catastrophe that had killed Medina Station and the *Typhoon* to a minimum or they had bigger fish to fry or both. And, she saw as she tracked their courses, the Laconian destroyers were heading for Auberon.

"You came close," she said softly, "but no cigar."

The Bara Gaon gate was on a secant that cut her passage through the ring gate to almost half what the maximum distance would have been. The gate wasn't quite where the navigation system expected it to be. The loss of the Thanjavur and Tecoma gates had shifted all the others just the smallest bit, but enough to make the software care about it. She went to correct the course manually... and paused.

My brother's sick, she thought. *And so am I.*

She corrected the skiff's course, aiming it for Freehold. And for home.

Chapter Thirty-Six: Teresa

The day Teresa finally broke began like most days now. With a nightmare.

She had been awake until the small hours of the morning, watching old movies and entertainment feeds that she'd seen before. Trying to squeeze comfort out of them because they were familiar. Knowing what was going to happen before it happened made the stories feel very safe. Not at all like her real life. She stayed awake as long as her body would let her. And when she could stay awake not one moment longer, the dreams came for her all at once, like they'd been waiting for her. Like they were hungry.

There were three main varieties. In the first, she was in a strange part of the State Building, and her father—or sometimes her mother—was in a room nearby being killed, and she could stop it if she found the right doorway. In another, the planet Laconia had gotten a disease of some kind and bits of the land had started falling down deep into the burning core. Nothing was stable and nothing was safe. The third was formless and violent, less a dream than variations on Ilich's murder of Timothy.

Each version came regularly enough that she'd begun to recognize them. The dreams had even started commenting on it. As some new terror reared its head, she'd think *It's just like in my dreams, only now it's really happening.* It made the nightmares worse because it made them feel inevitable. Her waking hours were poisoned by them. The violence and fear and loss could spill out at any moment, from any place, and nothing could be relied upon.

It was terrible because it was true.

She woke after not enough sleep to the gentle tapping of a servant and Muskrat's excited bark. Breakfast was a favorite meal for the old dog. Maybe every meal was.

The servant brought in a white ceramic tray with a plate of eggs and sweet rice, a glass of watermelon juice, and a sausage with the dark, grainy mustard that she liked. Or that she had liked. Food wasn't something that interested her now. Not the way it used to. She stirred the sweet rice and watched the official newsfeeds talking breathlessly about the Laconian ships offering assistance to local governments in the ongoing fight against separatist violence. Images of men and women in Laconian formal blues talking seriously with the governors of Earth and Mars. She wondered if anyone believed that. She wondered whether she had.

She knew that if she didn't eat, her failure would be reported to Trejo. It had happened before. She took a bite of egg, but the rubbery texture of the white made her gag. The rice would be enough. It had to be. She hadn't been able to get more than half of her dinner down the night before. She knew that starving wasn't good for her, and that Ilich and Trejo wouldn't like it. That was part of why she did it. She took a spoonful of the rice, sucked away the thick, sweet sauce, and spat out the grains. On her screen, Admiral Gujarat was talking about the completion of the *Whirlwind*, the newest *Magnetar*-class ship, as if it weren't the only one. As if the first two weren't already dead.

She picked the sausage up. The smell of grease and salt was repulsive. She couldn't see it as anything but a slurry of dead animals in a thin membrane. She tossed it to Muskrat. Instead of wolfing it down, her dog looked from the scrap to her and back again and whined.

"You might as well," Teresa said. "I wasn't going to eat it before. I'm certainly not going to now."

Muskrat swung her wide tail twice, uncertainly. She ate the sausage with something that looked like shame. Teresa's numbness slid away for a moment, and tears came to her eyes. The State Building was filled with people from every system in the empire. She had people whose only duty was to cook her food, to educate her, to see that her clothes were cleaned and put away. Nobody had the job of actually caring about her. The only one who even noticed her was a dog.

A voice spoke in the back of her head, as clear as if there had been someone in the room. It sounded like her own, but calmer. Drier. Somehow more adult than she thought of herself, like some later Teresa sending a stray observation back through time. *Muskrat likes Holden.*

The voice didn't go on. Teresa looked down at Muskrat's complicated brown eyes, and the sorrow lost its edge.

"You may have shitty taste in friends," she said. "Sorry, dog."

Another tap came at her door, and she didn't need to open it to know it was Ilich. She stirred her food to make it look like she'd eaten more than she had and let the door open. As soon as he saw her, his smile faltered.

"I know," she said, before he even spoke. "It's very important that we maintain the image that everything is normal. You tell me that every day." She stood up and put her arms out to the side. "This is normal. *I'm normal!*"

"Of course," he said with a practiced smile that meant he just wasn't going to fight her. "Your peer class is going to start soon. Dr. Okoye is going to be leading it today so that I can meet with Admiral Trejo."

So that I can do something more important, he meant. Even if he didn't say the words, Teresa heard them. Muskrat huffed and wagged her tail, anticipating the adventure of leaving her rooms. Teresa shrugged and walked toward the door, daring Ilich not to step aside. He stepped aside.

The State Building was the same as it had ever been. The archways, the colonnades, the gardens. Nothing about it had changed. It was her home and her kingdom. And somehow they'd made it into her cell, Ilich and all the others too. She was honored and revered and treated with total deference if she did what she was told, when she was told. Her opinion was listened to with seriousness and gravity, and then ignored. She stalked toward the lecture room, wondering what would happen if she marched in, took the microphone, and shouted *My father is brain-dead and nothing is all right*. It was enough to make her smile.

As it turned out, though, the fantasy wouldn't have worked. The lecture room had been rearranged for the day—six slate-topped tables stood in rows of three. The other students—her so-called peers—were already there. Apparently Ilich had come because she'd run late and hadn't noticed.

The room stank of something deep and caustic. Air recyclers were set up in all the windows, scrubbing whatever the volatiles were out and blowing fresh air back in. Small trays sat on each table, two each, with a variety of scalpels, tweezers, pins, and thin scissors laid out between them. Elvi Okoye was walking among the students, leaning on her cane, and chatting as she went. Teresa felt her anger shift again. She was supposed to be fixing Teresa's father, not teaching classes to a bunch of kids. But, of course, Teresa wasn't allowed to say that. Because that wouldn't look *normal*.

"Good to see you, Teresa," Elvi said, and touched her hand. "I'm glad you're here."

Teresa shrugged and moved away, leaning against one of the tables. Now that she was close, she could see the bodies spread out in the trays and held down with pins. Dead animals. Dead as Timothy. Dead as her mother. Dead as all the people in the ring space.

"So today Colonel Ilich wanted me to, um, give you all a little introduction to parallel evolution. So what we have here are two different species from two different trees of life. One of them is native to Laconia, and the other one's from Earth. They're both called frogs because they fill the same ecological niche and because they have some similarities in anatomy. So, yeah. Get in groups of three, I guess? And I'll walk you through the dissections."

Teresa looked at the frogs. They both had pale bellies and darker skin, though the one she recognized was considerably darker. The rear legs folded differently, and one had two forelimbs to the other's four. From where she was standing, the thing they had most in common was that they were dead. She took a scalpel between her fingers, considering the blade, and wondered whether she'd be able to cut the bodies open without vomiting. The upside was she didn't have much in her belly to puke up. So that was fine.

"Hey," Connor said. She hadn't seen him come up, but here he was. Sandy hair and soft eyes. She remembered caring what his opinion was. She remembered wanting to kiss him like it was in a film she'd watched, and not something she'd felt herself.

She pinched the flat of the blade between her fingers and held the handle out to him. "Want to cut?" she asked. He took it and looked away, uncomfortable. That was fine. Shan Ellison made up the third of their group. When all the rest had formed up, Elvi Okoye opened a volumetric display with an image of two idealized frogs to match the ones on their trays.

"Okay," Elvi said. "So one of the things that we see in both Laconia and Earth biomes is water. And there are animals that have found an advantage to living part of their lives in the water and part out. We call them amphibians. Both of your frogs are amphibians. And because water is chemically identical in both worlds, and the adult forms that we have here need to breathe air, there are some problems they both faced as they evolved. Some solutions look very similar, and some of their strategies could not have been more different. So let's start with looking at the Earth frog's lungs. Each team should make the first incision right here—"

Slowly, step by step, they began unmaking the frogs. Despite herself, Teresa found the process interesting. The way the Laconian frog cycled water in and out of its chest cavity to do the work that the Earth frog did with a diaphragm. The way the feeding mechanisms—mouth and esophagus for the Earth frog, chambered mouth and gut for the Laconian—served the same functions in different ways. She felt like it was all telling her something deeper than just biology. Something about herself and the people around her. Something about whether she could ever belong.

She realized she had been drifting off when Connor spoke to her again. His voice was quiet and tentative. "My mom."

Teresa glanced up at Elvi. She was across the room, talking to one of the other groups.

"What about her," Teresa asked.

"I was just saying that my mom, she's . . . You know. She watches the newsfeeds. With everything that's going on."

He glanced at her, and then away like he was shy. Like he was saying something shameful. Shan Ellison didn't speak, but watched with the intensity of someone expecting violence. It felt illicit and strange, like he'd said the first part of some password, and she didn't know the rest.

Then, a heartbeat later, she did. He was asking her to tell him something reassuring. His parents were scared. He was scared. And because they were in peer class together, and she was her father's daughter, he wanted her to tell him that everything was going to be all right. That she, knowing what she knew, wasn't afraid and that he shouldn't be either.

She licked her lips and waited to see what would come out of them.

"She shouldn't spend too much time on them," Teresa said. "I know everything looks really scary, but it's not that big a problem. Dad has the best minds in the empire working for him, and they're learning more every day. Everyone always knew there'd be setbacks."

"Yeah," Connor said. "Everyone knew."

So she'd lied. That was interesting. She'd told him what he wanted to hear, and it wasn't even because she wanted to protect him or keep him safe. It was just easier. She understood now why adults lied to children. It wasn't love. It was exhaustion. And she was like them now. They'd eaten her.

"Are you okay?" Shan asked, and it seemed like her voice was closer than she was. Like the girl wasn't talking from across the table, but whispering into Teresa's ear. It sounded soft and weirdly intimate. *I'm fine*, Teresa said. Only the words didn't come out.

She had the sense that she needed to leave now. That if she could get a drink of water and lie down for a minute, her breath wouldn't seem so loud in her ears. She felt herself walking. At the door, someone's arm appeared beside her, startling her. It was her own. She moved the hand, fascinated by her control of it married with the absolute emotional certainty that it wasn't her arm.

Elvi Okoye was there too, like something from a dream. She said something, asked something, but before Teresa could answer, she'd forgotten what it was.

I wonder if I'm dying, Teresa thought, and the idea wasn't unpleasant.

For a while, Teresa lost herself. A flurry of sensory impressions— voices, movement. Someone was touching her hands and her neck. A bright light shone in her eyes. When she came back, she was lying down. The room was familiar, but until she heard voices she knew, she couldn't quite place it.

"I'm not drawing any conclusions," the doctor said. It wasn't Dr. Cortázar. It was her old pediatrician, Dr. Klein. And he was talking to Elvi Okoye. "What I'm saying is she's dehydrated and malnourished. Maybe she got that way because there's some kind of uptake problem. Maybe she's had an allergic reaction to something. Or her stress levels are so high, she's somaticizing. Or— and I'm just saying maybe here—she's been starving herself."

She was in the State Building's medical wing, on a gurney. There was a line connecting an autodoc to a vein at the back of her hand. When she shifted, she could feel the needle under her skin and the coolness in her arm where it was feeding fluid into her.

"I skipped breakfast," Teresa yelled, and her voice sounded normal again. "It's my fault. It was stupid. I just lost track of time."

They were at her side before she'd finished speaking. Dr. Klein was a youngish man with wavy brown hair and green eyes that reminded her of Trejo. She liked him because he'd given her sweets after her checkups when she was young and because he'd never condescended to her. Now he was looking at the system readout from the autodoc and trying not to meet her eyes. Elvi, leaning on her cane, was ashen. She looked directly into Teresa's eyes, and Teresa stared back.

"It was the frogs," Teresa lied. It came easily. "Between not eating first and cutting them up, I got light-headed."

"Maybe," Klein said. "But if there is an underlying gastrointestinal issue, we should get on it quickly. There's some microbial life on Laconia that we're seeing fungal-model infections with. It's not something to take lightly."

"It's not what's going on. I promise," Teresa said. And then, "Could I talk to Dr. Okoye for a minute?"

There was a moment's hesitation that she couldn't quite read, like Klein might refuse. But then...

"Of course." He nodded to Elvi. "Major," he said, and walked away.

When he was out of earshot, Teresa whispered, her voice harsh,

"What are you doing bringing him into this? We're not supposed to be around other people. Dr. Cortázar is my doctor."

"He's not a physician," Elvi said. "His doctorate's in nano-informatics. He shouldn't be practicing medicine any more than I should."

"But he knows what's going on. Do you want Dr. Klein asking around about why I'm under so much stress? You want him to figure it out?"

There was a joy to throwing all the things they'd said to her back at them. A delight in seeing Elvi flinch. She watched the woman struggle with something, and then reach a decision. Elvi sat on the end of the gurney, sighing as she took the weight off her leg. She rubbed her hand across her forehead.

"Listen," she said. "I'm not supposed to tell you this, but you cannot trust Dr. Cortázar. I'm almost positive he intends to hurt you. Maybe kill you." Then, a moment later, "Probably kill you."

She felt a wave of vertigo, and the autodoc threw up a warning. It was just that she was hungry. That she needed water, that was all. Teresa shook her head. "Why?"

Elvi took a deep breath and spoke softly. "I think to give a well-known subject to the repair drones and see what they do. He has two others, but he didn't have the kind of scans and prep work that he has with you. That and…he wants what you and your father were going to have. He wants to live forever too."

Like the frogs, Teresa thought, and fought back cruel, despairing laughter. *He wants to treat me just like the frogs. Nature eats babies all the time.*

Holden had known too. He'd tried to tell her. That was two different people who'd warned her. Two different people who'd discovered the same thing. Elvi was holding her hand. The one that didn't have a needle in it.

"I've been trying to keep him away from you," Elvi said. "But Cortázar's very important. Without him…your father's recovery gets a lot harder. Everything gets a lot harder."

"We have to tell Trejo," Teresa said.

"He knows," Elvi said, her voice dark. "I told him. We're doing what we can. But you should know too. You should protect yourself."

"How?"

Elvi started to say something, stopped, started again. There were tears in her eyes, but her voice was steady. "I don't know. I'm in over my head here."

"Yeah," Teresa said. "Me too."

Chapter Thirty-Seven: Alex

You should rest," Caspar said. "How many double shifts are you now?"

"I don't know," Alex said, leaning his back against the galley bulkhead. "But I can't see that one more's going to kill me."

"Isn't until it is," Caspar said. "But that's not even all of it. As hard as you've been working, you're going to start making mistakes."

Alex scowled at the boy. He knew Caspar hadn't meant it as an insult. Knowing was what kept him from being angry. Or from showing it at least.

"When you catch me screwing up, I'll stop taking doubles," Alex said. "Until then..."

Caspar raised his hands in surrender, and Alex went back to his meal. Textured yeast paste and a bulb of water. It was his lunch if he was second shift, breakfast if he was third. So, in a sense, it was both.

The *Storm* had burned hard to get away from Laconian forces, but no one had chased it. No one dared to. To judge from the newsfeeds, most people weren't sure what they'd done to kill the *Tempest*, and no one wanted to risk that they'd do it again. Which was just as well, because the more they pushed, the clearer it was how much the victory had compromised them.

Every shift found new, unexpected degradations in the *Storm*. Vacuum channels that weren't transmitting power, regenerative plating that had stopped regenerating, atmosphere leaks so subtle that they couldn't be located except as the slow and steady loss of pressure. Alex was no engineer, but he'd been on the *Storm* as long as any of them and in space since well before many of them had been born. When he wasn't sleeping, he was working to keep the ship together. He stopped when exhaustion promised a fast, deep, and dreamless sleep.

It wasn't the first time he'd used work to keep his emotions at bay. On and off his whole life, there had been times like this when the danger of feeling what he felt was too much to face. Some people got drunk or got in fights or hit the gym until they collapsed. He'd done all those things too, but with the *Storm* as beat up as it was, and the crew as injured and sick as many still were, this was fine. It kept him busy and it kept the ship alive.

Even so, it was imperfect. He knew he wasn't healed, and he suspected he wasn't even healing. The pain came in odd moments. When he was just waking up or going to sleep and his mind wandered. Then, sure. But also when he was crawling through the access spaces looking for a broken line or at the medical bay getting his daily ration of medication to keep the lining of his gut from sloughing off again. It would sneak up on him, and for a few seconds he'd be lost in his own mind, and the oceanic sorrow there.

It was about Bobbie, of course, but it spilled over. In his worst moments, he also found himself thinking about Kit's upcoming marriage. About Holden and that terrible last run they'd had together on Medina when he'd been captured. Talissa, his first wife, and Giselle, his second one. Amos, who was the worst loss in this because he'd just vanished into the enemy lines. Alex might never know what had happened to him. All the families he'd had, and all the ways he'd lost them. It felt like too much to bear, but he bore it. And after a few minutes the worst would pass, and he could get back to work.

The passage through the ring gates into Freehold system went as well as they could have hoped. Alex let Caspar do the heavy lifting. It was going to be his job soon enough, and it was better that he get the practice. They came in hot, bent their trajectory hard for the Freehold gate, and shot back out into normal space. In theory, it was possible to hit a gate from the realspace side at the perfect angle and make the transit through the intervening space in a straight line. In practice, there was usually a little flex, but Caspar did a good job. As good as Alex could have managed. They threw a fast torpedo at the only thing that looked like a Laconian sensor array, blowing it to dust before they made their last course correction. It was as close to anonymity as they could ask without the shell game.

Freehold itself was a straightforward little system. The one habitable planet was a little smaller than Mars. Then a slightly larger one farther out with an unwelcoming atmosphere, and a series of three gas giants protecting the inner system. The *Storm*'s home port was there, in the shadow of the giant they called Big Brother when they were being polite and Big Fucker when they weren't. It was a fraction larger than Jupiter back in Sol, with a blue-green swirling atmosphere and constant electrical storms that created arcs of lightning longer than the Earth was wide. Alex watched it grow close on the *Storm*'s scopes, saw the black dot against it that was the rocky moon where they hid. Long-dead volcanism had left lava tubes big enough to land the *Storm* and a small fleet like her under the lunar surface, and that's where they were headed. Toward the permanent base of Belter engineers and underground operatives that Bobbie had called the "pit crew."

The knock at his cabin door was polite. Even tentative. Caspar stayed in the corridor, braced with a handhold.

"Hey," the boy said. "You coming?"

"Where to?" Alex asked.

"Bridge. You got to take us in, yeah? Tradition. A pilot retires, he takes himself to the last port."

"What kind of tradition is that?" Alex said with a chuckle. "I've never heard of it before."

"Made it up," Caspar said. "Just now. Can't turn that down, start your own tradition."

"You can take us in," Alex said. "You need the practice anyway."

"No," Caspar said. "It's you or we just plow the fucking thing into the moon and call it done."

"You're a shit liar," Alex said, but unbuckled himself from his crash couch all the same. "You should work on that."

"Just like everything else," Caspar said. And then, "You're really going."

"Yeah," Alex said. "I really am."

"You were good."

"You will be. You don't need me here."

He drifted out of his cabin, the light g of the braking burn making "down" a strong suggestion more than a real weight. He headed for the central lift and up to the bridge. As he floated into it for the last time, the rest of the crew braced their feet to stand at attention. Caspar, behind him, began to clap, and the others joined in. By the time Alex reached the pilot's station, his eyes were damp enough to obscure his display.

"On your order, Captain," he said.

"Bring us in, Mr. Kamal," Jillian said.

The actual landing was easy, from a technical perspective. Even as injured as it was, the *Storm* knew where the walls around it were, and where the encrustation of human structures would be. Alex felt a great weight falling away from his heart. The custom docking clamps they'd made back when the *Storm* was a recently captured prize of the war slid home with something between a sound too low to hear and a shudder.

"Welcome back, reisijad," the Belter-inflected voice said over the comms. "Looks like you fucked your ship pretty good?"

"It'll give you lazy fuckers something to do," Jillian said, the way Bobbie would have. Same inflection and all. It seemed right in a way Alex couldn't quite describe that the girl had paid so much attention to how Bobbie ran things. Even when they were gone, the next generation up would keep echoes of them.

The shuttle to Freehold was a single-hulled transport called the *Drybeck*. It had begun its life as an ore hauler and been retrofitted sometime in the last twenty years. The company that had owned it had a color scheme of green and yellow, and the ghost of its logo still haunted the bulkheads on the bridge. Its drive was small and touchy, prone to stutter when the burn changed, and limited by a tiny reaction mass tank. The hold was lined with crash couches, and the half dozen of the crew most compromised by the death of the *Tempest* were coming home more as cargo than companions.

The long fall down from the gas giants passed through the area that would have been the most trafficked space in Sol system. Hundreds of ships would have moved between Saturn and Jupiter and the inner planets. Maybe half a dozen did the same in Freehold. Alex plotted the course with a growing sense of the emptiness of the system that mere decades couldn't fill. It was too big. All of it was too big. He'd been there from the beginning, been part of blazing humanity's trail to the stars, and he still couldn't quite get his mind around how vast the spaces were.

He was surprised when, a few minutes before departure, Jillian came to the little bridge and sat in the couch beside his without buckling in.

"You coming down with us?" Alex asked.

Jillian looked at him for a long moment without speaking. She looked older than he thought of her as being, as if taking command, even for so short a time as this, had aged her.

"No," she said. "The family wants to see me, and I'd like to see them too. But there'll be time for that when the war's over."

I admire your optimism, Alex almost said, but the darkness was too much. He didn't want to bring her down with his own skepticism. Instead, he nodded and made a noncommittal sound in the back of his throat.

"There's a fast crawler waiting for you in port," she said. "It's got enough water, fuel, and starter yeast to get you going."

"That's good of you. I appreciate it."

"It's not altruism. Your ship," she said. "It's old, but it's a gunship. Still better than most of what the underground has burning out there."

"Maybe," Alex said. "It could also be a nest for whatever birds live in the desert down there. That's part of what I'm going to find out."

"When you do, you reach out. The only people who fly solo are slingshotters and assholes. You got to have someone with your back."

The comms clicked up. The shuttle was clear to leave. All Alex had to do was respond. He put the message on hold.

"What are you saying?" he asked.

"We're not done," Jillian said. "Not just that, we're winning. Underground is going to need every ship it can get, and yours would be a good one to have on the team. If you need a crew for her, you tell me. I'll get you one."

Alex didn't know what to say. The truth was, he didn't have a plan except to get back to the *Rocinante*. But she was right. There was going to be an after. An after Bobbie. An after Amos. An after Holden. Whatever he was doing, he wasn't going out there to die. Just to recover.

"I'll let you know what it looks like," he said. "We'll make a plan."

Jillian stood and held out her hand. He shook it without unstrapping.

"It's been good," Jillian said. "We've done good work."

"We have, haven't we?" Alex said.

After she left, he went through one last systems check. Flying single-hulled ships was a kind of gambling he usually avoided, but even if he hit a micrometeorite, they'd probably survive it. Anyway. Life was risk.

He flipped the comms back on.

"This is *Drybeck*," he said. "I am confirming clearance to launch."

"You're still clear, *Drybeck*," the voice on the other end of the connection said. "Not blowing nothing up, and no one floating out there to run into. Ge con Gott, yeah? Draper Station out."

Draper Station, Alex thought as he eased the ship through the lava tube on its maneuvering thrusters. It was the first time he'd heard it called that. He didn't hate the sound.

Freehold, like most goldilocks-zone planets, had a wide variety of environments. Freehold's salt deserts were on the same continent as the lush mountains he'd hidden in when they first came and the township that had grown to be a modest city. White dunes and mesas of red stone stretched from horizon to horizon. Tent rocks rose in some places, and knife-thick ridges that could have been artifacts of alien civilizations or just beautiful geology. The dawns were warm pink, and the sunsets were green and gold. Alex didn't know why. At night, the desert sang. High fluting tones as the temperature shift made the sand itself ring like a wineglass.

The fast crawler was mostly autonomous, and it took its navigation from the time and the position of the sun like an ancient sea captain on Earth. There was no signal coming in or going out that would give Alex's position away. The transport's wide titanium-and-rubber treads made the trackless badlands easier to cover than the simplest flight in a ship. The solitude was vast and consoling. He'd expected to feel lonely on the trip, but he wasn't. The effort of being okay around the crew of the *Storm* had, it turned out, been exhausting. He hadn't even known he was making the effort until he didn't have to anymore. He slept in the little bunk in the crawler's belly and spent his days sitting on top of the machine watching the sun and sky and stars and didn't even listen to the music he'd brought with him.

Twice, huge shambling animals with legs like slender trees and coats like yellow moss had walked with him for a while. The second had been with him almost half a day before it cooed three times and turned away. As far as he knew, he was the only human being who'd ever seen them.

He'd wondered more than once why Naomi had chosen to live in a hidden shipping container, but now, here, he thought he understood. The pleasure of being utterly alone made his mourning into something different and strange and humane.

The cave where they'd put the *Roci* was in the western quarter of the desert. He'd picked it because it was near a patchwork of radioactive ore that added a little camouflage if the enemy was looking for it and acted as a landmark for him.

The fears that haunted him now were that the *Roci* wouldn't be waiting for him. That the shelf he'd parked her under had collapsed in his absence. Or that the sealants they'd put on to protect the hull plating had broken down or been compromised by desert animals, exposing a ship built for vacuum to the erosion of wind and sand and salt. As the hours fell away, his anxiety started to grow. The peace of the desert rolled past until the crawler reached the edge of its automatic course and came to a shuddering halt beside a vast outcropping of stone.

Alex took a flask of water and a cloth to tie across his mouth and dropped to the salt-rich sand. The shade under the stone was cool. He followed the tracks of glass where the *Roci*'s thrusters had melted the sand, it felt like lifetimes before.

And there, dark and quiet and perfectly intact at the back of the cavern, was the old Martian corvette. Something had scratched at the sealant—maybe animals, maybe the sandblasting desert wind—but nothing had broken through. It was just his imagination that made him feel like the ship was welcoming him. He knew that. It didn't matter.

It took the better part of a day to cut through the sealing coat and get the airlock answering him, but after that, things moved faster. They'd drained the water out of the tanks before they left, but the crawler's supplies were enough to get the ship almost halfway to capacity. Getting the recycling system back online was harder. He spent half a day checking feed lines before he found the one that had split. And it took another half a day to replace it. It would have taken Naomi or Amos or Clarissa half an hour.

He didn't sleep in the crawler anymore, especially once the *Roci*'s galley was able to turn out a little food. With his limited supplies, the food was spartan and the drinks were water and green tea. The ship was lying belly-down on the ground, everything was at ninety degrees from where his mind wanted it to be, and he had to climb to get to his cabin and his crash couch.

Lost as he was in the work of hauling his old ship back to herself, he could almost pretend he was waiting for his old crew. That they'd be there in the machine shop and the flight deck, laughing and arguing and rolling their eyes like they had before. A week into the effort, he'd exhausted himself and fallen onto his couch without eating dinner. He found himself slipping between dreams and wakefulness, hearing their voices in the hallway. Clarissa's dry whisper and Holden's earnest concern like they were really there, and if he just concentrated, he'd be able to make out the words. The alert tone as the airlock opened and familiar footsteps in the halls.

When the silhouette bent into his doorway, he still thought he was dreaming. It was the sound of a living voice, the first since he'd left Freehold, that brought him back to himself.

"Hey," Naomi said.

Chapter Thirty-Eight: Naomi

H ey," Naomi said.
Alex shifted in his crash couch, and the hiss of the gimbals was like something made from memory. He blinked at her, confused and sleep drunk.

"No shit?" he said.

"No shit," Naomi said.

"No, no, no. I just...I didn't know you were coming." They were simple words. Commonplace. They carried a heavy weight.

Time and tragedy had thinned Alex's face and darkened the skin under his eyes. His smile was joyful, but it was a bruised kind of joy. The pleasure and delight that could only come to someone who understood how precious they were, and how fragile. She figured that she looked the same.

"I got your message about heading back here, and...well, I had some other plans, but the more I thought about it, the more sense coming back to the *Roci* made."

"Thought about it a lot, eh?"

"Ten, maybe fifteen whole seconds," she said.

Alex barked out a laugh and hauled himself up. She stepped into the cabin, and they embraced. The last time they'd touched had been on the deep transfer station back in Sol. There had been three of them.

After a moment, they stepped back. She was surprised by how good it felt to see Alex in the familiar environment of the *Rocinante*, even if the ship was ninety degrees from her usual orientation.

"How'd you get here?" he asked, still grinning.

"I have a crackerbox with an Epstein," Naomi said. "From Auberon to here. It's not rated for atmosphere, though, so I parked it at the transfer station and hitched a lift down on a shuttle."

"Planetside again."

"And my knees already hate it. But I'm in a ship, so it's not too strange," she said. "You're never going to convince me that this whole 'sky' thing isn't fucking creepy. I like my air held in by something I can see, thank you very much."

"You want a drink? The old girl's not all the way up to snuff, but she can make you some tea. Maybe even some maté by now, depending on how the recyclers are doing."

"I wouldn't say no," Naomi said, and then, because it felt stranger to leave it unsaid than to say it, "I am so sorry about Bobbie. I cried for a whole day."

Alex looked down and away. His smile shifted invisibly into a mask of itself. "I still do sometimes. It'll take me by surprise and it's like it's happening again, for the first time," he said.

"Thinking about Jim does that to me."

"You should have seen her, XO," Alex said, and he did something between a laugh and a sob. "Like a fuckin' Valkyrie, you know? Flying at that big-ass ship like she could take it down by herself."

"She did. Take it down by herself, I mean."

Alex nodded. "So did you have a plan now that you're here?"

He couldn't talk about it anymore. She understood that. She let the subject drop.

"I was following you," she said, turning to climb up the deck to the main lift—a corridor for the moment. "Now that Medina and the *Typhoon* are gone, we could actually move between gates again."

"That does open up some possibilities," Alex said. "My to-do list has two things on it. First one's put the old girl shipshape again, and the second's figure out what to do next."

"That sounds perfect," Naomi said. They reached the galley. The tables projected from one wall, but there were built-in jump seats for times like this. She pulled two of them out. "Let's do that."

It turned out that Alex's first entry gave her days of work to do. He'd gotten a decent start on the re-up process, but the *Rocinante* had been dry for a long time. Probably the longest since she'd been made by a Martian Navy that didn't exist anymore. A lot of the systems were old, and the newer ones were replacements that didn't ever fit together quite the way the originals had. There had been a little corrosion in the reactor shielding. Nothing that time and use didn't justify, but something to keep an eye on. She felt herself falling into a rhythm she hadn't known existed, and recognized perfectly. Normalcy. This was how life just was, and everything else she'd done, however comfortable she'd been with it, had been the aberration.

Day after day, she and Alex went through the ship, troubleshooting each system as it came back up. A full crew could have done the whole thing in ten hours, and there were only two of them. But they got it done—the reactor up, the comms, the power grid, the thrusters, the weapons. Some maintenance routines assumed there would be teams of four, but they found workarounds. One piece at a time, the *Rocinante* came back to life.

As they worked, she saw some of the ways Alex's time on the *Storm* had changed him. Whether he knew it or not, he understood electrical systems better than he had before. And he'd learned some tricks about checking the stability of carbon-silicate lace plating that shaved half a day off her estimates.

At night, they slept in their old cabins. She didn't know whether Alex went through his cabinets, but she went through hers. She'd never had much that she claimed as her own, but what little there was felt like the artifacts of some other, ancient Naomi. It was like coming across a favorite toy from childhood and being reminded of all the half-forgotten experiences that traveled with it. The shirts she'd worn that Jim had liked. The mag boots with the extra strap at the calf that helped stabilize her knee. A broken hand terminal she'd meant to fix before she went into hiding and hadn't ever gotten around to.

There were other cabins in the ship, with other personal supplies. Things that had belonged to Amos and Bobbie. Maybe even Clarissa. Maybe Jim. The trivial leftovers of a life. She was tempted to go through those too, but she held back. She wasn't sure yet that she'd be doing it for the right reasons, and it turned out that mattered to her.

As soon as the comms were up, the *Roci* started gathering covert communications from the underground. Three bottles had passed though Freehold gate since she'd left her shuttle. One from Sol, one from Asylum, one from Pátria. More would be coming. When she wasn't working, she paged through the information and listened to the reports of the leaders of the underground. Of her underground.

It was a week and a half after her arrival, and Naomi was out, sitting on the desert sand as the sun set. The truth was that as much as she enjoyed complaining about being planetside, there was a kind of surreal thrill to being under a vast dome of air. After an hour or so, she had to go back inside or she started getting anxious. But for that first thirty minutes, it was beautiful. The sunlight seemed to sink into the sand, lighting it from within. And the star field that bloomed above her head was familiar, even if the high air made the steady stars seem to flicker and shimmer.

It felt very strange to be in such a quiet, peaceful, empty place and also the middle of a war.

She heard his footsteps on the sand, soft and regular as an air intake gently cycling. She sat up and dusted the sand from the backs of her arms. Alex was wearing his flight suit, and it hung a little loose on him. Even with his usual beaming smile, he seemed a little deflated. He grunted as he sat on the dune beside her.

"You holding together okay?" Alex asked.

"I'm all right," Naomi said.

"Just asking because you've been spending a lot of time working the *Roci* with me, and then going straight to the reports and newsfeeds when you're done. You haven't taken much downtime."

Naomi felt an old, familiar touch of annoyance, and it was strangely delightful. If Alex had started his mother hen habits back up, it had to mean he was feeling better. Not recovered, maybe never that, but improved.

"Doing the briefings is my downtime."

"Coordinating a massive resistance to an authoritarian and galaxy-spanning empire is your hobby?"

"I didn't have an option. We don't have a golgo table, and... No offense? Even if we did, you play like a Martian."

He chuckled to show he knew it was affection. "Have you got a note back for them? Another bottle to pop out into the systems?"

It was a hard question. Even when she'd had her mind on the panels and wiring of the *Rocinante*, a part of her had been thinking about the grand strategy of the underground. About limiting Laconian reach and power, about taking advantage of the openings left by the enemy's mistakes.

And about the goal at the end. That was the trick of grand strategy. Knowing where the journey was ending even when you were making up all the individual steps to get there.

Working on the *Roci* had given the insight she'd had on the passage out from Auberon time to season. What had been a vision of a possible future had, while she worked with her hands and taken her mind elsewhere, become a bone-deep certainty. As long as Laconia had the capacity to make ships like the *Tempest* and the *Typhoon*, it could never grow past being an oppressor. The dream of empire could only die if the ancient Martian dream of independence through better technology was put to rest.

An attack on Laconia posed half a dozen unsolvable problems, and Naomi thought she had solutions to at least four of them...

"I've got some things I should send out. I can bounce a broadcast off the repeaters at Freehold and up to the *Storm*. Even if there aren't any ships closer to the gate than that, they can get one of their torpedoes going. And if they've been doing what they're supposed to, they'll have some bottles already on the float near the gates."

"Lightspeed is way better than the best drive," Alex said, nodding sagely. "Trying to send a bottle from here would take a pretty long time. You know, though, there is a way to shave a few seconds off the time it takes to get your messages out."

She shifted to look at him. The sun was gone, and the rose-and-gray twilight made him look younger. She lifted an eyebrow, inviting him to go on. He looked at her with feigned innocence.

"All we've got to do is be a few light-seconds closer, right?"

It hit her with a relief she hadn't expected. She looked up into the Freehold sky, past it to the stars.

"Right," she said. "Let's do that. I'm sick of walking on walls."

An hour later, they were strapped into their couches on the flight deck. Working the *Rocinante*'s displays was like singing with an old friend as she checked the maneuvering thrusters' output profiles. The reactor was stable. The thrust was good. Even after its long rest, the *Roci*'s power grid was solid.

"We're good," Naomi said. "Take her out."

"Oh yeah."

The ship lurched, and the crash couches shifted. Naomi had the familiar sense of motion as they accelerated and then slid out of the cave on maneuvering thrusters only. The deck swung around and down until it was under her, and she sank into the gel as Alex took them higher from the ground.

When the drive kicked in, the whole ship rocked and shuddered, and Naomi felt the prick of the needle and then the coolness of the juice in her veins, keeping her from suffering the worst of the g forces. Alex was grinning like a kid on his birthday as the old gunship rose again for the great emptiness. Naomi watched the external temperature as they rose, the atmosphere growing colder and colder, but also thinner and thinner until there wasn't enough there to conduct away heat at all. The shuddering stopped, and the only sounds were the ticking of the air recyclers and the occasional harmonic chiming of the drive passing through a resonance frequency. On her tactical display, the planet fell away behind them and they passed escape velocity. They weren't even in a long orbit of Freehold now. They were on their own. Free.

Naomi shouted, a wide, celebratory yawp. And Alex answered back. She lay back in the couch and let herself just be home. Just for a moment.

The *Roci* was an old ship now. She'd never be state of the art again. But like old tools, well used and well cared for, she'd become something more than plating and wires, conduits and storage and sensor arrays. Old Rokku had said that after fifty years flying, a ship had a soul. It had seemed like a cute superstition when she was young. It seemed obvious now.

"God, I missed this," Alex said.

"I know, right?"

An hour later, Alex put them on the float, and Naomi unstrapped. Freehold system was so empty, there was no traffic control authority. No flight plans or patrols watching for drive plumes without transponders. She started her diagnostics running, but she already knew from the sound of the drive and the taste of the air that they'd come back clean. She moved from station to station, checking the displays and controls as if there were other crew members who might be using them.

She didn't notice the change in Alex's mood until he spoke.

"I tried to keep her alive. I really did. Right at the end, she was out there throwing rounds at that great big bastard, and I was going to take us in. Burn the *Storm* right in there and try to get her back on board. But there wasn't time." His sigh had a shudder in it. "And it would just have fucked things up if I'd done it."

Naomi wrapped her hand around a foothold and braced. She turned to look at him, and this time he met her eyes.

"She was a hell of a woman," Naomi said. "We were lucky to know her."

"The thing I kept thinking all the way out was, *How am I going to tell Kit his Aunt Bobbie's gone?*"

"How did you?"

"I haven't yet. I couldn't stand to when we were in Sol system. And now...I still don't know if I can. I miss her. I miss all of them, but...but I watched her go, and...Shit."

"I know," Naomi said. "I was thinking about her a lot. I sent the okay for the mission."

"Oh, Naomi. No. This isn't your fault."

"I know that. I don't always feel it, but I know it. And it's strange, but the way I comfort myself? I think of all the other ways she could have died. Like oncocidal-resistant cancer. A reactor bottle failure. Just getting old and frail until the antiaging drugs weren't enough anymore."

"That's a little macabre," Alex said. Then, a moment later, "But yeah. I know exactly what you mean."

"It was Bobbie," Naomi said. "She knew we don't live forever. And if she'd gotten to choose a way to go, I bet this would have been in her top five."

Alex was quiet for a few seconds, then sniffed. "I miss her every minute of every day, but god damn, it was just so fuckin' *right*."

"Going hand to hand with a ship the combined strength of Earth, Mars, and the Transport Union couldn't beat and winning?"

"Yeah. If we've got to die, I guess that's a pretty good way to go. Still. I'm sorry we've got to die."

"Mortality does suck that way," Naomi said.

"What would be your way?"

"I don't know. That's not what I think about," she said, surprised that she knew her opinion about what aspect of her own death was important to her. "I don't care how I go. There are just things I want done first."

"Like what?"

"I want to see Jim again. And Amos. I want this war over with, and a real peace established. The kind where people can be angry with each other and hate each other and no one has to die over it. That'd be enough."

"Yeah," Alex said. "That would. I think about Amos a lot. Do you think—"

There was something like a great, soundless pop—a detonation without quite being a detonation—and Naomi fell. Would have fallen if direction still existed. Everything had gone the electric noncolor of eyes pressed too hard in the darkness. Nothingness buzzed around her like an assault. Somewhere nearby, someone was screaming. It might have been Alex. It might have been her own voice.

The bright void she fell into—falling in all directions at once—had shapes inside the light, jagged and shifting as a migraine halo. She felt something missing in herself, but couldn't tell what it was. That frightened her worse than the suddenness and strangeness of the transition. The sense of absence without an object, of loss without knowing what had been lost. She tried to close her eyes, but nothing changed. She tried to reach out, but there was nothing to reach for. Or with. She couldn't tell whether she'd just fallen into the light or if she'd been falling for hours.

She felt herself slipping into something else. Something like sleep but not sleep, and she resisted by instinct. A deep fear wrapped itself around her, and she held on to it as if it could save her.

And then, without any more warning than had come before, it was over. She was on the *Rocinante*'s flight deck. She'd drifted away from her crash couch. Behind her, Alex gagged. She grabbed a handhold and braced. Her body felt wrung out, exhausted. Like she'd been awake for too many days, and the fatigue had seeped into her muscles.

"Did we," she said, and her voice sounded weird in her ears. She swallowed and tried again. "Did we lose time?"

The soft tap of Alex's fingers against a control panel. She closed her eyes, grateful beyond words that the darkness came when her lids fell. A wave of nausea came over her and left again.

"We did," Alex said. "Lost...almost twenty minutes."

She pushed off, navigating her way to her couch by long instinct more than thought. She strapped in with a sense of deep gratitude. Alex's face was grayish, like he'd just seen something horrifying.

"That wasn't...that wasn't like the other ones," he said. "That was different."

"It was," Naomi said.

Alex checked over the *Rocinante*'s status and seemed to take some comfort in it. Naomi was tingling, the pins-and-needles feel of a pinched nerve, but without a physical location on her body. Like her mind was slowly coming back. It was a deeply unsettling feeling.

"Fucking Duarte," she said. "Fucking Laconia and their fucking tests."

"What do you think they did this time?"

Chapter Thirty-Nine: Elvi

Elvi's hand terminal chimed again. It was past time for her to go, but she couldn't pull herself away. Also, the girl in the glass cage didn't have a chair, and so Elvi had chosen to sit on the floor beside her. The prospect of getting back up with her aching leg wasn't pleasant.

"So," she said, "it wasn't a change in cognition?"

There was a moment of eerie stillness, the off-putting pause that they always seemed to have, and then Cara shook her head. "I mean, it's hard to be sure what it was like really, but I didn't have the feeling of being any different. Except for the library, you know."

The library was what Cara and Alexander—whose nickname in the family had been Xan—called the information that they carried with them after their re-creation by the repair drones. It was, according to them, like knowing things without having to learn them first. Sometimes the information was straightforward, like details about the local environment. Sometimes it was inscrutable, like the fact that substrate-level entities were difficult to refract through rich-light. That was the most interesting example, because Cara understood what the substrate was, and what refraction meant in that context, and the nature of rich-light, but the whole body of knowledge didn't connect to anything. There was no shared context with anything like food or trees or water. Any human knowledge. It was, Elvi thought, like finding a sea turtle who thoroughly understood Godel's incompleteness theorem, but didn't have any sea-turtley application for it.

That kind of cognitive artifact was a large part of why Cortázar had drawn the conclusion that Cara and Xan weren't actually the children they'd been before they were "repaired," but alien technology created using human corpses. It was a deep question, and one that Elvi struggled with. The children had clearly been transformed. The fact that they weren't aging or developing was evidence enough of that. The blackness of their eyes and the grayness of their skin dropped them straight into an uncanny valley that still made something in Elvi's hindbrain recoil.

But then sometimes when no one was observing them, Xan would put his head in Cara's lap so she could ruffle his hair. It was a moment that primates had been sharing back to the Pleistocene, deeper and more recognizable than mere humanity. Or Cara would crack a joke about something Elvi asked, and then smile almost shyly when Elvi actually laughed. Elvi's opinion shifted on them. Sometimes she was sure they were puppets of inscrutable alien technologies. Sometimes it seemed obvious that Cortázar had built his case that they weren't human just so he could keep them in a cage for a few decades and run tests on them. Elvi wasn't sure if she liked them or if they scared the shit out of her. If they were passing their Turing test, or if she was failing it.

But it was interesting that none of Cortázar's work on Duarte seemed to have resulted in the high consul's getting access to the library, and the weird turning-off of consciousness hadn't broken

Cara and Xan the way it had Duarte. There was a clue in there somewhere. She had the dataset. She just needed the right grid to put over it, and the pattern would make sense. She could feel it.

Her hand terminal went off again. This time with a message. Her transport had arrived. She was late for the briefing. She muttered something obscene and started levering herself up to standing. "I have to go."

"We'll be here when you get back," Cara said, and after a pause, Xan laughed. Elvi smiled too. It was silly to treat them like she'd been having lunch with friends and had to go too soon, but there she was. Sometimes she was silly.

She leaned on her cane as she made her way out through the labs to the fresh and open air. Her leg hurt. The regrowth, as simple as it was, was going slowly. Poorly. Fayez's new foot was already in place, the skin a little paler and softer, the new muscles still prone to cramp if he walked too much. But he'd regrown bones and tendons and nerves, and she was still leaning on a cane.

The difference, she knew, was the stress. Fayez was almost ornamental in her present life. He slept in, ate at the State Building, visited with whoever came through the gardens or read books or watched old entertainment feeds. He recuperated. Elvi was diving through Cortázar's data when she wasn't examining Duarte's condition or trying to keep Teresa from being murdered in the name of curiosity or going over her own data from the *Falcon*. She was barely sleeping, and when she did, it was just rolling the dice to see what flavor of nightmare was taking its turn.

There would be a point when it was all too much. When the intrusive image of Sagale with a part of his head missing wouldn't let itself be kicked down the road for her to think about later even one more time. When she'd break. It hadn't come yet, though, so she didn't have to deal with it. She was very aware that she was working on what Fayez called fuck-it-if-it's-not-happening-right-now protocol.

Worse than that, she was coming to a place where she enjoyed the intensity. She had never been under more stress in her life, except maybe once, back on Ilus. Everyone had been going blind, and there were neurotoxin-covered slugs crawling up out of the ground, and alien artifacts coming to life, and people murdering each other over political issues and personal pride. Everything had depended on her talent and the sharpness of her mind. And now it did again. And part of her loved it like it was sugar. Probably not a healthy part.

The driver waiting for her had an umbrella up to shield her from a light, misty rain. He didn't speak. When she got to the car, she leaned toward him. "Let Trejo know I'm on my way."

"I already have, Doctor," the driver said.

Drivers, Elvi thought as they pulled away, were a strange kind of affectation. It would have been easier to have a transport just pick her up and take her without another human involved. Having someone there whose job was to be deferential to her actually slowed things down. An extra layer of processing. Like that pause the children had. She wondered if it was like a stutter. She had to read up on that. Maybe there was something useful in it.

The State Building was wreathed in mist. The car's heater wasn't quite enough to push back the cold that radiated from the window. Early winter on Laconia—on this part of Laconia anyway—seemed to involve a lot of chilly days and bitter nights. As soon as the sun went down, all the mist would turn into an all-encompassing layer of ice. The local trees had all retracted their leaves. The imported ones had seen all their chloroplasts die out and were in the process of dropping red and yellow and brown remnants.

Inside, the climate was warm and dry, as controlled as a ship's, but the light from the windows was muted and gray. It still smelled like rain. A different servant took her jacket and asked if she wanted a snack or a cup of tea delivered to the briefing room. She said yes out of habit. Her attention was already divided between the past—sitting with the children or alien child-corpse puppet things—and the future—her report and analysis of the most recent mass blackout event. There was literally no room in her awareness for the present.

The briefing room was beautiful. Walls of polished rosewood with a subtle gold inlay, and lights set behind frosted glass that left the place shadowless. Trejo and Cortázar and Ilich were already there, seated around a malachite-topped table. Trejo looked as bad as she felt, and Ilich maybe even a little worse. Cortázar was the only one of them who was bearing up well under the stress. She was pretty certain that was because he didn't care whether any of the rest of them lived or died.

"Sorry I'm late," she said. "I'm sure you understand."

"We've all been busy," Trejo said, and either it was a subtle dig or it wasn't. She couldn't tell which. "Regardless, we're all here now. And we have to make a statement about this…latest event. What can the high consul say about it? What do we know? Colonel Ilich? Would you like to begin?"

Ilich cleared his throat. "Well, we experienced another event that appears to have simultaneously affected everyone in the system. And by simultaneous, again, I mean that it appears to have been a single, nonlocal event that happened…everywhere. We have reports that it also occurred in at least two other systems."

Cortázar raised his hand like a kid in grade school, and Trejo nodded at him.

"What happened in the ring space?" Cortázar asked. "Was it the same as in the systems?"

"We don't know," Ilich said. "We didn't have any of our ships in the ring space at the time. There's some indication that ships in the ring space may have been…um…eaten, if that's the term. The same way the *Typhoon* and Medina were. But I don't have confirmation. The event doesn't seem correlated with anything we did, but we only have an active naval presence in about one hundred and twenty systems right now. If something happened outside of those, we might not know."

"Seriously?" Trejo said.

"I can't overstate how devastating it's been to lose Medina Station, sir. Controlling that choke point was the leash we had on the empire. Without it…"

Trejo leaned back in his chair, scowling. He opened his hands to Elvi and Cortázar, giving the floor to them. Cortázar didn't seem to care, but Elvi found herself sitting forward to speak as if she owed the admiral something.

"If I can try to put this all in a wider context?"

"Please do," Trejo said.

"It's about the nature of consciousness."

"That may be a wider context than I was looking for, Major."

"Bear with me," Elvi said. "Unless we're reaching for religious explanations, which I'm not the person to comment on, consciousness is a property of matter. That's trivial. We're made out of matter, we're conscious. Minds are a thing that brains do. And there's an energetic component. We know that neurons firing is a sign that a particular kind of conscious experience is happening. So, for instance, if I'm looking at your brain while you imagine something, I can guess reliably whether you're imagining a song or a picture by seeing if your visual or auditory cortex is lighting up."

"All right," Trejo said.

"There's no reason to believe that a brain is the only structure capable of having that combination of structure and energy. And in fact, there's a fair amount of evidence that the gate builders had a conscious structure—a brain-like thing—where the material component wasn't at all the same kind of thing we use. Anecdotally, we've found at least one brain-like structure that was a diamond the size of Jupiter."

"I don't know what that means," Trejo said.

"Like we don't have a steel chamber in fusion reactors. We have magnetic bottles. Magnetic fields that perform the same basic function as matter. The older civilization appears to have developed its consciousness in a form that relied more on energetic fields and maybe structures in unobservable matter than the stuff we made a brain from. There's also some implication that quantum effects have something to do with our being aware. If that's true for us, it was probably true for them.

"My thesis—the one I was working on before I came here—explored the idea that our brains are kind of a field combat version of consciousness. Not too complex. Not a lot of bells and whistles, but takes a lot of punishment and keeps functioning. Our brain may actually have a kick-starting effect, so when the quantum interactions that underlie having experiences break down, they're easier to start up again. Does that make sense?"

Trejo said *Barely* at the same time Cortázar said *Of course*. The two men looked at each other. Elvi felt annoyed at both of them, but she went on.

"So, the scenario that James Holden brought back from the alien station in the ring space was of something systematically destroying the consciousness of the older civilization. Killing it. The previous civilization tried getting rid of systems. Inducing supernovas. That didn't help. They eventually closed all the gates, and that didn't fix the problem either, because whatever it was killed them all anyway.

"And that's where we came in. We found—and I have directly observed—things that we call bullets or scars or persistent nonlocal field effects. Basically a place where whatever hates the ring gates has done something to collapse consciousness on a planet or in a system. Or in all the systems at once. What I suspect—and I don't have any data for this—is that the enemy figured out how to snuff out all the systems at once, whether the gates were active or not. I believe that our travel through the gates is irritating to these beings. Maybe even damaging in some way. When that damage gets high enough, they react."

"So when I killed Pallas Station in Sol…," Trejo said.

"You also hit some weird, aphysical dark god in whatever passes for its nose," Elvi said. "And they did what you'd expect them to do. If you get sick and a penicillin shot makes you better, then the next time you get sick, you try another shot. Only it turns out we aren't the same kind of conscious system as the gate makers. We don't break as easy, and we recover better. What slaughtered their civilization just lost us a few minutes of time."

"How disappointing for the dark gods," Trejo said.

"Right? But then they're not done. Especially, and no offense here, when we start dropping bomb ships into wherever they are. Playing tit for tat. And the way this one *felt* different? Light and shapes instead of that kind of hyperawareness?"

"I did notice that, yes," Trejo said dryly.

"I believe that the enemy, whatever it is, is experimenting with new ways to break conscious systems. Brains. I think we're the equivalent of a penicillin-resistant infection, and the last event we experienced was an attempt at tetracycline."

"And the trigger?" Trejo asked.

"There doesn't need to be a trigger," Elvi said, "if the enemy has gone past being purely reactive. Maybe we just convinced them to take us seriously."

Trejo sank a little as the implications unfolded in his mind.

"Is this new information?" Cortázar said. "I feel we've covered this all before. I mean, nothing in this is really new, is it?"

Trejo and Ilich exchanged a look.

"It's useful to me," Trejo said, "to have Dr. Okoye's summary. So yes. Do we have any progress on healing the high consul?"

"It would be helpful," Cortázar said, "if I could examine Ilich's castoff. I don't suppose there's been any new word on finding it?"

Trejo's effort to hold his temper was visible. "Before we move on to that, if we could address the health of the high consul?"

"He's stable," Cortázar said. "Very stable. Perfectly fine."

"Improving?"

"No."

Ilich broke in, his voice tense. "Is there no way we can get him back?"

Elvi wasn't going to let Cortázar bullshit this one anymore. Either he had a plan he'd been holding back for his own reasons or he didn't. She leaned forward and put her hands on the desk, palms down, like she was revealing a hand at a poker table. "I don't see any realistic path toward returning him to his previous state."

Trejo nodded to her and shifted to Cortázar. "Do you disagree?"

Cortázar squirmed. "His previous state? Probably not. But moving him forward into a new state is much more plausible. Easy, even. And more than that, instructive."

Trejo went terribly still. A soft tapping came at the door, and the servant came in with Elvi's snack. She'd forgotten all about it. When the door was closed again and privacy restored, Trejo hadn't moved. His eyes weren't focused on anything in the room, and his skin was pale. It took Elvi a moment to understand what she was seeing.

All this time, Trejo had hoped. He'd believed that his leader would return, that the righteous king would rise and retake his throne. Despite everything Elvi had said, the admiral had believed Cortázar could Merlin his Arthur back from madness. She was watching Trejo realize he had just been letting someone play with the corpse. She was someplace between horrified for him and relieved that he'd finally heard what she'd been saying all along.

"All right," Trejo said. And then again, more slowly, "All right. The high consul is going to have to make a statement all the same. We'll draft something."

"We can say that the event was a test," Ilich said. "The high consul's elite team has made a breakthrough. A new weapon against the enemy."

"Or we could tell them the truth," Elvi said.

Trejo stood, his hands clasped behind his back. The anger and irrationality in his expression were grief. Grief made people crazy. When he spoke, his voice buzzed with barely controlled rage. Not at Cortázar either. At her.

"I don't think you understand exactly how precarious our situation is here, Dr. Okoye. I have a two-front war with no fronts. This is not a moment to undermine and degrade the confidence of our troops or embolden separatist terror. You have just outlined war on a cosmic scale. I can't prosecute a battle against your dark gods while guerrillas degrade our forces. We have to unify humanity for this. We have to strike with one will. We can't afford to fuck around knocking each other's comm relays down anymore. That is going to get us all killed. Do you hear what I am saying?"

"I do," Elvi said, and she was surprised by the steel in her own voice. Trejo heard it too. "I'm hearing you say you can't handle this. You want the fight with the underground over with? Easy to do. Surrender."

"Your jokes aren't funny," he said.

"They aren't when they're not jokes."

Chapter Forty: Teresa

Every night she went to sleep, Teresa thought that maybe the next day would be the one that brought her father back. Like with the story of Pandora's box, all the other fears and nightmares were made bearable by that one hope. Every morning that she woke, there was that sense of possibility that stayed bright as long as she could keep herself from checking in. And then Kelly, her father's personal valet, would tell her that nothing had changed because of course it hadn't. She'd feel let down again, and still, idiotically, stupidly, like a cartoon character with an empty grin, the thought would come up. Maybe tomorrow. Always maybe tomorrow.

His rooms weren't grand. They never had been. A bed frame of natural wood and a thin mattress that he would rest on, even after he'd outgrown sleep. A desk with metal, locking drawers and a screen built into its surface. The only decorations in the place were a picture of her as a child, one of her mother from when she'd been alive, and a simple glass vase big enough for a single flower that Kelly replaced every day. Winston Duarte, high consul and architect of the Laconian Empire, had taken pride in having a simple man's quarters. The greatness of Laconia wasn't in its gaudiness, but in its works. The vastness of the empire's ambition would have made any man seem small. Even him. That was how she thought of it, anyway. What she'd believed.

Now he sat at his desk, his head shifting as if he were trying to follow the flight of insects that only he could see. His hands rose sometimes and then drifted back down like he'd started to reach for something and then forgotten what he meant to do. Kelly had brought her a wicker chair to put beside him. Teresa sat on it, her hands clasped on her knees, watching him for any sign of improvement. Any hope that today might be the tomorrow she kept herself alive for.

"Daddy?" she said, and he seemed to react to the sound. He turned a degree toward her, and even though his eyes didn't meet hers, something like a smile touched his lips. Kelly kept her father's hair well combed, but it seemed thinner than she remembered it. Grayer. Greasier. The ancient acne scars on her father's cheeks made him seem rougher, more worn than he actually was. There was an amazement in his expression, like he was constantly discovering wonders that commanded his attention more than she did.

"Daddy," she said again, "he's going to kill me. Dr. Cortázar? He's going to *kill* me."

He turned toward her more, his brow taking on a gentle furrow. Maybe he'd heard her, maybe it was coincidence. He reached out his hands to pat at the air around her head the way he did sometimes, only this time she took his fingers in hers, pulling his hands down, pulling his face toward hers. "Are you there? Do you understand what I'm telling you? He wants to kill me. He wants to pin me down and cut me up like those frogs. And no one's help-ing. No one even cares."

She was weeping now, and she hated that she was.

"Come back," she whispered. "Daddy, come back to me."

He opened his mouth as if to speak, but only made wet click-ing noises. Like meat being moved by a butcher. He frowned for a moment, then looked away toward the window.

"Daddy," she said again. And then, *"Daddy!"*

He flinched at the sound.

The door opened behind her, and she heard Kelly's gentle cough. She dropped her father's hands and wiped her tears away. Not that she could hide the fact that she'd been crying. The best she could do was show that she'd stopped.

"Is there anything I can get you, miss?" Kelly asked. He wore his usual red porter's uniform. She'd known him forever, since she was a child gamboling down the halls with the puppy who would grow into her Muskrat. He'd brought her tea and served her meals. She'd cared about him the way she cared about doors and pieces of art. As a thing. A function. An object. Now they were in the room together, and she saw him as a person. An older man, as devoted to her father as anyone could be. As complicit in hiding what he'd become as she was.

"Does he change?" she asked. "Does he ever change?"

Kelly lifted his brows, looking for what to say. His sigh was soft and apologetic. "It's hard to say, miss. There are times he seems to know where he is. Who I am. But that may be wishful thinking on my part."

Her father had drifted back to following his invisible bugs through the air. His forehead smoothed. If he'd heard her at all, understood her at all, he'd been distracted from it. She shifted her weight, and the wicker chair creaked under her.

"I'll come back," she said. "If he changes. If he gets better..."

"I will see that they tell you immediately," Kelly said.

She rose, feeling disconnected from the motion. Like she was watching a Teresa-shaped balloon with its string cut. Kelly stepped over to take the chair away as she walked to the door.

"He would be glad to know you came," Kelly said. "I can't say if he knows we're here. But if he did know, he'd be glad. I believe that."

He meant the words as comfort, but Teresa couldn't bring herself to care. She walked out without thanking him or cursing him or doing anything but putting one foot in front of the other until she was out of the private rooms.

The public parts of the State Building where the mechanisms of government went on were as busy and efficient as ever. Like a beehive or a termite hill that was unaware that its queen was dead. No one stopped her or made eye contact. She passed through on the way to her own rooms like a ghost. All she wanted was to lock her doors and crawl into bed and pray for a dreamless sleep that would carry her to tomorrow. Or later. Or at least not now.

But when she get there, her door was open. Colonel Ilich was sitting on her couch. He didn't look up as she came in.

"Where's Muskrat?" Teresa asked.

"She's in the bedroom. You missed your tutorial this morning," he said, his voice pleasant and nonjudgmental and false as a mask.

Teresa folded her arms. "I was with my father."

"I respect that, but your father would want you to perform your duties. All your duties. That includes your education." Ilich stood, pulling himself to his full height like it might lend him more authority. "And your breakfast."

"I wasn't hungry."

"That isn't the issue. We are in—"

"Dangerous times," Teresa said. "A precarious situation. We have to keep up appearances. I know. Everyone keeps *telling* me."

"Then stop acting like a spoiled little shit and do your part," Ilich said.

It was fascinating to see his expression when the words were out. She was so used to him being in control, professional, approachable, friendly. The shock widening on his face, and the purse-lipped chagrin. And then the pleasure. Pride, even. It didn't take more than a few seconds, but it told its own little story.

"You," he said before she found the words to throw back at him, "are the high consul's daughter. You are the face of your family. That makes you the stability of the empire."

"The empire's fucking wheels are coming off," Teresa shouted. "Everything's falling apart. What do you want me to do about it?"

His voice was tight and controlled. "I want you to eat your meals. I want you to show up for your lessons. I want you to project normalcy and stability and calm to everyone who sees you. Because that is your duty to your father and the empire."

The rage felt like it was lifting her body. She didn't know what she was going to say. She didn't have an argument or a stance, only the power that came from being incensed beyond her capacity to contain it.

"But you can spend days running around looking for Timothy? You can have Dr. Okoye come teach because nothing she does is as important as making sure you can finish killing my friends? You aren't doing your work either, so you don't get to tell me to do mine. That's hypocrisy!"

Ilich looked at her, looked deep into her eyes, and he chuckled. He reached out and ruffled her hair like she was Muskrat and he was scratching her ears. It was gentle and humiliating. Teresa felt her rage stutter and die, and a vast embarrassment flood into the place it had been. She wanted the anger back.

"You poor kid. Is *that* what this is about? The spy? You're mad at me because of him?"

"I'm mad because of everything," she said, but there wasn't any power behind it now.

"He wasn't your friend. He was a spy and an assassin. He was here to kill us. That cave of his? He picked it as shelter for when he set the pocket nuke off. The mountain was a landmark for his evacuation team."

"That isn't true."

He took her arm just above the shoulder. His grip was tight enough to pinch. "You missed your tutorial this morning. We'll make it up now. You need to learn something."

The security offices of the State Building were familiar to her. They were offices like any other branch's, except for the occasional reinforced door and blast-resistant lock. There were cells there for political prisoners, though she didn't know if anyone was in them besides James Holden. The forensics lab, however, was new. It was a wide room with a high ceiling and movable partitions that could seal off a section and keep its atmosphere separate. Fume hoods with waldoes and blast-resistant glass lined one wall. The tables that filled the center of the room had aisles between them wide enough for specialized tool carts—chemical, biological, electronic, computational—to be wheeled to wherever they were needed. Half a dozen people stood at the workstations. And on them, Timothy's things. The carved wood tools. The cot. The cases and boxes that had been his. Even one of the repair drones that had apparently been damaged somewhere in the violence lay on a table, the size and rough profile of a dead animal.

Ilich cleared the room so they would be alone. The technicians left, trying not to be obvious in the ways they stared at Teresa. She saw the curiosity in their faces. What was the high consul's daughter doing there? What did it mean? The weight of their interest was like a hand on her shoulders, pressing down.

When they were alone, Ilich put her on a technician's stool and brought a data storage core over. She recognized it from Timothy's cave, though she hadn't thought about it much at the time. Ilich synced a monitor, pulled up a file directory, and stepped back, gesturing to it as if to say, *Go ahead. Look.*

Teresa found she didn't want to.

"Start with the notes files," Ilich said. "Let's see how much Timothy was your friend."

The notes were dates and times. At first, she didn't see any pattern in them, but the notations with the entries had a security note from the forensic tech. When she opened it, Timothy's entries matched the security logs for those dates. He'd been watching the State Building's guards. Working out their patterns and habits. Looking for a hole. And he'd been tracking James Holden. Those records were more scattered, because Holden had less of a pattern. He'd drifted through the buildings and gardens as he saw fit, and Timothy—Amos, his name was Amos—had marked every time Holden came in sight of his watching post on the mountain.

Once she'd gotten through the notes file, she didn't stop. She opened a tactical maps file and recognized the architecture of the city, of the State Building. A series of files showed blast radii of a small nuclear device. If it were planted at the wall. If it were set off in the city. If it had been smuggled into the State Building. Each one had notes speculating on deaths, on infrastructure degraded. She opened a file called "evacuation protocol." Topographical maps showed a primary evac site close to where she'd met him the first time and a secondary a day's hike away, with notes Timothy—Amos—had added about what parts of the visible defense grid would have to be taken out for each site to be practical.

Here is how he would have killed us. Here is how he would have left. Here is the man he came to save, here are the people he came to destroy. She waited for the rage to come back. She expected it. Instead, she thought of James Holden. *If he said he was your friend, then he was.*

"Do you see now?" Ilich said. "Do you see what he was?"

All these plans to kill her and her father. To slaughter them all. *You should lie down on the floor there. Flat as you can. Put your hands over your ears, okay?* Were those the words you said to someone you wanted to kill?

"I understand," she lied. "I do."

Ilich shut off the monitor. "Then we're done here."

He took her arm again and led her away. She hadn't seen him order up food, but when they got back to her rooms, it was waiting for her. A thick, white protein slurry like they fed to sick people. A steak of vat-grown meat seared black at the surface and warm pink in the center. Eggs. Cheese and fruit. Sweet rice with flakes of dried fish. It was all on a metal tray with a fork and dull knife. Muskrat trotted in, but caught the sense that something was wrong. When Ilich held his hand out, offering to scratch her ears, she ignored him and went to sit on Teresa's feet instead.

"Now then," Ilich said. "Eat your meal. Get some rest tonight. Tomorrow, you will be on time for your lesson. We will be in the east garden where everyone on staff can see us, and you will act as if everything were normal. Do you understand?"

"I don't want to eat this. I'm not hungry."

"I don't care. You're going to eat now."

She looked at the food in front of her. Reluctantly, she picked up the fork. She remembered something from an old film she'd seen about a girl in Sol system. On Earth. "I don't have to do this. Body autonomy is written into the constitution."

"Not ours it isn't," Ilich said. "You will eat this now, while I sit here and watch you. Then we will sit for another hour while you digest it. Or else I will call in Dr. Cortázar with a funnel and tube, and we force you. Am I understood?"

Teresa took a forkful of the steak and put it in her mouth. Intellectually, she knew it tasted good. When she swallowed, Ilich nodded.

"Again," he said.

After he left, Teresa didn't move. She just sat on her couch, feeling the weight in her stomach. She hadn't eaten a meal that large in weeks, and it left her feeling bloated and wrong. Muskrat sensed that something was off, and put her wide, furry head on Teresa's lap, looking up at her with complex brown eyes.

Teresa put on a feed. The same one she'd watched as a child. The nameless Martian girl and the fairy named Pinsleep. Familiar images washed over her, bringing something close to comfort. A sense of predictability, at least. She knew that at the end, the nameless girl would escape fairyland. That she'd go back to Innis Deep and her family. That in the last scene, she'd pack away all her girlhood toys and leave for upper university and an adult life. That was the sign that she'd won. She was free to make any life she wanted, and not be a prisoner of the elves.

She lay down on the couch, resting her head on a pillow. The girl was taken in by Pinsleep again, and ran, and fought to escape. And escaped. Teresa started it again from the beginning.

Prisoners and their dilemmas. She let the images play and took up her handheld. In her notes, she found Ilich's old diagram.

	TERESA COOPERATES	TERESA DEFECTS
JASON COOPERATES	T3, J3	T4, J0
JASON DEFECTS	T0, J4	T2, J2

She ran her fingers over it. She'd forgotten that Ilich's first name was Jason. She'd forgotten a lot of things.

The puzzle—the unsolvable part—was that no matter what she did, it was better for the others to defect. If she was good, they should take advantage of her. If she was bad, they still should. And the same logic applied to her, except she hadn't done it. Everyone else had defected, and when she didn't cooperate, they forced her to. Even though the thing that made sense was to defect.

Pinsleep discovered that the girl wasn't in her cell and screamed. Thin fairy fingers balled in stylized fists. Muskrat snored deeply, her fuzzy body pressed close to Teresa. She put her own hand down and scratched the old dog. Black with gray in her muzzle and at the tips of her ears. The thing she hadn't wanted to know pressed at her throat, welling up like a bubble rising from the bottom of the ocean. She felt like she could watch it come, and she knew that when it reached the surface, nothing about her life would be the same. Everything would have to change, because she'd changed.

And it happened, not with a scream, but with an exhalation. She leaned down, her lips almost against Muskrat's floppy ear. When she spoke, she whispered.

"This isn't my home anymore. I can't stay here. I have to leave."

Muskrat looked up and licked Teresa's cheek, agreeing.

Chapter Forty-One: Naomi

The Freehold gate, like all the gates, was stationary with respect to its local sun. That it didn't fall into its distant star was just one of its many mysteries, but since they couldn't hook a chain between it and the *Roci* and hang from it, they did not benefit from its gravity-defying properties. Instead, Alex parked the *Roci* close to it with the Epstein drive on a gentle burn to balance the pull of the sun.

The flight out to the ring gate had been eerie. The *Rocinante* had been her home longer than anyplace else. She'd slept more of her nights in these crash couches, and eaten more of her meals in the galley. She had breathed the air that passed through the ducts and filters more times than she could calculate. Being inside the ship now, she felt the presence of the others. Her memories of them. What surprised her most was that it didn't hurt.

She'd left the *Roci* not long after Amos took his covert assignment to Laconia. Alex was going to join Bobbie on the *Storm*. Naomi, they had all thought, would hire on a temporary crew for the *Rocinante* and keep her flying. Only she hadn't. At the time, she'd barely been able to explain why. She could still remember some of the rationalizations she'd used—*A gunship is harder to hide than one person* and *The* Rocinante *has symbolic value as a prize that ups the risk of using her* and *The underground on Freehold will be able to use her if the need for defense arises.*

They'd all been true, and none of them had. Looking back now, she saw that she'd left because staying would have been worse. She hadn't let herself feel the loss of Jim too deeply. Or of Amos. Or Clarissa. Bobbie had invited her to join the crew of the *Storm*, but Naomi hadn't accepted, and Bobbie hadn't pressed the issue.

Now, strapped into the spiderlike framework of a salvage mech and burning for the ring with her two transmitters and the spool of wire, she looked back at the ship—her ship—and it still ached. But it was bearable. She had taken her grief and locked herself away with it because she'd been skinless. It had been the best way she could find at the time to keep every new day from feeling like a little more salt on the wound. But that had been a different version of her. She'd grieved, but more than that, she'd changed. The woman she was now wasn't quite the one she'd been on the day that Jim left. Or even on the day she'd chosen not to accept Duarte's invitation. Between the loss of Saba and Bobbie's defeat of the *Tempest*, Naomi had been reborn so quietly she'd hardly even noticed. The only real evidence was that she could be on the *Rocinante* again. She could come home.

"You're almost there," Alex said. "How's it look?"

"Big," Naomi said.

The gate was only a thousand kilometers across. This close to the surface, it might as well have been half of the universe. This far from the sun, the mech's HUD needed to add some false color augmentation so that she could see more clearly what she was dealing with. She made her braking burn. She only had a little time before her orbit slid past her, but the transmitters were already wired together. She tapped through the initialization codes, and the compressed nitrogen thrusters took it from there. The primary transmitter shot out through the ring, and the secondary took up a stationary position relative to the ring gate except for a slow drift that would eventually snuggle it up against the physical surface of the ring itself. As repeaters went, it was about the simplest version there was—one step up from cans and string. But it didn't have to last long.

"How's it looking?"

"I'm watching," Alex said. "I've got sync from the local side. I'm waiting for a response from…Yeah, okay. We're looking good. Come on back."

"Copy that. I'm heading in," Naomi said. "So much for the easy part."

"Taking what I can get."

Naomi turned back toward the *Rocinante* and started her burn. The mech had enough power in the thrusters that she could have worked out there for a few hours without any risk, but she was just as happy not to. The cooling on the unit wasn't what it had been, or else she was less tolerant of being overheated.

By the time she'd gotten back to the ship, cycled through the airlock, packed the mech safely away, and floated up to the flight deck, the transmitter had been working for a little under three hours. The first cycle was passive, looking for signals coming from any ships in the ring space and identifying as many as they could. It looked like there were about a dozen at the moment, but all of them were recognizable as Transport Union or smugglers. Nothing had the comm signal or drive signature of a *Storm*-class destroyer, and nothing was the *Whirlwind*. No ships at all would have been better, but this was as good as Naomi could have reasonably hoped.

The connection request signal was the first real risk she was taking. If there were Laconian sensors in the ring space, this was going to give away what gates had active cells of the underground behind them. If things went the way she hoped, that information wouldn't matter much. It was a calculated risk.

For almost a minute, there was no reply. The farthest gate was only a little under a million klicks. The light delay should have been nearly trivial. Naomi had a sinking feeling—What if they were the only ones? What if the plan had already fallen apart?—and then the connections started coming through. First just one, then a handful, then a small flood. Fifty-three answers in all. Fifty-three systems with their full supply of ready warships, out of retirement and at her command. Easily hundreds of ships.

"Not bad," Alex said from his couch.

"It's excellent until you do the math," Naomi said. "Then it's ninety-six percent no reply." But she smiled when she said it.

Her plan, long since sent out via bottle and echoed from system to system, was larger than Laconia. Larger than the fifty-three systems that had sent ships for the fight. Even as she'd been setting out her makeshift repeater, an alert was going off at the transfer station on Nyingchi Xin. A pirate was breaking into Laconian warehouses on the largest moon of the smallest gas giant in Sanctuary system. A massive data breach was being reported from the new shipyards in Yasamal system. Hopefully dozens of other small actions and issues, anyplace that a *Storm*-class destroyer was in the system. After the death of the *Tempest*, Laconian forces and the factions that had thrown their lot in with them had to be nervous. That was her handle on them. It let her and her people distract them and draw them thin. They had to look strong now in every corner of the empire, because they already looked weak.

The next phase lost the anonymity and safety of the bottles. With a sensation like walking off her ship under an unfamiliar sky, Naomi chose the first of the connection requests and opened it. There was a hiss of static and the compression of sound that the multiple layers of encryption left behind.

"Nagata here," Naomi said.

"Zomorodi back to you," Emma's familiar voice replied a few seconds later. "We've got the *Cama*, a half dozen rock hoppers with rail guns mounted on 'em, and ten antipirate gunships recently liberated from the governing council's shipyard at Newbaker."

"Ammunition?"

The lag was present, but not so bad that she had to trade recorded messages. The immediacy felt almost intimate.

"Oh, damn. Knew I forgot something," Emma said, and Naomi heard the teasing in her voice. "Of course we're loaded up. The *Cama*'s got a full hold too. Anyone needs resupply, we'll be there. Unless they kill us all. Then, not so much."

"Fair enough. Send me the specs and transponder codes. And what happened to Captain Burnham?"

"Early retirement," Emma said. "Cashed out and bought part of a medical clinic."

"Probably smarter than all of us put together."

"I'm leaning toward coward."

"Good to hear from you, Emma. Keep drives ready. I'll be sending a flight plan as soon as I have everyone."

"Standing by until then, Admiral."

Naomi dropped the connection and took the next. Eight ships with old-style stealth composites and internal heat sinks. They'd have been the kings of space a couple generations back, but they weren't bad even now. The next group had a *Donnager*-class battleship they were pulling out of mothballs. A quarter million tons of pieces smuggled to an empty moon and welded back together like a child's model kit with a one-to-one scale. If she was lucky, there would be three or four more like it. Building them had been a pet project of Saba's.

Saba, who'd started it and hadn't lived to see it through. These people she talked with, whose lives she was now in a position to risk at best, spend outright at worst, were Saba's network. They were the sword he'd dropped on the battlefield that she had picked up.

Fifty-three systems. Four hundred and eighteen ships with five Transport Union supply ships and three *Donnager*-class battleships among them, and the *Storm*—still compromised, but able to fly, still on her way. The best hammer that the underground could put together.

And it still wasn't half the size of the force the *Tempest* had killed in Sol. Hopefully, if she'd done this right, it would be enough. If she'd been fooling herself, they'd all pay the price. But she was pretty sure she was right.

Once she had all the specs, she started sorting through by drive model, ship mass, and total energetic profile. Alex showed up with a tube of spiced lentils and a bulb of cold tea. She didn't know she was hungry until she started eating it, and then she was ravenous. She put the monitor aside, rolling the tube and pressing to get out every bit of the spicy, rich mush. When it was gone apart from a burning aftertaste and a pleasant pressure in her gut, she sighed.

"Just like old times," Alex said. "You never could remember to eat when you had a good problem to solve."

"My old problems were never like this. It was more how to make sure we get to the next port safely."

"That's not what we're doin'?" Alex asked with a grin.

"Nothing about this has any relationship to safety. This is exactly what I never wanted to be doing. Fighting? Getting people killed? I never even carried a gun."

"I knew that," Alex said, and the grin had turned into something softer. "There's still time. Call this off, head back to port. Go back to getting our people elected into the Association of Worlds."

Naomi was silent, her mind and her heart at odds the way they so often were. Alex misunderstood.

"I'm only half joking," he said. "There is time to pull back. We haven't committed these folks to anything. Not yet."

"No, we have to do this. If there was time...I don't know. Maybe. Maybe I'd have kept looking until I found a better way. One that wasn't this."

The comm controls alerted, a little orange strobe blinking with the incoming message. But it was only the *Storm*, updating her ETA. Naomi tucked the empty food tube into her pocket. She'd throw it in the recycler when she was done here. The bulb of tea cooled her fingers and pulled a tiny sheen of condensation out of the air.

"You feel like you owe it to them?" Alex asked, gently. "To Bobbie. And Saba. Amos."

"No," Naomi said. "And not to Jim either. This isn't guilt. It's…possibility? I don't want to fight. I don't want anyone to get hurt. Or die. Not our side, and not them either. I want to reconcile. That's why Bobbie always got so frustrated with me. She wanted to win."

"Looks like you do too, now."

"The problem is it's hard to reconcile when you've lost," Naomi said. "Someone takes all the power, and you try to bring them into the fold again? That's capitulation. I don't think violence solves anything, not even this. Not even now. But maybe winning puts us in a place that we can be gracious."

"Meet Duarte halfway?" Alex said. She could hear in his voice that he wasn't convinced. If she couldn't sway him, maybe there wasn't hope. But she tried.

"Make space for him. Maybe he'll take it, maybe he won't. Maybe his admirals will see something in it he doesn't. The point of this fight isn't to kill Laconia. It's to get enough power that we can close the distance they opened between them and everyone else. That may mean punishing some people. It may mean answering for old crimes. But it *has* to mean finding some way forward."

"You sure that's not owing something to Holden?" Alex said. "Because that sounds an awful lot like something he'd say. And then everyone else would roll their eyes at."

"I don't know," she said. "Maybe. There needs to be a Saba now, so I'll be that if I have to. But there's going to need to be a James Holden later. And if he's not there to do it, we'll have to pick that up too."

"What about a Naomi Nagata?"

"She should probably finish solving her traffic control problems. I don't want anyone going dutchman. Or setting off another lost-time incident. Not if we can avoid it," Naomi said. The comm alerted again, and this time she answered it. "*Rocinante* here."

"This is the destroyer *Gathering Storm*," a woman said. Her voice almost hummed with pride and the prospect of violence. "Requesting permission to dock and transfer crew."

Alex raised a hand. "I'll take care of this one, Admiral."

Naomi transferred control to Alex. "Hey there, Jillian. This is Alex. You are good for docking, but make sure Caspar knows to slide in from the side. It may not look like we've got the drive on, but we do. I don't want to prove it by cooking you."

"Like your little drive could burn us," the woman said.

"I'd feel bad about it, is all. I'll send the codes."

"It'll be good to see you, old man," the *Storm* said, and dropped the connection.

"Jillian Houston," Alex said. "She's a good kid. She'll make a fine captain."

"I remember her father being an asshole."

"She's also kind of an asshole."

It was three hours before the *Storm* sidled up beside the *Rocinante* and extended its docking tube. It was strange seeing the Laconian ship with its alien technology, but also with the same design history as the *Rocinante* itself. Naomi sometimes forgot that Laconia was in so many ways the heir to Mars until something like this reminded her.

She was still putting the final touches on her transit orders when the new crew came over, and Alex had to prod her more than once to get her down to the airlock. He was right, of course, but the project was complicated and so close to finished, it was hard to step away from it.

The *Rocinante* had run for years on a skeleton crew of four, and then expanded up to six. It was designed for twenty-two. The people who came in, drifting in the microgravity, were a mixed bunch. Belters and Freeholders and a gunner from Brazil Nova who'd joined up on Ganymede. She greeted each of them as they came aboard, hoping that she could commit each name to memory and put it to the correct face later. Belinda Ross. Acacia Kindermann. Ian Kefilwe. Jona Lee.

She felt a little odd about the deference and formality in how they saw her. She was Naomi Nagata to them, and that meant not only their captain, but also the admiral of the fleet and the leader of the underground. They also knew her as Captain Draper's old shipmate, and there was a respect there she couldn't quite convince herself she'd earned.

The odder thing was seeing Alex with them. One boy— Caspar, his name was—hadn't even come over to join the *Roci*. Just to see Alex. The admiration in the boy's face was impossible to miss. Watching them all together was like seeing an extended family that had come together for a wedding. Or a funeral. Alex hauled them all on a tour, showing them the *Roci*. He called it an orientation, but it was more like showing off a prized possession. Or no. Not that. A part of his life he'd only ever been able to tell stories about, and now could point to in the flesh.

She made her exit as he was leading them down toward the machine shop, pulling herself up to the flight deck and her nearly complete work. The distraction of the new crew left her unmoored for a few minutes, finding her place and her train of thought. There was less to do than she'd thought.

She put the final orders in. *There is time to pull back*, Alex said in the back of her mind as the real one, decks below, showed his friends and compatriots something about how the *Rocinante*'s PDCs reloaded or the way the power grid had been rerouted to support the keel-mounted rail gun or something.

Somewhere far below, an unfamiliar voice laughed.

This was what he'd done. Where Naomi had locked herself away, Alex had gone with Bobbie and made himself a new crew, a new family. It amazed her that he'd done it so naturally that he didn't even notice. The only reason he didn't have a place with them was that he chose not to. Even this brief contact told her that they would have welcomed him. He'd built another place for himself in the universe.

She hoped she wasn't about to take it away from him. She encrypted the orders, opened the broadcast, and sent them out.

Chapter Forty-Two: Alex

Staging was important, but Alex hated it all the same. They didn't know what was waiting for them on the other side of Laconia gate. For all they knew, the *Whirlwind* could be squatting just on the other side, ready to blast them all one by one as they came through. Sure, the intelligence they had showed it keeping close to the main planet, but that wasn't a promise. The faster they got through Laconia gate, the better off they'd be.

That sounded great until it meant trickling the assembled forces from fifty-three systems into the slow zone, bunching them together before the first one went through to Laconia, and then diving through the enemy gate one after another as quickly as they could without vanishing. Then it got a little nervous-making.

"Was it always like this?" Ian, the new comm tech, asked. He was a Freeholder born and bred. Draper Station was as close as he'd ever been to another system. "Caspar said it used to be different."

"That's true," Alex said. "It used to be different."

The station at the center of the slow zone was growing darker as the days and weeks passed. It had cooled from a point of sun-bright whiteness to a threatening shade of orange. The surface of the slow zone that had been black and featureless still had the strange aurora look. If anything, that seemed to be getting brighter.

"This is the *Deliverance*," a voice said from the open comm channel. "We have completed our transit from Hamshalim."

"Copy that, *Deliverance*," Ian said. "*Benedict*, you're clear for transfer."

A few seconds. "This is the *Benedict*. Copy that. We are starting our burn."

Two hundred of the ships had already come through. Like the *Roci*, they were making their way to the Laconia gate. The others were still stacked outside their gates with Naomi's transition order. Without Medina control to keep anyone from going dutchman, they had to rely on her for their script. Which would work as long as not too many other ships came through in the same time frame. And as long as the behavior of the gates hadn't changed.

That wasn't the slow zone's only new risk, though. Alex could still remember coming through the Sol gate the first time. Back then, the slow zone had been a place of mystery and terror, alien artifacts and death. Before Medina, he'd have said that the decades had tamed it. Made the place into something known and under-stood. That it was capable of changes they didn't understand tore the scab off that wound every time he thought about it. He kept reaching for the drive control, wanting to edge the ship out through the gate just a little faster, a little earlier. He was heading to a battle with a vastly more powerful enemy, but at least that was known. Being reminded that they'd been building roads through a dragon's mouth left him jumpy.

That was the thing about hubris. It only became clear in retrospect.

"This is the *Benedict*. We have completed our transit from Hamshalim."

"Copy that, *Benedict*," Ian said. "*Chet Lam*, you are cleared for transit."

Alex reached for the drive controls, pulled back.

"You okay?" Ian asked as Alex unstrapped from his couch.

"I'm going to go get some tea. You want some tea?"

"I'm good," Ian said, and Alex pushed off for the lift. He wished they were under burn, not only because he wanted to get out of there, but because being on the float made moving through the ship too easy. If he could feel the effort of motion, maybe it would do something for his anxiety. As it was, it was just having an itch he couldn't scratch.

In the galley, he pulled out his hand terminal. There was one message in his outgoing queue, flagged to hold. He braced with his right hand and foot and spun his terminal slowly in the air like a pinwheel while he thought about it. The display, reading his orientation, flickered to keep up with its own rotation. After a few seconds, it started to annoy him. He grabbed it again and opened the message. His own face appeared on the screen. His voice came from the speaker.

"Kit. I'm about to do something, and it seems like I might not come back. It's risky anyway. And the last time I did something like this, I thought about you a lot afterward. I know me and your mom didn't get along there towards the end, and maybe I haven't been as good a dad to you as I could have been—"

He stopped the playback, looked at it for a long moment, and deleted it without sending. There was this idea that one message could change a lifetime of decisions you'd already made. The truth was, he hadn't said anything in there that Kit didn't already know. If Naomi's plan worked, Alex could go back and say anything that still needed saying in person. If it didn't, it was probably better for Kit not to have had communications from his rebel pilot father.

Belinda and Jona came in together with the subdued glow of two people who've been enjoying each other's private company. Well, they were in the hours before action. Alex could still remember a time when he'd taken some comfort that way himself. They nodded to him, and he nodded back like he didn't suspect anything. Truth was, as long as it didn't affect the ship's function, a little affection in the crew was probably a good thing. Holden and Naomi's relationship had been the unstated center of the *Roci* crew for a long, long time. That was part of why losing Holden had broken everything apart.

Now, here he was, and here was Naomi, back in the ship, doing something dangerous. It almost felt like old times.

His hand terminal chimed. It was Naomi.

"Admiral?" he said.

"Captain is fine."

"Yeah, okay," he said. "Felt weird saying that anyway."

"So. I'm about to do a thing."

"A thing?"

"Speechy, rousing-the-troops thing, admiral-of-the-fleet kind of thing."

"Ironically," Alex said with a laugh.

"This is serious," Naomi replied, but there was no scold in her tone. "We're three transfers away from having the whole fleet in here. I've sent my group assignments to the other ships. I thought I should make a statement. Something to the crew. Did Bobbie do that?"

Alex had to think. "Sort of, yeah?"

"I was really hoping you were going to say no."

"Nervous?"

"I think I prefer being shot at."

"Well, if this goes well, you'll get to confirm that. So that's a plus?"

"Might be."

"Okay, I'm on my way up."

Alex took a last long pull from the bulb of tea and tossed the rest into the recycler, then pulled himself back to the central shaft and up toward the flight deck. He felt his anxiety starting to shift, but he wasn't sure yet what it was becoming. Maybe excitement. Maybe fear.

By the time he got to his couch, Ian wasn't on the open comms anymore. The kid looked grim, lips pressed thin and fingertips dancing at the edge of the control monitor like they were looking for something to do there. Alex gave a thumbs-up as he strapped in. He didn't know what he meant by it apart from general emotional support.

Naomi sailed onto the deck. She was in formal blacks that looked like a uniform without quite being one. Against it, her gray-white hair didn't look old. It looked striking. Her face was serious and hard, her movements fluid and strong. She pulled herself into her crash couch, pulled the tactical readout to her station, and looked over the data there. Her ships. Her fleet. Every eye on the flight deck was pointed toward her. She glanced at Ian.

"Open ship-wide," she said.

"Yes, Captain," Ian said.

Naomi cleared her throat. It echoed through the ship.

"This is Naomi Nagata," she said. "We are about to make our transit into Laconia. We will be going into the heart of enemy territory. We all saw what the *Tempest* did to the inner planets' combined fleet. I know that's in your minds now. It's in mine too.

"But what we're doing here is different. We were not able to stop the *Tempest* when it invaded Sol—"

Stopped the shit out of it later, someone shouted a deck or two below. Cheers and hoots followed, but Naomi ignored them.

"We aren't trying to stop the *Whirlwind*. We're trying to move it. How exactly this will play out is going to depend on what we find when get through that gate. The exact tactics, we will be figuring out on the fly. The grand strategy, on the other hand, is set. We're going to destroy Laconia's construction platforms. The tool Duarte has used to make the *Magnetar* ships. To make *Storm*-class destroyers. To generate antimatter. All of that ends now. And with that, Laconia's attempt at empire. We are going to do that.

"Every ship in this fleet has a part to play. The most danger-ous role is the actual attack on the platforms. With luck, that will be us. Our battle group will be the *Storm* out of Freehold, the *Cassius* out of Sigurtá system, and *Quinn* and *Prince of the Face* out of Haza. Five ships, but we won't be alone. Every ship, every battle group, every member of every crew will be at our backs.

"This will be a long fight. It will be hard. But it will be won. So if you need food, eat now. If you need to visit the head, you have five minutes. After that, we're going through."

She killed the connection to the sound of cheers. On the float, there was no way to sink back into her couch, but if she could have, Alex was pretty sure she would. He pulled up his controls, selected the course profile he'd already laid in, and typed in a message to her.

THAT WAS GOOD. DID EVERYTHING IT HAD TO.

It popped up on her monitor. She smiled thinly. A few moments later, he got her reply.

I HATE PUBLIC SPEAKING. HATE IT. NEXT TIME, YOU DO THIS PART.

GET ME A NEXT TIME, he typed, AND I WILL.

Her laugh was barely a chuckle. It was a victory, getting her to relax even that much. It was strange seeing her in Bobbie's role. It was stranger to realize that in his mind, it was Bobbie's role. Not Holden's anymore. He wondered what else had changed while he wasn't watching.

"All right," Naomi said loud enough for the flight-deck crew to hear. "It's time. Alex?"

"Aye, aye, Cap," Alex said. He triggered the acceleration alarm through the whole ship, waited twenty seconds for any stragglers to get into a couch, and the *Roci* jumped up, eager as he was. The gel of the crash couch pressed back, cool against him, and he felt himself grinning. His HUD marked the pathway to the gate, and he started wondering how bad it might be on the other side. As the fear of staying in the slow zone faded, the fear of leaving it for Laconia ramped up.

Behind him, another ship's drive bloomed. The *Storm*. And then the *Quinn*. The *Cassius*. They'd timed it all out to the second. He felt the needle and then the surge of the juice. It was a hard burn for him, it was going to be hellish for the Belters. For Naomi.

He kept his eyes on the drive status, on the maneuvering thrusters. They were making the transit much faster than usual, and a misfiring maneuvering thruster at the wrong moment could throw them off course and into the swirling nothingness at the edge of the slow zone. He didn't know whether that would be a good death or not, and he wasn't interested in finding out.

Without visual telescopy, the thousand-kilometer circle of the gate wouldn't have been more than a speck on the monitor before they were already through it. Almost before he could register the passage, the *Roci*'s thrusters fired. The crash couches didn't hiss so much as click as they snapped to his right and then sharply back again. Alex's vision clouded a little at the edges, the blood in his brain stirred by the shifts of inertia.

The first thing was enemies. The *Roci*'s radar was already sweeping the system, her telescopes looking for the drive plumes and her radio array listening for the transponders of Laconian ships. Already five had lit up, but they were identified as Transport Union ships with legitimate business in the system. There weren't very many points of interest in Laconia system. It was still too new for the spread of human stations that Sol system had. There were some, though. An ice moon around the system's single gas giant had a scientific outpost on it. One of the inner, rocky planets had been mining titanium for half a decade. Rumor was that Duarte had set aside one of the Ceres-sized dwarf planets as the site of a massive art project that was underway. The first real enemy the *Roci* found was almost halfway to the empire's home. A pair of *Storm*-class destroyers already burning out toward the gate. And then, behind them, close to the planet, the unmistakable heat and energy signature of a *Magnetar*-class battleship.

Alex pushed his fingers to the control pad at his side and typed out a message.

NO GUARDS AT THE GATE. THEY DIDN'T SEE US COMING.

A few minutes later, Naomi managed a reply. OR THEY COULDN'T IMAGINE ANYONE BEING THIS DUMB.

He would have laughed if he could catch his breath. They'd been at eight gs since they came through. He'd done worse, but he'd been younger when he did it. The *Storm*, *Quinn*, *Cassius*, and *Prince of the Face* were all behind them, their trajectories making a thin fan pattern. At the gate, the first of the *Donnager*-class battleships emerged into normal space and angled off on a vector different from their own. The threshold level on Naomi's model dropped slowly on his screen, measuring mass and energy and safety. The moment it was low enough, the second battleship arrived. The light delay from the ring to Laconia was almost three hours. So everything they were seeing in system was from the past. But it also meant that the closest Laconian ship wouldn't know the enemy had arrived for a little over an hour and a half, and Laconia proper twice that. Alex didn't let off the burn. By the time the response came, their fleet needed to be scattered as far through the system as it could be.

If it had been football, Laconia would have had a world-class goalie and a couple of professional strikers against Naomi's team of four hundred grade school children and three *Donnager*-class football hooligans. Any head-to-head battle was a win for Duarte. So it was better that there not be any. Not until Naomi could pick them.

Alex switched over to visual telescopes and looked back at the receding gate. It was already tiny, but he could make out the drive plumes of the emerging ships when they came through like new stars being born. And behind them, the real stars and the wide, beautiful smear of the galactic plane. The same, more or less, as it always was.

Three hours later, the enemy destroyers killed their drives. Light delay meant that they'd seen the intrusion into their space and reacted, and the evidence of response was only just arriving. Alex wondered if they'd cut drives when they saw the *Roci* come through or if it had taken a few unexpected drive plumes lighting up their gate to make them nervous. If he'd cared enough, he could have done the math and figured it. He did enough to know that the news of their appearance hadn't reached Duarte and the Laconian capital and that it would very, very soon.

In his couch, Ian grunted. For a moment, Alex was afraid it was a medical problem. Some people reacted pretty badly to their first extended high-g burn. But then the message came from Naomi.

DROP THE BURN. WE HAVE A MESSAGE.

Alex thumbed the *Roci* back down to half a g. All around him, he heard the others gasp and sigh. He did a little of the same himself.

"Kefilwe," Naomi said. "Let's have that message."

"Yes, Captain," Ian said. "To your station?"

"I think we'll all be interested."

A woman not much older than Ian appeared on their monitors. She had sharp features, pale lips, and the blue uniform of Laconia, and her forehead was furrowed. Confused. Not alarmed.

"This is Captain Kennedy Wu of the Laconian destroyer *Rising Shamal* to the unidentified destroyer and its escort. You have made an unauthorized and unscheduled transit into Laconian space. Please cut your drives at once. If you are in need of assistance—"

Someone behind Kennedy cried out in alarm. Alex thought they said *It's the* Storm or *That's the* Storm. Something along those lines. The Laconian captain's concern changed to fear and anger in a heartbeat. Alex tried to put himself in her place. The stolen ship that had murdered the pride of her navy, killed the unkillable, and was now showing up where it had no business being. He and Naomi knew all their antimatter supply had gone up with the *Tempest*, but he watched Captain Kennedy wonder.

"Attention, *Gathering Storm*. You are to cut engines immediately and surrender control to me. Any attempt to approach Laconia will be treated as hostile and met with immediate and—"

A different voice called out. This time Alex was sure of the words. *More contacts. This one's big.* That had probably been one of the *Donnager*-class ships coming through. Captain Kennedy looked away from the message, checking something on another monitor, and the message ended.

"Well," Alex said. "I think they noticed us."

"Got to think High Consul Duarte's going to be having a distressing day, don't you?" Ian said.

Naomi pulled up the tactical display. The vastness of Laconia system simplified so much that all their ships pouring through the gate were a single, minuscule yellow dot.

"Orders?" he asked.

"They're coming for the *Storm* first," she said. "Bring us on a slower burn toward the gas giant. And get me a tightbeam to Captain Sellers on the *Garcia y Vasquez*. We'll make it look like we're open for a fight there, and the *Neve Avivim* can burn like hell to get around like they're going to make it a pincer. As soon as the destroyers commit to that, we'll change it."

"Copy that," Ian said.

Behind them, another ship came through the gate. Hundreds of drive plumes arced in shallow curves or wide, spreading like dust in a high wind.

The siege of Laconia had begun.

Chapter Forty-Three: Elvi

If she could have, Elvi would have moved her work someplace else. A lab of her own would have been best, her rooms with Fayez a damned close second. But the data was at the university and the Pen, so that was where she went. And at first, she resented it. The breakthrough came when she could finally put aside Cortázar's work on changing Duarte and get back to her own data.

Her reports from the dead systems felt like letters from a past life. The breathlessness she'd felt upon realizing that there were literally rains of glass on the one semihabitable planet in Charon seemed almost childish now. She looked back at it and saw her own wide-eyed wonder, and even felt an echo of it. The massive crystal flower with filaments running though the petals like vacuum channels, gathering the energy of Charon system's wildly fluctuating radiation and magnetic fields like daisies collected sunlight, if daisies had been thousands of kilometers wide. She still thought the crystal flowers could be a kind of naturally occurring inter-stellar life. And the massive green diamond...

She looked at that one for a long time before she understood what she was really thinking. Then she took a tablet with the readouts and data to Cortázar's private lab. She hated being in the room with him, hated having him at her back, but she didn't have an alternative.

"Yes," Cara said, when she looked at it with her flat, black eyes. "I know about that."

Xan was sleeping. Or resting with his eyes closed, which was probably the same thing from where Elvi sat. Cortázar, at his desk, scowled at the two of them—Cara and Elvi, leaning against different sides of the clear plastic cage like girls comparing lunches at university. He went back to eating a sandwich with an air of disapproval.

"Is there anything you can tell me about it?"

Cara frowned. Even that had a moment of extra processing that went into it. Like the girl, or the thing that had been a girl, needed to remember how to make movement first. Or maybe it was more like a kind of gross motor stutter. Elvi really needed to get back to that line of research at some point...

"It does...record?" Cara said. "That's not the right word. It's not like memory, exactly. It's more like everything all at once? Like the way a film is all the pictures that tell the story, and they're all there even when you only see one at a time? I'm not explaining this right."

"A gestalt," Elvi said.

"I don't know that word," the girl said.

Her hand terminal chimed at the same moment that Cortázar's system threw an alert on his monitor. Trejo informing them of an emergency meeting in his offices in half an hour.

"Problem?" Cara asked.

"Too many masters, not enough time," Elvi said. "I'll be back when I can."

Cortázar was already heading for the door. She had to trot

to catch up. A driver waited for them outside, managing to look obsequious and impatient at the same time. A cold wind was blowing in from the east, stinging Elvi's earlobes. It was her first winter on Laconia, and she understood it was likely to get a lot colder for a very long time before the warmth came back.

In the back of the car, Cortázar folded his arms and scowled out the window. The city was glittering, and there were banners up for some kind of cultural celebration. Elvi didn't know what it was. The streets they passed had people rushing down them in thick coats. A pair of young men ran alongside their car for a moment, hand in hand and laughing, before a security guard in Laconian blue waved them off.

It was hard for her to remember that a whole population—millions of people—was spread across the planet, living lives in a new environment while she tired her head in reams of data. In that, it felt a lot like pretty much every other city she'd spent time near.

"I heard you talking to the older subject," Cortázar said.

"Right?" Elvi said. "This is awesome." She lowered her voice, roughened it, and put on a fake Martian accent. "We thought it was two cases, but it's been the same case all along." Then, when Cortázar didn't respond. "Like Inspector Bilguun? How he and Dorothy were always on different investigations, and it turned out they were related?"

"I never watched those," Cortázar said. "I'm concerned about how you're treating the subjects."

"Cara and Xan?"

"You treat them like they're people," Cortázar said. "They aren't."

"They aren't rats. I've worked with rats. They're very different." Again, he didn't get the joke. Or didn't think it was funny.

"They are mechanisms created from the corpses of children. They do some things that the children did because those are the parts that the repair drones had to work with. Eros was only different in scale. The nature of the protomolecule and all the technology related to it has the same logic. On Eros, when it wanted a pump, it co-opted a heart. When it needed tools to manipulate something, it repurposed a hand. This isn't different. Cara and Alexander died, and the drones made something out of the dead flesh. When you talk to that girl, she isn't there. Something is, maybe. And it's made from parts of a human, the way I could stitch together a model catapult from chicken bones. You're anthropomorphizing them."

"Is it a problem?"

"It's inaccurate," Cortázar said. "That's all."

At the State Building, an escort led them to a conference room where Trejo and Ilich were already sitting. Ilich looked worse than usual, and the way things were, that was saying something. Trejo, on the other hand, seemed almost at ease. He gestured at the chairs, and Elvi and Cortázar sat. A display on the wall showed a map of the system—sun, planets, moons, and ships—like a virtual orrery. It seemed to her like it had a lot of ships in it.

"The research?" Trejo asked curtly. "Where do we stand?"

"Making progress. Steady progress," Cortázar said.

"Do you concur, Major Okoye?"

"We're finding new connections," she said. "You don't really know what's critical and what's just nifty until after the fact, but sure. Progress."

"We've had a development," Trejo said.

"What's up?" Elvi asked.

That was how she learned that the underground had launched a full-scale invasion. Trejo brought them up to speed as quickly as he could, then opened the floor to comment.

"The thing I care about," Ilich said, "is what they know that we don't. That's why this is a problem."

"I understand your concern," Trejo said, one palm up as if to say, *Please stop whining.*

"First, they all saw the *Tempest* stand up to their fleet. They knew what it was capable of. And we saw them destroy the same *unkillable* ship. We don't know what else they're capable of."

"The readings from Sol are consistent with the full complement of antimatter resupply we sent having been used," Cortázar said.

"And there isn't any more missing," Trejo said. "All that still exists is either being isolated on the construction platforms or was shipped to bomb ships in other systems. It's possible that they've been appropriated by the enemy since the loss of the *Typhoon*, but we haven't heard of any that have gone missing."

"So if it's not that," Ilich said, "then what is up their sleeve that they're willing to throw three hundred—"

"Four hundred," Trejo said. "More came through."

"Four hundred ships at us? Because unless they've all suddenly become suicidal, we have to assume they know something."

Elvi tended to agree with Ilich's point, if not with his tone. She also understood why Trejo seemed more at ease. After all the alien strangeness and political intrigue, a nice simple shooting war was a move back into his comfort zone. Not into hers, though.

"You let me worry about that," Trejo said. "I've already been in touch with Admiral Gujarat. The *Whirlwind*'s still not at a hundred percent readiness, but she's comfortable taking it out so long as it stays in-system. I have no interest in putting our last *Magnetar* through the gates anyway. We're ready for this. What we aren't ready for is the high consul's silence."

"Would seem strange," Cortázar said.

"Leading a secret task force focused on the things that killed Medina is plausible," Trejo said. "Reassuring, even. Staying silent in the face of an invasion is not. We need his face on this. No options."

"I'm not sure how we do that," Elvi said. "He hasn't had a really lucid moment since—"

"We make it," Trejo said. "I understand that this is a little below your collective pay grade, but I'm not interested in bringing a media team into the fold. We'll scan the high consul, get recordings of his voice, and generate a message to enemy and empire. You have some experience with imaging, yes?"

"I've run a bunch of animals through sampling pouches," Elvi said. "It's not really the same thing."

"We can make it work," Ilich said.

"Good," Trejo said, and stood. For a moment, Elvi thought the meeting was adjourned and started to head for the door herself. "Dr. Okoye. We're not waiting on this. We're doing it now."

The scanning device wasn't particularly bulky, but Duarte's room wasn't built for it. Kelly had dressed the high consul in his formal uniform and was helping him to his chair. The thought, as Elvi understood it, was that if they scanned the uniform into the same profile as the man, creating the false version would be simpler.

"There are going to be forensic traces," Cortázar said. "There always are."

"We have very good imaging programs," Trejo said as he tried to fit the lighting stick into its base.

"Other people do too," Cortázar said. "I'm not objecting to the plan. Just be prepared to discredit the people who say it's faked."

"Already on that," Trejo said, and stood. The lighting stick cycled through its spectrum, getting ready to catch the subtleties of Winston Duarte's skin and hair. He'd grown thinner since the break. His eyes still had an intelligence to them if not a focus, but his cheekbones had become more prominent. Elvi felt like she could see the skull beneath the skin, and she didn't remember thinking that before. Kelly brushed his hair, trying to put it into place the way he probably had before other addresses and announcements. Only Duarte wouldn't keep still. His hands were thinner, gray and dusty-looking, and he moved them constantly. His eyes rolled in his head like he was following butterflies no one else could see.

"Is there any way to make him sit still for a minute?" Trejo asked.

"He does sometimes," Kelly said. "Having people around agitates him. Give him a little time to settle."

Trejo muttered something but didn't object. Elvi waited with the others, watching the man who had, however briefly, been the god-king of a galactic empire. All she saw now was a lost man.

She remembered feeling the force of his personality the first time they'd met. The sense of being in the presence of something vital and irresistible. She saw something in the way his jaw fit against his neck that reminded her of Teresa. It was easy to forget that they were also people. Father and daughter. The same complicated, fraught relationship that human beings had been navigating since they'd developed language. Before that, probably.

Without really knowing why, Elvi stepped forward and took Duarte's hand. He considered it like it was a pleasant surprise. She knelt, smiling gently, and his gaze swam through whatever dark waters he lived in now until he found her.

"We just need to scan you, sir," she said. "It won't hurt."

His smile was gentle and filled with an unspeakable love. He squeezed her fingers gently and let them go. She stood back, getting out of the light and the scanning radius. Duarte looked around the room like a beneficent king in his dying hours until his attention landed on Cortázar.

"All right," Trejo said. "Let's get this done before—"

Duarte stood, his head tilted at an angle like he was remembering something half-forgotten. He stepped away from his chair. Ilich made a small, frustrated hiss.

"All right," Trejo said. "It's okay. Let's just get him back in position and try this again."

Duarte stepped over to stand before Cortázar. His attention seemed as focused as Elvi had seen since his fall. Cortázar smiled and bowed his head like it was something he knew he was supposed to do. Duarte's jaw worked, his mouth opening and closing, but the only sound he made was a small *oh*. He moved his hand in a soft gesture, like he was fanning away smoke, and Cortázar's chest bloomed out at the back. It was so slow, so gentle, that Elvi couldn't understand what she was seeing. Not at first.

It was as if Cortázar were an image projected on mist, and the mist was being blown away. Nothingness swirled through his chest, his face. And behind him, floating on the air, spirals of red and pink, gray and white, as ornate and beautiful as ink dropped into water. The air filled with the smell of iron. Of blood. Cortázar sat on the floor, his legs folding under him, and then slumped to the side with a long, wet exhalation. The left half of his head was missing from the jaw to the crown. His heart was still trying to beat in the open theater of his ribs, but the man was gone.

They were silent and perfectly still. Duarte looked up, his attention caught by something that made him smile like a child seeing a dragonfly, and his hands rose aimlessly. Trejo put the scanner down on the bed, turned, and walked quietly out of the room, pulling Elvi along with him. Ilich followed, and then Kelly, shutting the door behind them. They were all pale. The State Building was shaking under them, tremors that matched Elvi's heartbeat. She fought to breathe.

"All right," Ilich said. "Okay. That happened. That just happened."

"Major Okoye?" Trejo said. His normally dark face was pale and gray.

"I have never fucking seen anything like that. Ever," she said. "Holy *fucking* shit."

"I agree," Trejo said.

"He knew," Elvi said. "That's what this was. He knew about Teresa. Did you tell him?"

"What about Teresa?" Ilich asked. "What did he know about Teresa? What did she have to do with this?"

"Let's not lose focus here, people," Trejo said, leaning against the wall. "Mr. Kelly, would you escort the high consul to fresh quarters until we can get these cleaned?"

Kelly looked like Trejo had just asked him to put his hand in a meat grinder to see if it was running. For a moment, Elvi thought the man would refuse, but Laconians were a breed apart. Kelly nodded and walked stiffly away.

"We can do an announcement without him," Trejo said. "I can do it. As his...acting military commander. Pleased to accept the position. Thank him for his faith in me. Like that."

"We need to shoot him," Ilich said. "Whatever that thing in

there is? That's not the high consul. I don't know what the hell it is, but the only sane thing any of us can do right now is put a bullet in its brain."

Trejo drew his sidearm, took it by its barrel, and held it out toward Ilich. "If you're sure that'll kill him, be my guest."

Ilich hesitated, then looked away. Trejo holstered his pistol. "Major Okoye."

"I know," she said. "Another top priority. I'll get right on it. But..."

"But?"

"I know you told Cortázar to give me full access. I've never been entirely certain he did."

Trejo considered it. From the far side of the door, something rattled. A thump, like a piece of equipment had been bumped into, knocked over. If it had been a sound of violence, it would almost have been better. Trejo pulled out his hand terminal, thumbed in a code, and adjusted something she couldn't see.

"Major Okoye, you *are* Paolo Cortázar. You want to go through his room and check his underwear, you go right ahead. See what he's been eating. Check his medical records for sexual diseases. Read his letters to his God damn mother, I don't care. That man's life is an open book to you starting now. Find something useful in it."

"I'll do what I can," Elvi said.

"And Major? I know you were a civilian before you were appointed. You didn't come up like the rest of us, so I'm going to make this clear for you. If you say one more word about surrendering the empire? I will have you before a court-martial, and then I will have you shot. This is a war now. The rules have changed."

"Understood," Elvi said. "They've been doing that a lot lately."

"Ain't that the God damn truth," Trejo said. Then, "Colonel Ilich, you're with me. Let's draft this announcement."

Elvi walked out of the State Building like she was in a bad dream. Even the bite of the wind felt less real to her. Shock, she thought. I'm in emotional shock. That happens when people die in front of you.

At the lab, Dr. Ochida waved to her as she passed, and then looked concerned when she didn't wave back. She knew that she should have stopped and talked to him, but she didn't have any idea what she'd have said. In the private lab—*her* private lab— Xan and Cara were sitting in their cage playing a word game they used to pass the time. They paused when she came in, but didn't ask her what had happened. What was wrong.

The uneaten half of Cortázar's sandwich was still on his desk, wrapped in brown paper. Elvi threw it in the recycler and opened her work environment. All the reports and data feeds she'd been poring over for weeks. She split the screen and, with her new permissions, pulled up Cortázar's. She backed both up to the functional index.

His was a hundred and eighteen entries longer. Elvi felt something like anger, something like dread, something like the mordant pleasure that comes from being proven right about something shitty.

"What an asshole," she said.

Chapter Forty-Four: Naomi

The burn was long and it was punishing. Even with the crash couch distributing the pressure along every possible square centimeter of her body, Naomi ached her way through the hours. The only solace was the breaks for food and the head, and she kept those brief.

Laconia was a slightly smaller heliosphere than Sol, with nine planets, only one of them habitable. A single gas giant with somewhere between eighty and a hundred moons, depending on where the line was drawn. Two large planets out past that in the deep, and a rocky captured planet hardly larger than Luna with a retrograde orbit that swung high above and far below the plane of the ecliptic. Five planets in closer to the sun, the second of them being her target and the heart of the empire. A transfer station at the gas giant, and the alien construction platforms that orbited the inhabited world. That was her battleground, and she meant to have her forces diffused through it. On the enemy's side, the *Voice of the Whirlwind* at Laconia proper, the *Rising Shamal* and her sister ship, plus four more *Storm*-class destroyers.

Her couch on the burn was almost as isolated as her old shipping container. Her time, even if it was painful, was her own. She studied the maps until she could see them with her eyes closed.

And in the back of her mind, Bobbie waited. The memories and habits of decades spent breathing the same air, drinking the same water, being part of the same organism had made the woman a part of her. And the Bobbie in her head had a lot to say.

A campaign like this is an argument. You're trying to persuade the enemy of something. Talk them into it. And this time, here? You need to teach them that the danger of staying in place is greater than the danger of coming after you. For it to work, every lesson needs to support that one single thought.

The Storm-class destroyer *Mammatus ended its assignment in Arcadia system and rotated back to Laconia for resupply. The transit from Arcadia to the ring space was uneventful, apart from the now-familiar annoyance that the most recent set of repeaters had been sabotaged.*

The Mammatus' *transit into Laconia was very different. The moment the destroyer emerged into normal space, its sensor arrays were swamped by massive jamming from multiple sources. Half a dozen ships positioned just outside the ring gate flooded the* Mammatus *with radio and light. It took fewer than three seconds for the ship to reset, but by then five torpedoes—already launched and waiting for a target—were slamming into the ship. Informed by months of analysis of the captured* Storm, *the torpedo strikes were devastating. The* Mammatus *lost maneuvering thrusters along her port side and six PDC emplacements. Worse, it began venting atmosphere.*

Its counterstrike was late and weakened. The enemy PDCs took out the torpedoes as soon as they were launched, and with its mobility limited and its port vulnerable, the destroyer fled. Its burn toward Laconia and the prospect of safety was the obvious strategy, and easy to foresee. Compromised as it was, it failed to register the field of stealth composite–coated debris in its path until a swarm of uranium micrometeorites peppered its already-stressed hull, peeling back a section of the plating. A maneuvering thruster misfired as the power grid tried to compensate, sending the destroyer into a spin. Despite all that, it took five more torpedoes and a constant stream of PDC fire to kill it. The Mammatus *fought well and died ugly, but it died. Everyone in the system saw its last hour, even if the light delay meant they saw it far too late to act.*

Lesson one: You can't rely on reinforcements.

Days under burn stretched. Naomi slept when she could, studied the movements of the enemy and the reports of her fleet when she couldn't. Her knees ached from being bent just slightly backward by the acceleration. It hadn't all been in the same direction. Twice now, Alex had shifted them. Not a full flip-and-burn, but a change of vector that brought them closer to the gas giant. The Laconian destroyers in the system started a burn to match, and Naomi's three *Donnager*-class battleships—the *Carcassonne*, the *Armstrong*, and the *Bellerophon*—had redeployed as if to make a full engagement just outside the transfer station there. And then they had all broken off, scattering, while a dozen smaller ships dove sunward to the inner planets. The *Whirlwind*, capable of slaughtering any of them, stayed in place, leaving the chase to the destroyers.

She'd expected the battleships to draw off the Laconian forces, but they didn't. The destroyers followed her hunt group, pushing them to a long, arcing retreat up above the ecliptic. The destroyers turned back quickly, never venturing past the gas giant's orbit. It wasn't the repositioning she'd wanted, but it worked. It would do.

When the burn paused, she took a long moment before she

unstrapped, just to enjoy the physical relief of a gentle half g. Walking down the hall to the galley, her legs felt shaky and her neck ached.

The others—her crew—were already there, wolfing down bowls of noodles and mushrooms, talking and laughing. They sobered when she came in. She was the adult. The commander. Who she was mattered less than what.

She didn't mind that.

She found Alex in the cargo bay, opening an access panel. He looked like he hadn't showered in days. Probably he hadn't.

"Issue?" she asked.

"No. We're good. I was just getting a little less pressure on the water feed to this thruster than I'd wanted. Thought I'd tweak it while I had the chance."

"Good thought."

"I was hoping we'd be getting down to the inner planets by now."

"Early days," she said. "There's time."

The Bhikaji Cama *lumbered through the void, well behind the other ships. Its hold was open to the vacuum.*

Two groups of ships, eight in one and fourteen in the other, fired long-range torpedoes at the transfer station. The missiles burned hard, then went ballistic. Slightly fewer than three hundred warheads screamed through the black, all aimed at the transfer station, and all timed to arrive within seconds of each other.

And all of them, of course, were intercepted. Most were killed by the transfer station's PDCs, but a handful also fell to long-range countermissiles launched from the Whirlwind. *It didn't use its field projector, and wouldn't. Despite its power, the range was short, and the last time one had been fired in normal space, Sol system had lost consciousness for three minutes. The Laconians didn't want to risk their defense with a blackout.*

When the last of the torpedo barrage died, the expended hunt groups looped back, burning for the Cama. *There the crew put on mech suits and loaders, made their way into the cargo ship's vast belly, and came out with fresh torpedoes and water and PDC rounds.*

A week and a half into the campaign, at the time Naomi had specified, the Verity Close—*sister ship to the* Bhikaji Cama—*made the transit into the system and bent its path to the opposite edge of the system and opened its hold.*

Lesson two: We have thirteen hundred systems to resupply us. You have one.

"They're following the *Storm*," Naomi said. "I need to split you off."

On the screen, Jillian Houston scowled. "When the time comes, and you lure that murderous bastard of a ship away from Laconia, you're still going to have a planetary defense system trying to shoot you down. That's at minimum. You need me to eat that flak for you."

"If you're with the attack group, the *Whirlwind* won't budge. Not ever. I don't like it any more than you do, but your ship used to be theirs. They know it's the best tech in our fleet. They're not going to take their eyes off it. They think you're the number one threat because you are."

Despite herself, the younger woman smiled. "They're right about that."

"I'm redeploying you. Move to accompany the *Armstrong*. When the time comes—"

"I'll be part of the bait," Jillian said. "I don't love it."

"It's a risk. But it's worth it."

"Understood," Jillian said, and dropped the connection. Naomi stretched and checked her system. Eight more minutes before the next burn. She tried to decide if she wanted to wash off or get a bulb of tea. If she didn't pick soon, she wouldn't have time for either.

Or maybe she could do both.

"Alex. Postpone the burn for half an hour. There's something I want to do."

"You bet," Alex said.

Naomi went down to her cabin and her private shower, the map of the system in her mind. With the *Storm* on its own, she could reroute the *Carcassonne* and fifty or so of the other, smaller ships toward the transfer station. The *Roci*, *Quinn*, *Cassius*, and *Prince of the Face* would be a minor threat and could loop down sunward, using the innermost planet as a gravity assist.

There was a way that the whole process was like playing golgo. Judging her shot, how the ball would bounce and spin off the other balls, how the next person would react to that. How each decision changed the state of the table. The Bobbie that lived in the back of her head said: *A challenge of intellect, technique, and skill.*

Naomi saw how easy it would be to forget that the stakes were people's lives.

When the Laconian capital was surrounded—ships answering to the underground and the Transport Union at every angle throughout the system—the barrage began. The transfer station was forgotten. Not just long-range missiles, but rocks. Cheap, deadly. Every ship in the group sending nukes and accelerated titanium rods and holds full of gravel into intersecting orbits. Some moved fast, some would take months to arrive at Laconia—which was a message in itself about how long the underground was prepared to draw out the fight. Nothing targeted major population centers, but there was no way for Laconia to know that for sure. To be safe, they had to defend everything.

The barrage kept going, day after day. Rock after rock to intercept. Torpedo after torpedo to shoot down. An endless rain of threats, wearing them down hour by hour by endless hour. That was the third lesson: Playing defense means being endlessly ground down. Someday something will get through.

The Whirlwind *stayed in its place, guarding the gravity well over Laconia, but the destroyers ranged farther and farther. When the enemy came too near, Naomi's fleet scattered like children running from the police. Not everyone escaped. The* Tucumcari, *a rock hopper retrofitted to fight pirates in Arcadia, caught a torpedo on its drive cone and died in a ball of fire. The* Nang Kwak, *a private security company stealth ship two generations out of date, didn't dodge a line of PDC fire. Disabled, it tried to surrender. The Laconian ships destroyed it instead. There were others. A handful. Each of them one too many. And every chance Naomi had to strike back at the enemy, to lure them out and end one or two of them, she let pass. It was the cardinal rule that she sent to every ship, all through the system. Laconian military that came out after them went home intact.*

Because that was the final lesson she taught her enemy: It's safe to chase after us. It's how you'll win.

And it was a lie.

The first sign of fresh cheese in the mousetrap was the *Bellerophon* changing its drive signature. The *Donnager*-class battleship was burning away from Laconia, heading in the rough direction of the *Verity Close*. Even from half the system away, the drive plume would have been visible to the naked eye, a faint but moving star.

And then, for a moment, it blinked out.

The *Roci* and her three escort ships were on the float, skating on the far side of the sun from Laconia. She'd led them in toward the corona until even with pumping spare water onto the ship's skin and letting it evaporate, the built-up heat was at the edge of tolerance. Even when the temperature was in the error bars of normal use, it baked the resins and ceramic. The air smelled different, and it left Naomi and the rest of the crew jumpy and uncomfortable. But with Laconia's fighting ships near the planet, they were in a blind spot. Out of sight.

When the *Bellerophon*'s drive lit back up, it was dirty. Half a minute after that, it went off again. The way an apex predator lured lesser hunters by mimicking the sound of wounded prey, the *Bellerophon* called out for help. And Naomi's fleet answered. The *Storm*, the *Armstrong*, the *Carcassone*, and almost a quarter of the other ships started burning on courses that would meet the *Bellerophon*. The *Bellerophon* wasn't halfway to the *Verity Close*, but the light delay from it to Laconia was still over seventy minutes.

A malfunctioning ship would be interesting to Duarte and his admirals. An escort fleet coming to its aid looked like something more. It looked like a mistake. And an opportunity.

"Come on," Naomi said.

"Should I start up?" Alex asked.

"Put us at half a g," Naomi said. Even if it didn't work, they'd want to be out of here soon. As comms officer, Ian passed the word along to the other ships, and the *Roci* eased up from beneath her.

Two hours later, the *Whirlwind* moved. At high burn, she headed out toward the *Bellerophon* and the gathering escort ships. For anyone who'd seen the *Tempest* destroy the combined forces back in Sol, it was like seeing a shark darting toward a beach full of toddlers.

Three hours after that, several hunt groups on the other side of the heliosphere started burning in toward Laconia, and the destroyers went on intercept courses, ready for a slice of their own glory.

There was a point long before any battle came that was her window. Not just how long it would take the *Whirlwind* to get back, but how long it would have to decelerate before it could even start to reduce the distance to Laconia again. And the same for the destroyers. It was a window of time defined by mass and inertia, thrust, and the frailty of the human body. The time it would take even long-range torpedoes to reach them. Naomi ran the numbers, and she knew when they would see her and her little force diving in from sunward. And that it would be too late.

"Alex?"

"Ready when you are," he said.

"Let's go."

The burn was punishing, and it lasted hours. The distance from the sun to Laconia was slightly less than an astronomical unit. If they'd kept the burn going the whole distance, they'd have snapped by Laconia too quickly to see it. The flip came at the halfway point, and the braking burn was just as bad. Worse, because now the planetary defenses had seen them. Torpedoes darted out toward them, and died in the web of four ships' coordinated PDCs.

The planet itself was beautiful. Blue and white as Earth, with a greenish cast at its edge that was almost pearlescent. Naomi could make out the clouds. A cyclone forming in its southern hemisphere. The jagged, black-green line of its coast where the forests stood. Naomi fought to keep them in focus. The force of the burn was deforming her eyes.

THE WHIRLWIND HAS TURNED. STARTED ITS BRAKING BURN. IS FIRING LONG RANGE.

The message was from the sensor ops. One of the new people. She checked it herself all the same and agreed. If this didn't work now, it wouldn't work later. This was her only shot. Fingers aching, she sent a message to Ian, suffering in the next couch over. SEND THE EVACUATION ORDER. EVERYONE GOES FOR THE GATE NOW.

She heard him grunt and took it as assent.

Alex shouted, his voice strangled by effort and the g forces pressing at them. "Rail-gun fire. Brace. For. Evade."

The *Roci* bucked, lurched. At this distance, the rail-gun fire could still be dodged. The closer they came, the harder that would become. She pulled up the targeting arrays, and the beautiful blue-green sphere sprouted five red lines, as bent as tree limbs. The platforms. The targets.

TARGET ALL FIRE ON THE PLATFORMS, she typed. FIRE AT WILL.

It was too soon, but only by a little bit. And there was a chance for a lucky shot. Every second they spent in the firing arc of Laconia was another chance to die. Worse, another chance to fail.

INCOMING TORPEDOES FROM THE WHIRLWIND. ETA 140 MINUTES. Naomi deleted the message. By then, everything would be over.

"Cut the brake," she shouted. "Do it now."

The *Roci* fell onto the float and snapped around 180 degrees, ready to accelerate again. Ready to flee as soon as the enemy was finished. There would only be one run past the planet. If they missed, they lost.

The ship jerked, and Alex took them out of the path of another rail-gun round. The chatter of the PDCs ran through the flesh of the *Roci* like the ship was talking to itself and it was angry. Naomi's jaw ached with the tension and fear and the joy. The small, jagged red lines grew a fraction larger.

"Captain?" Ian said. "I have something."

"Not as helpful as you think," Naomi snapped. "What do you have?"

"I'm not sure," Ian said, and passed the comms controls to her monitor. It was an incoming message from the surface of Laconia, coded with an out-of-date underground encryption schema. An evac request.

Amos' evac request.

"Alex?" she said, and the ship jumped again, slamming her left and then right again, her crash couch whipping like the seat in a carnival ride. *"Alex?"*

"I see it," he shouted. He was out of breath. "What do we do?"

Chapter Forty-Five: Teresa

The *Mammatus* died, burning through Laconia's gate and being dismembered by the enemy ships, two nights before her birthday. The celebration was held in one of the minor ballrooms, with the same tasteful and understated decorations she always had. Silk banners with bright designs, glass candles that she'd loved when she was eight and been saddled with ever since, flowers raised in hydroponic farms in the city proper.

Soft music played over hidden speakers, all of it by composers and performers living on Laconia. Half of the guests were politicians and cultural figures—adults who'd come mostly to say they'd been there and to see who was in favor. The other half were her peer class and their families. They were dressed in stiff formal blues, just like she was. None of them seemed happy to be there. That was fair. To them, it was like having to go to school an extra session. They were nice to her. They had to be.

The sense of strained pleasure almost made her happy. All the adults had smiles like masks. They made a show of congratulating her, as if not dying for fifteen years in a row was an achievement to be proud of. But even while they pretended to be impressed by how mature and composed she looked, their eyes were darting around the room, trying to find her father. She had to play her role, but at least so did they. No one talked about the invasion. Not even Carrie Fisk, wearing a champagne-colored gown and a fixed grin, looking like she wanted to bolt for the door. Camina Drummer wasn't there, and Teresa wondered what had happened to her. Either she'd lost control of the Transport Union and wasn't anyone anymore, or she'd been part of planning the invasion, in which case she was lucky if she wasn't in the pens.

Teresa didn't care. She had her own problems.

It was still thirty interminable minutes before the dinner was served when Ilich escorted her to the dais at the back of the room. The crowd got quiet without being prompted. Like they'd been trained. She'd been trained too. She knew what to do.

"I want to thank all of you for coming tonight," she lied with a smile. "I am honored to be in your company now, and for all the years that I've lived here among you. My mother, as you all know, died when I was very young. And my father carries his own burdens. He can't be with us here tonight because his duties to all of us don't allow him time even for simple, honest pleasures like this."

Plus which, he's out of his fucking mind. Lost to all of you and to me as well, but I'm the only one who knows it, you poor fuckers. She grinned widely at the pattered soft applause, taking an angry pleasure in the raw perversity of the situation.

Teresa caught sight of Elvi Okoye in the back of the room. Yellow gown, and her husband at her side. She was holding a wineglass in her fist like she was trying to break the stem. She knew too.

"All of you have been a family to me as I grew up," Teresa said. Ilich's words didn't sound like something she'd say, but none of them knew her well enough to catch it. "I am humbled. And I am grateful." Another round of applause, and Teresa bowed her head like she was actually grateful. Like she actually cared whether the enemy ships burning from the edge of the system reduced everyone in the room to ash.

You're one of the angriest people I know. She wore the words now like a shawl, smiled and made her little bows as if they weren't statements of contempt.

"Please enjoy this evening as both my guest and my father's," she said, and stepped down. The guests turned back to each other, oppressed and anxious and thinking less about her than the return of the *Gathering Storm* and its pirate fleet. Reminiscing less about Teresa Duarte's childhood and more about the violent death of the *Heart of the Tempest.*

Teresa made her way across the ballroom, avoiding Ilich and Connor and Muriel. She found Elvi and her husband not far from where she'd seen them. From the dais, Elvi had looked stressed. Close up, she looked angry.

"Is everything all right?" Teresa asked.

Elvi started, snapped out of whatever other place her mind had been by Teresa's voice. For a moment, she didn't speak, and when she did, it wasn't convincing. "Fine. Everything's fine."

"Well," Teresa said. "Except."

Elvi nodded, the movement hinging in her chest so that it seemed less like agreement, more like someone preparing for violence. "Yes. Except," Elvi said.

The chime rang, calling them all to the dining room like the most privileged cattle in the universe. When they started walking, Teresa stayed at Elvi's side. Her husband was using a cane and wincing as he walked. That was fine. Teresa wanted to go slowly.

"I was wondering, Dr. Okoye," Teresa said. "The *Falcon.*"

Again, it took Elvi a moment to come back. "What about it?"

"I wondered how the repairs were going. With everything that's going on ... I mean, it is built for sustained high burn. It has breathable liquid crash couches."

Elvi shuddered.

"Those are unpleasant," her husband said.

"But still. If the fighting got close? You'd be able to use it to get away?"

Elvi and her husband exchanged a look that Teresa couldn't quite read. Like there was another conversation going on that she couldn't quite hear.

"Unfortunately," Elvi said, "the *Falcon* was deeply, deeply compromised."

"I got a new foot, toenails and all," her husband said. "But that ship's still in pieces."

"I really don't think it'll come to evacuation," Elvi said. "None of those ships are even going to get close to the planet. And everything Admiral Trejo has at his disposal will be used to keep us all safe."

"Maybe you should put a push on the repairs, then," Teresa said. It came out sharper than she'd meant it to, but Elvi laughed. That was interesting.

"Maybe I should," she sighed, and then they were in the dining room, and Teresa was escorted to the high table with Ilich and a half dozen guests more honored than Elvi Okoye.

The meal was a feast. Fresh pasta. Lobster tails taken from actual lobsters. Gently marbled steak grown from the finest samples. The centerpieces were all Laconian flowers, and they smelled of mint and iron and resin. No one asked after Dr. Cortázar. That, Teresa had come to understand, was one of the unwritten rules. When someone disappears, don't ask why. She wondered if they'd mention her after she left. Assuming she could find a way.

She looked over at the table where Elvi Okoye sat. Her husband was telling a story, his hands shifting in exaggerated gestures for the delight of their tablemates. The doctor was lost in her own thoughts. Teresa wondered whether they'd been lying about the *Falcon*. She wasn't sure, and she wasn't even sure how she'd find out.

Regretfully, she discarded the plan to have them escape the invasion and take her along. She'd have to find another plan.

Days passed. Weeks. The invasion proved harder to stop than anyone liked. The state newsfeeds kept a brightly optimistic view, treating the threat as more of an annoyance by disgruntled idiots than an actual danger to the empire. She still had the access her father had given her to high-level secret reports and briefings, but even if she hadn't, she'd have known the reports were bullshit.

Apart from the peer class, her lessons were ignored now. She only saw Ilich at meal times. He didn't repeat his threat to force-feed her, but he didn't need to. She understood the terms of their relationship now. Having lost control over so many other things, he made up for it by controlling her. There was nothing she could do about it.

"They've slipped this time," Ilich said. "They panicked. That great huge ship of theirs lost part of its magnetic bottle, and they're all going to defend it."

"That doesn't seem like a bad idea," Teresa said, forcing herself to take another spoonful of the corn chowder. It should have tasted good, but the texture was slimy and it was too sweet. She swallowed and didn't gag.

They were sitting in an enclosed courtyard with ivy growing up the walls and artificial lights that mimicked the sun. The actual weather was a snowstorm that was covering the gardens in white up to her ankles. Muskrat had been running through it with a wide canine grin and little balls of ice forming on her coat. Ilich hadn't let her in with them while they ate because she stank of wet dog.

"It wouldn't be if there was any way for them to actually mount a successful defense. They've survived as long as they have by running away. We could kill any of them whenever we chose to, but Trejo was waiting."

"For what?"

"For this," Ilich said. He did love the sound of his own voice. The calm, patient instructor unfolding for the clueless little girl how the universe really worked. It had seemed like kindness for so many years. Now it looked like condescension. "The three Martian battleships are the irreplaceable core of their makeshift fleet. And when you have something that important, it's natural to try to protect it. But it's an emotional response, not a tactical one. And that's why they're going to pay for it."

He had said all the same things at breakfast—eggs, sweet rice with fish, seared spinach with almonds—and she let him repeat himself now. Nothing he said mattered to her anymore.

"The *Whirlwind* will go through them like they weren't there. There'll be some cleanup afterward. We won't get all of them. But their major ships? They're even putting the *Storm* in harm's way for this. It'll be a bloodbath. And I—"

His handheld chimed. Ilich scowled and accepted the connection. Teresa put down her spoon and took a sip of water. Trejo's voice was clear, and it was tense.

"I'd like a word with you in the tactical office, Colonel."

Ilich didn't speak, only nodded, rose, and walked away. Teresa was forgotten behind him. Which suited her just fine. When he was around the corner, she got up and opened the door for Muskrat. The dog trotted in, huffing under her breath. Teresa took out her handheld and opened the tactical reports.

There was a moment of sorrow. They came now and then. The memory of her father telling her that she could be the leader they needed her to be. That he wanted to train her with all the things he knew, just in case. She'd been a different girl then. He'd been a different man. She missed both of them. But the pain faded quickly, and she didn't lose anything by letting it go. It always came back.

The tactical reports were strange, and it took her a moment to understand what she was looking at. The broken-down battleship had repaired itself somehow. And the fleet of enemy ships was running away, but not for the far edges of the system. They were going to the gate. Most of them, anyway. Almost all of them.

All of them but four. And those were in a path to Laconia. It was suicide. Four ships against the *Whirlwind*. Unless they had a secret weapon the way they had in Sol system…

But no, the *Whirlwind* couldn't stop them. It had already gone too far, and even with the braking burn, its vector was still away from the planet. It was fighting its own mass and momentum like a swimmer struggling against the outgoing tide. The destroyers were in the same position. They'd been tricked. Lured away with only the planetary defense grid to protect them.

Which, in fairness, it probably could. Four ships weren't much. They'd do some damage, though. And there was only one target. She was sitting in it.

She knew she should be scared, but she wasn't. She put down her handheld, scratched Muskrat's back, and thought. It didn't even feel like solving a problem so much as remembering something she'd always known. She pulled up a map of the system and added in the enemy ships, their burn times. A lot would depend on how they made their braking burns, but Ilich had taught her enough about battle tactics that she could make an educated guess. Make a plan. If she called the enemy down, they'd kill her or take her as a prisoner. She needed something she could trade for passage. She didn't know what that was.

And then she did.

Muskrat looked up at her when she laughed. The thump-thump-thump of the dog's tail against the ground was reassuring. Without thinking, Teresa took another spoonful of chowder in her mouth, frowned, and sprinkled some salt over the bowl.

Her next bite was better.

The timing was bad, but it could have been worse. She left out the window as if she were sneaking out to see Timothy again. It felt familiar. Comforting. She knew it was the last time she'd see her room or her things. The last time she'd sleep in the bed that had been hers since she was a child. But her father had been dead for months, and it turned out she'd already done her mourning.

Muskrat whined as she slipped out, dancing from one paw to the other.

"You can't come this time," Teresa said. "I'm sorry."

The dog whined, lifted graying eyebrows, and wagged hopefully. Teresa leaned back in and gave Muskrat one last long hug. Then she was out the window and gone before she lost her resolve.

The first step—the hard one, really—was getting to the cell. It was night. The snow was still falling lightly, but it wasn't up past her shins. Getting out wouldn't be the problem.

There were two guards watching over the cells, a man and a woman. They braced as she walked into the room.

"I wish to speak with the prisoner," she said.

They looked at each other.

"I'm not sure—" the man said.

Teresa made an impatient sound. "Trejo has asked me to question him before. It's about the assault. We don't have time."

The fear did it. The sense of an enemy almost at their gate, and the confidence that someone in power was taking care of it. Even if the voice of authority had just turned fifteen. They led her into the cell. She felt shaky with excitement. It was like being one of the adventurous women she'd watched on her screens, only it was real. She was doing it.

Holden sat up, blinking against the sudden light. His hair was standing at odd angles and his face had pink lines across it from the pillow. Teresa turned to the male guard.

"You stay," she said. Then to the woman, "You have something to subdue him? An electrical prod?"

"Yes," the woman said.

Teresa held out her hand, and the woman drew a black, shining weapon with a grip all along its length. It looked like an ear of burned corn. The female guard showed Teresa where the safety was and how to trigger it.

"That's really not called for," Holden said. "Whatever this is? I'm not going to fight it. You won't need those."

"I'll decide that," Teresa said. She nodded the female guard out.

Then it was just the three of them: Teresa, Holden, and the male guard. It was the last chance to turn back. She could still change her mind...

Teresa flipped the safety clear.

Holden flinched, prepared for the pain and shock, and Teresa drove the weapon into the guard's belly and pulled the trigger. He went down hard, not even trying to catch himself.

"Okay," Holden said after a long, stunned moment. "That was weird."

"We don't have much time. Come with me."

"Um...no? I mean, I think I'm going to need a little more explanation about what's...ah..."

Teresa felt a burst of anger, but there wasn't time for it. She started stripping the male guard's uniform off, undoing zippers and buttons, tugging at his sleeves.

"Your people are coming. Your old ship. The whole invasion was a ruse get them close."

"There's an invasion?" Holden said. And then, "They don't tell me much. But you're saving me?"

"I'm *using* you. I need to leave. You're my ticket onto those ships. Now hurry. We don't have time."

Holden pulled the uniform over his prisoner's jumpsuit. Confinement had left him thin enough that the extra cloth just about filled out the difference. Teresa took the stunner from the fallen guard's belt and his access key, and opened the door. They marched out together. The woman at the guard's station had time to look confused before Teresa put her down.

"This is actually happening, right?" Holden said as she led him down the hall toward the forensics lab. "Because this is a very realistic dream if it's not happening."

"This is happening," Teresa said. And she meant, *I'm really doing this.* "I have an implanted tracking device. They're going to be after us as soon as we go."

"Okay," Holden said.

"Here," Teresa said. The door was locked, but the access key opened it. She stepped into the dim room. Timothy's belongings had been moved around in the weeks since she'd been there, but they hadn't been taken away. She walked from table to table, her fingertips brushing each container they passed. It was here. Someplace. It was right here.

"Hey," Holden said. "This is…the pocket nuke? The one Amos had?"

"Yes," Teresa said.

"And I'm standing right here next to it."

"You are."

"And you're comfortable with that," he said. "This is a *really* weird night."

She found what she was looking for. The screen glowed as it powered up. She felt the seconds slipping away. Somewhere far above the planet, the rebel ships were already coming close. Already engaging with planetary defense. The files came up, lockouts and protections broken weeks ago. She looked for the file for evacuation protocol and, without hesitating, shifted the call to active.

"What was that?" Holden asked.

"I called for evac," Teresa said, liking how adult the word felt in her mouth. Not *evacuation. Evac.* "All we have to do is get to the pickup."

"Sure," Holden said. "Sounds easy."

Chapter Forty-Six: Elvi

Going through Cortázar's hidden files was the work of days. It was horrifying. Winston Duarte had believed in Cortázar's ability, but more than that, he'd assumed that he had the man's loyalty. And that the things Cortázar told him were true. The experiment to change Duarte's body using the tamed protomolecule had been the worst kind of science—uncontrolled, unethical, speculative, and risky. He had overstated his certainty to Duarte, underplayed the risks, moved ahead on therapies based on best-guess understandings of Cara and Xan, and collected data obsessively. His notes and records read like a horror story.

As the unexpected changes had come—Duarte no longer needing sleep, developing new senses—Cortázar's comments shifted. Elvi wasn't sure the man himself would have seen it, but a plaintive quality started coming into them. A sense of jealousy about all the things he could only experience secondhand. A hunger was growing in Cortázar's mind that he didn't seem aware of.

Elvi tried to go though it all in more or less chronological order, but that was harder than it sounded. For one thing, the enemy fleet in Laconia system shook her concentration. Trejo was reassuring. No more antimatter was missing, and the mere nuclear warheads raining down on the planet were a trivial danger, easily avoided. Elvi started having nightmares about it, and her sleep suffered.

Also, chronology wasn't how Cortázar had structured his work. Notes and results on the protomolecule-modified telomerases that had been one of the first steps were in the same files as preliminary scans and data on Teresa Duarte. NIR and magnetic scans of Cara and Xan from his initial research had annotations about Duarte's blood protein structures from as recently as the day before Cortázar died.

There were some advantages. Bouncing back and forth in time, Elvi began to feel the shape not only of Cortázar's obsession but also of the path he'd gone through. The change. His earliest notes on Teresa had been much like his plan for Duarte with some variations. His decision to instead kill her and give her to the repair drones hadn't come until fairly recently.

It was almost out of character too. Everything she saw about Cortázar had been about pushing forward, trying things that were new. He was a discoverer at heart, and the choice to pull back and study something foundational more deeply was unlike him.

It was a long time before she figured out who had convinced him to change from his usual strategy.

When she did, she only told Fayez.

"Holden?" her husband said, incredulous. "James Holden put Cortázar up to killing Teresa?"

"I don't know," Elvi said. "I think so. Maybe."

They were getting ready for Teresa's birthday party. The dress Elvi had ordered up was a yellow that had looked good on the screen, but she wasn't sure about it now. It was the first time she'd seen Fayez in days. She'd been going to the labs early and leaving them late. Would have done so again if Trejo weren't insisting on keeping up appearances. Between Duarte's conspicuous absence and the breaking news that the enemy had gutted a destroyer called the *Mammatus*, it was a harder and harder job.

"That doesn't make sense," he said, but the way he said it meant he believed her. "Why? Why would he do that?"

The note hadn't been hidden. It was in with Teresa's medical scans and blood data, as simple and open as a reminder to get fresh socks. *Holden's argument correct? Consider restarting protocol with additional subject.* And every note after that, wherever it had been added, assumed that Teresa Duarte began the process already dead. Another note seemed to be a list of talking points for breaking the news to the high consul.

With your life span, she was going to die before you did anyway.

The important thing is that we learn as much as we can from her ~~death~~ *sacrifice.*

Children die in nature all the time. This is just like that.

But the one she kept returning to was *Holden's argument correct?*

"She was...*is* heir to the empire," Elvi said. "If Cortázar turned her into a lab rat, it might destabilize Laconia. Take away the clear line of succession?"

"That's an awfully long game," Fayez said, pulling on his shoes. "It explains how Holden knew. But then why did he warn us?"

"Couldn't go through with it?" Elvi said. "Holden's a decent person. Decent people have trouble with murdering children. Second thoughts. Doubts. I don't know. I don't understand anything anymore."

"That's the thing about alien biologies and transdimensional monsters," Fayez sighed. "At least they're not *supposed* to make sense."

Elvi sighed in agreement and looked at herself in the mirror. Her leg was healed in that it didn't hurt, but the gouge the aliens had left in it still showed. A lighter patch of skin with a puckered edge.

"Pass me the cane?" Fayez asked. And then, as she did, "Are you going to tell Trejo about it?"

"I don't know. I'm not going to keep it from him, but...Cortázar's dead and Holden's under guard. There's nothing for Trejo to do about it, and he's juggling enough already. How do I look? Do I look like a wrapped candy? I feel like I'm dressed up as caramel chocolate."

"You look beautiful," Fayez said, rising to his feet. "You always do. Also, that you care at all what any of these people think is charming beyond words."

"What makes you think I care about what they think?" she said. "I asked *you*."

He laughed and stepped close to her. She put her arms around his chest, leaned her head against his shoulder, closed her eyes.

"I hate this," she whispered. "I hate all of this so much. I'm so tired of being scared and overwhelmed."

"I know. I'm a little adrenaline-sick myself. Maybe we should leave."

She chuckled. "Tender my resignation? Say I'm exploring options elsewhere? Maybe go back to teaching."

"I'm serious," Fayez said. "You still have command codes for the *Falcon*, don't you?"

She pulled back to look him in the eyes. He wasn't joking. She knew all his smiles, and this was a serious one.

"There are two separate navies out there ready to shoot us down," she said.

"Maybe. Or maybe we could defect. Or just run and take our chances. It couldn't be worse. This place is made out of palace intrigue and fear as much as it is concrete. And that's before it was the target of an ongoing rebellion looking to nuke it to glass. Say you're going to look for residual transdimensional radioactive ectoplasm or something. They won't know. With the shooting war going on, they're not going to come after little old us. We could make a break for it."

It was crazy, and worse, it was tempting. Elvi imagined waking up under some other sun. In a hut on a mountain on a world without a name.

"You've wanted out since you got here," Fayez said. "You've put a brave face on it, and I have too. But this is killing you by centimeters."

"Let me think," she said. "I'll think about it."

They walked to the ballroom together. For a quinceañera, there weren't many teenagers. Even as large as the room was, Elvi felt like the air was close, stale, rebreathed. She got a glass of wine, hardly aware of who she'd gotten it from. Pulled by her exhaustion, trying to make sense of Holden, her fear of the fighting in the system, and the beautiful dream of leaving Laconia behind, she was in a fog.

"Is everything all right?"

Teresa Duarte was at her side. Elvi had been aware the girl was speaking, but she hadn't listened. "Fine. Everything's fine."

Teresa smirked. "Well. Except."

"Yes. Except."

The dinner chime came, and Elvi tried to move away, but Teresa stayed at her side. The girl was working herself up to something. With a forced casualness, Teresa said, "I was wondering, Dr. Okoye. The *Falcon*."

Elvi felt a chill of fear. "What about it?"

"I wondered how the repairs were going. With everything that's going on…" The girl put on a smile that was meant to be calming. Innocuous. "I mean, it is built for sustained high burn. It has breathable liquid crash couches."

"Those are unpleasant," Fayez said, trying to move the subject away.

Teresa would not be turned aside. "But still. If the fighting got close? You'd be able to use it to get away?"

Elvi glanced at Fayez. His expression went blank. So he was wondering it too. They'd been in their private rooms, but that didn't mean they couldn't be monitored. Was Trejo watching them? Was this a test?

"Unfortunately," Elvi said, choosing her words carefully, "the *Falcon* was deeply, deeply compromised."

Fayez followed suit. "I got a new foot, toenails and all, but that ship's still in pieces."

Teresa's expression shifted, but Elvi wasn't sure what it had shifted into. Elvi kept going, saying the things someone who had never thought of fleeing would say. "I really don't think it'll come to evacuation. None of those ships are even going to get close to the planet. And everything Admiral Trejo has at his disposal will be used to keep us all safe."

"Maybe you should put a push on the repairs, then," Teresa said, harshly. *As if there is anything I would rather do*, Elvi thought, and chuckled.

"Maybe I should," she said as they entered the dining hall. Teresa finally had to go her own way. It felt like escaping something. Fayez put his arm around her waist and let himself be guided to their table.

"That was uncomfortable," he said.

"Don't read too much into it," Elvi said as they found their chairs. "Also? Don't forget it."

The dinner proceeded, the conversations stayed on safe ground. Elvi put Holden and his role in Cortázar's murder plot out of her mind. She didn't think of it again for weeks, and by then things were already out of control.

"Holden escaped," Ilich shouted. The speaker on her hand terminal overloaded a little, flattening his voice. She tried to bring herself back to consciousness. It was hard to believe she'd actually drifted off, but the dreams still had their claws in her.

"The attack," she said.

"They're here. They're fighting right now, and Holden's free."

She sat up on her bed. She was still wearing her uniform, though it was creased from sleep. She rubbed the back of her neck with an open palm. Holden was out of his cell at the same moment that the underground's strike force was engaging with the defense grid. There was no way that could be coincidence. Somehow, he'd known it was coming. And he was getting out before the bombs hit the State Building.

Her gut clenched. The fear that had been growing since the enemy's gambit became clear tightened her gut. *I'm going to die. Fayez is going to die. We're not going to see dawn.*

"Tell Trejo," she said. "You need to tell Trejo."

"He's busy commanding the defenses. Holden stunned the guards. They're still unconscious."

"Jesus Christ," she said. "What do you want me to do about it?"

Ilich stammered for a few seconds. "I don't know what to do."

"Secure the pocket nuke that's in the same facility, then get a security team and start looking for him," Elvi said.

"Yes," Ilich said. "Right."

He dropped the connection. Fayez was sitting on the edge of the bed, his eyes wide and alarmed.

"That man," Elvi said, "is not great in a crisis. I'm starting to think he's got the wrong job."

"Elvi," Fayez said. "Holden. *Teresa.*"

It only took a moment. "Shit."

She went for the door, Fayez close behind her. The air was cold and wet and stinging. It numbed her face instantly. Flakes of snow swirled down from the sky like ashes from a huge fire. The distant ground-based rail guns made a constant rolling thunder, and the clouds flickered red and orange in the north as they fired. Far above the clouds, a battle was going on. Elvi put her head down and ran. Fayez came along just behind her, his footsteps falling in and out of sync with her own.

An alarm sounded, screaming out across the State Building and its compound. She didn't know if it was about the war or the escaped prisoner.

At Teresa's rooms, she pounded the door with her fist and shouted the girl's name, but the only answer was frantic barking. The thunder of the planetary defenses grew louder, almost deafening. Something terribly bright happened somewhere above the clouds and turned the white snow-struck landscape to noon for three long seconds.

"We need to take shelter," Fayez said, and Elvi kicked Teresa's door. Fayez did too. It seemed like it wouldn't be enough. They'd beat themselves against it forever and never get through. And then the frame gave way, the door slammed inward, and Teresa's dog ran out into the night, barking madly.

"Get inside," Fayez shouted, but Elvi was already following the dog. It bounded through the fallen snow, throwing up ice like dust. Its bark was urgent, and it led Elvi on. She couldn't feel her feet well, and her wounded leg burned and ached, but one foot went in front of the other.

Snowfall and the battle light had changed the gardens into a vision of hell. She didn't know where she was, didn't know where the State Building was, couldn't tell where she was going, except that she was following the trail of paw prints and broken snow.

She should have gotten a gun. She was a major. Someone would have given her one if she'd asked. Better, she should have called Ilich and the security team. It was too late, though. She couldn't turn back, and she had to believe that the James Holden she knew would listen to her. Would hear her. Would stop whatever his plan was before the girl got hurt.

The dog vanished into the gloom ahead, barking and howling. She'd been stupid. She'd been overworked. Duarte and Cortázar and the war and the things from beyond time and space. They'd overwhelmed her and she'd lost sight of the girl who was right in front of her and the man who'd planned to kill her.

All the panic and the fear and the driving need to flee distilled into this moment, this doomed rush, the snow, and the howls of the dog.

And voices.

"Stop!" Elvi shouted, and her voice was hoarse. "Holden, stop!"

The trail led almost to the fence. High in the darkness, the mountain beyond the State Building reared up, transformed by snow and darkness into a vast gray wave. And there, in a snow-filled gully, James Holden stood in a black guard's uniform. His hair was wild and his skin was pale except for two bright-red patches at the cheeks where the cold had bitten him.

The dog capered and yapped at his side, and Holden raised a hand like he was seeing an unexpected friend at a cocktail party. But there was another voice. Teresa's voice, scolding the dog and telling it to be quiet.

"Holden," Elvi gasped. Now that she was slowing down, her side hurt like someone was stabbing her. "Holden, stop. Don't do this. You don't have to do this."

"Do what?" he said. And then, "Are you okay?"

"Let her go. It won't fix anything to hurt her."

Holden's forehead furrowed, and for a moment, she could see the young man he'd been the first time she'd met him, decades ago on a different planet. She held tight to the chance he might still be the same man, somewhere deep inside.

"Hurt who?" he said, and pointed at Teresa. "Her?"

"I know what you did," she said, trying to catch her breath. "I know you put Cortázar up to it."

"We have to go," Teresa said. Elvi noticed for the first time that the girl was doing something in the gully. Digging away a drift of fallen snow. Holden's sleeves were crusted with ice where he'd been doing the same.

"She's just a kid, Holden. Whatever your plan is, she doesn't have to be part of it."

"I'm more part of *her* plan at this point," he said.

"We have to go!" Teresa said. "We don't have time for this. Muskrat! Shut up!"

The dog wagged, happily ignoring the order. Footsteps came from behind Elvi. Fayez, stumbling through the snow. A deep, rolling sound came from the north. The earth trembled, and the rail-gun flashes stopped. Without their voices, the night seemed weirdly silent.

"What's going on?" Fayez said.

"I'm leaving," Teresa said. "I'm trading their prisoner for a way out, and I'm leaving. His ship is coming for us right now, and we have to get to the rendezvous."

"He tried to get you killed," Elvi said. "You can't trust him."

"I can't trust anyone," Teresa said, and the weariness and bitterness in her voice belonged to a much older woman.

"No," Holden said. "That wasn't about Teresa. That was about you. Hey, Fayez."

"Hey, Holden," Fayez said, and dropped to his knees at Elvi's side. Snowflakes landed on his hair and stayed there, unmelting. "I don't understand."

"This has all been about you," Holden said. "Literally from the minute I found out about the alien rip-in-space thing that showed up on the *Tempest*, I've been trying to get Cortázar out and you in his place. All this?" He gestured at the now-quiet sky. "I don't know anything about it. I haven't been in touch with anybody. None of it's been me."

Elvi shook her head. "I don't understand."

"I got you the job," Holden said. "I'm the one who told Duarte you'd been studying what killed the protomolecule engineers. And yes, I talked Cortázar into getting himself in trouble. And then I tried to rat him out. It was the only thing I could think of that Duarte would care about enough to get rid of his pet mad scientist. And since you were the expert, you'd get the promotion."

The punch in her chest was betrayal. She felt betrayed. She'd seen Sagale and Travon die because of Holden. She'd almost lost her leg, almost lost her husband, suffered through everything because of him. "Why would you do this to me?"

"I wanted to get someone sane and rational in charge before Duarte did something stupid that we couldn't take back." He lifted his hands and then let them fall, a gesture of powerlessness. "I'm not sure it worked, but it was all I could do."

Teresa stood up. Her black sweater was white with ice. "We can get through. The space is big enough. But the second I'm off the grounds, security's going to know it. We can't stop running once we start."

Holden nodded, but his eyes were on Elvi. "I'm sorry," he said.

Make up for it. We're here. Take us with you. And in the other half of her mind, the labs. The pens. The *Falcon* and all the data she'd acquired with it, still waiting to be sifted through. Was Ochida going to take it up if she left? Would he be better than Cortázar?

Was there anyone, anywhere she'd trust with this more than she trusted herself? And the enemy—the deep enemy—had tried to hurt them already. Was looking for a way. Her leg throbbed like it was reminding her of the black things between the spaces. Was someone else going to stop them?

She looked at Holden's face. He was one of those men who was going to look boyish until the day he died. *Fuck you for putting me in this position*, she thought. *Fuck you for making* this *the right thing for me to do.*

It wasn't what she said aloud.

"Go."

Chapter Forty-Seven: Naomi

A^{*lex?*"}
          "I see it," he shouted. "What do we do?"
A wave of disorientation washed through her, like she had started floating again without having stopped the first time. The ship jumped and shuddered around her as she pulled up the record of Amos' mission and cross-checked. It looked real. If it was false, it was convincing.

The plan was to hit the platforms and then burn hard to get away before the enemy forces could get back. She'd given them a wide window for it. Adding in a surface landing and extraction...

But if she didn't, and Amos really was waiting. Or Jim.

"Naomi?" Alex asked again. "What do we do?"

"Take out the platforms," she said. And then, "First. We take out the platforms first."

"If we're going to land, we have to slow down," Alex said.

She needed time. She didn't have it. The *Roci* shifted hard, then fell away, slamming her against her straps as their rail gun fired.

"Get me options," she said.

"Coming up," Alex said, and the thrust alert came on. They were flying into the enemy barrage, and she was slowing them down. "Ian! Tell the others to match my course. We're putting on the brakes."

She pulled up the tactical, and the drive came on, pushing her back into her couch and the coolness of the gel. She couldn't tell if it was the evasive dodging or the changes in acceleration or her own sense of doom that left her feeling nauseated, but it didn't matter. She pulled up the tactical display, ran it through the *Roci*'s system, and prayed to nothing in particular that a solution existed.

Their information on the defense grid was pieced together from Transport Union ships that had moved through the system. Five weapon platforms, flat black and resistant to radar. They were in higher orbits than the alien construction platforms, and spaced around the planet in a web that put any approaching ship in the sights of at least two and usually three. They were already firing at Naomi's little strike force, and whatever technology they were using to compensate for the rounds they fired, it didn't make a heat or light plume that she could use for targeting.

The construction platforms were closer to the planet, long and articulated, with filaments coming off of them like something in a microscope slide of contaminated water. They shimmered with light. There were five of those too, all of them in near-equatorial orbit.

The plan had been to approach with the ships close together so that they would all be covered by the same defenses and dilute the incoming fire between them. Then, when they were close, the *Cassius* and the *Prince of the Face* would split off, wrapping around the spinward side of the planet while the *Roci* and the *Quinn* cleaned up anti-spinward. Then they would all burn hard for the ring gate and the hundreds of systems beyond to hide in.

That had been the plan. Now it was the same, but slower. More time in the enemy crosshairs. Less chance of escaping unharmed.

Ian shouted over the din of PDC fire, drive resonance, and thruster burn. "*Cassius* is requesting permission to break off. They're ready to make their run."

"Confirmed," Naomi shouted. "Let's do this."

"With them gone, the bad guys are going to have more guns for us," Alex said. "We're about to get real bumpy."

"What the hell has it been up to now?" Ian asked.

"Walk in the park, kid," Alex said.

On her tactical display, the *Cassius* turned, its drive plume leaning in toward the other three as it slid toward the far side of the onrushing planet. A few seconds later, the *Prince of the Face* did likewise. As they slid away, a new bloom of fast movers jumped up from the Laconian defenses.

"How many of these missiles can we take?" Naomi shouted, and a voice she didn't know yelled back, *PDCs at sixty percent* as if that answered her question.

"We can start doing damage of our own in eighty seconds," Alex said. "Seventy-nine."

"Lock on the construction platforms," Naomi said. Her legs felt like they were on the verge of cramping. Her monitor was throwing three low-priority medical alerts. She ignored them. The ship moved hard to port, fighting to get out of a rail gun's firing arc. They were getting close enough that dodging after the rail gun fired was getting hard.

"Permission to hit their weapons, Captain?"

"No," Naomi said. "The construction platform goes down first." She might die. They all might die. Even if they did, they didn't have to lose.

She fought the temptation to grab weapons control herself. The fear and the tension left her muscles trembling, and the evasive shifting was coming faster and harder. She wanted a sense of control. Of being able to bend the next minutes to her will. Trusting a crew she'd barely met with everything was like flying blind.

"*Prince of the Face* reporting that the *Cassius* took a rail-gun hit," Ian shouted.

"How bad?" Naomi asked, already pulling up the sensor array data to see for herself. By the time Ian spoke, she knew.

"The *Cassius* is gone."

The odds shifted in her mind again. If the *Prince of the Face* was lost too, it would mean looping around Laconia to catch the surviving platforms. She'd only just taken on the risk by slowing down, and she was already paying the price.

She took comms control and opened a connection to the *Prince of the Face*. As soon as it went through, she started talking.

"This is Naomi Nagata of the *Rocinante*. Kill your braking burn. Go back to the initial strategy. In fast, kill the construction platforms, and burn for the gate. Do not decelerate further. Do not wait for us."

"Reconegut, *Rocinante*," a voice came back. The accent was pure Ceres Station. "Geh cahn Allah, sa sa?"

On her tactical display, the *Prince of the Face*'s drive plume died, and the ship seemed to leap ahead, rushing toward its target by burning less.

"We're almost in range," Alex said.

"I don't care how much you have to dance," Naomi said. "Just get us there."

"Ten more fast movers coming from the defense platform," Ian said. "PDCs are at fifty."

"Alex?"

"Doing what I can," he said. "Give me thirty more seconds."

Naomi opened a channel to the *Quinn*. "Report."

"We took a few rounds in engineering and our machine shop," a young man's voice answered. "We're okay for now."

"*Rocinante* is lining up a shot. Cover us."

"Copy that," the *Quinn* said.

The *Roci* slammed to port, and then again. Naomi's crash couch whirled, keeping the impacts against her back no matter what direction they came from.

"I really. Wish. They had fewer rail guns," Alex said from between clenched teeth.

"At least we can dodge," Naomi said.

"We can until we can't," Alex said, and the *Roci* stuttered under her as their own rail gun fired. She pulled up the image of the alien platform, still much too far away to see with the naked eye. Even with the *Roci*'s system stabilizing the image, it jumped and vibrated. Naomi leaned in, willing the shot to hit. At this distance, even a mistiming in the shot, a small unanticipated vibration, could mean they'd failed.

The image whited out for a second as an enemy missile died close enough to their line-of-sight to confuse the sensors. It came back in time for her to see the platform shudder and shift. The complex structure seemed to pull in like it was wrapping itself around an injury. It thrashed once, a widespread spasm. The shimmer of lights danced along its spine and out through the structures of its arms, and then it began to unspool. Like a tight-wound thread dropped into water, it relaxed and spread. The rigid shape softened and collapsed on itself, scattering through the emptiness over a vast Laconian ocean. Bright lines of energy like lightning or dying nerve impulses shot along it as it grew dark and drifted apart. The *Roci* shook and shuddered as the alien structure gently, gracefully died.

Alex let out a sigh that was part relief and part awe. Naomi knew exactly what he meant. She tried to open a connection to the *Prince of the Face*, to report the kill and check in, but the body of the planet blocked it, and there weren't any repeaters she could use. From here on in, she had to go on faith.

Alex turned off the drive. They'd braked. If they'd kept it going, the *Roci* would have started moving away from the planet again. They were in orbit now. Being on the float should have been a relief. It felt like a threat.

"Where's the next one?" Naomi asked.

"Coming up," Alex said. "It's behind the horizon line now. We'll have it in eight and half minutes."

"Let's start knocking down some of these weapons platforms. See if we can get a little peace."

The *Roci* kicked again, and the PDC chatter was joined by the deeper, subtle thrum of the torpedoes launching. Naomi found herself grinning despite the pain.

"What's that?" Naomi said. On the surface of the planet, near the center of one of the continents, a brightness was lighting the thick clouds from beneath. City lights. The capital. Laconia. And just north of it, a bright and burning light, rising up through the atmosphere in a perfectly straight line of fire and smoke.

"Huh," Alex said. "That's surface-based rail guns."

"Were we expecting those?"

"First I've heard of them."

"That's going to make landing a lot harder."

"Yes, it is," Alex said, and dragged the *Roci* out of the path of the incoming fire. "Kind of makes you wish the pickup was a little farther from the most guarded part of the planet, really."

"We'd meant to do this a long time ago," Naomi said. "It looks like they built up in the meantime."

She checked her maps. The city was almost beneath them now. This was as close to Jim as she had been in years. If the *Prince of the Face* was on time and target, there was only one platform left. On her monitor, one of the Laconian weapons platforms blew, taken out by a combination of a rail-gun round from the *Quinn* and two of the *Roci*'s remaining torpedoes.

It would be so easy to order the drop. Fall through the rough Laconian air, make the pickup, and kill the last platform on her way out.

If she was sure she'd make it. If she was so convinced that she'd live through it that she could risk wasting everything they'd done until now. And she wasn't.

"Steady as she goes, Alex," Naomi said.

A sudden bang like a detonation shook the ship, deafening her. She waited for the hiss of lost air, the silence of the vacuum, and it didn't come.

"What was that?" she shouted.

"Debris hit," Ian said. "We've got a hole in the outer hull."

"Watch our pressure. If we start leaking, tell me."

"You got it."

"I've got the last one," Alex said.

Fast movers on our back. PDCs at thirty percent. Naomi pulled up the visual tracking. They were so close now, she could see the curve of Laconia in the scopes, the milkiness of its high atmosphere.

A connection request came in. The *Prince of the Face* had cleared the planet and had line of sight for a tightbeam. She accepted it.

"Give me good news," she said.

"Clar y muerte," the *Prince of the Face* said. "Up to you now, boss."

"Thank you for that," Naomi said.

Another rail gun from the surface.

"Another what?" the *Prince of the Face* asked.

"We're getting fire from the surface," Naomi said. "It's fine. Continue with your flight plan. Get out of here. Do it now."

"Maybe etwas can can do," the *Prince of the Face* said, but before she could ask what they meant, Alex said, "I've got lock."

"Do it," Naomi said.

The *Rocinante* bucked again. The rail-gun round left a faintly glowing trail, superheating the almost-absent air that it passed through. Naomi held her breath. The rail-gun round touched the distant platform, and her sensors went dead. She pulled up the ship status. All the sensor arrays had tripped to safe. Overloaded.

"What's—" she started, and the ship screamed. She grabbed the edge of the crash couch as it whirled crazily. They were tumbling. A shock wave moved through the barely present gas out past the edge of turbopause, still strong enough to send them spinning like a kid's toy that had been kicked. The lights flickered, died, and came back on again. The bones of the ship creaked, and the roar of maneuvering thrusters filled her ears as Alex fought to bring them back to stability. The sensor arrays were still resetting, and Naomi felt the rail-gun rounds cracking up from the surface unseen. She waited to hear them snap through her ship. Hole the reactor. End them.

When the sensor arrays blinked back, the construction platform was gone. A corona of superheated air danced where it had been, green and gold and red.

"I think they may have been making some more antimatter," Alex said, dryly. "Not sure that was the best idea."

Naomi didn't respond. Something was happening on the surface of the planet. The ground defenses where the rail-gun rounds had originated was reading hot. Nothing was firing. She tried to connect the death of the platform with it, but the pieces wouldn't fit. Something else had happened.

A connection request came. The *Prince of the Face* again. Naomi took it. "Did you do something? What did you do?"

"Still had demi-hold á plasma torpedoes, yeah?" the other ship said. "No use for. Dropped them on your rail-gun base, que? Clear your way. Question is what did *you* do? That a *nuke*?"

"Nothing so trivial as that," Naomi said. "Thank you, *Prince*. We're good. Now get out."

"Already gone," the ship said, and the connection dropped. She sent a tightbeam to the *Quinn*. It answered immediately.

"We're seeing all enemy weapons platforms in the hemisphere disabled," a young man said. "We have a half-hour window before anything cycles to this side of the planet."

"Go," Naomi said. "We have a pickup to make on the surface."

They were silent long enough Naomi thought she might have lost the connection.

"We're your escort, *Rocinante*. Do what you need to do, we'll be here. If we were rated for atmo, we'd go with you."

"Negative, *Quinn*," Naomi said. "Burn for the gates. That's an order."

A moment later, the *Quinn*'s drive plume bloomed out bright and huge, and the *Rocinante* was left alone in the wide sky over Laconia. Naomi looked around her. There was smoke in the air, but no alarms were going off. Her crash couch had pushed one of her medical alarms back to normal, but the other two showed elevated cortisol and blood pressure. No one was shooting at her, and it felt strange.

"Alex?" she said. "Are we ready to go down?"

"Checking," he said. "That debris hit fucked up our aerodynamics, but...I can make it work. It'll be choppy as hell."

"Can't scare me," Naomi said. "Get us down. As soon as you can."

Below them, Laconia was in night. There was a beauty to it. Apart from a faint bioluminescence where the distant sea met the shore, the land was dark. The only light was shrouded by clouds. This was what Earth would have looked like, more or less, before the first electric light. Before the first satellite, the first orbital shuttle. Before Mars. Before Ceres. Before the Belt. It was the heart of a galactic empire, and still as bare as wilderness. Auberon and Bara Gaon had more cities. Earth had more history. Every place had the dream of what it could become.

Dreams were fragile things to build with. Titanium and ceramic lasted longer.

"Captain?"

She looked over at Ian. He was a boy. He was probably older than she'd been when the *Canterbury* died and she'd first set foot on the *Rocinante*, and he was just a boy.

"Kefilwe," she said.

"I was wondering if I could take the comms controls back," he said. "I...It's my duty. If you..."

"Sorry," Naomi said, shifting them back to his station. "Old habit. That was rude."

"Just trying to feel useful," he said through a tentative smile.

"All right," Alex said. "We're as close as we're going to get. And more time won't help us."

"Take us down," Naomi said. The maneuvering thrusters fired, slowing the ship and letting it drop. Alex turned them back toward the cloud-blanketed city already carried hundreds of klicks away by the planet's rotation, tilted down the nose, and tapped his controls. The maneuvering thrusters roared again.

Less than a minute later, the *Rocinante* hit air.

Chapter Forty-Eight: Teresa

Teresa pushed through the cold and the darkness of the flood channel, hunched down. A slush of almost frozen water and slime soaked her shoes and the hem of her pants. Clearing the entrance had numbed her hands, and now her fingers were starting to hurt. Not bringing gloves when she left only felt like the most recent in a long line of terrible choices.

Behind her, Muskrat whined.

"I told you to go back," Teresa said, but the dog ignored her. If anything she stayed closer. And behind Muskrat, the heavy footsteps and rough breath of James Holden.

The slush under her feet grew thicker, more solid. A few more steps, and she was standing on solid ice.

"We're almost there," she said.

"There?"

"The other side of the flood channel."

"Is that the pickup?"

"No, we have to get to the mountain."

"Mountain. Right," Holden said. "Okay."

A thin oval of gray the size of her pillow swam out of the darkness ahead. A drift of fallen snow blocked the way out, but not enough to stop her. Teresa stamped forward, pressing the snow down, compacting it, then scrambling forward to do it again. Somewhere in the State Building, an alarm was going off. The security forces alerted to her escape. She hoped that the battle would be distraction enough to lend her time.

"You're going to get soaked," Holden said.

"I'm going to get *out*."

He was quiet after that.

She scrambled out into the world. The wall of the State Building was behind her, the stretch of the wilds ahead. Holden emerged more slowly, and Muskrat with him. The trees had pulled in all their leaves, and the snow stuck to their trunks like a million featureless masks. Everything was transformed. The same and not the same. For the first time, she felt a prick of uncertainty. This was her place. She knew it and how to navigate it. Or at least she had until now.

She headed down the first path. Her breath plumed white and thick with every exhalation, and moving helped to keep the cold at bay. She wished that the flashes and roar of battle were still there, if just to help light the way. She told herself that it meant the rescue ship was almost there. And that she had to hurry.

The path through the forest seemed brighter than the sky above them. The snow was thicker here, rising up almost to her knees. Muskrat huffed and pushed, forging a path beside hers, and Holden followed along in the furrows they made. The snow was still falling. Small, hard flakes that tapped against her cheeks and melted down like tears.

There were tracks in the snow where animals had passed, and one of the trees had a long, fresh rip in its bark where something looking for food had dug deep into the hibernating flesh. Teresa wondered if animals did that on other planets, or if it was only here. For a moment, the implications of what she was doing rose up and threatened to overwhelm her, but she pushed the thoughts aside. She wasn't going back now. Not even if she could.

Something moved in the trees to her left, and she felt a moment of panic. A bone-elk leaped across the path and away, the exoskeleton of its legs clattering like stones rolling down a hill. It was nothing.

She made what she thought was the right turn, and the path grew steeper. The mountain loomed up in the darkness. Not really a mountain. An artifact so ancient it was covered in stone. Or one that had been made that way. History so deep, a forest had grown over it, and seasons passed against it like days.

She pushed into the clearing where the evacuation ship was supposed to land. It was wide and flat, with a slope that rose toward the distant summit on one side and a clear view of the State Building on the other. In the falling snow, the buildings with their softly glowing windows seemed farther away than they were. Like something seen from fairyland. With the flash and roar of the battle gone, it looked peaceful. It wasn't, but it looked that way.

Behind her, Holden came to the clearing. He had pulled his arms inside the shirt for warmth, the sleeves flapping empty against his sides. He squatted down in the snow.

"Are you all right?"

"Out of shape," he said. "Next time, I'm working out more. I'll convert a corner of my cell into a gym or something."

She'd had enough conversations with him now to know he was telling a joke without his voice signaling that it was a joke. No one else in her social life did that, and she found it irrationally annoying. It made every exchange into a puzzle that had to be decoded to see if it was sincere or not. She pushed the irritation away. There were a lot of things people did that she'd never had to be patient about. It was time to start learning that skill.

"This is where I met him," she said.

"Met him?"

"Timothy," she said. "Amos."

"Oh," Holden said, and looked around. For a moment, he was silent. "It's beautiful. I mean, weird. But also beautiful. I wish I'd seen more of Laconia. Not just the gardens."

"Me too," Teresa said, and stared at the low, gray sky. "Where *are* they?"

Without the trees to shelter them from the wind and the effort of pushing through the snow, the cold grew sharper. Holden seemed to fall in on himself, arms wrapped tight, head resting on his knees. Muskrat went and sat beside him, the dog's wide brown eyes concerned.

Teresa knew about hypothermia. She didn't feel bad herself, but Holden was older and he'd been in prison for a long time. It had weakened him. She thought about going and sitting beside him too. She remembered stories about people caught in the wilderness making structures in the snow to capture and share body heat, but she didn't know how that worked. She wondered, if the evac ship came and Holden was already dead, what they would do with her...

A blast of frigid air came down the mountain, pulling the top layers of snow up in brief whirlwinds. Teresa took a step toward Holden. Maybe she could take him to Timothy's cave. Just until the ship came. Take him there, and then she could come back herself and lead the rescuers to him. If there were rescuers. If this worked.

A trickle of black dread seeped through her body. This had to work.

"I'm sorry you had to find out that way," Holden said.

Teresa looked at him. She couldn't remember if delirium was part of hypothermia, but it seemed like it might be. "Find out about what?"

"The whole killing-you thing. Pushing Cortázar into it. It wasn't personal."

Teresa looked him. A miserable man, hunched in the snow. She knew that she should feel angry. She was angry all the time these days, and at everyone. She tried to summon up the rage, but it didn't come. She could only feel sorry for him.

Holden took her silence as something it wasn't. He kept talking. "It wasn't supposed to get you hurt. I was putting a wedge between your father and Cortázar. That was all. You were the only thing that would do that. Everyone saw how much he loved you."

"Did they?"

Holden's nod was slow to start, like he was already turning into ice. "There was a woman I knew. Long time. She used to say you can't judge anyone by what they say. You have to watch what they do."

"She *said* that."

"I recognize the irony. But I watched what she did too. How she made people like her. How she made them afraid. I'm not good at the second one, but I was pretty good at the first part."

"Because of her?"

"In part. And I watched what your father did with you. How he treated you. And I used that. I'm sorry."

"Yeah?"

"Not repentant," he said. "Just sorry."

"So sorry that you'd do it again the same way?"

"I'd try to move it along a little faster, but yes. Sorry that it was my best move."

Teresa looked up into the clouds again. The snow swirled down at them. Her fingers and toes were starting to burn. There still wasn't a ship.

"It's okay," she said. "I knew you were the enemy. You did what enemies do. It's worse when it's your friends."

"That's true," Holden said. And then, "Cart's coming."

She listened and heard it too. The electric whine of a security cart. The way the snow muffled sound, it had to be close. She looked around for someplace to hide, some way to escape, but the snow would give her away no matter where she went, and Holden couldn't run anymore.

"Stay calm," she said. "I'll handle it."

A moment later, Holden rose to his feet, and Muskrat looked up at him, concerned. The dog's expression said, *Maybe you should sit back down. You don't look steady.* Holden scratched between her ears.

There were voices now. She made out two of them. Maybe a third. Down the path that led back to the State Building, a light began to dance. Headlights on a cart moving fast through the fallen snow. Voices calling her name. The cart rolled into the clearing and stopped. Three men in it. Two wore guard uniforms like the one Holden had stolen. The third was Colonel Ilich.

Ilich leaped out, pistol raised at Holden.

"Put your hands up," Ilich shouted. "Now!"

"Okay," Holden said, poking his arms back into his sleeves, then lifting them. "I'm not armed."

"Teresa, get in the cart."

"No, you get in the cart," Teresa said. "I'm not going anywhere with you."

Ilich turned toward her, shock in his eyes. She watched him understand, confusion slipping seamlessly into rage.

"Get in the fucking cart," Ilich said.

"Or you'll shoot me?"

The two guards looked at each other nervously, but Ilich walked toward her. He kept his pistol trained on Holden, but his eyes were on her.

"No, I won't shoot you. But I'll put a guard on you every moment for the rest of your life."

"You don't control me anymore," Teresa shouted, and Ilich laughed.

"Of course I do. That is literally my first duty. Make sure the girl eats. Make sure the girl sleeps. Educate her. Socialize her. I am your fucking mother, and I am telling you to get your spoiled, egotistical, self-centered ass into that God damn cart!"

"I won't," she said, and crossed her arms.

Ilich seemed to deflate. For a second, she thought she'd won.

"You will," he said, "or I'll kill your dog."

He lowered his pistol a degree. It was like the volume of the world turned down. Teresa could still hear everything, but at a distance. She waited for the gunshot, sure it was coming. That she wouldn't be able to stop it. *Don't do it, I'll come* tried to find its way to her throat, but she was frozen. Her throat wouldn't work any better than her legs. Ilich shook his head once, just a centimeter one way and then the other. He turned to check his sights on Muskrat, but the shot that rang out wasn't from him.

Back at the cart, something was happening. Teresa couldn't tell what it was at first. Her mind tried to make it into the two guards wrestling with each other, except one of them toppled out the side of the cart and fell into the snow. The violence in the cart kept going on. In her peripheral vision, she saw Holden step in front of Muskrat, his arms still lifted, but Ilich wasn't paying attention to that now.

"Captain Erder! Report!" Ilich barked, but no one answered. Instead, the guard still in the cart shrieked once. Something wet snapped, and the screaming stopped. Everything was perfectly still. Ilich took a step toward the cart, then another.

Timothy boiled out from the shadows behind the cart, sprinting through the snow. His eyes were black, his skin gray. Ilich fired and a smear of blackness appeared on Timothy's bare ribs. He hit Ilich like he'd fallen from a great height and sent the man's legs up in the air as Timothy bore his torso down into the snow.

It had all happened too fast. She didn't know if the pistol belonged to one of the guards or if he'd taken it from Ilich. Only that it looked smaller in Timothy's hand. Muskrat barked happily and wagged her tail, scattering the snow.

Holden slowly let down his arms. "Amos?"

Timothy—Amos—stood up over Ilich and went perfectly still for a moment, then said, "Hey, Cap. You look like shit." Below him, Ilich gasped, the wind knocked out of him by the violence of Timothy's charge.

"You've been prettier yourself, one time and another."

"Well, you know how it is." Amos turned his dark eyes to her and nodded down at the snow where Ilich lay, still wheezing. "Hey there, Tiny. This guy a friend of yours?"

Teresa started to say yes, and then no, and then she understood what he was asking.

"No," she said. "He's not on my side."

"All right," Amos said, and fired the pistol twice. The muzzle flash was the brightest thing in the world.

"How did you find us?" Holden asked, swaying on his feet.

"This asshole," Amos said. "I been tracking him every time he came out from the compound over there. Figured sooner or later, I'd get a shot at him. You made a good distraction."

"Did you have to kill him?" Holden asked.

"Just evening up the score, is all. Are you sure you're okay, Cap? You seem kind of fucked."

A dozen questions pressed at Teresa's mind—where have you been living, how did you survive without any of your things, how badly are you hurt, why aren't you dead—but what came out of her mouth was, "Aren't you cold?"

Amos looked at her, thought about the question. Snowflakes were landing on his bare chest and melting there. The hole in his ribs where he'd been shot wasn't bleeding. After a moment, he shrugged. "I'll live."

Before Teresa could say anything more, a powerful, deep roar came from somewhere high above them. Her first thought was that they'd started an avalanche. She imagined herself and all the others wiped away by tons of snow rushing down the mountain. But then she saw the lights in the sky.

Amos took her elbow, leaned close, and shouted in her ear, "We should get back to the tree line."

She let herself be led, Holden and Muskrat following close behind, as a huge ship fell from the sky. The plumes of its maneuvering thrusters melted the snow in the clearing away in an instant and set the security cart rolling. Teresa huddled back among the dormant trees, her hands over her ears, until the roaring stopped and Amos tapped her shoulder.

The ship was a fast-attack frigate. A very old Martian design. Its sides were a patchwork of different plating materials. Steam rose all around it, and the cooling metal and carbon-silicate lace ticked and popped. Teresa walked out toward it with a sense of awe and joy and profound accomplishment. She'd done it.

The airlock opened, and a man in no kind of uniform looked down into the darkness and the mist and the snowfall.

"Who's there?" the man's voice called.

"Alex?" Holden shouted.

Almost conversationally, the voice said, "Well, holy shit."

A rickety metal stair ladder descended. Holden went up first, his steps unsteady at first, but more sure the higher he went. Muskrat paced at the bottom of the stair anxiously.

"I don't know," Teresa said to her. "This is why I told you to stay in my rooms."

"Go on up," Amos said. "I got this."

Teresa put her hands on the bright metal and climbed up toward the hands of strangers reaching out to help her aboard. And behind her Amos, balancing without his hands because his arms were filled with dog. The black wound on his side didn't appear to bother him. The man waiting for them laughed when he saw Muskrat, and the dog wagged uncertainly at first.

The locker room seemed to be on its side, Holden and a bald, dark-skinned man embracing and grinning at each other. Timothy—no, Amos hauled up the ladder, and the airlock door closed behind her.

She'd practiced for this moment. *I'm Teresa Duarte, and I'm giving you back this prisoner in exchange for passage out of Laconia.* Now that it had arrived, it seemed like that was all just given.

"You got to come up to the flight deck," the dark-skinned man said. Alex, Holden had called him. "We gotta get out of here, but I'm not letting either of you two sons of bitches out of my sight."

Teresa followed them, unsure what else to do. Amos walked with her through the sideways lift and flight deck. A beautiful older woman with curly white hair pulled down almost over her eyes was waiting there. When she saw Holden, she took a long, shuddering breath. The prisoner took her hand.

"All right," Alex said. "Everybody strap in. We're off this mudball."

A rough cheer rose all around her, and Teresa surprised herself by joining in. Amos took her by the shoulder and led her to an ancient-looking, thoroughly disreputable crash couch.

"You're gonna need to strap in, Tiny. I got an idea what to do with this one," he said, pointing a thick thumb at Muskrat. "So you just stay here with Naomi and the captain."

"Naomi," Teresa said. "That's Naomi Nagata?"

"And this is the *Rocinante*," Amos said. "And I don't know who most of the rest of these people are, but one way or another, we're home."

And then he was gone, leading Muskrat into the belly of the ship and leaving her to stare up into the monitor. It felt strange, like she was in a dream, but also mundane as walking down a slightly unfamiliar hallway. She was here. She was leaving.

The ship shuddered, hissed, started to rise up.

"You want me to kick on the main drive?" Alex asked over the sound of the thrusters burning. "I could slag that whole palace if you want."

"No," Holden said, "leave it be. We still have friends there. Elvi, for one."

"Oh," Alex said. "Should we go get her?"

"No," Holden said. "She's where she needs to be."

The *Rocinante* rose, pushing Teresa back into the cool, blue gel of the couch. The ship shuddered and hummed as it rose, and then when they were high enough from the ground, a new, deeper thrum began, and they leaped upward. Into the darkness of space. Leaving everything behind. She closed her eyes, trying to decide what she felt. If she felt anything, or maybe everything all at once.

Her home, everything she'd ever known, was falling away behind her, and all she was certain of was that she never wanted to go back. The princess was getting hell and gone from fairyland.

A sharp alert caught her attention at the same moment the pilot—Alex—said something obscene. She looked over at him, and his face was ashen.

"Alex?" the woman said.

"We been target locked," Alex said. "We took too long. It's the *Whirlwind*."

Chapter Forty-Nine: Naomi

Because the *Rocinante* was built to land on its belly, Holden stepped onto the flight-deck wall. He looked thin. More than thin, he looked like he'd been ill for months. The lines around his mouth were deeper than they'd been, and his grin looked less like his usual easy joy and more like surprise that anything good had actually happened. He looked bruised at heart, but only that. Not broken. He didn't look broken.

He met her eyes, and something in her chest that she didn't know could relax relaxed. She took a long, shuddering breath. Jim took her hand. She'd thought that would never happen again, and here he was, touching her again.

"Hey," he said, too softly for anyone to hear but her.

"Hey," she said back.

Amos, behind him, looked wrong. His skin was gray and his eyes were a uniform black. She'd seen kids on Pallas affect the same look with dyes and scleral tattooing, but on Amos it didn't look like an edgy fashion choice.

Also, he was carrying a big black dog with a gray muzzle and a perplexed expression. The girl beside him seemed familiar, but not so much that Naomi could place her. There would be time for stories later.

Alex climbed up to his crash couch, grinning. "All right. Everybody strap in. We're off this mudball."

The crew cheered, not quite drunk with success, but maybe a little tipsy. Or maybe that was just her. Holden slipped into one of the other couches, staying close to the girl. Protective of her.

Slowly the ship tilted back to its normal, upright position.

"You want me to kick on the main drive?" Alex asked. "I could slag that whole palace if you want."

Before Naomi could answer, Holden did. "No, leave it be. We still have friends there. Elvi, for one."

"Oh. Should we go get her?"

Holden shook his head, even though Alex wasn't looking at him. "No. She's where she needs to be."

He'd been on the ship for less than fifteen minutes, and he was answering like he was the captain. If she'd pointed it out, he would have been horrified. And apologetic, and maybe in some other context she would have expected the apology. She was, after all, the head of the underground, the engineer behind the campaign and a hundred other operations besides. The pleasure of having him back, of feeling herself and Alex and the ship falling into ancient patterns, was more than she could express. It was like waking up after a long and terrible dream to find that whatever it was hadn't actually happened.

In all her long life, it was maybe the most beautiful moment she'd ever had.

It couldn't last.

She felt Alex flying the ship inside Laconia's atmosphere, sliding them above the landscape and rising up above it until the drive plume wouldn't be a danger to anyone below. When the main drive kicked on, they shot up, rising through the last of the atmosphere and into the light of the Laconian sun. As Alex laid in their course for the ring gate, Naomi checked the tactical map for her fleet. The burns they were all under were punishing. By keeping on the edge of what human endurance would allow, they made it less likely that the Laconian ships would reach them. And the enemy ships themselves...

She pulled up an overlay that showed the destroyers and the *Magnetar*-class battleship. It was like looking over and finding a centipede on her arm. The target-lock alert came on, cutting through the merriment and joy like a scalpel.

"Alex?"

"We been target locked. We took too long. It's the *Whirlwind*."

Naomi laid down a sensor feed over her tactical display. The *Magnetar* was still almost nothing without magnification. Hardly more than a pale spot of darkness in the middle of the steady star that was its drive plume. With only a little magnification, though, it was the same eerie almost-organic shape as the *Tempest*. The bone-pale vertebra of an unimaginably huge animal. A ship like that had brought two navies to their knees. A single frigate with its supplies nearly drained already didn't stand a chance. All her joy collapsed to ashes. She wondered whether Duarte would let her see Jim when they were both in prison. Whether they'd even be allowed the option of surrender. Fighting down through the planetary defenses had taken four ships and cost one of them. Or, depending on the next few minutes, maybe two.

At least the *Whirlwind* was the last *Magnetar* that would ever be built. She'd broken the construction platforms, so at least that. If she died in the effort—if they all did—Bobbie would still have approved. Some sacrifices were worth it.

"We have a tightbeam request incoming from the *Whirlwind*," Ian said. His voice only shook a little.

"Let's have it," Naomi said, and Ian looked at her. The uncertainty in his eyes was clear. He didn't know if she was going to surrender or lead them all into death. She wasn't perfectly certain herself. "Now, Kefilwe. This won't get better by waiting."

He put the incoming message on every display, though only Naomi's was live. She didn't know if he meant to pressure her by letting the whole crew see the exchange or if he was nervous and screwed up. It didn't make a difference.

The woman on her screen was young, with dark skin and straight, close-cropped hair. She wore Laconian blue and the rank insignia of an admiral, the same style that Mars used to use. The rage in her eyes gave Naomi very little hope.

"I am Admiral Sandrine Gujarat, commander of the Laconian battleship *Voice of the Whirlwind*. You have thirty seconds to drop core, deactivate your weapons systems, and open your airlock for boarding. Failure to do exactly as you are told will result in the destruction of your ship."

Thirty seconds. Naomi raised her chin in defiance. If she was taken, they would get everything she knew eventually. The networks and contacts in dozens of systems. The long-term plans and strategies. Everything she'd built in all the time she'd spent working for Saba and then taking his place. It had made her into a perfect asset for the enemy. A ship full of her people stood breathless, waiting for her to decide whether to give them all over or let them all die. It was like being crushed under a hundred gs and weightless at the same time.

The voice that answered wasn't hers. It wasn't even one she knew.

"No, Admiral Gujarat. It will not end in anybody's destruction. You will stand down at once."

On her screen, the admiral's eyes widened in anger, but also in confusion. Naomi craned her neck to see the girl who had spoken. She was in a crash couch, gesturing that the comms control should be transferred to her. Naomi hesitated for a moment, then went with it. When the *Roci*'s feed showed the girl's face, the Laconian admiral paled.

"Do you know who I am, Admiral?"

"I don't... The high consul—"

"Yes, I am the high consul's daughter and heir," the girl said. "You understand now. Good. I am on the *Rocinante* at my father's request. Your threat is ridiculous and your orders are to return immediately to your assigned mission protecting the homeworld."

The girl couldn't be sixteen yet, but her voice had an easy arrogance. Naomi turned to Jim and mouthed, *Is that true?* He lifted his hands in a Belter shrug.

"Miss," the admiral said, unconsciously bowing as she did, "you are... I was unaware... This is very irregular, miss. I'm afraid I can't allow this ship to go anywhere."

The girl rolled her eyes dramatically. "Is there a protocol? A security protocol?"

"I'm sorry?"

"If I am in distress, being held against my will. Threatened. Whatever. Is there a phrase I use to indicate that? Something innocuous I can slip into any conversation without my captors knowing it?"

"I... That is—"

"It's a yes-or-no question, Admiral. This isn't hard." At this rate, the *Whirlwind* was going to nuke them to be rid of the girl.

"There is, miss," Admiral Gujarat said.

"And have I said it?"

"You haven't."

"Then we can take it as given that I am not here under duress. That something is going on between the high consul and the leadership of the underground –something with which I have been entrusted and you haven't. With that in mind? Go. Back. To. Your. Post."

The woman on the screen squared her shoulders. "I have orders from Admiral Trejo that—"

"Stop," the girl said. "What's his name?"

"Whose?"

"Admiral Anton Trejo. What is his last name?"

"Trejo?"

"Yes," the girl said, and leaned close to the camera so that her whole face filled the screen. She spoke softly and with an incandescent rage. "Mine is *Duarte*."

"I'm sorry, miss," the admiral said. "I can't let your ship leave."

"No?" the girl said. "Then shoot me the fuck down." She dropped the connection and turned to Alex, staring down at her slack jawed. "We can go. That woman is scared to death right now."

"Prepare for high burn?" Alex announced over the ship-wide channel, and the girl nodded curtly and settled back in her couch.

"Jim?" Naomi said.

"I know," he said. "It's been a really weird day."

"We thought you were dead," Naomi said as she stepped into the lift.

Amos blinked his unnerving black eyes, then shrugged. "Yeah, I can see that, Boss. What can I tell you? Sorry."

Eight hours of high burn had taken them out of the *Whirlwind*'s effective range. Fifteen had increased the distance to the point that she almost felt safe. Not *safe* safe, but close enough that she could imagine stepping away from the ops deck and starting to make sense of everything that had happened, hearing everything that had brought Jim and Amos back. And how Teresa Duarte fit into it.

And also to tell them what had happened during their long and separate pilgrimages. What they had lost. With the four of them together, Alex had asked for the ceremony. As if the universe had given them a chance, and he was worried that if he didn't take it now, it would somehow slip away. And she and Amos were heading to the airlock together again, as if the past had returned. But as if it had returned changed.

The changes to Amos were odd. His skin was somehow pale and dark at the same time, like a thin coat of white paint over black. His eyes were darkness, and there was something strange about the way he moved. But after so long, being able to think of him without grief and worry made the alterations only interesting. It was so much better than what she'd already carried with him. With losing him.

"I'd have called earlier, but... Well, I wasn't ready to go. I was being patient."

"What happened?"

He shrugged. "One thing and another. Good to be back, though."

The lift stopped, and she stepped off. Amos followed just a step behind. "You're different."

"Yup," he said, smiling amiably. It was such an unmistakably Amos-like thing to say. Such a familiar way to say it.

"Did the bomb fail?" she asked.

"Nope, it was fine."

"So why didn't you follow through on the mission? No blame, but... What was your thinking there?"

Amos went still for a moment, like he was listening to something she couldn't hear.

"I met the kid," Amos said. "Seemed kind of shitty killing her. I thought maybe it was the wrong call." He shrugged.

Naomi stepped over and put her arms around him. It was like hugging a metal strut. "Good to have you back."

Alex and Holden were at the interior door to the airlock. Alex had changed into an MCRN uniform. An artifact from another age. Jim was in a white formal shirt. He'd washed his hair and combed it back. He looked distinguished and somber.

The coffin in the airlock was just a shell, hardly more than a body bag with slightly hardened sides. And it was empty.

"This is way we always did it," Alex said now that they were together. "When we'd lost someone and couldn't recover the body. We'd still take the moment."

He cast his eyes to the deck. Jim did the same. Amos put on the same somber face he always did at moments like this. A flood of complex feelings washed through her. Sorrow and joy, relief and the emptiness of a loss that would never be made whole.

Alex cleared his throat and wiped his eyes with the back of his hand. "Bobbie Draper was one of my best friends. She was a Marine right down to her bones. Anything else she did was built on that. She was brave and honorable, and she was strong. She made a hell of a captain. I remember when Fred Johnson tried to make her into an ambassador back in the day, and she kept calling it the way she saw it instead of playing politician. She was always like that. She took on the impossible, and she made it work."

He took a deep breath, opened his mouth like he was going to go on, then closed it again and shook his head. Jim was weeping now too. And so was she. Amos' newly black eyes shifted like he was reading something in the air, and he lifted his chin.

"She was a badass," he said, then paused and nodded, satisfied.

"She will be missed," Naomi said. "From now on. And forever."

They stood in silence for a moment, and then Jim stepped forward and cycled the exterior door. When it was open, the little chemical boosters on the coffin slid it to the edge of the lock. And then it was gone. Jim cycled the lock closed again, turned, and stepped in, putting his arms around her and Alex. A moment later, the solid mass of Amos' arms looped around her too. The four of them held each other there with the hum and rumble of the *Rocinante* around them. They stayed there for a long time.

The elements of her little ragtag fleet that had been closest to the ring gate were through long before the *Roci* was even halfway through the system. Alex kept them at a punishing burn, balancing the reaction mass they still had and the distance to a friendly resupply depot in Gossner system. If they took breaks a little more often than during the dive into the system and burned a little less heavily, it was to conserve mass and because the *Whirlwind* and her cohort of destroyers were parked close in to Laconia, still knocking down the torpedoes and long-arc rocks that

Naomi's people had flung at the planet. Three days into their burn toward the gate, someone somewhere had grown the balls to issue an order, and the *Whirlwind* flung half a dozen torpedoes at the retreating *Roci*. The PDCs took them all down, and no more followed.

When they were burning, Naomi used the time to calculate a safe transit schedule and tightbeam it to the other ships. From the start of the campaign to its end, they'd lost thirty-two ships, and just shy of two hundred lives. They had retrieved Jim and Amos, taken in Teresa Duarte, and destroyed the mechanism of production that Laconia depended on for its high-powered fleet. The *Whirlwind* was still a massive killing machine capable of taking control of any system it chose. But it was only one ship. It couldn't attack through any of the ring gates without leaving Laconia underprotected. It was pinned.

The *Storm* reached the gate and sent back a formal salute to Naomi before it passed through. Jillian Houston taking her ship back to Draper Station and waiting for new orders. That was a strange thought. Naomi had spent so much of her mental energy and focus on winning the battle she'd almost forgotten about everything that came after. Freedom from Laconia didn't— couldn't—mean a return to de facto rule by the Transport Union. For one thing, Medina Station was gone and no one would be setting up a permanent base in the ring space again. For another, Laconia had replaced the structures of trade and control with its own.

But still, there were ways. There wouldn't be a choke hold on the ring space the way there had been, but there could be a network of cheap, easily replaced relays that announced incoming and outgoing traffic. Ships could know, at least, what the chances were of going dutchman before they made the transit. There weren't many people who'd choose to go through a ring gate if they knew they wouldn't come out the other side. Give the people enough information, and they'd be able to make the right decisions on their own. That was a problem for later, though. For the moment, she could watch the drive plumes of the ships that had broken Laconia touch the gate and escape, one after another, and think to herself, *Safe. Safe. Safe.*

In the breaks between the hard burns, the crew celebrated and, unfortunately, fought. In the tension before the attack, Ian Kefilwe and another young man—an engineer named Safwan Cork—had fallen into bed together and were now negotiating the difficult romantic territory of having survived. She tried to keep out of it, but once she saw Jim sitting with Ian in one of the now-empty torpedo bays, listening while the young man wept. It seemed right.

The ship was only about three hundred thousand kilometers out from the ring gates, and the remaining burns were all braking, making sure that when they did the transit, they had time on the far side to maneuver and not just slam into the other side of the sphere and vanish. The Laconian forces hadn't come after them. Not even to throw more long-range torpedoes.

Teresa Duarte was an astounding beast of a human being. Naomi tried to make a connection with her, but only once. They were in a pause, Alex making a gentle quarter g, and Naomi was getting dinner. It still felt strange to her, seeing the galley full. In her mind, there were still only six crew on the *Roci*.

Teresa was by herself, leaning against one of the walls, a bowl of noodles in one hand and chopsticks in the other. Her hair was braided back, and it made her face look harsher than usual. No one was sitting with her. No one was speaking to her. Probably because no one knew what to say.

Naomi served herself a bowl of white kibble and sat down across from the girl. Teresa looked up, and there was a flash of outrage before she reined herself in.

"Is this okay?" Naomi asked.

"It's your ship. You get to sit where you want."

"Got to be a little strange, being someplace like this, yeah?"

Teresa nodded. Naomi took a bite of her kibble and wondered if they were going to sit in silence. Teresa shook her head. "There are people everywhere. And there's nowhere to go. Back home I could be alone. No one's ever alone out here."

"There are ways," Naomi said, thinking of her cargo container. "But there are usually fewer people here. It does get a little full."

"You should have a crew of twenty-two."

"We usually made do with six. Sometimes four."

"I don't like it here," Teresa said, standing up. "I'll want to find someplace else once we leave."

She walked away without saying anything else. She didn't put her uneaten bowl in the recycler, so when Naomi was finished with her own meal, she cleaned up after both of them, then walked down the corridor to her cabin.

To theirs.

Jim was in the crash couch. His jumpsuit was drenched in sweat at the armpits and down the back. He looked at her and shook his head.

"I will never, ever get this out of shape again," he said. "This is miserable."

"You'll get better," she said, and lay down beside him. The couch shifted to account for her added weight. Every time she saw him, she felt herself not quite trusting it. Not quite letting herself believe he was really back, in case it was all a dream or a false reprieve. As if the universe would take him away from her again. It was getting better, but she wasn't sure it would ever completely go away.

"I saw your friend in the galley," she said. "She's having some trouble adjusting, I think."

"Well, she was the only child of a galactic god-emperor, and now she's eating oatmeal in a half-antique gunship. That's got to be a hard transition."

"What are we going to do with her once we get to the supply depot? You know she's too important to just let her go, right?"

"I don't know that we can make her stay. Not unless we're

talking about throwing her in a prison. But there are other options."

"Are there?"

"There were plenty of Martians who didn't take off with Duarte back in the day. Some of them will be cousins of hers. If we're lucky, some of them may be counselors and therapists. Or... I don't know. Run rehabilitation centers."

"If not?"

"If there aren't, some can be made. Everyone's related to everyone, if you go back far enough. We'll just go back until the right people are connected to her."

"You sound like Avasarala," Naomi said.

"I've been thinking about her a lot. I feel like I built a little version of her in my head. You ever have that feeling?"

"I know the one," Naomi said. And then, "Teresa doesn't just need a place to land and some sort-of relatives. She needs love."

"She had love. Her father loved her. He really did. What she didn't have was a sense of proportion."

"And then you brought her here."

"She brought herself," he said. "Just like we all do. And it's a pain in the ass for each and every one of us, every time it happens. Outgrowing your family? Hard work under the best of circumstances. Which these aren't."

She lay down, snuggling into his arm. He was sweat-damp, but she didn't care. She stroked her fingertips across his forehead and down his cheek. He turned his head, pressing into her hand like a cat that wanted petting.

"Do you think she'll be okay?" Naomi asked.

"No idea. She will or she won't. Either way, it's going to be up to her. I'm pretty sure she'll be herself while she does it, though. That's a victory for her. We'll help if we can. If she'll let us."

The alert went on. Ring passage in five minutes. Jim sighed, stood, and started changing into fresh clothes.

"What about you?" Naomi said.

"What about me?"

"Will you be okay?"

Jim smiled, and there was only a little weariness in his eyes. Only a little sorrow. "I played a long, terrible, shitty game, and I won. Then after I won, I made it back home. I'm waking up in the morning next to you. I'm perfect."

Chapter Fifty: Elvi

The day after Teresa escaped, Elvi spent the hours before dawn watching the feeds. As soon as the violence ended, even before the wounded and the dead were sorted, the stories began taking shape. The differences between the state newsfeeds and the security reports Elvi saw in the aftermath made it sound like there had been two different battles. The separatist terrorist forces, each of them tracked as they fled for the ring gate, had been driven back by the overwhelming power of the Laconian Navy. Or else the enemy had achieved all its apparent objectives and withdrawn of its own accord. The orbital weapons platform network and land-based rail guns had successfully protected Laconia from the enemy's last-ditch suicide attack. Or else the underlying assumption that the platforms and the base would be support for a naval defense had, in the heat of the moment, been ignored. And the enemy losses, while real, hadn't been catastrophic. The enemy was in flight, and the threats to Laconia required little more than a mopping up. Or else the *Whirlwind* was going to be stuck close to the planet for the foreseeable future while a handful of destroyers hunted down the stray torpedoes and rocks that had been launched at the planet, any one of which could cause massive damage.

The most breathtaking lie—the one that put all the others to shame—was that the construction platforms had been taken down before the attack could reach them, and were being brought back to full operation in a secret location to protect them from further attack. The other stories about the battle might be extreme readings of the actual text, but the construction platforms were no more. There was no version of reality that supported the state's claims that they had survived. The former shipyards of Laconia were a collection of junk scattered in orbit around the planet, and no number of horses and men were going to put them together again.

Added to that were all the things that the newsfeeds simply didn't mention: That a fast attack frigate had landed within spitting distance of the State Building. That the high consul's daughter had run away with the enemy in what might perhaps be humanity's newest record-setting act of teenage rebellion. That the prisoner held in the State Building had also escaped.

Or that one prisoner had, anyway.

"Major?" the young man said. "Admiral Trejo is ready to see you."

The lobby was a wide space with sandstone-colored columns and enough sofas and chairs to seat a hundred people. She was the only one there.

"Doctor," Elvi said.

The young man looked confused. "I'm sorry?"

"I'd prefer you call me doctor. Major is an honorary rank. I earned my doctorate."

"Yes, Dr. Okoye. Of course. The admiral..."

"Is ready to see me," she said, standing up and pulling her tunic straight. "Lead the way."

The meeting wasn't in one of the usual rooms. No formal desk, no volumetric display, no small crowd of men bowing to the power of the state and jockeying for their status in it. It was just her and Trejo in a private dining room. He had a simple breakfast of coffee and fruit with a sugar-iced pastry, and another like it set aside for her. A window almost as wide as the whole wall looked out over the snow-covered grounds and the land beyond all the way to the horizon. It felt a little obscene to think about the violence that had shaken it all. That they weren't both underground in a high-security shelter felt like another kind of lie.

"Admiral," she said, sitting. The young man left immediately. Trejo poured her coffee himself.

"We found Ilich," Trejo said instead of hello. "Well, his body anyway. He and two of the state guard were assassinated by the separatists."

Elvi waited to feel something about that. The familiar, professionally thoughtful man she'd worked with was dead. She would never see him again. It wasn't the first time she'd lost a colleague. Back before anyone called her major, she'd taught at an upper university that had three of her fellow faculty members die in the same semester. She'd lost most of the science staff of the *Falcon*, and it had been devastating. This wasn't. Where the shock and sadness should have been, there was just an oceanic depth of resentment. She wasn't even perfectly clear whose name belonged on it. Duarte. Trejo. Holden. All of them together.

"Too bad," she said, because she felt like she ought to say something.

"He was loyal to the empire," Trejo said. "Whatever his failings were, he was that."

She didn't know what she could say to that, so she didn't say anything.

"Our situation has once again changed," Trejo said, and paused to blow across the surface of his coffee. He didn't just look exhausted. He looked ten years older than when he'd arrived, and things had been broken beyond repair back then. Another few years like this, and Trejo would be the oldest man alive, no matter his age. She remembered a myth about someone wishing for eternal life, but forgetting to ask for youth to go with it. In the story they'd gradually shrunk and withered until they turned into a cicada. She wondered if Fayez knew who the story was about.

She realized again that Trejo was waiting for her to respond. She didn't know what he wanted her to say and didn't care much either.

"Are you feeling all right, Major?"

"Doctor," she said. "I think it would be best if you called me doctor. And I'm fine. I've had a lot on my plate recently. I'm sure you understand."

"I do. I most certainly do," he said. "The construction platforms. The stick moons, they called them. They were what drew the high consul's attention to Laconia in the first place. Did you know that? He saw them in the first wave of scans that came through when the gates opened. There was a vessel—something like a vessel—halfway built in one of them."

"I'd heard that," Elvi said. The coffee was good. The pastry was a little too sweet for her liking.

"They are the foundation of Laconian power."

Jesus Christ, Elvi thought. Had Trejo always been this sanctimonious and she just hadn't noticed? Or was she just really irritable right now?

"They stole a goal on us," he said. "I will give them that. They found a dirty trick, and we fell for it. Once. It won't happen again. I need you to put aside the other issues you're looking into. For the time being. I know what you're going to say. 'Another first priority.'"

"That's where I would have started, yes," Elvi said.

"The loss of those platforms is the loss of the most powerful ships humanity has ever made. It's the loss of antimatter production. It's the loss of the regenerative tanks. Without them, we lose the ability to project our power out beyond the system. Whether we're fighting against the terrorists or the things beyond the ring gates, we need that ability."

"So whatever the high consul has become gets shelved," she said. "Figuring out the nature of the enemy and the weird system-wide attacks gets shelved. The secret of immortality? Shelved."

"I can hear your frustration, and I share it," Trejo said, "but the fact remains—"

"No, I'm good with that. But making more weapons isn't the first priority," she said. She took out her handheld, pulled up her notes, and passed it over. "That right there? *That* is my first priority."

Trejo scowled at the display like she'd handed him some particularly unpleasant insect. "Adro system?"

"The big green diamond that looks like it might have a record of the entire protomolecule civilization. Rise and fall. I would probably get the best results if the *Falcon* were repaired and crewed with a team specifically chosen for this project. I have some names drawn up. I'll send them to you."

"Dr. Okoye—"

"I understand I'm not in a position to force you to do anything. But I'm comfortable in the belief that all of the issues we're trying to deal with are connected, and that"—she pointed at the schematic of the massive diamond—"looks more like the Rosetta stone than anything else. So that's where I'm putting my efforts. In my professional judgment, it makes more sense than building bigger explosions or chasing after the fountain of youth."

Trejo put down the hand terminal. His coffee sloshed over the lip of its cup, staining the white linen. "We are in a war—"

"Yes, you should fix that too."

"Excuse me?"

"You should stop being in a war. Send the underground a fruit basket or something. Start peace talks. I don't know. However that works. I said it before, and I meant it. If you want peace, lose gracefully. We have bigger problems."

She took a last bite of the pastry and washed it down with the dregs of the coffee. It tasted better with the bitter following the sweet. Trejo was stone-faced. She stood.

"Do what you need to do," she said. "I'm going to get ready for work, and then I'll be in the lab at the university. If you want to throw me in prison for insubordination or whatever the military term is, that's where you'll find me. If you want to fix this, let me know when the *Falcon* can be ready, and I'll brief you on everything I find."

He didn't respond. She nodded curtly and walked away. She'd hoped she would feel better, and she did. But only a little.

The wide sky of Laconia had cleared. The snow clouds were gone, and the air was crisp and bright with just a hint of the spearmint smell of freshly turned Laconian earth. A flock—or swarm—of something flew high in the sky, vanishing against the sun and reappearing on its collective way to the south. Some organism following a temperature incline or a nutrient gradient or some other more exotic drive she didn't know about. That no one knew about. Not yet.

They would, though, someday. If she could fix all this.

Fayez was awake when she got back to the rooms. He sat on the edge of their bed in the soft cotton pajamas that the Laconian Empire provided them gratis. He was massaging his new foot the way the physician had told him to. He looked up at her, worried. He hadn't slept since the night before either. They'd gotten back to their rooms cold and weary, and also in another kind of shock. She had been a pawn in Holden's chess game. And Holden had gotten her to the last rank and promoted her to a queen.

"Well? How's Trejo?" Fayez asked, mordant and hopeful. "Are we exiled?"

"No such luck," Elvi said. "Maybe later."

"We could still leave." He was only partly joking. She imagined what it would be like. Getting the *Falcon* back. Or any ship, really. If they got off Laconia, they could go anywhere. Trejo wouldn't have the resources to chase them. Not now. They could go back to Sol or Bara Gaon or one of the new, struggling colonies. They could leave all this bullshit behind.

Except that something out there was looking for a way to snuff out their minds. And there wasn't a better place to fight against that than right here. Her prison wasn't Laconia. Her jailer wasn't Trejo. The thing that had taken all her choices away was that this mystery so clearly needed to be solved, and she was so clearly the best one to do it.

She kissed her husband softly, and on the lips. When she pulled back, the humor was gone from his eyes. They'd been together for so long. They'd been so many different people together. She felt the change coming again. She was entering a new part of her life now. It meant packing away all her stories about how she was only here from fear of the authorities. The authorities were broken. She was here because she chose to be, and that changed everything.

"I'm sorry," she said. "I know you were hoping for a gentlemanly retirement someplace that would give us both tenure."

"Or just one of us," he said. "I'm not greedy."

"We don't get to have that. And I'm sorry."

Fayez sighed, crossed his legs. "If we don't, we don't. I still have you?"

"Always."

"Good enough," he said, and patted the mattress at his side.

"I have to go."

"Mixed signals," he said.

"I'll be back after work."

"You say that now, but I know you. You'll find something interesting and stay up until midnight chasing it, and by the time you come home, it'll be time to leave again."

"You're probably right."

"It's why everyone needs you," Fayez said. "It's why I need you too. When you get back, I'll be here."

"Thank you," she said.

"I'm sorry we couldn't run away together."

"Maybe in our next lives."

The universe is always stranger than you think.

It didn't matter how broad her imagination was, how cynical, how joyous and open, how well researched or wild minded. The universe was always stranger. Every dream, every imagining, however lavish and improbable, inevitably fell short of the truth.

Elvi had been born in a system with a single star and a handful of planets. She'd studied exobiology when it was still theoretical. When she'd been a newly minted PhD, her greatest dream was that she might get a research fellowship on Mars, and maybe—the pinnacle of all her wildest hopes—find some hard evidence that life had evolved there independently. It would have been the most astounding, important thing she could imagine. She'd be in the scientific histories as the woman who'd discovered living structures that came from someplace besides the Earth.

Looking back, the dream seemed impossibly small.

At the labs, she stopped to have a long talk with Dr. Ochida. She wanted a rundown of all the research being done—where it stood, who was heading up the projects, what his opinions were of the experimental designs. Even after Cortázar had died, she hadn't done that. Hadn't acted as though the labs were hers to run. Now she did, and Ochida didn't object. That probably made it true.

At any rate, he answered everything she asked, and Trejo hadn't sent any guards to drag her away. So she was effectively in control of the most advanced research facility in the history of humankind. And if there was one thing that her decades in academic science had drilled into her consciousness, it was that power meant policy.

"We're going to need to make some changes," she said. "We're shutting down the Pen."

Ochida actually stopped walking. She could have said that all the science teams were now required to walk on their hands, and the man would have been less astounded.

"But the protomolecule...The supply..."

"We have enough," she said. "Our reason for collecting more died with the construction platforms."

"But...the prisoners. What do we do with them?"

"We're not executioners," Elvi said. "We never should have been. When the guards come, tell them we don't accept the transfer. If Trejo wants to line people up against the wall and shoot them, I'm not in a position to stop that. But I can say we won't support it. And we won't base our research on it. From here on in, informed consent or work with yeast."

"This is...This will..."

"Speed isn't the only measure of progress, Doctor," Elvi said. But she could tell from his eyes he didn't know what she meant. "Just get it done. All right?"

"Yes, Dr. Okoye. As you see fit." He almost bowed as he retreated.

The universe is always stranger than you think. Elvi went to her private lab. There were so many things to do, so many possible pathways to follow in the research. She could keep the secret of Duarte's condition, or she could make her own research group, pulling from the best minds in Laconia. Trejo's conspiracy was down to just the two of them and Kelly anyway. And with Teresa on the run with James fucking Holden, treating it as a state secret was more and more ridiculous.

The chair seemed more comfortable now that it was hers. She knew it hadn't actually changed, but she had. She pulled up her waiting messages and ran through them. The most recent one was from the shipyards, giving her an unscheduled update on the status of the *Falcon*. She took it as an olive branch from Trejo.

As she went through the list, she felt herself growing calmer. More focused. The complicated, obscure world of politics and intrigue fell away, and the complicated, obscure world of research protocols and alien biology took its place. It was like coming home. Fayez had been right. She was going to be there until morning if she wasn't careful. But whatever she did, whatever path she took, the first step was the same. Even if it was a bad idea, it was necessary.

The black-eyed children watched her as she went to their cage. Cara stood up, coming to meet her the way she often did. When Elvi undid the lock and slid the cage door open, Cara stared at it, confused. Her little brother walked to her side, slipped his smaller hand in hers. Elvi stood back, nodding to them. For the first time in decades, the two children stepped out of their cage freely. Xan's little chest was heaving in and out with the emotion of it. A tear slipped down Cara's grayish cheek.

"Really?" Cara whispered. She meant, *Are we really free?*

"There are some things I have to figure out," Elvi said, and her voice was trembling too. "I hoped, if you're willing, that you would help me."

Epilogue: Holden

Holden lay strapped in the autodoc, his eyes closed. The ship was on the float, conserving the last of their reaction mass. He didn't mind. Weightlessness was a visceral reminder that he wasn't on Laconia anymore. He loved it for that.

The machine ticked and hummed in a vaguely disapproving way, like it was trying to tell him to exercise more and cut back on salt. There were voices in the background. There were always voices in the background these days. After so many years with a skeleton crew, having a full complement felt like having a party where too many people had showed up and no one was leaving.

A needle slid into his left arm, and the autodoc chugged to itself, pumping in his own peculiar cocktail of oncocidals and antiagathics and blood pressure stabilizers. And probably something for psychological distress. Lord knew he had that coming. The coolness gave him a pins-and-needles feeling on his lips, and he tasted something that his brain tried to interpret as peanuts. When it was done, the needle withdrew and a thin scanning bar on an armature came out and waved a wand along his face. An image of his skull and lips appeared on the screen, with the new growth in green.

"All the parts in the right place?" Naomi asked from the doorway.

"Most of them," Holden said, and the scanner beeped at him, chiding. He stayed still while it finished. When the armature retracted, he said, "It does feel pretty fucking undignified to be teething at my age."

"Well, they knocked your tooth out," Naomi said. Her tone was mild, but he could hear the murder behind it. He played it all down, but she knew. All the time he'd been under Laconian control, he'd made light of things. He'd made rules for himself so that his powerlessness didn't turn into despair. He'd plotted and planned and watched for opportunities. Now it was over, and everything he'd been careful not to feel was still waiting for him.

"My dad used to say something when he'd been traveling," Holden said as the autodoc finished its run.

"Which one?"

"Father Caesar. He used to say that when you went too far too fast, your soul took some time catching up to you."

Naomi frowned. "I thought that was how religious fanatics argued that Belters didn't have souls."

"Might have been that too," Holden said. "Father Caesar was talking about jet lag. Anyway, I was thinking about it with just... change. You know?"

He didn't talk about the day he'd been arrested much. Not with anyone besides Naomi. He'd been taken into custody on Medina Station, held for questioning. Not sure if he was going to live the rest of his life in a box or be slaughtered as a warning to others. And Governor Singh had shipped him back to Laconia for questioning about the aliens that had made the rings and the other aliens that had killed them. And through the first part of it, and then again on and off all the time he'd been gone, he'd had the sense that none of it was really happening. Or that it was, but not to him. He'd become someone else. Being a prisoner had driven him a little crazy for a while, and he still wasn't right. Not really. But every day he woke up on the *Roci* with Naomi beside him and Alex in the pilot's chair, he felt a little closer to sane. His soul a little bit nearer, in a wide and metaphorical sense.

Naomi pushed off, floating to him, and catching herself with the unconscious grace of someone born to it. She took his hand. She did that a lot these days. He liked it too. Especially when he woke up in the middle of the night, too groggy from sleep to know where he was, and started to panic that the guards were coming to beat him again. Her voice calmed him down, but her hand in his worked faster.

"We're going to start the braking burn in about forty minutes," she said.

"Hard?"

"Alex says about three-quarter g. We'll be fine. But I thought I'd let you know anyway."

"We won't be trapped in the same couch for hours."

"Well, not by that, anyway," she said. He didn't know if the sly sexual banter was sincere or just another way of telling him he was home. It soothed him either way.

"Just between us?" he said. "I'm going to be glad when it's just us again. These are nice folks, but they're not family, you know?"

"I do," she said. "We might... we might need to talk about hiring someone on, though. With Clarissa and Bobbie both gone."

"Yeah," he said. "We'll look at it." He meant, *But not now. Later. When I can.* She heard it all.

"I'm going to go check the coolant feed lines," she said. "These kids all grew up on newer ships. They're not used to our heat tolerances."

"All right," Holden said. "I'm going to finish this and head for the flight deck."

"Sounds good," she said, and pushed backward, keeping her

eyes on him as she moved away to the door and caught herself without even looking.

After she was gone, the autodoc chimed, giving him permission to unstrap himself. He moved slowly not because he hurt, but because he liked the sensation of freeing himself. The report was on the screen when he got there. All in all, it was pretty solid. He pulled up a record going back to his return to the *Roci*, and all the trend lines were going the right way. So there it was in clean, glowing lines. His soul on its way back.

It would be good to feel like himself again. Naomi was stuck as the central planner for the underground as it transitioned to whatever came next. But she'd made it very clear that one run as captain of a gunship on campaign was more than a lifetime's worth for her. The captain's chair of the *Rocinante* was his. Though, since she was still nominally the admiral of the resistance fleet, his captaincy felt a bit like an emeritus title. Even so, there were responsibilities that came with it. If not now, then soon.

He hesitated, then pulled up Amos' record. There was no data. He thought about it for a moment. He didn't want to have the talk, but he was going to have to. If he was going to be the captain again, he was going to have to be the captain again.

He stopped by the galley first for a bulb of coffee and a printed length of something that the system called mushroom bacon. Three of the new crew were floating near a table, and he felt them watching him in the same way people sometimes did in bars or the corridors of stations. *Is that James Holden?* He'd been able to be oblivious to it before. Now he felt their attention like they were pointing a heat gun at him. He pretended not to notice their interest and headed for the machine shop.

Muskrat floated in the middle of the room, a complex diaper on her haunches with a hole for her tail. She started wagging as soon as Holden came in. It made her gyrate around a center of mass defined by her larger and mostly still body and her lighter and fast-moving tail. Holden tossed a thumb-sized bit of the bacon at her mouth, and she caught it.

"You're getting better at that," he said to the dog as it chewed noisily.

The machine shop was perfectly familiar. The smell of high-grade lubricants and the residual heat of the machine printers, the old sign still in place where it had been. SHE TAKES CARE OF YOU. YOU TAKE CARE OF HER.

A clanging came from inside the deck, two sharp, percussive strikes, and then a grunt. The slide of a body moving through a crawl space.

"Hey, Cap'n," the thing that had been Amos said, pulling himself out from under the decking. He had a wrench in one hand and an air filter in the other. His skin was still a sickly gray, and it left him looking cold. Like someone who had just drowned.

"Everything going all right?" Holden said, gesturing at the dog with a forced cheerfulness.

"So far. Turns out there's a lot of people been thinking about how to have dogs on a ship. I'm just looking at what kinds of solves they've come up with." He let the tools float and scratched the dog's ears, stabilizing her jaw with his other hand so she didn't drift.

"Seems difficult," Holden said.

"It ain't all dignified. I'm putting together a traveling kit for Tiny. Figure anyplace she heads for, she's taking this one. Hard part's the filters. Turns out these dogs throw off a lot of fur. Gums the standard recyclers up pretty quick if you don't catch it first."

Holden braced himself with a handhold. Muskrat tried to turn toward him, but didn't have anything to push against.

"Have you heard about Teresa having any plans?" Holden asked, avoiding the conversation he'd come here to have.

The mechanic took the filter and started running his thumb along the edge, inspecting it by touch. The blackness of his eyes made it hard to know what exactly he was looking at.

"Nope. Last I saw, she and Alex and one of the new kids were all talking about Martian entertainment feeds. Apparently one of the ones she was into, Kit watched when he was her age. I think

Tiny likes having something in common with people, even if it's just the films they've watched."

"So I was at the med bay just now," Holden said. "I noticed you hadn't been by."

"Yeah, well. Autodoc isn't so clear on what to make of me these days."

"Yeah," Holden said. "About that." He hesitated. He didn't know how to ask if the thing in front of him was really Amos anymore.

"What's on your mind?"

"Are you really Amos anymore?"

"Yup."

"No, I mean. Amos…died. He got killed. And then the repair drones took the body, and…I need to know, are you really Amos Burton? The Amos I knew."

"Sure am. Anything else?"

Holden nodded more to himself than to anyone else. Muskrat whined and tried to swim over toward him, paws flailing in the air. He reached out and pulled the dog over, bracing her against his knee and patting her back. "I just think it's important."

"Seems like you're having a hard time taking yes for an answer, Cap. Here's how I look at it. Yeah, I went through some weird shit. It changed me. I know some things I didn't know before."

"Things like what?" Holden asked, but Amos waved the question away.

"Thing is, you went through some weird shit too. You got changed. Know some things you didn't know going in. Naomi and Alex? Same. Hell, Tiny's barely related to who she was the first time I saw her. That's just life." Amos shrugged. "I guess the dog didn't change much, except she got a little gray around the muzzle."

Muskrat wagged.

"You want this to be a philosophy question, that's fine," Amos said. "But if you're asking am I still me? I am."

Holden nodded. "All right. I had to ask."

"No problem," Amos said.

Holden scratched Muskrat one last time. A little cloud of hair floated free, the strands clinging together in complex webs and drifting toward the air recycler. "I see what you mean. Alex is starting our braking burn in twenty-five, thirty minutes."

"I'll make this all safe by then," Amos said.

Holden pulled himself to the door. As he was about to leave, Amos' voice pulled him back.

"One thing, though?"

He braced in the doorway. Amos' eerie black eyes were on him. "Sure."

"Those things that Duarte pissed off? The ones that ate Medina?"

"I know the ones you mean," Holden said.

"One of the things I know now is that they're going to kill everybody."

They were silent for a moment.

"Yeah," Holden said. "I know that too."

Acknowledgments

While the creation of any book is less a solitary act than it seems, the past few years have seen a huge increase in the people involved with The Expanse in all its incarnations, including this one. This book would not exist without the hard work and dedication of Danny and Heather Baror, Bradley Englert, Tim Holman, Anne Clarke, Ellen Wright, Alex Lencicki, and the whole brilliant crew at Orbit. Special thanks are also due Carrie Vaughn for her services as a beta reader, the gang from Sakeriver: Tom, Sake Mike, Non-Sake Mike, Jim-me, Porter, Scott, Raja, Jeff, Mark, Dan, Joe, and Erik Slaine, who got the ball rolling.

The support team for The Expanse has also grown to include the staff at Alcon Entertainment and the cast and crew of *The Expanse*. Our thanks and gratitude go especially to Alex Cabrera-Aragon, Glenton Richards, and Julianna Damewood.

A particular debt of gratitude is also owed to Jeff Bezos and his team at Amazon for their support of the project in all its forms.

And, as always, none of this would have happened without the support and company of Jayné, Kat, and Scarlet.